PLUTOSHINE

PLUTOSHINE

LUCY KISSICK

First published in Great Britain in 2022 by Gollancz
an imprint of The Orion Publishing Group Ltd
Carmelite House, 50 Victoria Embankment
London EC4Y 0DZ

An Hachette UK Company

1 3 5 7 9 10 8 6 4 2

A CIP catalogue record for this book is
available from the British Library.

ISBN (Hardback) 978 1 473 23314 0
ISBN (Export Trade Paperback) 978 1 473 23315 7
ISBN (eBook) 978 1 473 23317 1
ISBN (Audio Download) 978 1 473 23318 8

Typeset by Input Data Services Ltd, Somerset

Printed in Great Britain by Clays Ltd, Elcograph S.p.A

www.gollancz.co.uk

Prologue

Some time in the not too
distant future

One-two-three.
One-two-three.

A series of short, high, piercing whistles, then again. Like a bird call, or an SOS. The pattern was familiar now, and the three figures listened for the sequence's final part: *one-two-three-four*, lower in pitch. Then the cycle repeated.

Their breaths were short and close in the confines of their suit helmets. Out there, under the black of the ice and far from the comfort of the stars, one thing was certain: this was no bird call, and if it was an SOS, it was the most distant ever heard by humanity.

A shot of colour in the torchlight, gone as fast as it appeared. The sound of breathing stopped.

Red flooded their vision.

'Well,' said one. He said it all wrong: calm, cool, blithe. 'This changes everything.'

Phase 1

Chapter 1

Some time in the not too distant future + one year

The first time Nou saw the Sun she was a little girl, barely 0.02 years old, and ungainly on the soles of her heated boots. Her brother Edmund was her whole world at that age, and she was in his arms. He was pointing to one pinprick in the star-speckled sky. To Nou, it seemed indistinguishable from the rest.

'They're all stars,' he said, voice intimate in her ear across the helmet intercom, 'but this one's special.'

'That one?'

'Yes. That one's *our* star. We call it the Sun. And one day that star is going to change the face of our world.'

Nou considered this for some time. On her world the skies were dim and the nights long, and starlight saturated the ice plains that disappeared over the horizon. No warmth came from those points of light, nor—as far as her no-nonsense grasp of the world could gather—did anything else.

It was pretty, though, this Sun. She liked how colours splayed across her vision when she squinted at it. Whenever someone would take her she would return to that frozen shore, pulling them by the hand, then sight along her arm as her brother had. She would connect the starry dots, searching with cross-eyed concentration until she found the right one—the brightest one, yes, but finding it Edmund's way was like following a winding path only they knew.

If it was so special, though (she concluded, aged 0.03), then why was it so tiny? What did it *do*?

The oldest of Stern's villagers—those raised on Earth—told her of wondrous things like warm light on bare skin; of blinding sparkles on oceans falling beyond the horizon; of life's humble origins as chemicals in the glittering waters of tidal pools.

The Sun could *melt ice*? And create *life*?

The youngest villagers—those raised on tales of Earth— told her of terrible things like blinded astronomers in ancient history; of giant mirrors cracking and melting Mars; of fried pioneers on Mercury.

Nou would sit hugging her knees, listening wide-eyed. This was no mere pinprick. The Sun, she decided, was definitely something special.

And if life had been found on two and a half places beyond Earth (no one was quite sure if the suspiciously bacteria-like forms of Mars counted), to her it followed quite logically that her world must have life, too.

And she was going to be the one to find it.

By the time the terraformers arrived on Pluto, Nou— now aged 0.04, and small for ten Earth-years—had almost suc- ceeded.

Calling Pluto *cold* was like saying it was a bit of a trek to reach, or a bit dark: when you've travelled four billion kilometres, or thirty times the Earth–Sun distance, to land on a surface more than two hundred degrees below zero, normal methods of de- scription tend to break down.

For Lucian, Pluto's cold meant a permanent, non-tune-out- able humming from his spacesuit's heat packs, and losing all sense of bodily extremities if he stood still for mere seconds.

The distance from home meant a kind of vertigo, a mild panic that hitched his breath if he considered it for too long. He didn't think he would ever get used to the gravity: each footfall a soaring rush, a brief moment's flight, then its antithesis—a half-second's terror, a tremulous fight to touch back down, a rush of relief with each landfall.

But most of all it was the skyline that got him. On this distant world that snowed nitrogen and never reached brighter than Earth's predawn, the sky was blue. Not an Earthly blue—not the cornflower of a clear high noon—but darker, diluted, almost indigo as it faded upwards.

He was in love with this place already.

Lucian was bursting with excitement. He was giddy with it. He was standing on *Pluto*. The world they called the New Horizon. On his every side was a vast plain of battered, buckled white ice—and what ice! Not your average water-ice as on Earth, nor carbon dioxide as on Mars. Pluto's ice was nitrogen; a little methane; a smidge of carbon monoxide. He was walking across ground so cold it was literally frozen air.

The ice sheet's actual name was Sputnik Planitia, or Sputnik Plain, outside of the Latin. But ever since its sighting in the early years of the twenty-first century, the iconic landscape had been better known simply by its shape: as one half of Pluto's Heart.

Up ahead on the tight curve of the horizon loomed the al-Idrisi Montes: icebergs the size of mountains, long ago beached upon the eternally frozen shores of this Heart. And there, growing at the foot of their serrated cliffs like tiny crystals, was the gleaming base of Stern.

Lucian's own heart leapt at the sight. Humanity's furthest outpost. He kept tripping over his feet, half-skipping, half-leaping, catching the ground at odd angles and delighting in each short burst of adrenaline that followed. After one particularly close

7

misstep sent him soaring for a good ten seconds, a terse voice came through his earpiece:

'Are you aware,' it said, 'that approximately one hundred people are about to watch you dash yourself against their base like a fly on a windscreen?'

'Ah, well,' Lucian returned cheerily over their personal line, still catching his breath. 'It's never too early to start building a reputation.'

'With that balance anyone would think you were born on Earth.'

Lucian was dimly aware of his gloved hand reaching to self-consciously ruffle his hair, encountering only helmet.

'Think of it this way, Halley—it's a bit like walking up a staircase that's just a little tilted. Even though you know it, you're going to forget and trip every step of the way.'

He turned around to wave at her, one of a handful of fireflies off in the distance. Looking forwards again and the base's main airlock was scarcely two broad leaps away. Beyond, through the glass walls on either side, it looked like the whole of Pluto had come to greet them. They pressed close against the windows and thronged the inside, some beaming at him, some waving, some leaping up and floating, featherlike, to get a better view. Their curiosity was easy to understand: newcomers out here at the frontier of civilisation were rare, and some of those faces had spent their entire lives with only one another for company. A shining banner momentarily caught his eye: *Welcome Sunbringers!*

'*Sunbringers?*' Halley scoffed—as usual, with more venom than was really called for. The old professor appeared in an even more bitingly unsociable mood than usual. 'Do they take us for a pantheon of ancient deities? We're terraformers, for Earth's sake.'

Lucian pulled the facial equivalent of a shrug, momentarily forgetting his audience.

'Well, I tend to go by solar engineer, but I suppose that's not an inaccurate description? I mean, if we landed on Earth a thousand years ago people'd probably think we were gods, the things we can do these—'

'No.' The *click* of disconnection, then she continued, on the public line: 'Dr Harbour, we'll be there in two minutes . . .'

Lucian's heart stuttered as his helmet whipped around. For a horrible moment he feared he'd leapt right past the man, but no: as he turned his body more properly he saw a tall, slender figure just emerging from the airlock.

Now Lucian regretted his haste: he'd have to face the greetings alone. He fumbled on his wrist-pad for the right frequency.

'Dr Harbour? Hi. To your right.'

The figure turned. Beneath the harsh shadows from his helmet's lighting the face was unsmiling and, in the nearly sunless gloom of high noon, Pluto's cold seemed to bite harder.

Edmund Harbour. The man they called Prince of Pluto, and son of the legendary Clavius Harbour. Lucian had met Edmund remotely countless times during the planning phase, of course, but even in an age where everything was virtual, there could be no substitute for the raw intimacy of face to face. Well, helmet to helmet. Lucian bounced carefully over.

'Hey.' He was still smiling from the run, at least, so didn't need to force one. He almost flinched as their gloves made contact, half-anticipating a shock of cold. 'Great to finally meet in real life.'

'My regards to you also.' Harbour's grip was solid as he bowed slightly. His voice, like his bearing, was full of stately, solemn grace. 'Our people have awaited this day for a generation.'

'I feel like I have, too,' came Halley's voice as she and the rest of the team joined them. She shook Harbour's hand firmly. 'It's excellent to finally meet in three dimensions. Can we take this inside? I'm losing all feeling in my feet.'

As the new arrivals headed into the base Lucian held back, turning for one last, quiet look out across the crinkled plain of the Heart. He would have that same view for the next undetermined number of years, but for now, every crevice and crevasse was new, and everything about the sight was a joy. Above were the stars, exactly as they shone in his own neck of the Solar System. It seemed a kind of celestial joke to find their positions, too, were just the same: a good-humoured reminder of the relativity of distance. He focused himself then, scanning the sky in search of one in particular.

It was then, as he returned his eyes downwards, that he saw a slight figure watching him from ahead: someone else who had ventured outside the airlock. Lucian peered at the face and saw it was a child, maybe a girl, face pale among the anonymous huddle of suits from his own ship. She stood awkwardly, a feather-light bird poised for flight, but held his gaze with intense concentration. She looked to be on the cusp of asking something.

'Hi.' Lucian spoke across the public proximity line and gave her a little wave. 'How are you doing? I'm Lucian.'

With a jerk she spun to look behind her, as though called, and before he could speak again she had vanished into the airlock.

'Hey, Lucian?'

Lucian looked around. Spacesuit audio capabilities were improving near-daily, but they could never quite pinpoint direction the way an ear in open air could. He jumped as he came face to face with the source behind him.

'Too close, Stan.'

Stan was Lucian's PhD student. The boy was wringing his thickly gloved hands, and Lucian felt a little twang of relief at seeing he, too, moved with awkward steps.

10

'Sorry. Um. They're not going to get me up to speak, are they?'

'Oh, no, no.' Lucian put a confident hand on Stan's shoulder, more for his own stability, as the pair headed inside. 'It's just a town meeting. Probably only a few representatives will go. I imagine they'll just want Halley to say a few words.'

Ten minutes later he had a microphone attached to his face, a name badge attached to his chest, and a jug of sparkling water in his hand, which was making its way down a long table in what was probably the canteen. Four speakers besides himself sat along it, and before them, standing room only, were the Plutonians. Apparently, every last one of them.

'How big will it be?'

'How bright will it be?'

'How risky will it be?'

'How can we get involved?'

Lucian had worked on a dozen, far smaller terraforming projects in his career, and never before had the reception for one been so unanimously hopeful and excited. Their questions were valid, insightful, and endless.

'Next question.' Edmund Harbour, chairing the talk, extended a hand.

Out of his suit he wore smart black in contrast to the bright base, had the kind of physiognomy that evaded age (twenty-eight? Thirty-eight?), and spoke with such calm understanding that Lucian felt his own expertise was just about superfluous. He could have been handsome, but all Lucian saw were straight lines and grim sharpness: sharp jaw, sharp brow, sharper eyes. Everything from his motionless poise to his immaculate hair seemed held too rigid to permit so much as a smile.

The question-asker rose.

'What temperature rises can we expect, and over what time-scale?'

'It's something like thirty Celsius over the first hundred years, more or less over the whole planet.' Lucian took this one, swallowing half a ginger nut from a packet that was making the rounds. 'But for the three-hundred-kilometre design, we're talking fifty at the mid-lats. As for the timescale—'

'Consider a light switch,' Halley interrupted drily. 'For the light, that is. There's a lag for temperature, a slow exponential growth. We anticipate it will stabilise at around'—she wiggled her hand—'minus seventy, minus fifty Celsius, and that's after something like five hundred E-years. What you've got to remember is Pluto has never had a sun before. We go bringing one straight to it and some geological systems are going to react right away, and others . . . Well, they're called "geological" for a reason, and that's because they operate on far longer timescales.'

'It's perfectly safe,' Lucian added, seeing hands rise. 'Nitrogen-ice melts first, then the methane-ice more gradually. Hydrosphere activation is always going to involve a certain amount of planetary . . . *upheaval* . . . but remember we're talking about a controllable way of wielding crazy amounts of power here.'

Another hand.

'How long before it's operational?'

'Give us two Earth-years.' This was the project's chief engineer, a spry, eighty-something man named Parkin who Lucian liked and knew well. 'With the citizens of Pluto's permission, we're good to go just as soon as we've finished these biscuits.'

Parkin was an original Plutonian, hand-picked by Clavius Harbour himself, and an old hand at megaconstruction. Where Halley was the titan in scientific design, Parkin was the counterpart who engineered her worlds to life. Not for the first time, Lucian, sat between them, contemplated the surreality of his situation.

12

'One final question.' Edmund Harbour nodded towards another hand.

The speaker rose. 'We've all been following the search for indigenous Plutonians very closely, and many of us still continue that search. If there *is* life on Pluto, what effect might this project have upon it?'

A charge seemed to sweep through the room then, like wind disturbing a field. Murmurs passed from one bowed head to the next. Lucian managed to catch Halley's eye without turning his face, but his confusion was met only with calculated blankness.

'I'll take this one.'

The smooth, fluid voice of a woman from the other end of the table. Lucian had said hello in the whirlwind of introductions earlier without taking anything in, but now he saw her nameplate read Mallory Madoc . . . *She* was Mallory Madoc? It was one of those names everyone in his field knew, but whose face he had never thought to look up. She looked so young to have led the first team to discover extraterrestrial life.

'What we saw consistently on Europa were independent colonies of thermophilic methanogens clustered around deep-sea hydrothermal vents,' said Madoc, in brisk tones better suited for scientific symposia. 'It's a similar story on Enceladus, wouldn't you say, Yolanda?'

A dark-haired, dark-eyed woman in the front row responded with a nod as Lucian felt the name click. He had been agog when he'd first heard Pluto had Yolanda Moreno as well: the woman who, only months behind Madoc, had found life on Saturn's moon Enceladus. They called themselves xenobiologists—researchers of extraterrestrial life—and it was only now Lucian thought to wonder how some backwater dwarf planet a year's journey from civilisation had got the duo who'd literally incepted the subject.

Well . . . for the same reason it got people like him out there, he supposed. Because it was a frontier. Precisely *because* it was a year's journey from civilisation.

Madoc continued. 'Including Earth, we now have three data points, four if we count Mars, for how life operates in light-poor, ice-rich environments. If Pluto does harbour life, we'd expect to see it, first'—she held up a finger—'focused at plumes of either heat or geochemical activity. Second, deep beneath the surface. And third, as with Europa and Enceladus, as a very simple microscopic form. I firmly believe the steady influx of heat provided by Project Plutoshine would nourish any life, even draw it from its hiding places and into the open.'

'Thank you, Dr Madoc, and I'm afraid we are out of time.' Harbour was on his feet. 'With that I'd like to conclude today's panel. Please join me in thanking once more our speakers, both familiar faces'—he indicated Parkin and Madoc—'and our newest residents.'

Newest residents. Lucian gingerly considered the words as hands fell and applause rose. There was still that slight head rush at considering himself an inhabitant of this furthest-inhabited outpost of humanity. Or maybe that just went with his aching bones, and eyes that felt like they hadn't closed since passing the orbit of Neptune.

It was only later, after Edmund Harbour personally saw the dozen or so newcomers to their quarters and bade them good-night (*night* marked by the dimming of the lights and ended by their gradual return upon *dawn*), that Lucian got to ask Halley what all the fuss was about the life question.

Her eyebrows rose, but she didn't turn from her study of their shared living room's livestream.

'You really have to ask?'

Lucian looked up from the act of throwing a fuzzy blanket across Stan, who was upright in an armchair and breathing stead-ily in that deep, wholesome manner only sleep could achieve.

14

'Well, clearly I *do* have to ask,' Lucian said, 'otherwise I would be saving myself the pain of admitting to you my fiercely raging ignorance.'

'It's only been a year since the accident.' Halley continued to watch the on-screen tide of a seashore ebb and flow. 'A planet this small for drama that big? Kid, they're still talking about it on Earth.' She gave the screen a pinch and the camera footage—at least nineteen hours old, if the live feed had travelled at light speed—zoomed right in to waves soaking the sand. 'Didn't you see the empty place set beside Edmund?'

Lucian had. It had been extremely uncomfortable to sit alongside, as though he were its equal.

'Do people really resent the entire discipline of xenobiology just because one search party for it went wrong?' He angled himself upon the arm of a sofa and folded his arms. 'Even now I'm here I don't get that.'

'There were many who said they shouldn't have been searching at all, or that it was a waste of time.' Halley's shrug became a stretch. She was a lioness of a woman, bony but strong, with an unflinching stare that seemed to dissect, then reassemble, everything in its path. 'I agree with you, but remember nothing's ever "just" anything when it comes to Clavius Harbour. Pluto's still adjusting to his absence.'

'Make that "Solar System".' Lucian slumped into the sofa's depths. 'Remember when we heard on the ship? Out in the middle of nowhere in the Asteroid Belt, and every one of us knew about it.'

'These altruistic genius types, they—' Halley stopped at the call of their doorbell.

It was Lucian who opened it and saw her standing there. The little bird girl. Somehow he knew it was her, minus the suit: the same height, the same huge eyes, the same anxious, hesitating intensity. She was even tinier face to face, with neat, delicate features and scrawny shoulders that hunched her arms close, as though to ensure she took up as little space as possible. She was staring up at him with what Lucian could later only think of as unblinking panic.

'Hi,' he said, somehow in that one word adopting the well-meaning, slightly patronising tone adults reserve just for children. 'I remember you. How are you doing?'

The girl didn't speak a word—only held out her hand, in which was pressed a note.

'Oh! Thank you . . .'

She bowed slightly as he took it, and then, somewhere within the moment of him looking at his hands and back up, vanished.

He blinked. It must be a Plutonian thing, bouncing with the gravity just right.

Halley peered over with interest.

'Did I just see you trying to talk to Nou Harbour?'

'*Harbour?*' Lucian spun around. 'Edmund Harbour has a daughter?'

'You really didn't read any of those social and culture pages I sent, did you? She's his sister—there's a twenty-something age gap.'

Lucian recalled the severe figure of Harbour earlier, phlegmatic, impenetrable, and struggled to find anything about the man either fraternal or paternal.

'Wait.' Something had just registered. 'What do you mean, "trying to talk"? I'm great with kids! I resent that—'

'Nou Harbour hasn't spoken two words in more than a year.'

Lucian's mouth opened in a silent 'oh'.

'Actually, that's an understatement.' Halley cast her eyes up in thought. 'She hasn't said a single word.'

'Well, OK then.' Lucian shook his head. 'What does that to someone? What happened?'

16

'Physically she's fine. It's common knowledge that it's some kind of psychological trauma.' Halley regarded him with deadpan patience, letting him figure it out.

It took Lucian a moment to pick up what she had put down.

'*Oh!* One year ago . . . The accident. Her dad's accident?'

'Magnificent deductive reasoning. Edmund says she was there when it happened. They both were. Clearly they each deal with it in different ways.' Halley stared at him. 'Well, are you going to open it? I'd like to see what she has to say, as rare an occasion as that is.'

He unfolded the note:

Can I please help?

The words were written . . . *oddly*, somehow. Cursive but disjointed, as though each letter had been torn from her fingers, slowly and painfully written in time for the ink of the previous to dry.

'Well, I'm not dealing with her if she wants to help.' Halley had read upside down and was already turning away. 'I don't do small children and I've repeatedly made that quite clear.'

'Help with what? With us—with Plutoshine, you mean?' Lucian looked up in surprise.

'Presumably.' Halley was heading towards a white door with her nameplate at its side. 'Get Stan to give her a micro-internship or whatever they're called. He can put himself as supervisor on his CV . . .'

'Goodnight, Halley,' Lucian called to her sliding door.

He looked down at the note in his hand again, at the disjointed letters, the childlike curls, the careful neatness. He was thinking, if she hadn't spoken for a year, why was she taking the effort to communicate with them?

*

17

Nou's heart was thumping so hard she could swear it was lifting her from the ground. Scarcely three minutes had passed since she had stood with trembling hands at the Sunbringers' door. It was three minutes since she had fled, unable to help herself, and run to her darkened room the corridor over. Two minutes since she had reached her desk and burrowed under it, feeling the tight space pressing against her sides, her back, the crown of her head. One minute since she had pulled off her socks and pushed the soles of her feet into the solid warmth of the floor—felt it ground her. She was hidden. Safe. Her hands felt bereft, clutching and unclutching at the space where the note had been.

But she'd done it. She'd given it to them. The big man, the one with the wild hair. And now maybe—just maybe—she could help them draw life from its hiding place.

And maybe—she squeezed her eyes shut until even the rosy glow of her nightlight went out—maybe that would be enough to undo the mess she'd already made by trying to do so.

Chapter 2

Lucian never slept too well through his first nights back on solid ground. It was the view that did it: though his eyes were closed, and though the porthole was covered, beyond the window was a world that did not move. No endless pinwheeling of the ship; no arcing of the stars in perfect clockwork, each second faster than a night's worth on Earth. He went dizzy if he thought about it too long—as though he'd spent the past year not in spaceflight but spinning on the spot, and only now was standing still with a head that reeled.

Besides which, he was a child in the small hours of Christmas morning. How was he supposed to spend his first hours on Pluto sleeping?

Lucian told his family all this as he sat upright in bed, blinking at the miniature self staring back at him from his wrist-pad screen. Where to begin? He was in Clavius Harbour's Stern, on the world he had colonised, in the base he had created, even in the beds he had designed: above Lucian was a dome of glass, a little out of reach from outstretched fingertips, ensconcing him within the snug pod of a snowless snow globe. Little controls by his pillow even cast dancing visions across this bubble: pelting rain, drifting auroras, favourite films. Pure magic, yes, but critically, also an infallible seal against depressurisation. Clavius

Harbour was—and hadn't everyone known it?—a genius.

And Lucian had been so excited to think he'd actually get to meet him.

But he didn't tell his family that. Instead, he told his mum about the peanut soft-bakes he had hidden under her bed, freeze-dried for freshness, especially for this day. He told his little sister Felicity how the lab group all had bets on how long till they could swim across Sputnik Planitia, ranging from 'with the heat death of the universe' to 'next week if we build a big enough water-slide'. He asked his other sister Joy—also younger, but so damn competent he tended to forget it—how the finances were holding with the family's foster care, and which of the kids had got a home since they'd last spoken. He asked them to hug the cats for him, even the angry ones.

'Love and sunshine,' their son and brother told them, kissing his palm for the camera. 'I miss you all so much.'

Lucian hit *send* on his wrist-pad. Nineteen hours later—the longest wait for human-to-human contact across civilisation—his family would see his face.

And by that time, he would have explored all of Stern. Excitement set the roots of his hair tingling. A kid wide awake in the dark of Christmas morning can only resist for so long.

Where to first? Lucian was well versed with the base's layout: he'd had the blueprints on his wall as a student. What could be more unthinkable and morbidly gripping to a boy who'd grown up under the dictatorship of the Sun than a world devoid of one? He was thirteen when the settlers had first arrived on Pluto and even then, at an age where everything new seemed to him the biggest, the furthest, the most exciting, Pluto getting its first little town had deserved all the superlatives. He and his mates had raced around these halls in virtual reality games; had traded metadata on Clavius Harbour's interstellar ship plans; had memorised the names and skills of the scientists working alongside him; had taken turns role-playing the man himself off on adventures.

Were kids at home right now playing at being him? Lucian shook his head with a smile. The terraforming debate had certainly piqued interest from tip to toe of the occupied Solar System, but that honour would be reserved for the likes of Halley or Parkin. Those who designed and executed these grandest of plans were elevated to household names, to rock star status—and rightly so.

Soft lights started up a glow about his feet and moved with him to guide the way, like bioluminescence following a wader in seawater. All automated, of course, but still, it was all too like being watched . . .

Lucian actually gasped in delight as he remembered.

'*Gen!*'

At once a polite, androgynous voice suffused the air.

'Hello, Lucian. Or, as I better know you, Quickestsilver-underscore-seventy-four.'

Lucian grinned. 'So it really was the real you plugged into that game—the real server, or whatever, I mean. The conspiracies called it an advertising rumour. I was forever coming to you looking for clues and secret rooms.'

'I was pleased to be of service where I could,' the base's AI responded. Lucian was still walking; the voice kept up as seamlessly as mental narration. 'I hope you enjoy your stay here in Stern, Lucian.'

'Certainly intend to, Gen. I'll catch you around.'

'Catch you anywhere, Lucian.'

Long, shallow steps wound down a coiled staircase, their dimensions directly proportional to the gravity much the way Earth's short, stubby steps corresponded to the short, stubby steps of its inhabitants. Lucian took them two at a time, looking up as he did: stars awaited him, stippling the sky beyond a dome, bordered by just a silver sliver of those guardian mountains on one side. Hanging in the dome was a full-scale replica of *New Horizons*: the first spacecraft to visit Pluto, and the eyes through which humanity had first glimpsed the world that would become a home.

This floor—level 0—was the largest, the airiest, the brightest, the place where everything happened. Sharp shadows bent in the wake of his entourage of personal lights as Lucian crept in, patches of light and dark leaping together down the plaza, miming the bustle his imagination supplied of its daytime. Silence reigned for now, but here they would host festivals, birthdays, gigs, chilled afternoons off, catch-ups with friends, animated debates over exceedingly esoteric tributaries of science. This place was the true heart of Pluto.

He moved on to a nearby door, where a little silver plaque read . . . (he got closer) . . . *The Parks*. A swipe of his hand and the door swished into the wall. Lucian slipped inside.

And stepped straight into a forest.

Green. Dew. A dawn chorus. For a moment he was rooted where he stood, the breath stilled in his lungs. A year was a long time to spend in a rotating tin can. All the virtual reality in the Solar System, all the green in all the spacefaring greenhouses— none of it could touch the graze of bark beneath fingertips, nor the clean, peppery scent of rain upon loamy earth, the distant, mournful chirrups of a robin. Every surface was radiant with life. Peeking through the trees' tallest boughs was the latticed framework of a great bubble, and up ahead through the undergrowth, a well-trodden path curled enticingly between the trunks.

Socks lightly damp underfoot, Lucian disappeared along it.

And so he passed his pre-morning. He found a dedicated video diary room backdropped by postcard-perfect views of the Heart; he found a swimming pool the shape of a hamster wheel, the centrifuge turning its waters to hold the surface level; most foot-to-foot-hoppingly of all, he found a sizeable music room with all the essentials for a start-up band. Drums, guitars much like his own, a gorgeously 3D-printed grand piano, bizarre percussion pieces whose sounds he could scarcely conceive. His home-made didgeridoos would be in good company.

Buzzing from head to toe, Lucian wound his way back to the plaza and delighted in taking the long route via several missed turns and dead ends. But when he breezed back to the dome, he realised his trail of lights were no longer the only ones there.

'Hello,' called a woman's voice, rich and warm as the room's gradual onset of dawn. 'It's Lucian, isn't it?'

Lucian started as he recognised the silky hair of Mallory Madoc, the xenobiologist who had spoken last night—the one who had discovered life on Jupiter's moon Europa. She was sitting on a bench, ankles crossed and hands in her lap. She was smiling at him.

'Dr Madoc, yeah, hi, that's right.' Lucian returned the smile and bobbed over. He was suddenly excruciatingly aware that he was unshaven and dressed in a greying T-shirt that he was pretty sure (he didn't dare check) featured an indie band from two hundred years ago. He rifled among the morning's memories in the vain hope he had brushed his hair. 'It's . . . Wow. It's fantastic to meet you. Your work on Europa was incredible.'

Mallory Madoc was, Lucian was helpless to notice, lovely. Elegant as a tall glass of gin and tonic, perhaps somewhere in her forties, with eyes that sparked with dry wit. The Solar System's most famous xenobiologist extended a hand.

'Please—Mallory.'

Lucian accepted. Her grip was firm.

'May I?' He indicated the seat beside her and she inclined her head invitingly.

'You've been brought to me by g-lag, I take it?' She arched

an eyebrow. 'I was just the same when we arrived last year. It was days before my body remembered it was designed to experience gravity and let me sleep through.'

Mellifluous. The half-learned word drifted to the forefront of Lucian's mind. Maybe she'd just talked to the Europan ice, and its little creatures had sprouted up to meet her.

'Ah, it's not a bad morning to be up,' he told her with a shrug. 'My mum tells me there's only one known cure, and that's to stay at home.'

'Wouldn't that be to the loss of us all? Here.' She poured dark liquid into a cup and passed it to him. 'I'm an early riser, but it always helps me.'

'Oh, cheers, much obliged,' said Lucian with sincerity, then felt rather than tasted the coffee assaulting his system. A subtle aftertaste lingered: a sweetness like honey, like cantaloupe.

'I've got to ask . . .' He hesitated. Social etiquette between scientists always seemed a little muddied: how much small talk could be leapfrogged to reach the good stuff? 'I know you must get this all the time, but . . . How did it feel, the moment you discovered them? The first life off Earth?'

Mallory laughed once—a delightful sound. 'Please ask away. I'm far more frequently asked if I felt how people imagine *they* would feel. Can you guess what that is?'

Lucian imagined encountering new life. He had often fantasised of such a moment, and was familiar with the sudden quickening of his pulse and dilation of his pupils that followed.

'Euphoria,' he said on a breath. 'That, and vertigo, and awe, and . . . ah. So I'd imagine, at least.' He self-consciously scrubbed his hair for something to do. 'So, go on then. What does everyone imagine you felt?'

'You think far too highly of people as a collective.' Mallory was looking at him with something like amusement, or pity. 'It's fear. People ask if I was afraid.' She gave him a wan smile, as though inviting him to share this disappointment. 'In popular culture, extraterrestrials equal battleships and laser guns and . . . oh . . . existential weapons. Our media had hardly prepared our species for so ordinary a first contact as via a microscope.'

Lucian considered this. Nothing about the discovery of the first xenoforms—as they had come to be known, *xeno* for foreign, and *form* for shape—had seemed ordinary to him. He'd been writing up his thesis at the time, and could still recall with vivid clarity how he'd checked his feed and the room had swung upon a pendulum, how his ears had roared, how his flatmate had run in asking what he was caterwauling about . . .

'Now, Lucian, here's one you'll get asked all the time now you're here . . .'

'Oh?'

Mallory fixed incisive eyes upon him. 'What brings a man who has lived his whole life either beneath the Sun or studying its powers all the way out here?'

So much for small talk. Lucian exhaled.

'Well . . .'

'Won't you miss it?'

'Well, yeah, of course I will. But it's more like . . .' He fought to organise his thoughts. He tried staring at a figure beyond the window, out for a morning jog upon the ice. Rather them than him. 'I had to come,' he said eventually. 'Halley put the ad out and I knew that was it. I couldn't say no.'

'Why?' Mallory's gaze was relentless.

'I don't know.' He shrugged. He did know, but he was again self-conscious. He spoke with this woman as though they were two strangers at a hotel bar whose paths would never cross again—which could hardly be further from reality in this base the size of a university department. 'What about you?' He asked it in defence, to steer the conversation away from himself, but his curiosity was genuine. 'Europa's far enough out for most. Why did you leave?'

'Oh, come now.' Mallory laughed. 'If life can emerge independently around Jupiter and Saturn, then I'll hardly be weak in the knees if it transpires it emerged elsewhere across those two planetary systems.'

'Well, *heck*.' Lucian held back a stronger word. 'I mean, it's *life*. I'd be bloody dislocated in the knees from cartwheeling if another couple of worlds joined the "active habitat" category.'

'Really?' Mallory frowned. 'Gosh. I quite disagree. I'd much rather understand life's tenacity across the cosmos by exploring worlds less and less likely to host it.'

'What, like here?' Lucian sat up a little. He had known there was general interest from the xenobiologists about Pluto as yet another ice-rich—maybe water-rich—body, but attracting the two top leaders in the field was something else. 'Why?' He asked the question he'd wanted to last night, when she had first spoken. 'Why Pluto? What's so special about it?'

'Why not?' countered Mallory. 'The Sun plays no role in the lives of the Europans and Enceledans, so why should it be different out here? Clavius Harbour certainly considered it possible.'

Considered. Past tense. Lucian almost pointed it out, but there was something about discussing the man here in his own kingdom that seemed sacrilegious.

Instead he said, digesting this: 'He invited you here? Clavius Harbour?'

'And Yolanda. I dare say Clavius showed more excitement than the pair of us at the prospect of finding indigenous Plutonians—you might say it was one of his primary leisure pursuits. Though perhaps'—her voice lowered dramatically, and needlessly in the empty plaza—'perhaps, if one is to believe the rumours, he had already found it.'

Lucian paused mid-swallow; coffee shot up his nose.

'What?'

'Bless you. You know the story about the accident, of course?'

'Bits and pieces. Every newspage said something different.'

'Everyone knew Clavius was looking for life. He was dedicated to it. He would speak passionately of . . . What was it? Our *moral duty* to assure life's absence before tampering with wilderness. And how native life must always take precedence.'

Lucian nodded; everyone knew this. It was one of the many reasons kids were role-playing Harbour back home—the good guy sticking up for the small.

'He was always out on some expedition or other. Even once I arrived, he insisted on joining us as often as he could spare. And he was such a *busy* man . . .'

'They put us to shame, these industrious types.'

'It was a normal outing one morning last year. If I remember correctly, Clavius's daughter—'

'Nou?'

'Oh, you've met her already, then? Although perhaps "met" is a little generous when the conversation is one-sided. Yes, Nou—she was positively chatty back then. I heard her that morning claiming to have found life not a stone's throw away, wanting to show Edmund and Clavius. Off the three of them go for a pleasant family walk, then the next anyone hears they're calling an SOS.'

'You think they found it? Life?' Lucian was leaning forward now, coffee growing tepid between his cupped hands.

Mallory raised her shoulders in an elegant shrug.

'She could, of course, have been lying. Clavius Harbour for a father —imagine! Perhaps she wanted a normal family excursion, and found a reason he couldn't resist. All *we* know is that since that day, one hasn't smiled, one hasn't spoken, and the other hasn't moved.'

27

'There's been no response at all from the coma?'

Mallory's answer was a slow nod. She looked to be enjoying this—watching him put it together. Although sorry to disappoint, Lucian only held up his hands, unconvinced.

'Has anyone thought to actually ask them what happened?'

'Certainly. There's an official story, of course, but one doesn't need to be an investigative journalist to see the holes. Edmund hasn't said a thing about what really happened, but if the girl could speak . . .' Mallory casually brought her coffee to her lips. 'I'd be most interested to hear what she had to say.'

The door to the canteen slid open. Even from half the plaza away, it took scant seconds for the smell of hot bread and cinnamon to reach their noses, and barely another for the unreasonably strong stirrings of hunger to awaken. People were just starting to appear now, lone figures and twos or threes, their light conversation collecting into a sleepy, cheery hum.

'My colleague, Yolanda.' Mallory was looking beyond Lucian, one hand raised in a wave. 'I promised her my company for breakfast.'

Lucian turned: there was the sombre-faced woman who hadn't participated in the panel discussion the day before, the other leading xenobiologist.

'Right. Well, then.'

He drained his coffee, repressed a splutter on finding it cold, and rose to his feet as Mallory did. She came up to a little above his shoulder—the exact height, Lucian noticed, as the girl he'd once loved with a doomed and eternally secret crush in high school.

'Lucian.' She held out her hand. 'Thank you for sharing your time.'

Lucian stuck out his own and their palms met. There was something intimate about the action—about touch—after such a conversation.

'Thanks for giving me a fair bit to think about. And for the coffee.'

'I'm here any time you want to talk conspiracies. Oh, and Lucian?'

He met her eyes.

'You were right.' Mallory still had hold of his hand. 'It was euphoria. Take care.'

'Life on Pluto?' said Halley and Stan together, as Lucian related the morning's events over lime marmalade toast. The one was as credulous as the other disbelieving.

'It's minus two hundred and sixty Celsius out there,' said Halley, dusting crumbs off her fingers. 'Do you know what happens to atoms at those temperatures? *Nothing*.' She drew a line in the air before her, as though it were a graph with *things happening* on the y-axis and *time* on the x. 'Chemical reactions cease to exist on all thermodynamically relevant timescales. It would be trillions upon trillions of years before you had so much as a ghost of a thought of meiosis.'

'What about the Wimmer–Scheuring Effect?'

Two sets of eyes whirled to Stan. The young scientist visibly shrank, but continued:

'I read chemical reactions can happen at a few nano-Kelvins far more efficiently than at room temperature.' He blushed under the combined weight of their stares. 'Newman *et al.*, last year, if you want to check.'

'You understand quantum statistics?'

Judging by the raise of Halley's eyebrows, the professor was either sceptical or impressed; it was impossible to tell.

'Never mind that.' Lucian leant forward intently. 'Tell me how you can so perfectly memorise these references. Who taught you this power? *How can I learn it?*'

'I don't know if *anyone* understands it,' Stan mumbled around his coffee mug. 'It's just interesting.'

'Well, this place may feel colder than entropically possible, but we're still tens of degrees Celsius above those levels.' Halley turned to Lucian. 'Clavius Harbour is a property developer. We terraformers are his architects. Madoc and Moreno are surveyors checking for Japanese knotweed. The pair of them are only here to satisfy the Court of Planetary Protection, and they know that full well.'

'Yeah.' Lucian hid his disappointment behind an emphatic nod. 'Yeah, that's . . . I figured as much.'

But as he buttered his second round of toast and good morninged two of their lab mates, he couldn't help but wonder: if he was Madoc and Moreno, would he have crossed the Solar System if he was so sure it was for nothing?

That evening there was a gathering in the Parks, a warm welcome for the newest residents. Lucian was in his element. It was a far cry from the quiet midday meal shared earlier with their tour guide Edmund, whose flawless etiquette and ramrod-straight back rendered the event stiff and formal. In the Parks there was music—fiddles, guitars, a penny whistle—and there were raised voices and unchecked laughter. Within ten minutes he was deep in conversation with a chap named Vasily on the bulk berry composition of their cider; within another ten, once it transpired the man was the band's guitarist, he had met possibly every musician on Pluto and been heartily invited to play at their next practice. He met the chief chef and promised her a dinner of traditional dishes from his homeworld; he met the chief horticulturalist and was offered an early morning tour when the fuchsia-pink grow-lights were brightest. He agreed to more bake-offs, lab tours, and team sporting nights than he doubted he'd ever find time for.

30

As the dimming lights simulated the warmth of sunset, then the chill of nightfall, Lucian gathered the base's children to him and brought forth his greatest scientific instrument—and greatest party trick. The gauntlets were his invention, and no doubt the reason Halley had chosen him for the job over someone with a shinier academic record. They were increasingly the main tool used in his research, but also a source of enchanting spectacle.

'Look up, look up!' Lucian's voice was hushed and fervent.

He held his arms before him, with the cobweb-fine metalwork of the gloves reaching his elbows.

The children did, some with blinking, overtired eyes, others with glancing, self-conscious nonchalance, most with staring, stupefied wonder. And small wonder why: just above their heads, catching the light like glitter in a snow globe, was a gently rotating cloud of dust and light. Though barely stretching further than the children huddled cross-legged below, in reality that incandescent cloud would have spanned light-years across in every direction.

Lucian felt the familiar thrum of anticipation guide his hands to position.

'You see that glow right there, that big dusty haze above you?'

There were whispered yeses, hands reaching up to touch, but for the most part there was rapt silence.

'That's us.' Lucian didn't need to fake the awe in his words; the darkened dome, the stars burning above, the glow of the simulation like campfire sparks, all worked their magic on him, too. 'That right there is how we began. That cloud of dust and gas is just about to start clumping together to make our Solar System. Look, watch . . .'

The three-dimensional projection was simple enough: it wasn't real, and it couldn't touch them, but it certainly looked

31

as though it could. The spectacle was something like an immersive planetarium. Where the gauntlets came in, and why they were so powerful, was their ability to control every tiny detail of what the simulation did. A twist of a finger: the dust began to spiral to a disc. Curling his hands to fists: the disc began to collapse. Faster and faster as his hands closed in and in, until they were clenched, until the speckled cloud glowed fiercely, until a clump of embers grew at its centre, until those embers ignited with a flash . . .

The children sucked in a breath as one. Behind them, their shadows were long and radial.

'And now we have a Sun.' Lucian grinned. This was his favourite part. The illuminated faces stared up at the rippling, roaring, gargantuan beast that was their distant Sun, perhaps for the first time with this much detail and power. 'Watch your eyes and don't look too close, mind,' he cautioned. 'If you start seeing purple and green splotches, then look away and be the first to point out a new planet to everyone.'

Of course, at this the hunt was on, every face swivelling this way and that, eyes sparkling in the darkness in the search for the first tiniest leftover speck.

Every face, Lucian saw, except one. Nou Harbour's eyes were still ablaze with sunlight, unblinking, entranced. She was following the burned sunspots, the angry flares, the soaring magnetic arches. Her expression was one of awe and of terror.

Me too, kid.

Lucian knew better than most the unbearable, unimaginable power of the Sun. Fifteen million degrees, ninety-nine times more massive than the rest of the Solar System put together, capable of burning your skin a hundred million kilometres away. And the people of Pluto had better get used to it, because its power was heading straight for them. That was why he was there.

32

He flicked a surreptitious finger and a proto-planet zoomed Nou's way. She jumped as it crossed her vision, then watched as it carried on hoovering up dust along its orbital trajectory. Lucian was talking about magma oceans and atmospheres of vaporised rock when the worldlet passed between the two of them—the man canted against a tree with gloved arms held steady, the girl on the outskirts of the nest of cross-legged children, almost hidden behind the hanging orb of the Sun.

She met his eyes as it did—focusing and unfocusing from the dust-speck to him—and looked away as fast. Then, with care, she looked back again.

Lucian held her gaze for a moment. He was talking about the first solid surfaces just then: the first places, the first plains, the first oceans . . .

'The first habitats,' he told them. Above, fully formed planets now orbited their Sun in clockwork perfection. 'It's still going to be a bit hairy—there's still quite a few bits of rock hanging around that might bash into our new worlds—but for the most part, now is the time. Now, *right now*, there are weird chemicals forming and unforming at the edges of little pools getting washed by the sea on Earth. Right now, there are tiny little things at the bottom of Europa's ocean that're just learning how tasty the volcanic gases there are. And Enceladus has got them, too, and maybe Mars, maybe other places. Now they've learned to make copies of themselves. Now they're learning to grow. Now they're learning to spread themselves out and make a sticky green lawn over the bottom of the sea . . .'

The planets continued to rotate gently along their orbits, unheeding, uncaring, as species rose and evolved and fell and started all over again. Below the flame of the Sun, Nou's eyes were fixed upon him.

'Until eventually you get something like us.' Lucian spread his hands wide and the simulation blossomed, quadrupling in size and soaring high to the dome's latticed heights. 'Four and a half thousand *million years*,' he said, 'to make a human. That's how long it took for us to arrive. I wonder . . . I look at all this space, all these places, and I can't help but wonder—what else managed to happen in all that time?'

He saw it because he was looking for it: out of the corner of his eye, he saw Nou Harbour look away. And that, Lucian decided, was interesting.

He clapped his hands together and, like the bursting of a balloon, sparks replaced his orrery and rained from the ceiling to shrieks of delight.

Halley had called him a romantic before. A good scientist— one of the best of his generation—but with the terrible affliction of imagination. Optimism.

Why couldn't there be life on Pluto? he thought, watching the planet's children as they dispersed, some coming to thank him, some to ask questions, some to show him school science projects on their wrist-pads. There was no Sun out here, granted—no heat, no liquid water, no obvious source of energy. But that hadn't stopped the human Plutonians.

Maybe it hadn't stopped non-human ones, either.

Interlude 1

'I've found life on Pluto.'

Nou Harbour, nine years old, pyjama-clad, with a firmness of voice that belies her limpness of limbs in her father's arms. It is the end of a long day—the longest of any Plutonian's year, the one with the latest bedtime—and with her chin on his shoulder and her arms around his neck, her eyelids are drooping as though under Jovian gravity.

Clavius's response is a conspiratorial smile. 'Have you been at Daddy's Scotch, pickle?'

'I found it. I promised I would.'

'Did you, now? Hey, Ed, did you hear that? Nou's found us life.'

Edmund, a little out of breath, is right behind them. He is flushed in the cheeks from dancing, and a small flick of his hair has come loose to tickle his temple. He looks from Clavius to Nou, slumped, half asleep in his arms, and feels himself relax.

'I couldn't find you,' he says, his eyes resting upon Nou before meeting Clavius's own. Then, as the words register: 'Life?' His sister has talked of little else besides the search for weeks—she does this, joins in on their latest obsessions, not wanting to be left out—but this is something new. He regards Nou very soberly as he crosses his arms. 'Did you check the encyclopedia like I taught you?'

'I looked everywhere,' Nou tells them as Clavius lowers her into her bubble-pod. She keeps her hand tight around his as he does. 'I looked at all the bacteria on Earth—'

'Every one of them?' Clavius gasps theatrically.

'—and then I looked at the slime they found on Europa, and then I looked at the things they found on Encelsius—'

'Enceladus,' Edmund corrects gently.

'—and then I looked all over Earth again, and I looked at all the glaciers and the ice caves and the deserts, and I couldn't see anything like it anywhere.'

'Wow, Nou, that sounds amazing.' Clavius throws the duvet over her. Her quilt is the same rich navy as the sky outside, adorned with silver crosses for stars and patches of wool and silk for planets—Edmund's gift the day she was born. 'I tell you what—there's no school tomorrow, so why don't the three of us go for a nice walk and you can show us your new friends, hm?'

'I don't think we're friends yet,' Nou mumbles. Her eyelids spasm in the fight to stay conscious. 'I think they like me, but they haven't told me anything about themselves when I tell them about me, so maybe they're shy.'

Clavius coughs once and brushes a hand across his smile. He meets Edmund's eyes, but Edmund is thinking too fast to return one.

'Well, pickle,' Clavius says easily, 'you know most of humanity doesn't speak English, so maybe these guys are still coming up with a translation system.'

'More likely they're cryptoendolithic chemolithoautotrophs with no evolutionary incentive for communication,' Edmund deadpans.

'No.' Nou shakes her head sleepily, eyes still closed. 'They don't talk. They whistle.'

Edmund feels his eyes narrow. For a story, or a game, such a detail is oddly specific.

'Whistle?'

Nou's only response is a soft hum.

'And here I thought it was our job to tell you the bedtime stories,

36

Nou.' Clavius grins from son to daughter. 'So did you have a good Tombaugh's Day, sweetheart?'

No answer.

'Wow.' Clavius blinks. 'You never told me bedtime was so easy, Ed. I should do this more often.'

Edmund sidesteps him to tuck Nou's blankets closer—she tends to wriggle, then gets cold—then draws the pod's hood down for the night. He checks the seals twice, then turns on her rose-pink night-light before following Clavius out.

The celebrations for the anniversaries, both of the day of Pluto's discovery and their settlement upon it (not coincident by coincidence), are muffled above in a bassline thump. Outside their quarters, the usually spotless white halls are dotted with orphaned plates and footprint-shaped patches of glitter, and the air smells of dry ice and spiced tarts. In unspoken agreement at the hub, the pair travel not up to the source of these sensations but down, on to the lab level, down a quieter, fresher corridor. It is only once they are inside Clavius's office and the door has sealed itself shut that both turn to speak.

'Now, you know I love Nou to pieces,' begins Clavius, 'but the kid hasn't got a shred of imagination.'

Edmund is silent for a moment, his hands by his sides.

'In this context I agree,' he says eventually, a fixed point of stillness as Clavius begins to pace. 'She spoke too quickly and consistently to be recalling another child's tale or crafting her own.'

Clavius steeples his fingers and continues his slow pacing. Out of the soft lighting and warm pastels of his daughter's bedroom, he has emerged as another man entirely: taller in body and sharper in eyes, a lean, powerfully built figure of lupine grace, made for larger skies and stronger gravity than those of his adopted world. He isn't quite handsome, but there is a faded attraction about him: his lightly creased face; the crow's feet around his eyes; the small upwards flick of hair at a receding widow's peak. He is a man quick to laugh, as readily with warmth as without—quicker still to turn suddenly serious—and when he speaks he has the gift of making all beside him fall silent to listen.

'All right.' Clavius spreads his hands. 'Let's say she's telling the truth. Life on Pluto. How would she find it?'

'Inquisitiveness. Persistence.' Edmund keeps his response curt, businesslike. There's something surreal about discussing this in complete seriousness. 'She's spoken of nothing but the search for weeks.'

'Kids can leave the base unaccompanied.' Clavius seems to be thinking aloud. 'Stay within twenty kilometres, tell an adult where you're going, keep in contact. I'd know if she'd been flagged for disobeying those.'

'The immediate vicinity of Stern has been thoroughly searched multiple times,' interjects Edmund, inflectionless, 'not least of all robotically prior to the base's founding. Are we to believe that native life exists in our own back garden?'

'Well, how about we find out now . . .?'

As Nou's parent, Clavius can access her location history as easily as his own. The alternative to monitoring Pluto's children was to imprison them indoors, a precedent no Plutonian had been willing to set.

He brings up his wrist-pad, taps open a field directory, then projects the resulting map upon a glass wall. Bluish-green glows from his wrist across the darkened room, lone dots like snipers' targets lit red upon a skeletal blueprint of Pluto's surface. Topography, morphology, with a light dusting of anthropology in Stern and its scant web of thoroughfares to various places of interest. Red is clustered in the base to the point of obscuring it entirely; zooming in reveals lines that represent corridors, circuits for park laps, smaller clusters for bedroom, classroom, canteen.

'Let's see where you've been, Nou . . .' Without looking away: 'Are we crazy?'

38

'For taking the claim of a nine-year-old seriously regarding a fourth emergence of life?' Edmund does not smile.

'Fifth including Mars.'

'No. Every lead must be followed. The terraformers will be here in barely a year.'

'Right answer.'

The red specks upon the ice outside are far fewer and less ordered. Edmund squints at them as Clavius leans in, face lit a ghostly blue.

'All the highways to the mountains. Tartarus Dorsa. Picullus Dorsa. Up the shoreline . . .'

'Look within the past day, not week,' Edmund says. 'She would have come immediately to us after the discovery.'

'You think so, Edmund?' Clavius raises a brow. He is amused. 'You really think our little girl tells us everything she gets up to?'

Edmund bristles. 'The dependence of a child—'

'Is no match for their secrecy,' finishes Clavius. He smiles, sharp canines glinting. 'Didn't you keep secrets from me at her age?'

Edmund shuts his eyes.

'Pandemonium Promontorium.'

Clavius points to one place on the map, a headland along the shoreline of the Heart within twenty kilometres north of Stern. It is the most distal end of one dot-joined line leading from and to the base, and it is the only one within twenty-four hours.

'Pandemonium Promontorium is part of the Cousteau Rupes.' Edmund's brows crease together. 'That whole region was systematically ruled out as a xenohabitat candidate during the first robotic search. There's nothing there.'

'Would you be willing,' says Clavius, with precision, 'to stake your life on that?'

Their eyes meet.

'No.' Edmund shakes his head in answer to another question, the one posed by Clavius's eyes. 'We can't. It's too late tonight.'

'Then stay, and babysit what's left of the party.'

'Our absences will be noticed—'

'I know you're going to come with me. You're ticking off your rational, sensible check boxes.'

'One of us ought to,' says Edmund around tight lips.

'Ten minutes. Meet me at the minus two back door.'

'There is an airlock at minus two?'

'You're standing in its porch.'

Within ten minutes, two pale figures are crossing the pale plains of the Heart of Pluto and fast disappearing over the tight curve of the horizon. They move in slow, arching leaps, and they move together, and they are unobserved, so they do not exist at all.

Chapter 3

Solar mirrors were old hat to the great terraformer Halley. This was the woman who grew oceans, tamed volcanoes, resurrected worlds. She captured comets, crushing them into atmospheres; she generated external magnetic fields, bringing the aurora back to Mars; she had the forces of nature wrapped around her finger. Lucian was just a solar engineer, but one could be forgiven for thinking of Halley as an ancient deity: by classical standards of omnipotence, she was.

Again like an old god—or perhaps an old cat—she was also irascible, capricious, and possibly the least desirable companion for an extended mission. She had also, after ten years, yet to let him forget the time he once flooded her lab as a graduate student. Lucian welcomed any other company.

'So I heard you don't talk much, but that's OK, because I can talk plenty enough for two,' he said cheerfully to Nou, who had showed up at the simulation of daybreak and remained until its nightfall.

They were in the team's sparklingly new workshop, which presently looked as unmanageably huge and bare as new offices universally are wont to do the day of moving in. A half-made shelving unit, a glass screen atop a desk; these might have pointed to a more conventional use for such a space. Three concentric pillars in the room's middle, each at least two metres high and arching to connect in their centre, suggested otherwise. They formed a cleared space on a raised dais wide enough to swing a cat, though the closest one for testing this was presently snoozing on the room's single functioning chair, and would never have consented anyway.

'Five phases to create your sun.' Lucian pointed a spanner at the girl. 'Phase One—raw materials.' He raised an eyebrow. 'You're not attached to your moon Styx, are you?'

Nou was a skinny thing who came up to about his elbow, with a feathery crop of hair she tended to hide behind. She did so now, looking so worried as she always seemed to—perhaps thinking he expected an answer from her.

'Is that the one they call the baby potato?' piped up Stan, who was passing with several boxes of flat-packed machinery atop his shoulders that would each flatten a man on Earth.

'I will take that as a no,' Lucian said to Nou with a conspiratorial smile.

Which was just as well, because Pluto's third-smallest moon was about to be peeled, chopped and fried—or at least a sliver of it—to create a mirror two hundred kilometres across. That was four hundred *thousand* tonnes of pure aluminised mylar right above their heads. Some had suggested they hack up Acheron or Lethe, the two tiny moons discovered decades after the *New Horizons* survey, but Styx had the sweetest compositional cocktail for the job. And Pluto practically sprouted more moons the longer you looked at it; no one would miss one little bit of space dust.

Lucian felt the old spark of excitement kindling within his eyes. He wrapped his hair in a knot atop his head and speared it with a pencil.

'All right. Let's get this mine on the moon.'

*

'The mechanics are simple enough.' Earlier that morning, he had stood in the middle of the darkened amphitheatre, zooming in on the holographic speck that represented Styx. 'Sixteen by eight kilometres across, with a density of two point two grams per centimetre cubed, meaning it's about eighty per cent rock with just a veneer of water-ice on the surface.'

'This type of asteroid—it's unusual for this region?' Edmund Harbour asked. He had his arms folded across a polo neck— black again, Lucian noticed—that accentuated the ghostly blue glow of his skin through the projected moon.

'Here—catch.'

He went on as Harbour held the rock up in the wan light.

'It's not your typical Kuiper Belt Object. There's too much silica in it—metals, too.'

'And you can manufacture all the necessary materials from this?'

Harbour curtly threw the rock back; Lucian had to move fast to catch it.

'Your mirror's going to be one hundred per cent Styxian,' he assured him. 'And there's about two billion metric tonnes of that material up there.'

'We'll require less than a twentieth of a per cent of that.' Parkin, the old engineer, took over in his deep, slow voice. 'Gen?' he called to the base's AI. 'Would you kindly move the moon to surface view?'

The little holographic potato stretched flat before them like a round table, zoomed right in—a crumbly, misshapen horizon of boulders and gaping craters.

'Extracting the raw materials themselves is an entirely automated process, powered in situ by fusion.' A neat little power station appeared upon the crater-pocked surface, hiding the writhing coils of electromagnetic vortices seething inside. 'We require a month to set this up, followed by another few months' extraction and processing, before the tile manufacturing can begin.'

'But that's only the first half of Phase One.' Later, in the workshop, Lucian accepted the proffered Allen key from Nou. 'Cheers. That's just my role, and making the mirror itself is a lot easier than you'd think. Really, it's Halley who does all the heavy lifting . . .'

'May I ask,' interrupted Mallory Madoc from the other side of the amphitheatre, 'where is this two E-years figure you cited in the plan coming from? I'm failing to understand how collating a simple wall of mirrors can take so long.'
    'It's not "simple"—' began Lucian.
    'The mirror is only one half of Project Plutoshine,' interjected Halley. 'We build the mirror to enhance your watts per square metre—or, translated, to get you extra sunlight. But that's no good without an atmosphere sufficiently substantial to keep hold of all that heat. Gen, bring up Pluto.' At her words, Gen replaced the computerised Styx with the familiar, tan-hued globe of Pluto. The room felt warmer for it. 'Look at your atmosphere. Even after a decade of artificial greenhouse gas release, you're still at a hundredth the pressure of the Martian surface, which is in turn a hundredth that of Earth's. Combine that with your average surface reflectivity of point six—which is pretty reflective as far as space rocks go—and any sunlight we throw at you is just going to bounce right back. If you're going to make the most of this mirror, you need to up your atmospheric partial pressure by at least two orders of magnitude.'
    'Your proposal described capturing several KBO asteroids'—Harbour focused his stare on Halley—'and grazing them against the outermost shell of what modest atmosphere we have. Do I understand that correctly?'

44

'Yes, with "graze" being the key word here. Sunlight first, atmospheric renovation second—that's our Phases Two and Three. Gen?'

Gen seemed to know what he, she, or it was doing, because now the translucent Pluto was gone, replaced by three reddish, irregularly shaped projections. Halley pointed to one.

'Meet our new favourite asteroids—one-nine-seven-seven-oh-four-three'—pointing to the next—'one-eight-three-eight-four-six-nine'—and lastly—'two-oh-three-nine-four-eight-five.'

Lucian realised his mouth was open.

'Did . . . ? Did you really have those memorised?'

Someone began feeble applause, which quickly died off.

'You'll be relieved to hear the Interplanetary Astronomical Union has let us name them Mortimaeus, Silvasaire, and Jovortre.' Halley smiled wryly. 'We call them the gards. I'm assured it's some literary reference. Now, their densities range from nought point four to nought point six, meaning they're about as close to clean ices as you're going to get. Those red patches you're looking at are photo-dissociated gases that later froze, probably things like methane and ammonium hydrates. These rocks are full of them, and they're what will be liberated once we scorch them through your atmosphere. The plan is this. What we intend to do first is capture them . . .'

Little propulsion systems flared into existence at a wave of her hand at the table.

'We then get them into orbit . . .'

The orb of Pluto appeared once more.

'We manoeuvre them into position . . .'

The projected Pluto grew larger and larger.

'They then enter the planet's atmosphere . . .'

Each gard-asteroid began to flash, just lightly, as it degassed in the planet's tenuous air—more of a sparkler than the fireworks of shooting stars on Earth.

45

'. . . where they then break up under the subsequent friction. We call this the termination point.' Halley spelled it out for them: 'Capture, orbit, manoeuvre, enter, terminate.'

'I bet that makes a nice acronym,' someone remarked.

'Always helps with funding.'

'She calls it COMET, and she's done this with something like fifty of them across the Solar System. Did you know they calculated she almost single-handedly accelerated Mars's terraforming by half a century with it? Man, you'd look at her CV and just retire . . .'

'Now.' Halley turned to the projection once more. 'The solar mirror and the asteroid capture go hand in hand. By the time the mirror is assembled in six months, we'll have moved the first gard into position ready for atmospheric entry and have the other two well on their way. Parkin here kindly deployed remote propulsion vessels to reach and transport the three while we were still in transit, so that's a bonus head start. Mortimaeus is the smallest and nearest—it should reach Pluto in eight months.'

'And it won't take much longer than that to complete the mirror itself,' rumbled Parkin, 'which forms the other part of Phase Two—the mirror's first test. The time waiting for the rest of these asteroids will be well spent with simulations, improvements, and test runs.'

'Something worth mentioning as well,' Lucian added, 'is that it gives us leeway to get the fusion reactor powered up at a gentle pace. Fusion's an excruciatingly exact science and it's not the kind of thing you want to rush . . .'

'So, there you have it. That's Plutoshine. Phase One is get all your materials. Phase Two, get the first asteroid in and test the mirror. Phase Three is get the other gards in. Four is turn the mirror on for good, and Five is leave it on long enough for all Plutonians to need swimming lessons.' Back in the workshop now, after the morning's meeting and a long, satisfying day's de-flat-packing, Lucian beamed. 'Basically, it's my job to make the mirror, Halley's to make the atmosphere, Parkin helps us with both, your da—brother oversees everything, and you, Nou . . .' He racked his brains. Then he raised his pencil with a bright smile. 'You get to be my apprentice.'

'Hang on a minute!' Stan cried. 'I thought I was your apprentice! I had to have a panel interview and everything.'

'Stan.' Lucian grabbed the boy by the arm as he passed and clapped a paternal hand on his shoulder. 'You are so much more than an apprentice. You are my first and only student, and you make me proud every day—'

'Is the simulation supposed to be on fire, by the way?'

'The hm? Ah!'

In the midst of the workshop's part-assembled production line of 3D-printed furniture was that one cleared patch, a perfect circle guarded by its three arcing pillars. And within this, reaching up past the mezzanine to the ceiling, was a burgeoning, gargantuan fireball.

'Nope!' Lucian jumped to his feet. 'Nope, *nope*, initiate reset, *reset system*!'

'No simulation can achieve perfect fusion every time, so this is the one aspect we've got to go full twenty-first century with and do manually.' Lucian looked from one colleague to the next in the darkened amphitheatre and winced. 'And I really mean manual—you cannot take your eyes off the merging of atoms for even a moment . . .'

'Stan, quick, toss me those gauntlets . . .'

In the workshop, Lucian snapped on his circlet with one hand and regained his balance with the other.

'Catch!'

He caught the contraptions mid-air and pulled them on. The gloves came to his elbows, delicate metal wires snaking up the length of his fingers and around his wrists, more an intricate computational mesh than gloves. Then, with the same urgency one would deploy for retrieving burned muffins from an oven, he plunged his hands straight into the fireball.

Nou, flattened behind a pop-up chair set, looked on in flabbergasted horror.

Lucian breathed in deeply through his nose and tuned out the white-lit room around him. The simulation's flames licked up his arms, unable to so much as tickle, but the sight still raised goosebumps every time. He slowly lowered his eyelids, letting all his concentration slide down his arms and into the tips of his fingers, focusing on curling and uncurling them . . . on drawing his hands together . . . on snapping them apart. Each millimetre counted.

The gloves' projection in the Parks had just been the beginner's mode; fireworks to a rocket propulsion engineer. Standing with feet firmly apart, gauntlets extended, encircled by their triangulating transmitters, Lucian the terraformer was now engrossed in the virtual world of planet-making. The silver band across his forehead was studded with white circles pressed close against his skin, each fine-tuned to the slightest move of those gloved hands. Each thought had a consequence in this world. Each thought could build a world.

Nou was standing up now, watching in fascination. Stan was watching, too, in his case with scholarly interest.

The whirrs and hums ubiquitous in artificially maintained atmospheres began to fade away for Lucian. His whole forearm seemed distorted, rippling, as though moving through some heavy, insubstantial force, but it was the sensing that counted. And the sensing, in his mind, drew into the clarity of a still lake.

He snapped his eyes open and—just like that—the fireball vanished. He blinked himself back to the world.

'Well, I made a right pig's ear of this one, didn't I?' he called cheerfully over his shoulder. The fireball was a phantom now, a bleached ring of green and purple upon the insides of eyelids. 'Stars above us. Just nobody tell Halley, OK?' He inclined his head at Nou. 'That includes you.'

'Did you blow the field coils again?' said Stan with interest. 'Can I rewind it? I keep doing that, too, it's the outer poloidal ones that catch me out . . .'

'Don't you go learning from my example, I taught you better than that.' Lucian pulled his hands out and gave them a shake. A shudder ran through him. 'I always half-expect molten plasma to come flying off when I do that.'

He started a little when he turned around to find Nou right there, closer than she'd let herself come before. She was staring at the gauntlets, one hand carefully raised. Lucian brought his own before her.

'They're gorgeous, aren't they? Go ahead and touch them, I know they look delicate. It's all carbon optics, just wires and crystals and electrochemical signals. I'll teach you some time.'

'It doesn't look like the field coils,' called Stan. He had goggles on with glass so dark they appeared opaque-black, but the white light of the rewound simulation must have been telling him something. 'There's a pressure loss somewhere.'

Lucian's eyebrows shot up. 'Eh?'

'If this simulation is accurate, it's saying there's a nought point nine per cent probability of magnetic containment cohesivity disintegration over the next week with no action taken.'

Lucian carefully folded his arms.

'So, in English, you mean an explosion?' He held up one finger to Nou—*one minute*—and hopped over to his student. 'All right, let's have a look, show me on the screens. Point out where . . .

'Oh, *come on*,' he sighed, a moment later. 'Bloody argon again. See the liquid lithium vessels here? They're not getting the pressure they need to operate because *somebody*'—he jabbed a finger at that part of the screen—'isn't playing ball.'

Behind him, Nou was standing on her tiptoes to see, but their dozen screens all displayed mathematical code. To the trained eye, none of it looked good.

A probability of 0.9 per cent over a one-week timescale didn't sound like much, but that was about as high magnitude a catastrophe as one could ever hope to avoid in one's lifetime. And there was more—something Stan hadn't noticed. That 0.9 per cent probability was *cumulative with each passing week*.

'All right . . .' Lucian clapped his hands together and stood up—then paused at a soft hiss from around the corner. It was the stirring of inrushing air with the opening of a door; it was, for now, all they had for a doorbell.

Maybe Halley or someone in the adjoining room was calling it a night. Then a cultured, disembodied voice:

'Pardon me for disturbing you. I was told I would find my sister here. I wonder, have you seen her this evening . . .?'

Edmund Harbour! Lucian's eyes flew to his wrist-pad—it had gone 10 p.m.—then to Nou. Her frozen stance and round eyes confirmed his split-second hypothesis: it was past her bedtime. And Lucian, as the supposedly responsible adult, felt just as caught out as she.

They had but moments; Harbour would round the corner and be upon them in seconds.

'Quick!' Lucian mouthed to her. He spun on the spot, then,

spying inspiration, plonked both hands on her shoulders and pressed. 'Sit!'

Barely had Nou slumped into the chair behind her than he darted two leaps, scooped up what he was after, and all but flung the thing upon her lap. Then, straightening up, speaking up: 'OK, maybe if I try the mop, maybe we can *sweep* him—Oh, Edmund, hi.'

'Lucian.' There was Edmund Harbour all right: hands behind his back, posture zero degrees from vertical, eyes exquisitely devoid of expression. 'May I ask if you—Ah.'

Nou was pinned—*half-buried* was perhaps more accurate—beneath a great mass of coarse fur, which rose and fell beneath her hands with a cyclic wheeze. The cat twitched a torn ear and stretched out his paws; Lucian swallowed his breath as the girl flinched before resuming her brushing.

He spread his smile and his hands wide in apology.

'Captain Whiskers,' he said in indulgent fondness, as though this explained everything. 'He shreds anything that moves. We've been waiting for him to get up for hours so no one gets hurt. I'm guessing you've come to see who commandeered your sister past her bedtime?'

Lucian caught Nou's eye just for a fraction of a second—and hoped her startled eyes were at the speed of his ingenuity, not a mortal terror of battle-hardened toms.

Edmund, meanwhile, was looking inscrutably from his sister to the cat.

'I . . . see.'

'We'll have her returned to you in just a jiffy, honest. Stan was going to find us a broom or something—'

'We can try these.' Lucian swelled with gratitude: Stan was pulling on the gauntlets as though they were industrial washing-up gloves. 'I got to know him on the ship over, so maybe he won't mind so much if I try.'

Lucian gave Edmund his brightest smile—'Give us ten minutes'—but the other man did not see: Edmund was looking down at his sister, and Nou was looking up at her brother. She had stopped stroking the cat. The look the two shared was only a moment, but it was time enough for Lucian's smile to slide loose.

He rushed over the instant their guest had departed and swept Captain Whiskers into his arms.

'You marvellous, darling old man,' he declared, cuddling his dear savage close. 'Nou, don't you ever fear this cat. He's a cantankerous grumbler, and the claws do come out when deserved, but he's got a heart of praline ganache.'

Nou got to her feet; Lucian watched her over the crest of the Captain's head. She drew in a breath, her expression distant—then she smiled.

She looked up at Lucian. He smiled right back. There was something conspiratorial about it: a shared gratitude, shared secret. They had got away with it.

Lucian inclined his head the way Edmund Harbour had gone.

'Now off with you. Your brother was right to come looking. And you're going to need your sleep for tomorrow because we've still got that fusion error to fix.'

'More gauntleting, then? Oh, can we call it gauntleteering?' Stan was ruffling the Captain's chest through said gauntlets; tufts of fur clung like dandelion heads between its wires. 'Or will we be coding, getting into the source?'

Lucian raised his eyebrows from Stan to Nou.

'Actually, I was thinking more along the lines of a little field-work.'

Chapter 4

The seat was trying to swallow Nou whole. Padded cushioning rose either side of the chair but too distant to offer support; armrests pushed her elbows almost eye level; her feet dangled some way above the floor. She gave them a surreptitious swing, feeling like a mouse in a lion's throne.

When Lucian and his apprentice had sought Edmund for permission over breakfast the following morning, her brother had seemed only perplexed they had bothered to ask. Every child on Pluto was considered safe with another adult, and largely even without one: adults far more parental than her brother trusted them with their freedom. As such, Nou was now in the aircraft hangar, being strapped into a chair that really could have used a child-sized add-in, and apparently she was going to Styx.

The Sunbringer came to stand in front of her, hands on hips, and frowned at the sight. The action set a little dimple in each cheek.

'No, that's not quite right, is it?' He stroked his chin. 'All right, keep still, I'll have this sorted in a tick . . .'

Why had she gone along with this? Nou cringed to herself as he disappeared behind her. She was being slowly bound to a chair so large she could barely see the windows, a chair within a craft that would propel her from the surface of her home and for the first time—the first time ever *ever*—into space. A place where there was no ground and no gravity and no home.

Of course she had gone along with this. It was her perfect in with the Sunbringers. Besides—

'Ah! Here's the armrest lock, there you go . . .'

She jumped at a sudden sensation: there was the close-by whirr and vibration of a drill.

With a click they slid to a good grippable height. Nou gripped them in gratitude.

Lucian was struggling with something behind her. He sounded in his element, happily chatting away with a screwdriver behind an ear.

'Just hold still a sec, let me see if these belts will go any tighter . . . A*ha* . . .'

Nou jumped as two solid strips of metal appeared behind her shoulders and crossed in a firmly anchored *X* across her chest. With a click they locked into place, too tight to inhale a full lungful of air. She fought the instinct to tear herself free.

'Much better!' Lucian had come back around to admire his work, his great mass of hair lagging behind him as though in a current. 'Oh!' He pointed the screwdriver at her dangling feet. 'Leg rests. Let's have a look . . .'

It was another ten minutes until Nou was so securely strapped in that she might have been swaddled. Satisfied, Lucian began leisurely clipping himself in with considerably more ease.

'One last thing.' He leant over to her. 'Here . . .'

He attached what looked to be an oversized wristwatch to her suit's arm. Nou looked from it to him, perplexed; in place of numbers or hands it had only a pure red face.

'It's a panic button,' he explained over the hiss of the airlock. 'You lift this cover here'—indicating a casing above the face—'and you press this button if you need to get my attention

54

for any reason. OK?' His forehead creased as he raised his eyebrows. 'And I mean *any reason*. I get that communication isn't your gig, and I know that space travel is no more dangerous than stepping out your front door and all that, but I will get in serious trouble if anything happens to you up there. So, we need some way to talk. OK?'

Talk. The concept felt like a fundamental impossibility—no more within her reach than the Sun itself. Behind her, anxiously flicking through *An Introduction to Introductory Hydromagneto-dynamics* on his glasspad as though it was the morning before an exam, Stan had not been given his own button. It was only her who was the liability. Nou felt her cheeks burn with shame.

That would have been a good moment to nod back at Lucian, to talk in actions if not words, but as she looked up she was held rigid by his eyes. There was something in them that froze the breath in her throat, something unplaceable. It wasn't disappointment, or impatience, or irritation—those she knew well. It wasn't even pity in the Sunbringer's eyes; that was worst of all, when the adults would look at her with exaggeratedly saddened eyes, as though she was a sorry-looking stuffed animal at a tea party, one nobody loved but felt too bad to leave upon the shelf. Nou shied away from Lucian's eyes and it was several long moments before she could place the look in them as something like genuine concern.

'All right.' Whatever she had done, Lucian appeared satisfied. He gave her an encouraging nod, then looked over his shoulder. 'Stan, book away. Let's go.'

In the wake of his words was gaping, empty silence. Nou felt a spurt of anxiety: the airlock's depressurisation hiss had stopped. They were ready.

The hangar doors were sliding open. A sliver of the curved horizon was spreading across the windscreen, black pinpricked sky above, dimmed white ice below. With a nudge of the joystick, Lucian pressed them forwards and Nou felt as much as saw the movement, felt it in the vibration of her seat, in the shifting weight of her body within it. They slid into the near-vacuum of the night, out beneath the tenuous shadows of Stern and its mountains, out into vast, open space.

Nou's harnesses seemed to be tightening across her chest, constricting her more with each breath. They were clamped hard around her waist, holding her fast against her will, the headband a clammy palm against her forehead. Her world was outside and it was out of reach: no ghost of a chill beneath her boots, no numb tingling at the touch of her gloved fingertips, no feather-light skip in her stomach with each footstep. She was leaving it. Leaving home. Never before had she left the surface of Pluto, and never had she wanted to.

'It's a little like the old biplanes of Earth, this Sagittarius,' Lucian was saying, and Nou started as she realised he had been talking for some time. 'They just take off straight from the ground and into space. The engineers were so clever, they had to completely rethink the way planes worked once you get into a micro-vacuum . . .'

The words were slipping away as fast as she caught them. She failed to understand how anything this massive could fly at all, whether on Earth or on Pluto.

'That's our runway right there.' Lucian pointed to a strip of white up ahead, carved and smoothed from the ice. He turned to Nou and she felt his gaze like the heat of the greenhouse grow-lamps. 'Are you OK?'

It was no polite question or silence-filler: he spoke the words precisely, fixing her again with that bewildering stare of kindness.

Meeting his gaze steadily with her own was the only answer she could give. A nod would have been dishonest.

Lucian returned his eyes to the runway.

'All right. Styx, here we come.'

A tug at the base of her spine, the backs of her legs, the nape of her neck, and the little plane accelerated from a trot to something increasingly like a zoom. Armrests dug convulsively into her palms as they jostled with the rocking horizon ahead. Nou squeezed her eyes shut as a wave of panic washed her skin in sweat.

With a sudden lurch of power they shot forwards, too fast for her to gasp or cry out, and she was shoved hard into her seat by an invisible hand. The world outside her window was a blur; something was rattling ferociously like a wing about to snap. In that moment she felt caught in the belly of some great behemoth, too massive to lift a foot from the ground.

We're not going to make it, she thought wildly. *We can't take off, we're too heavy . . .*

Onwards they went, faster and faster, until the pressure pinning her to the seat began to feel disorientatingly familiar somehow, as though she was not streaming forward but lying down, and flying upwards . . .

'We're at Earth *g*-force now!' Lucian called over the racket. He was grinning from ear to ear. 'This is how our ancestors lived for millions of years!'

In a flash of clarity Nou had the thought, *But how did people live if they couldn't breathe?* before all the air was sucked from her lungs and she was tilted back in her seat, and with a paralysing surge of force from below they were airborne.

Beside her, Lucian was cheering, and Stan was shouting in excitement, but Nou couldn't register their words. She craned her neck towards the window against the tide of acceleration, her head spinning and heavy—so peculiar a feeling, *heaviness*—and froze at the sight beyond.

For her whole life her world had only had two dimensions: a surface and a sky. Ice and starlight. Pluto and elsewhere. The world beyond her window was all of these at once. Shapes were taking form in the Heart: great crevasses criss-crossed it like palm-lines; dark dune-fields of methane ice curved and aligned along wind-paths like fingerprints. Climbing higher, now she could make out the edges of ice polygons like creases in ancient skin: tens of kilometres across, the plates separated by deep gulfs made by some upwelling fluid, long, long ago frozen solid, the surface the hide of some sleeping and benevolent being.

Nou drank in every square metre of it. A tingle grew from the roots of her hair and swept down her limbs to each fingertip. Warmth, then shivers, raised her skin in goosebumps. Her heart felt ablaze, jumping from sight to sight as fast as her eyes.

The curve of the horizon was tightening like a bow pulled taut. A bone-deep thrill coursed through her: this was her world as she had never known it before, and it was more beautiful—it was *more*—than she could have possibly imagined.

A wall was growing higher on the edge of the horizon. A cliff: the beginning of the plateau that bound the Heart on all sides. Nou felt a lurch of alarm: had Lucian seen it? Were they flying high enough? Her hand stretched out towards him.

We're not going to make it! She willed him to understand with her eyes. *We're not high enough!*

Up close the cliffs were serrated knives, off-white and dusted with the blood-red snow of irradiated particles. They were almost level with its summit but not quite . . . Her fingertips skimmed his suit . . . They were too low . . . !

With a scream that froze in her throat and a hurtling rush of adrenaline, they soared clear, glancing so low her whole body tensed for impact. And now, above the cliffs and above Pluto's vast plateaus, there was nothing between them and the stars.

'Did you see that? Did you see it?' Lucian cried, whooping for joy. 'No automatic pilot, that was all human!'

That would explain it, Nou thought, but meeting his eyes she was startled by a hiccup, then another, rising and bubbling in her throat. It was laughter. She was trying to laugh. She stared at Lucian in wonder, and realised she was smiling. He smiled back at her with eyes that glowed.

They listed to the side now, and Nou's attention jumped back below. The landscape was every shade of tan, cream, gold, rust, whorled together like marbled paper. There were wide, stretching plains of each colour and crooked, scarred terrain where they met. She saw crumpled mountains catching the feathery atmosphere; she saw deep moats of maroon where organic material had gathered between their peaks, and she saw their glassy, translucent summits barely reflecting the weak starlight. The highways of glaciers scoured down sinuous valleys and poured out where they met their sea; the ice spikes of Tartarus Dorsa, each barely metres across but hundreds high, rose to the sky in tightly aligned bristles tiny enough to sweep her fingers through. Details, so many details, more than her eyes could soak up. They banked further and soared above the mountains now, back over the Heart, and there at the base, nestled into their steep sides . . .

Stern! Nou pointed excitedly.

How tiny it looked from up here! How isolated, how precious. There was her life below, rotating gently, each new angle revealing more: there, the great honeycombed dome of the Parks . . . there, the silvered skin of the central hub . . . the warm glow of the canteen . . . the domes of the greenhouses . . . the observatory's huge black eye . . . the neat rows of comms dishes. Wonder took liquid form and pooled, foaming and golden, in hollows within her she hadn't known existed.

Now it was Lucian's turn to point: a scattered handful of orange dots out on the ice, visible only as the tiniest of specks like broken pixels.

'I heard there was a search party organised for today—looks like that's them.'

A search party? Nou bit down a habitual stab of anxiety as she looked closer. How many dots . . .? One, two, maybe three or four. Her brother would be among them. He always joined the searches for life on Pluto.

Now they soared over the Heart again, this time so high that something of its legendary shape could be discerned. Nou stared and stared, grappling to understand that what was, on the ground, an endless expanse of creamy white, pooling like milk over the horizon, could up here be cupped within a gloved hand. Abruptly the scene blurred, lines softening and colours melting. She didn't realise she was crying until her hands hit the front of her helmet; she had unconsciously moved to dry her eyes.

The tenuous blue line of micro-atmosphere was fading now. Nou was stretched to the limit of her harnesses, leaning as far out as she could; when she settled into her backrest the surface disappeared completely. She raised her eyes. The blackness of space was waiting. Their journey to Styx had just begun.

Chapter 5

It was perhaps an hour before she noticed the patch of sky devoid of stars. As it grew, Nou understood how naive it was to think of Pluto's third-smallest moon as small at all. An elongated shape—more sweet potato than baby—began to emerge, dark rust in colour, saturated with craters so large it was a wonder it was still in one piece.

Lucian pointed ahead. 'You see that big hole right there, just coming into view?'

Nou looked, forgiving the use of *hole* rather than *crater*; he meant well.

'That's Condatis Crater. It's where the base is being set up. We're going to dock just above it, on a satellite station linked to the surface.' He tapped the control centre's touchscreen out of sleep and entered a series of commands too fast to follow. 'We'll be there in fifteen minutes. I'll ring Parkin, shall I? Tell him to get the kettle on. Tea or coffee?'

'Ooh, tea please,' called Stan over his book. 'Do they take tea with biscuits round here?'

'They'd better, or I'll be penning a very serious letter . . . You all right, Parkin?'

'Not quite,' came a woman's voice over the line.

'Halley!'

Nou watched Lucian physically straighten like a soldier roused from sleep.

'I didn't know you were up here, I didn't think fusion was your business,' Lucian gabbled. 'We'd have offered you a lift.'

'That's very kind of you, but incompatible with how I value my life. I would rather have walked here than risked being your passenger again.'

There was a splutter from somewhere; Stan must have got something stuck in his throat.

'Well, anyway,' said Lucian. 'Did you get to check out this argon leak? Have you localised it yet?'

A deep male voice took over: 'Oh, it's nothing a hard day's nanty narking can't solve. What do you say, Professor?'

'Parkin! Any chance of a cup of tea in ten minutes? Any shortbread?'

As the engineers threw unfamiliar words back and forth over the line like *cryostat* and *tokamak* and *deuterium–tritium*, Nou watched the little moon steadily fill their vision, so poorly lit it was easier to discern when not looked at directly. Condatis Crater was a deep, bowl-shaped depression that dwarfed their ship as its walls rose about them. Lights climbed in a mooring line from its central peak to a base about level with the crater walls: their destination.

'All right,' said Lucian once the plane had successfully docked. He beamed at her. 'Are you ready for zero-*g*?'

Nou's mouth fell open. After all the commotion with take-off, and with being strapped down so firmly, she had entirely forgotten Styx was capable of only the slightest gravitational pull, essentially equating to zero gravity. Lucian laughed at her dumbstruck expression.

'You're going to love it, I promise,' he assured her, unfasten-ing her safety belts with a series of intricate *click*s. 'You've felt it all the way here, except you've just been sat still. Moving around is the fun bit. Watch . . .'

And with the slightest push from his hands on the back of his seat, he streamed to the rear of the plane. Nou spun to watch this graceful dance but moved too fast: the frictionless momentum carried her, light as a feather on a breeze, right into mid-air.

The instant, seizing rush in every part of her body was almost violent. It was like being slammed into a solid wall of pure euphoria. She wanted to yell, to sing, and she wanted it so fiercely her chest burned and brimmed.

'You're fine, it's fine.' Lucian was right there, voice easy and calm. 'You can get yourself back down as easily as you got up.'

Nou felt as though she had taken too deep a breath, or jumped too high and had yet to fall. Her stomach and ears seemed to think she was free-falling.

'Brace your feet against the ceiling and push yourself forward. Then you see the headrest? Use that to pivot your feet back to the floor.'

Regaining your bearings in zero-g was as simple as remembering which way was normally up and repositioning yourself accordingly. Which was not simple. To Nou, bracing her feet against the ceiling as instructed and trying to remember what *pivot* meant, it was she who was touching the floor and Lucian and Stan who were upside down and grinning at her. Very carefully, she did as Lucian instructed. The correct perspective, and correct seriousness, followed with the suddenness of cold water to the face.

Lucian gave her a thumbs-up as she caught her breath.

'Nicely done! You'll have plenty of time to practise. Zero-g for me is a normal day in the office, so watch what I do and you'll pick up some tricks.'

'Is that really wise?' said Stan. 'I've heard the opposite said more than once.'

'Just you watch yourself.'

Beyond the airlock, free-floating within a padded tunnel, Parkin and Halley were waiting for them. Nou had never stopped to consider zero gravity architecture before: even under Pluto's light tug its residents were still mostly confined to *left-right, forwards-backwards*; here, *up-down* was a fully fledged reality. The corridor was circular and winding, with others angling off on all sides, and weaved out of sight down a gradient that made her stomach lift just looking at it. It all felt like a fantastical science trick, this weightlessness: as though any moment Lucian would turn to her and say *Time's up, it's someone else's go*, and flick gravity back on.

'Parkin, you old lifesaver.' Lucian swung himself effortlessly forwards and accepted a sealed pouch of tea. 'The sooner you can take this stuff intravenously during flight the better.'

'Or intravenously full stop,' said Parkin. 'Hello, Stan, hello, Miss Nou. I hear the best solar engineer on Pluto has taken you under his wing.'

'And the worst,' the solar engineer in question pointed out. 'I'm the only one, after all.'

Science, Nou was beginning to grasp as the talk immediately turned to the problem at hand, had a language of its own. Just like when she overheard Russian and could interpret the odd word, so it was with the scientists as they discussed nuclear fusion—even Stan, surely only in his early twenties. They used the same *and*s and *the*s, but in between these were indecipherable, syllable-laden words such as *gyrokinetic* and *magnetohydrodynamic*. She watched them pass the words between them like a shuttlecock, effortless, revelling in keeping the rally up. How could anyone become so skilful in something? Maybe that's what the *Doctor* before their names meant. Maybe it was something you were given that granted you this power and cleverness.

Edmund had one, so that would fit. She didn't think her dad did, but then he was so very clever that it would probably have been too easy for him. Her dad probably could have built the mirror all by himself if he'd wanted to.

'Nou, are you up for it?'

Nou started. Everyone was looking at her.

'The space walk,' Lucian added without missing a beat. 'Our argon's escaping from some kind of leak, and we're going to go plug it. Want to come along for the ride?'

A direct question. Nou felt her skin grow cold. Answers burst across her mind so clear they were almost tangible, but her mouth would not respond. There was not so much as the preparatory drawing in of breath, or the pursing of lips.

A nod. That she could do. Move your neck, your head follows. So why had her whole body turned rigid, and why could she feel the familiar seize of panic in her throat?

Only a second had passed, too soon for anyone to notice yet. But they were all watching her.

How about it?

That direct question, that pressure to communicate, not even to speak but to convey something . . . anything. The adults were all waiting. All she had to do was nod.

Please don't let me do this in front of Lucian.

The thought was abruptly there, overwriting all others. To Lucian she was still a novelty: where the other adults had long ago lost patience or interest, Lucian felt like the one person on Pluto not bored with her.

Don't let me embarrass myself. Just nod. Nod!

'All right!' Lucian clapped his hands together.

Nou blinked.

'Just so long as you remember your big red button and don't go too far from us, we'll be fine.'

Nou didn't move. Had she nodded? She couldn't recall. It was entirely possible. In her growing panic, perhaps she had moved spasmodically . . .

'Shall we meet back here in ten minutes once we've suited up?' Parkin was already collecting his equipment.

As the others nodded and did the same, Nou bowed as best she could in the weightlessness, then reached for a handrail to propel herself as fast as she dared back to the ship. Hot shame burned her eyes and hunched her shoulders close. Never mind that she'd got out of the situation: it shouldn't have happened at all. The desire to curl up small and find some dark, tight place to hide overrode and interrupted her every thought. She shook with the effort to resist.

Her helmet was where she had left it, clipped to her headrest. Inside would be some limited privacy. Whatever had happened back there, however she had got out of it, her behaviour was unacceptable.

Your behaviour is unacceptable. The hooded sparks of Edmund's eyes, always only a thought away. He would always find her unacceptable.

Nou swallowed the thoughts and swell of her throat as hard as she could. Not now. She pulled on each glove, clasping them in place with the safety checks, pretending she was Lucian pulling on his magical ones. She needn't assume her present company would think so little of her as did what remained of her family.

'Thank you for that, Lucian,' said Halley, eyebrows raised in a slight grimace, the moment the smallest member of their party was out of earshot. 'That was getting painful.'

'Is she OK?' Stan, bless his heart, sounded concerned. 'Is she always like that?'

Lucian looked to Parkin. 'Has there been progress at all since the accident?'

'Oh, yes.' Parkin pressed his lips together in a facsimile of a smile. 'Anti-progress. Edmund enlisted the help of a specialist psychologist last month, in fact. Though I can't help but wonder if the effectiveness is rather diluted when one's psychologist is at the end of a multiple-hour delay . . .'

Lucian felt one eyebrow furrow as the other rose.

'She's been like this for a year and it's only now he's calling in the professionals? And from another *planet*?'

'He must have thought she would improve on her own.'

Lucian turned his head: it was Halley who had risen to the man's defence.

Halley continued, 'From what I've heard, mutism is a common ailment in children and they usually grow out of it.'

'Yeah, but what about scared kids, damaged ones?' Lucian surprised himself with more vehemence than intended in his words. 'It's not like she's just shy—'

'The lass will talk when she's ready.' Parkin cut him off, with gentleness. 'Good days like today will help, I'm sure.'

Lucian met Stan's eyes. It was childish and unfair to put the boy in this position, but he wanted backing. The student looked from the Solar System-leading, comet-wielding, planet-resurrecting professor to his adviser, expression impassive but eyes slightly too wide, and winced in silent apology.

'Let's meet outside in ten minutes.' Parkin clapped Lucian easily on the shoulder. 'Two cubic metres of argon lost per minute isn't going to fix itself.'

In the privacy of his helmet, Lucian tried and failed to follow his companions' reasoning. *She'd* come to *them*: she had sought him out, sought the terraformers out, and it had looked extraordinarily uncomfortable for her. That didn't look like waiting to talk when ready: that looked like trying, like pushing, like wanting but not knowing how. There was an *urgency* about Nou Harbour somehow: something in the permanent crease of her brows, her unblinking stare, the disconcerting way her eyes never left what she was focused on. Lucian had grown up around kids well enough to know: Nou was bursting with something, or *for* something. He'd bet his right arm on it.

What was it Mallory had said? *If the girl could speak . . .*

He snapped his gloves into place and snapped back to the task at hand.

In the womb of weightlessness, in pure silence but for her own breaths and the pulse of her heartbeat, Nou was floating among the stars.

The charcoal-black of Styx was above her. Strange: being tethered to a planet your whole life meant you were always upside down in a sense, clinging with your feet to a surface and praying for gravity to hold you there. She knew it now, knew it as clearly as she knew gravity by weight: she knew weightlessness as vertigo. Just lightly, mind: as lightly as gravity on Pluto. But it was there behind her eyes, reminding her, cautioning her.

'*crrk* . . . No reading yet . . . *crrk* . . .'

Lucian, above her, following the umbilical cord that connected their landing port to the moon. It was a pipe of sorts, or so she had gathered, too thick for her arms to meet around its other side. Machines below the surface were digging for silver and silica and all the other precious things you built a mirror out of, and they passed these up the cord to build in the three dimensions of space.

'I'm getting something over here, on starboard . . .'

Stan. The figures moved swiftly, gracefully, as though born in this alien vastness. As she watched, one of them caught hold of a rung and propelled themselves into a scissor-kick that fired them in the opposite direction.

Nou stared, dazzled. Like them, she was tethered to the cord, but where they floated carefree she was rigid against it, one hand secure around a handle and one foot slotted within another. Her other limbs she let drift as they pleased, to a pleasure and wonder that conflicted with the rest of her body's seizing dread.

'Got it,' called Halley over the line, inside with Parkin as counterparts. 'If you switch your visual to infrared you'll see it. Slight heat anomaly at floor five-oh-five.'

'That fissure there?' It was Lucian: he was the scissor-kicker. Nou trained her eyes on him. '*Heck*.' He sounded more amused than upset. 'Small wonder we were getting suboptimal plasma rotation . . .'

Nou let her eyes drift down. There was one other reason she felt Styx was her *up*, and that was because all of Pluto was below, and it was always your world beneath your feet. Pluto was an illuminated globe about the length of her outstretched arm (were she to stretch it out, which she was not quite brave enough to try). From this distance the Heart, straddling the crescent horizon, was a bright, featureless plain. Nou had once read that Pluto had some of the brightest and some of the darkest surfaces found anywhere, all patchworked alongside one another; now that knowledge was not in a book but verified with her own eyes. There was no sign of the al-Idrises, let alone Stern; no evidence of humans at all. Abruptly she spun her head back around, back to people and machinery and signs of civilisation, and closed her grip harder around the handle. All of it still existed. Stern, she told herself, still existed.

'Stan, have you got it? OK—three, two, one, *now*!'

Nou looked up in time to see the figures of Lucian and Stan working together to open a panel. They weren't far away—maybe ten metres above. She could go to them. Perhaps they could do with a third pair of hands, or perhaps she could learn something.

'That's . . . weird.' Lucian's voice, tugged low in confusion. 'Doesn't look like a mechanical failure at all. If I didn't know better, I'd've said this pipe had been . . .'

Nou looked about her, searching for a way to join them. Perhaps there were . . . Yes, handholds, she could see them. She could climb her way to them as simply as ascending a ladder.

'. . . *hacked into*,' Lucian said, as Stan offered, '. . . ripped open?' Lucian continued, sounding deep in thought. 'Let's try cutting away some of this ice. Get a bit closer to the break.'

The stars twirled around Nou as she lifted her ankle free, then spun to wrap both hands around a hold. Pluto's relative glare caught her full in the eyes, and she winced as her pupils contracted.

'Do you feel . . .? Lucian?' Stan, with some anxiety. 'Do you feel that?'

Nou looked up: the next handhold was a little way above. If she could just use the arm that held the handle to launch herself up, then let her own momentum propel her . . .

Vibrations grew beneath the pads of her gloved fingertips. The cord began to thrum like a plucked string.

Somebody in her earpiece swore.

In the flash of the moment, Nou's perception was of explosion after explosion, *one, two, three*, more still, surging towards her up the cord like fire up a match, only there was nothing to see: no sparks; no fire; not even the bits of cord, blasted off too fast to catch. But it could be *felt*, in bones, in blood, in instinct. There was no time to comprehend, to feel fear, before the wave hit her.

The closest blast was somewhere just below her—too far to hurt, too close to escape. Time came in discrete pulses: useless padded fingertips grazing the handhold; a body punched to breathlessness; the cord narrowing, narrowing further in the distance, as she was hurtled loose into the empty canopy of space.

A scream scraped up her throat as nothingness closed in on all sides, but all she heard was a choked hiss, clamped off as sure as a hand throttling her into silence. Pluto was spinning madly, everywhere at once, a blur of silver and burgundy with meteor streaks of stars wheeling at its sides, and everything was melting together, her eyes stinging with sick panic, her throat sealing shut in panic . . .

The panic button.

Nou blinked, scattering the globes of tears cohering as one mass across her eyes. Her hands were free: she could see the red button through the veil across her sight. She could call for him. She could call for Lucian. She could communicate . . .

A memory erupted across her senses.

She was somewhere dark. She was by herself and she shouldn't have been. She was nine years old. She was cold . . .

Pluto continued to wheel. The stars continued to streak.

Her suit was shutting each system down one by one to save power. Heat was the last—heat equalled life—but still she cried for help.

Her hands would not move. Her lungs would not open. The memory was so vivid as to split her consciousness in two.

Blackness on all sides. Cold, eating her from the outside in. And still no one came.

Nou's hand felt electrified, every nerve charged, simultaneously reaching to hit the button and pulling itself back in a perfect stand-off. She shook with the effort. Red filled her vision.

No one came. Until he did. Until he did, and she wished she had been left to die after all.

A direct communication. Not words, but it meant as much. The button grew brighter, bigger, redder, flooding all thought. *Go ahead*, it said. *Cry out for a protector to save you. And if someone comes—if, if someone even comes—then watch them despise you for it forever.*

71

Lucian had no reason to come. No reason to care. Why should he? She was nothing to him. She was nothing, even to the ones she loved. Nou squeezed her eyes shut as they burned. No sound, no sign. No one had noticed. No one would come.

A different kind of scream boiled within her then, not one of terror or panic but of miserable, exhausted frustration. Why silence? For how much longer must she remain a ghost? When she got her voice back that was the first thing she would do—she would turn off her radio and go out into the mountains and she would scream as hard as she could, and—

When. Nou froze. *When* she got her voice back. Her lips parted as her breath and her pulse and her world grew quiet. She had thought *when*. Not *if*. She blinked in wonder and mouthed the word. She could almost taste it.

'Nou!'

Colour flooded Nou's vision and with it came a second Pluto, a bright blur growing larger, now eclipsing it, now filling her vision, now taking her by the arms. Everything else washed to grey but he was in blinding colour.

'Hey hey hey, you're OK, all right? You're OK . . .'

Lucian's face came into focus. He was right there, helmet hitting helmet, as close as could be.

'I've got you,' Lucian said, and as he stared into her eyes she realised abruptly that they were blue, as blue as pictures of the skies of Earth, so bright it seemed unreasonable she hadn't noticed sooner.

'I'm right here,' he said. 'You're just fine.'

There was warmth seeping from his gloved hands up her arms, across her shoulders. Nou stared into his eyes, at the knot between his eyebrows, and saw they were just a touch too wide, his hands a touch too tight, and it took her a moment to place his expression not as annoyance, or impatience, but relief. He was relieved. Her chest spasmed oddly in that moment, a series of tight, airless gasps, as though she was on the verge of hiccups, or sobs.

'You've got nothing to worry about, all right?' Lucian held her against him with one arm and pulled at his tether with the other. 'We'll be back at the base in two seconds. And, you know what? I don't know whether to be impressed or cheesed off because, despite all the acrobatics I get to do up here for a living, you just roll along and somehow effortlessly get yourself into a gyroscopically perfect pirouette with no prior experience . . .'

Nou was still staring as he chatted away, something now about sleeping tops and positive torques. He still had hold of her, carrying her close like one would a child . . . 'Like'? She was ten years old: was she not a child? The thought was there, gentle but firm. Nou blinked back at herself, fish-eyed across Lucian's helmet. And with her answer came release, like laying down a load under the deepest gravity well in the Solar System. Her head moved forward slightly, then came to rest against his shoulder. Her eyelids twitched, then settled closed. For the first time in a year, she felt and let herself feel as small as she was.

She could not have said when she slipped into sleep, but when she awoke she was still in her suit. She shouldn't have slept; she knew not to—all children knew that. If you were asleep you couldn't check your oxygen. You couldn't check your pressure, your power, your environment. They were taught this as rigorously as sealing doors behind you in case of depressurisation, or never travelling beyond twenty kilometres from the base. But Nou knew she was safe. Opening her eyes, she saw the Sagittarius control board, glowing buttons of red and blue on glass screens, and outside the stars, more lights than darkness, carrying them home. She closed her eyes again.

Later, when she awoke, she was in her bedroom, and the soft rose glow of her nightlight was warm velvet settled upon her like a blanket. There were memories—or dreams?—on the tip of her mind's tongue: fragments of the landing, of feeling heavy, of hushed conversation. On a little shelf notched into her bubble-pod was the panic button.

Barely conscious, she slipped it back on. If she ever needed him, for anything, Lucian would come.

Phase 2

Chapter 6

Once again, the canteen had been commandeered as a town hall—this time as an emergency one.

'Why wasn't this caught in the simulations?'

'Why wasn't this possibility identified earlier?'

'Is the reactor stable?'

The questions were valid, insightful, and relentless.

'What was the cause?'

That one, at least, Lucian could answer.

'OK,' he began, addressing the room from the same ankle-high dais as his first night. No chairs had been laid out this time, and Lucian didn't suppose ginger nuts were exactly a priority. His heart was thudding in his chest. 'So, the problem started out as a hairline fracture down a conduit for piping argon. The danger *was* flagged,' he stressed. 'I keep a twenty-four-seven simulation going that forecasts the current phase of Plutoshine one week in advance—that's the furthest ahead you can get reasonably accurately, and that gives us time to anticipate any problems. The problem with *this* was that it all happened so fast.'

Lucian already recognised many—if not most—of the faces in this hall, but every one of their tense, anxious expressions was new. They were technicians, electricians, glaciologists, cosmologists, their children, hand-picked for life in humanity's loneliest outpost. One face was missing, he knew that—but still he found his eyes drawn to elbow height.

He went on tightly.

'Within . . . I don't know . . . ten hours of noting the issue, we were up there trying to find this fracture and seal it.' He looked from one face to the next. 'And we did find it. The simulation said we'd have no problems for another week, but the pipe began rupturing within minutes of us checking it out—'

'*One* fracture?' Somebody raised a hand. 'But multiple ruptures? Multiple explosions?'

That one question punctured through Lucian's facade of understanding.

'I don't—'

'What caused the fractures in the first place?' someone pressed.

'How can you be sure it won't happen again, if you plan to resume work?'

The room was growing restless. Lucian was finding it harder to blink the flashbacks from his eyes: the pipe shaking beneath his gloves—exploding towards them, *bam*, *bam*, *bam*—exploding at regular intervals, with regular force, in a regular sequence . . .

Sabotage.

'Multiple ruptures, indeed, but most probably with a unifying cause . . .'

Parkin had stepped in, but Lucian could barely hear him over the roaring silence in his head. Again he replayed the action: he and Stan opening the pipe cladding, finding the leak—*a* leak, singular—finding the sealing plug of frozen argon, *then* feeling the vibrations . . .

Lucian surreptitiously pulled down his rolled-up sleeves as goosebumps crept over his skin. It was only when he'd raised the pipe's cover that the chain reaction had begun: the first explosion, then the next.

Sabotage.

'How do we know the rest of the project is safe?'

The question snapped Lucian back to the hall. To the canteen, with its salad bar pushed to one side, and its trays piled in the galley, and with his hundred colleagues. All shaken and alarmed.

Except maybe one of them. A someone. Or *someones*. Lucian looked from face to face—faces he knew, names he didn't—and realised he really knew none of them at all.

'Are we just going to end up another Mars?' someone called—not provocatively, but with genuine dismay in their voice. 'A lot of us signed up to this thinking the business had got better since then. We all thought it was safer.'

Lucian opened his mouth—*That was one accident fifty years ago*—*This wasn't our fault, this wasn't our failing*—but was cut off:

'We don't *have* to restart the project.'

One hundred faces whirled to the speaker, Lucian's with them.

'There are many who advocate for the preservation of wilderness,' came the monotone voice of Yolanda Moreno, Mallory's fellow xenobiologist. Lucian couldn't remember having ever heard her speak. 'As one whose work concerns this wilderness, I cannot claim utter indifference to such a position. So . . .' She shrugged, setting her viewpoint loose. 'That is something to consider.'

'Pluto already had that referendum ten Earth-years ago.' Halley's voice cut immediately through the turbulent murmurs. 'So you don't get to play that card. You want to talk pros and cons of terraforming itself? I'll give you the pros.' She stuck out a finger. 'Mercury.' Another finger. 'Mars.' A third. 'Earth. The sooner we reduce our dependence on artificial habs and survive out on the surface, the sooner we reduce preventable deaths via technological failure. And the sooner we get people off Earth, the sooner the only known planet with multicellular life gets to pick itself up again.' She glared about the room—there was no other word for it—as though daring a challenge. 'I could go on,' she warned, 'if I must.'

'This is really not the time or the place.' Lucian found himself stepping forward with his hands spread between their general directions—just as, in the corner of his eye, he saw Edmund Harbour move to do the same. He could hear the pleading in his own voice. 'The important thing, the *good* news, is that we got the explosion under control, and nobody got hurt.'

'How is Nou?'

Lucian followed the soft voice; it was Vasily who had spoken, the Russian guitarist he had befriended in the Parks.

'She's fine,' Lucian told him, and his own voice softened in turn. 'Bit shaken, but . . .'

He bit his tongue. Nou would have been fine on her tether, hurtling from ground zero even if he hadn't seen her for ten minutes—but that didn't matter. The responsibility he felt was staggering.

'She needs more care,' he heard himself saying, and his own eyebrows rose at the words. They weren't the only pair; Edmund Harbour's were heavy and dark against his pale skin, and Lucian couldn't help but distinguish that one face among the many. Though Lucian's eyes remained firmly upon the crowd, it was for Harbour that he now spoke. 'I know it's not my place, but'—he was burningly aware of Halley's scowl, deepening with each word—'but if she could talk—'

'Thank you, Lucian.' Harbour was a blur as he transitioned from seated to standing. 'If you would like to come by my office at some point in future, I would be keen to explore this discussion with you. Now, unless anyone has any remaining pressing questions for our terraformers, I would suggest we all return to our routines and ensure no further disruption occurs owing to this accident.'

Now, and only now, as the people of Pluto bustled and flowed for the exits, did Lucian let his eyes rest upon Harbour. The man was already striding off, long legs and shiny shoes, and Lucian found himself gripped by a foolhardy impulse. He'd not three hours ago survived a near-death experience; if he couldn't be excused, then he could at least be understood.

He rushed forward and tapped Harbour twice, firmly, on the shoulder.

'Hey, uh, could I have a minute?'

Harbour glanced over his shoulder but did not pause; Lucian had no choice but to fall into step with him.

'I will be co-ordinating a thorough inquest,' Harbour told him with a curt nod, 'into exactly what occurred today. If you have any further information beyond what you have already imparted, please do draw it to my attention.'

'What you said about exploring the discussion on Nou.' Lucian pushed on, skipping to keep up. 'How about right now? 'Cause it seems to me it's kind of urgent, you know, that a kid can't talk even in a pretty life-threatening situation—'

'So you admit it?' Edmund's tone was conversational. 'You admit you put a child who was not your responsibility in a life-threatening situation?'

'I put my student up there, too,' Lucian pointed out, 'and myself, and I'm very fond of both those people. I wasn't exactly anticipating an act of sabotage—'

'Sabotage?' Harbour stopped dead and faced him; on either side, a river around an island, the current of people behind them parted. 'That's what you think this was?'

Lucian bit the inside of his cheek.

'I don't have proof,' he said, and he couldn't have said why he hesitated, 'but what I saw up there . . . It wasn't random. It was ordered, and you tend not to get order without conscious interference.'

The custodian of Stern regarded him with incisive attention.

'Thank you for this information. Now, if you'll excuse me . . .'

'Just a second.' Lucian cut in front of him; held up his hands as Harbour, eyes steadfastly elsewhere, attempted a sidestep. 'About Nou . . .'

Lucian could have sworn that the momentary flash of teeth counted as exasperation.

Harbour said tightly, 'Is this the most appropriate time for this discussion?'

'All I'm saying is maybe something more could be done to help her get through this. The whole not-speaking thing.'

'As I said,' Edmund's words were clipped, 'if you would like to come by my office—'

'Great! Where's your office?'

Edmund Harbour's workplace was almost exactly as Lucian would have predicted: stark, sparse, and cold. The dominant feature was an enormous screen that curved the full length of the desk; no sooner had Lucian tried to read its reversed writing then the glass went blank and slipped into the wall like a drawn blind.

Harbour's arm cleaved the air as he indicated a set of chairs around a table.

'Please.'

Lucian pulled one out and shuffled to find some comfortable position, but the thing was all too like its master: hard, blank, functional. As he did he couldn't help noticing—rather plaintively—a pair of velvet winged armchairs to one side. They were placed below the room's only concession to personalisation: a large photograph of a vivid, snow-swept landscape framed like a window. As he watched, he realised the image was moving, the howl of some silent wind brushing the trees with long fingers.

'Is that a simulation? A video?' Curiosity had the words out of his mouth before his brain could stop him. 'It's . . . beautiful.'

Harbour gave it a glance. 'A livestream,' he said. 'Earth. Nineteen-hour delay.' He focused his stare upon his guest in a manner that burned away all superfluous talk. 'You wanted to talk about Nou.'

'Right, yeah.' Lucian pulled himself together. 'Well, look, I've had an idea I think might really help. With learning to talk again.'

Lucian hadn't had any such idea two minutes ago, but there was something profoundly inspirational about the perfect order of Harbour's world. Inspirational in a way Lucian did not want his own to ever imitate. The idea had crystallised there in his mind as though he had known it all along.

Harbour's expression did not change.

'In psychology Nou's condition is called selective mutism, which refers to when a person is physically able to talk but in certain situations cannot, or chooses not to. It is common in anxious or disturbed children and usually resolves itself.'

'But it's all the time with her,' Lucian felt compelled to point out. There was something about the way Harbour had said *chooses* that he disliked. 'It's every situation.'

'In Nou's case, yes.' Harbour's nod was barely perceptible. 'Mutism almost always manifests itself as a coping mechanism for extreme social anxiety, which the child usually acclimatises to with time.'

'But hasn't it been a year . . .?'

'If you have concerns you should speak to the base's doctor. She oversees all medical and psychiatric cases, and is more than capable in her assessment abilities.'

Lucian opened his mouth, then stopped himself.

'OK. But as Nou's guardian, I figured you'd be interested to hear this idea. Or maybe you'd like to get involved? I think she'll like it, it should be fun—'

'That is considerate of you,' Harbour monotoned. 'However, I trust the doctor to know what is best for Nou, and I am satisfied leaving this to her.'

He had sidestepped the *get involved* bit entirely. A real politician. Lucian became aware of his eyebrows trying to twist themselves into question marks and fought to keep them smooth.

'OK,' he said. 'OK, great. I'd better go find this doctor, then.'

'Please do.'

There was a pause.

'Righto then . . .' Lucian slapped his knees.

Both men, understanding this universal social cue, rose to their feet and shook hands. There was something intensely awkward about the act—two people making physical contact who never otherwise would.

'Thank you for seeing me.' Lucian let go the first moment it was acceptable. 'I'll, uh, catch you tomorrow.'

'Lucian.'

Lucian paused in the act of turning and dying inside.

Harbour stood with his hands by his sides. He was watching him with steadfast attention.

'Why are you doing this?' His eyes flicked down and he pressed his lips together, as though considering the right phrase. 'Why are you helping her?'

Lucian looked back at him. Whatever emotion he had hoped to inspire during their meeting—enthusiasm, perhaps gratitude, at least *interest*—he saw now the foolishness of this thought. Those skeletal pines in the storms of Earth were as likely to grant him emotion.

So he lied. He shrugged his shoulders and said, with equal disinterest:

'I heard she knows something about native life around here.'

Perhaps he only imagined it because he was looking for it, but he thought he saw something flash across Harbour's face. Too fast to catch.

Then that face was at once a blank mask again.

'Very well. Good evening to you.'

The whole encounter had taken less than five minutes. Back in the bright of Stern's corridors, with folk still heading in knots from the hall, he could almost have passed the whole thing off as a moment lost in thought.

At least he had a lead. The doctor. Though some lead that was, if she'd been ineffective for a whole year. Well—Lucian nodded to himself, and as he did a rush of determination set his features as rigid as Harbour's—he'd just have to make this happen on his own. Get Nou talking again. It was what his mum would do. You help people who need it. Especially when they've been let down by others. And—the thought was there, he'd admit—if Nou *did* know something about life on Pluto, well . . .

'Lucian! There you are.'

Lucian's heart did a little pirouette: Mallory Madoc was bobbing over, her fine hair trailing, then settling as she stopped before him. He blinked at her for a moment, scooping up his scattered thoughts.

'You ran off,' she said, as an explanation. She reached out and touched him, very lightly, on the upper arm. 'It sounds like you may well have saved a few lives this evening. It must have been a traumatic day for you.'

'Oh. Well. You know.' He attempted a shrug. 'What can you do, eh?'

'Listen.' Mallory clasped her hands earnestly before her. 'You were talking to Edmund just now about the little girl, weren't you?'

'Nou?' Lucian couldn't hide his surprise. 'How——?'

'Pluto's a small town, Lucian. I heard you'd taken her under your wing. And you did just announce your dissatisfaction with her progress to the whole base.'

Lucian had the good grace to cringe at that.

'Well, I've got an idea I think might help her. Not even to get her talking again, just . . . communicating.'

'Then count me in,' Mallory told him firmly, and Lucian's eyebrows flew up. 'I have a daughter of my own back home.'

'You do?' Lucian couldn't hide his surprise.

'I know if it was my child I would welcome all the help I could get.'

'I . . . Wow. I had no . . .' Lucian found himself grinning at her. This was good. This was a better lead than the doctor. 'Have you, uh, got a partner or someone, someone looking after her?'

'Oh, just my ex.' Mallory flicked her eyes and hands upwards in a synchronised wave. 'Alexandra's only a year into high school. I couldn't bear to uproot her—even for so great an adventure as Pluto. Let's have coffee tomorrow morning. You can tell me all about this plan of yours.'

'Yes. Great. Fantastic.' Lucian realised he was still grinning, doubly now. 'All right. That sounds like a plan.'

'Nou, you know Mallory, right?' Lucian looked from one to the other, then to Mallory. 'There's me giving introductions—I keep forgetting you were here a year before me.'

'It's all right.' Mallory smiled with courtly grace at their small charge. 'Our paths have not crossed as often as I would like. It's a pleasure to be here.'

'Mallory's a xenobiologist,' Lucian added, redundantly. 'She gets to search for life on other planets for her job.'

'That's right,' said Mallory warmly. 'And from what I know of you, Nou, you're as interested in the search for native life as I am. We might learn something from each other.'

The three of them were in one of the topmost rooms of Stern: up a spiral staircase, past a snug common room beneath a great glass dome, off to one side, and into a private study nook. Not too big, nice and cosy—and most importantly, nice and quiet.

Lucian floated himself onto a sofa—a big, squashy thing that rose and settled like a sea sponge around him—as Mallory did the same. Nou took one of the opposite armchairs, tucking her legs beneath her and balling her hands into a cushion.

She looked a little nervous, Lucian thought: hunched shoulders, arms hugged close, even her gaze—flicking from the cartoon planets on her socks, to Mallory, to him, back again—never taking up more room than needed. But there was something encouraging in her eyes when she met his: something open, and curious. And there under the glitter-lined wrist of her jumper, giving him a little start, was the square protrusion of what Lucian knew could only be his panic button.

'All right.' He clapped his hands together. 'Nou, thank you for coming to hear me out, and, Mallory, thank you for going along with what might end up being an utterly silly idea.'

'I sincerely doubt it will be,' Mallory assured him, 'so do continue.'

'OK.' With a nod Lucian turned to Nou and brought up his hands. He tended to express with them when animated, and he did so now. 'So I had this idea,' he began, 'and I think you're going to love it, because I already love it, and I'm pretty sure I'm a genius for thinking of it.'

Nou trained her usual intense look of concentration on him. Her hair was settling about her ears like fine down.

'It goes like this.' He leant forward. 'There are a hundred different ways for humans to communicate. Actually speaking out loud is one, but there are whole communities who talk to each other without ever saying a word—and these are people who otherwise might feel very alone, who don't need to be.'

A touch of colour lit Nou's cheeks, but she held his gaze without faltering.

'So,' he went on, 'what I propose we do is give you those same tools. So you can communicate, but only if you want to. So you can be safe.'

Safe. Lucian tasted the word and in a flash was back in his spacesuit, back as the saboteur did their work. Back with that jump-start of fear in his chest.

'*So*,' he said again, drawing cheer to his voice, 'here's what I propose.' He extended his hands before him as though poised for a magic trick. 'I'm going to teach you sign language.'

He hadn't expected any notable response to this statement: it was the subtle, subliminal cues he was watching for. Nou sat up a little straighter; her brows quirked just slightly; her knuckles lessened their grip on the cushion. Lucian felt a tiny fist bump occur in his mind: she was definitely interested.

'So,' he went on, emboldened, 'the really wonderful thing about sign language is just how much of it *makes sense*—a lot of the time you'll guess what the signs mean before I've told you. For instance, if I do this . . .' He pointed his index finger into his chest. 'I'm talking about me. So then, if I do this . . .' Now he pointed his finger outwards, across to her. 'What do you think I'm talking about now?'

This was a risk. He was putting her on the spot, perhaps too soon. To his side he could feel Mallory's eyes resting neutrally on him.

Nou's eyes focused from his own to his hand.

He waited.

She brought her hand up. Her right hand, he noticed. That would simplify the teaching, if she was right-handed like he was.

88

She turned her hand to point, slowly, uncertainly, at herself. *Me?*

Lucian could see Mallory in his peripheral vision, looking from Nou to him and back again. There was Nou for both to see, copying his gesture. *Communicating.*

'Brilliant,' Lucian told her, with sincerity. 'Very well done. And it's the same for anyone else, too. Like if we were going to talk about Mallory, we'd go . . .'

They did it together this time. Lucian kept pace with her, until the pair of them were both pointing. Mallory put her hands up in feigned defence.

'I feel I've wronged you both in some terrible way.'

She caught Lucian's eye and they shared a smile.

'Now,' he continued, shifting slightly—even on worlds where he weighed far less, adults were definitely not meant to sit cross-legged for long. 'Let me show you some more of what I call the *makes-sense* signs, those ones you can guess.'

There was a little velvet bag by his side, not much bigger than a closed fist, which he brought into his lap and untied. Lucian was a woefully sentimental man, and for most of his life had held on to useless trinkets that held priceless memories: the metal name badge his father used to wear; his first guitar plectrum; the now-shining copper coin he'd found on his first trip to Earth; the blue kyanite earring he'd worn every day through a regrettable phase in his undergraduate days.

He laid the knick-knacks out one by one on the floor between them. He could have used cards, but where was the fun in that? Nou was watching each piece of miscellanea as it emerged with fascination.

'Hm.' He frowned. 'I forgot yellow. Not to worry . . .' He reached behind his neck and fought his way through hair to reach the fish-hook clasp. He pulled the little oval locket out from behind his shirt and held it up. It glinted in the warm light, catching the ornate etchings of *C. M.* on its back. 'Well, it's more of a white-gold, but we can use our imaginations.'

There were now ten objects lined up along the floor. To anyone besides Lucian, who knew their origins, their only common factor was that they were all different colours.

'Colours tend to make sense in sign language because they're things we can see and point to,' he said. 'Watch, I'll show you . . .'

He pointed to his lower lip with his index finger, then lifted the finger away and curled it down past his chin. He repeated the action: lip, curl, down.

'Mallory.' He turned to her; he didn't want to push his luck with Nou too soon. Just saying the name *Mallory* was still a little thrill, as was the sight of her, ankles crossed, hair over one shoulder catching the light. 'You do this first example. Will you please point at what colour you think this is?'

Lip, curl, down. She watched him intently—watched the pads of his fingertips, the brush against his mouth. His hands grazed the beginnings of stubble on his jaw, and Mallory watched that, too. Lingering—barely a half-second too long, but plenty enough to set his cheeks the very colour he was describing.

She released him by turning to the line of objects. Her hand passed over orange coin, green carabiner clip, blue earring, before hovering between red plectrum and a thumbnail-sized cat carved from rose quartz.

'I'm vacillating between red or pink,' she said after a moment, and her eyes returned to his. 'If I must, let me choose red, as in the red right here.'

She had touched her own lips as she spoke. For another half-second too long, Lucian couldn't quite collect himself to react.

'All right, so it's not *overwhelmingly* obvious,' he managed with an exaggerated huff. 'But you're right—it's red. The lips are . . . are very red, and I was pointing to them. Makes-sense signing. Let's do another one. Nou, you're up.'

Back to the task at hand. He went with the next-easiest one he could think of: this one didn't point to anything actually its colour, but the sign was unmistakable with context.

He stretched his thumb away from his hand, then with his other drew a line down the skin between thumb and forefinger. All, all the way through, trying to blur out Mallory's gaze. He was spelling out the letter *y*.

Nou watched with rapt attention. He repeated the action. *Thumb out, line down, y.*

She leant forward and extended her hand. Lucian leant with her unconsciously. She settled her hand above the locket. *Y* for yellow.

'Fantastic,' Lucian breathed. '*Brilliant.* You're doing great.'

He made it into a game. He would sign, she or Mallory would guess. And when all ten colours were established, they would race each other to reach one first. Nou made a strange sound every time she tried to laugh: a sharp exhalation through her nose, her expression all the regular motions of laughter, just with the sound on mute. In those moments she looked like any happy child.

'Lucian, from what I've seen of her, that was quite phenomenal progress,' said Mallory, the moment their charge had run off with one last shy bow. 'She actually engaged with you. She *communicated.*'

Lucian didn't answer as he carefully placed each of his colours back into their bag, thinking both of the successes of the session and how he really should get his miscellanea framed to see them more often.

'Do you think she was pushing herself?' he said after a moment. He had his locket between his fingers, skimming it between them in thought. 'Or did we trick her? Did she realise she was talking to us?'

'Either way'—Mallory was shaking her head—'I rather think you're on to something with this. She looked to be enjoying herself as much as I was.'

'Ah, we'll see.' Lucian ducked his head to hide the glow of his cheeks.

'How in the world do you know all this? It's not very common these days, is it? I heard auditory surgery has become astonishingly advanced.'

'No, it's not,' Lucian agreed. 'My sister lost her hearing in a nasty accident.' He looked down at the locket in his hands; fastened it back in place and tucked it into his shirt. 'A really, really nasty accident.' The metal was cool against the skin between his collarbones. A familiar comfort. 'Here's what I'm going to do—I'm going to reinforce those colours as I see her over the week, and I'll start speaking the names as I do. Sign language is as much about lip-reading as the signs themselves. That's the next key leap.'

'To bridge from miming to speaking.' Mallory nodded.

'Even just miming would be worth a song and a dance at this stage. But we'll see. This is already far, far more than I'd expected.' Lucian could feel his thoughts closing about him, a thick forest of plans and schemes and practice sheets. 'Practice sheets! Yes, that's it. I could set her homework, or little tasks, or I'll make up songs like mnemonics . . .'

Mallory laughed. 'Well, remember you've got a sun to build among all that. And . . . Lucian?'

'Hm?' Lucian paused in pulling out the pencil in his hair.

'Don't forget you're not her brother. Or her father. You're not responsible for her.'

'Ah, I know.' He sighed.

He'd been thinking a lot about this himself. For a moment there was only the melodic hissing of the overhead air control; the chatter of the people flopped on sofas down the hall; the

92

approaching whirr of a vacuum bot making its rounds. Lucian found what he wanted to say.

'But no one is responsible right now, you know? And I'm a project person. My mum takes in kids from Earth—refugees, they come from the worst places—and some of them . . .' He tried to think; the reasons were there in his head, but they were so much a part of him that it was hard to put them into words. He curled his hands, then opened them up in the air. 'It's just what I do. It's what I've grown up doing. You help a person out. Even more reason to when someone else should have, and hasn't. And Nou's a good kid. I want to help her. Somebody should.'

Lucian cringed a little. Soliloquising. Not a good look. But Mallory was smiling her slow smile at him, as though he was a little secret to keep close—so that was all right. He managed a self-conscious grin back.

'Coffee? Want to grab . . . aah, I forgot.' Forgot they'd just got coffee before they came, as their cold mugs caught his eye. 'Right, not coffee, OK, is it lunchtime yet? Or has enough time passed that more coffee's acceptable?'

Mallory's eyes narrowed as her smile widened.

'Let's call it second coffee, shall we? I'm sure we'll find something to talk about.'

As they headed down the stairs in single file, Lucian brushing his hand against the banister just seconds behind Mallory's own, already his mind was ticking away—ideas to plans and plans to strategies. Maybe they could start on numbers even before the next session, just from getting Nou to do odd jobs around the workshop. Better still, he must teach Stan at the same time—Parkin, too, and his lab-mates; they all had good hearts—and who knew, maybe even Halley, acidity aside, would be willing to help . . .

Of course, there was also Styx to think about. And—a chill

like a draught of Pluto's thin atmosphere shuddered up his spine—a potential saboteur at large. with the asteroid Mortimaeus well on its way, and two more gards to come, there was already plenty enough to worry about.

Chapter 7

Halley ran in long, sweeping strokes, her body an arrow lancing above Pluto's surface. It was more flying than running, each brief contact propelling her a further five metres, ten, knives of ice crunching like old leaves beneath the balls of her feet. No air resistance to tug her back, barely a ghost of gravity to pull her down. She was tireless. She could keep this up all day.

Lucian knew this just by looking at her. He knew it as plainly as anyone looking at him must know the opposite.

He glanced to his upper left: the figure across the gorge was keeping easily apace with Halley, the pair ahead of him and only growing smaller. Lucian pressed down harder with each footfall, surging onwards with arms rigid beside him. His heaving breaths blew with a crackle against the suit microphone but the rest was tuned out: the white noise of the heat packs; the urgent ticks of his pulse monitor; the occasional voice in his ear warning he was consuming oxygen fifty-six per cent faster than recommended. There was no superfluous energy to be wasted: his every sense was on the icescape around him, on perceiving obstacles in the twilit gloom, on *not dying in front of Halley*.

A dead end up ahead: their methanol-ice cliff ledge was narrowing. Sudden friction as Lucian's elbow scuffed the wall caught him off guard and he stumbled, only one wrong footfall but enough to break focus, to trip again, and searing through his head was the incongruously upbeat bass of a song he'd loved in college, 'Death Without Dignity'. In a split-second decision he pressed his feet to the ground, coiled his knees, and jumped before his lost balance could force his hand.

There is a recurring dream humans have shared, perhaps for millennia: a dream of flight, of remembering some lost art to catching your breath, then soaring in one clean leap to the sky. As though flying was an old trick, one humanity had only forgotten the knack for. Lucian felt a disorientating wave of déjà vu in that moment, or the sense of being tumbled from his bed seconds before sleep: he was in that dream.

A lurch of his stomach signalled the fall's beginning. He felt it in the prickling of his scalp, in the dry back of his throat, in the quickening of his heart. He was twenty metres above ground with nothing to catch his fall—it was the rational response. But out here, gravity could not hurt him.

The gorge opened wide as he floated into it. Up ahead, Halley was a vision of grace executing the same move. Lucian swallowed hard as the fissure's walls rose to block out the silvery horizon, and had the sense to brace his knees for touchdown. Any second now . . . *Contact!* And—oh, Earth, why did he do this to himself?—he was running again.

'You run like a native,' remarked an appraising voice in his ear—and whether from a brain starved of realism or oxygen, it took Lucian a moment too long to realise Edmund Harbour was not, in fact, referring to him.

'I could say the same for you,' Halley retorted.

Lucian glanced up and saw with a start of anxiety just how far he was falling behind: Harbour up on the cliff and Halley in the gorge, perhaps just ahead of her competitor.

For that was what this was, Lucian realised. And he had been stupid enough to invite himself along and get between that. How sensible it had sounded in his head: the perfect occasion to chat with both the base's head and Plutoshine's head, in a setting where they wouldn't be overheard, to talk about Styx.

The ground was growing tacky beneath his boots now, blood-red organics a coating like wet sherbet upon the ice. *Star-tar*, the beloved astronomer Carl Sagan had almost named it, before settling on *tholins*, a derivation from the Greek for 'muddy'. Lucian had analysed them in their first week and found Sagan was bang on with that: the sticky mess of irradiated hydrocarbons was about as easy to analyse as it was to clean off your boots.

Halley said, 'We both have the weight of Earth in our bones, and the body doesn't ever forget gravity as tough as that.'

'Everything seems easier in comparison,' Harbour agreed. 'We're nearing the opening to Inanna Fossa now. You're in some kind of tributary fracture.'

'Good stuff,' Lucian gasped, more to remind them he still existed than from having anything worthwhile to say.

The walls were pulling apart now and rising ever higher, so Harbour ran from his vantage point to join them. His steps kicked sinuous arcs of tholins into the air, raining red snow back down at an accumulation rate several orders of magnitude above the background levels.

'We must be getting pretty close now,' Halley said. 'These layers are crazy. So many colours . . .'

'We had a visiting stratigraphist here perhaps a decade ago who documented this region,' said Harbour on the tide of his breath. The two ran side by side now, matching strides like synchronised swimmers. Lucian might as well have been wearing armbands. 'There's over four billion years' history preserved in these strata, everything from migrating cryo-volcanic hot spots to colliding glaciers . . .'

Lucian let them go on ahead; if he eased off now, his dignity might have time to dust itself off. He'd volunteered for the hike thinking it would just be a hike. A brisk walk, a bit of sightseeing, a bit of exercise, and with his old mentor at that. But what Halley had carefully omitted was the 4 a.m. rise; the according lack of breakfast. And possibly even worse than missing buttery, steaming, raisin-studded cinnamon bagels was the hardship he had known he was letting himself in for: their tour guide in the form of Harbour.

'So it's some kind of conduit?' Lucian called when he could trust his breath not to get in the way. 'Some kind of surface extrusion?'

Harbour and Halley were skidding to a stop and Lucian adjusted his own stride, scuffing his feet into the ground, gradually closing the gaps between each step. Fifty metres, twenty, ten . . . Oh, perfectly done, not two metres from his companions, and first go, too! But neither Halley nor Harbour saw his grin: both were already preoccupied with the cliff face before them.

'All right, what have we got?' Halley's voice was taut, excited. Light washed the scene as she snapped on her suit torch. 'Is this it, this section right—? Holy *smokes* . . .'

Lucian leapt to their side.

The landslide had excavated a notch like chipped flint in the towering cliff face. Those same gorgeous ice layers of the chasm walls ran through the freshly cut face: the murky reds of tholins, the greenish greys of methanol, maybe nitrogen for the bluish ones. But at the very base of the sequence was something different.

That was where all three now trained their torches.

'How old is this slide?' Halley murmured.

'I was hoping you might tell me.' Harbour's voice, like hers, was hushed. Like it would be before an exhumed tomb.

Halley bobbed forwards a careful step and held out her arm. Touched the surface with her fingertips.

The white vein at the sequence's base was as thick as a hose and anabranching, slipping up then between individual strata.

'Water,' she said on an exhalation, and she laughed.

Frozen water, here on a world of frozen nitrogen and frozen methane. If he squinted, and ignored the airiness of his limbs, Lucian could almost convince himself he was in the twilight of Earth.

There was a smile in Harbour's voice as he crouched on his haunches beside her.

'There are plenty more exposures, but this was the closest. I trust this will be sufficient for your research?'

'I'll say' Halley's voice was alight. 'You know, when you find ice in some new reservoir on Mars, people go crazy for it. Ice in a world of rock. And here's me losing it . . .'

'. . . for ice in a world of ice.' Harbour nodded. 'Only, Mars's water-ice has not been expelled from a buried ocean.'

'Is it deep, this ocean?' Lucian bobbed closer. The white cracks were spiderlike in the gloom, and this close he could see where the fracture system disappeared under their feet. 'And it's definitely still active?'

'That's what the seismic data tells us.' Harbour looked him in the eye. 'Liquid water, ammonium salts, organic matter . . .'

Lucian's eyebrows shot into the edge of his helmet's balaclava. 'A good place for life. I had no idea.'

Halley shrugged off her backpack and unloaded her toolkit: hammer, pneumatic chisel, sample boxes.

'Let's hope we don't need explosives to get a piece of this bad boy out.'

'The compositional data has been well constrained,' Harbour went on. 'But the isotopic has never been touched. It's about time someone did something about that.'

99

Tap tap tap. Down came the hammer on the chisel. Lucian bent for a closer look. The ice seemed to take its colour from its surroundings: blue, pale green, off-whites, now the orange of Halley's gloves. Up close it was glassy, almost transparent.

'Must have quenched too fast to form a crystal structure,' Halley was muttering, apparently to herself. 'But shouldn't it have devitrified by now? Unless the cracks are young, unless the liquid has been forced up only recently—or perhaps, in the cold temperatures . . .'

Oh, Earth, Lucian thought, *I'm an engineer. If you want anything intellectual from me, and I have to pretend to understand any of this . . .*

'I feel compelled to announce that, as a biologist, this is not a debate I can contribute to,' came Harbour's voice very patiently, and Lucian blinked in surprise.

'Was I speaking out loud?' Halley wrapped her hands around a loosened block. 'Don't mind me, it's been decades since I've got to be a geologist . . .'

She began wriggling it back and forth, and Lucian almost winced at the sight: the ice must be −240 °C at least, the kind of temperature the brain could only interpret as scaldingly hot. It looked as jagged as rock as she prised it free.

Both men leant closer.

Halley was holding a piece of Pluto's ocean.

Her eyes flicked to Harbour's. 'That box just there, please.'

Harbour obliged and swiftly brought the silky-smooth polytetrafluoroethylene beneath her hands. Carefully, painstakingly, she lowered it in.

'All right.' She exhaled and began tidying her equipment away. 'We've got it. You reckon we'll make it back in time for breakfast if we push it?'

Harbour looked up at the stars. Bloody show-off: Lucian couldn't have done that even back home, let alone where the sky only ever shifted its variation of darkness.

'Well, at my estimate it's something like five-twenty now,' he said, 'so if we push it—'

'Edmund Harbour, you're an execrable liar.' Halley had brought the time up on her wrist-pad as Lucian did the same: it read 05:20 exactly. 'I'll save a spot for you in the hall . . . if you make it back in time.'

'Wait,' Lucian began desperately, 'why don't we just . . . just amble, just take in the scene . . . ?'

But Halley had taken off like a greyhound and the race was on. Long, low-angle leaps, a slow-motion dance of speed and power, her and Harbour's steady breaths in tandem. In five swift bounds the pair were up the chasm walls and back on the plains, and Lucian couldn't even groan as he kicked his legs to work because they would hear it.

There were one or two decent things about being up at such an unearthly hour. The vague sense that everything he did was slightly more purposeful, for instance. And the scenery, even as it flew past him into a tunnelling vision, was really something. The ice was numbing his toes, and the stars were sweeping overhead, and his breath was close in his helmet. He was flying across the surface of Pluto, over four billion miles from home, and when he got those cinnamon bagels not too far in his immediate future he would have bloody *earned* them.

Stern emerged in lieu of a rising sun as the three eventually crossed into familiar territory. The base seemed a shadow nestled at the foot of the al-Idrises, pinpricked here and there by lights like a little fishing village. They shone as bright as the stars above, as though a handful had slid down the mountainside and stayed to dock.

It could be home, Lucian thought, given time. The floors of Stern were always blood-warm beneath his socks. The air was always cool and clear and lightly scented to match whichever season the Parks were emulating (presently autumn: wet leaves, ripe apples, damp skies). And the people were pure sunlight.

But it wasn't home just yet. Where was it . . . ? Swivelling his head across the sky. The brightest star. That was home. Right there.

The others were almost out of sight, Lucian realised with a jolt. He had been so distracted he had let his already meagre pace slow. Biting down a curse—they would hear it—he pushed his protesting calves until he thought they would tear.

'All right, you got me,' he gasped once they were inside the airlock. '*Earth*, you're both absolute comets.' Nausea chilled the sweat on his palms and face as he braced himself against a wall. He felt sticky, feverish, faint; he was either going to have to do this more often, or never do it again. 'So who got here first—who won?'

Halley nodded at Harbour, and Lucian was somewhat gratified to notice her own chest rising and falling heavily, too.

'We're a good match,' she said, 'except for that burst of speed you always get at the end.'

Harbour spread his hands graciously. 'You would have caught me had we another kilometre to go.'

The green light flashed for stable pressure with a beep; all unclipped their helmets and tore off their balaclavas with relief. Lucian ruffled his hair into a sphere of frizz and savoured the coolness on his scalp; opposite him, Harbour did the same. His hair was black with sweat and stuck to his forehead—far from the Prince of Pluto's characteristic immaculateness.

Halley and Harbour pulled off their gloves and clasped hands.

'Thank you as ever, Professor,' said Harbour. Then, turning to Lucian: 'And thank you, too, for your company this morning.'

Lucian tugged off his own glove. 'Yeah, you too. For letting me third-wheel on your hike.'

Harbour glanced out of the porthole window, then said,

straight-faced, 'By my estimate it can't be more than five past ten, but I'm sure some breakfast will remain.'

Lucian lit up his wrist-pad face: *10:05*.

'How . . . ?' he began, then stopped as he looked up.

Harbour had his own watch lit up—*10:05*—and he was smiling. The smile was more in his eyes than his lips, but Lucian thought it was like watching a stone wall warm in the Sun.

Halley pointed a cautioning finger at him.

'We'll see you at breakfast.' Then, rounding on Lucian, 'You wanted to talk to us about something?'

Lucian, easing off clutching his side, waved a nonchalant hand.

'My mistake was assuming there would be conversation. Let's just call a meeting some time.'

Neither the prospect of that conversation nor even cinnamon bagels (slathered with hazelnut butter and minced apple, counterbalanced by the bitterest of coffees) could hold Lucian's attention for the rest of the day quite as tenaciously as Halley's sawtoothed piece of ice. She was going to cut bits off, she said, and melt them down, and tease out all kinds of isotopes held within it. Imagine. From a sample of Pluto's *ocean*.

What exactly those isotopes would tell her, Lucian knew about as much as the bagels. Cosmochemistry wasn't really his field: he knew isotopes were atoms of the same element, just with different numbers of neutrons inside them; he knew that different types preferentially accumulated within different environments, within different regions of the Solar System. OK, so a bit more than the bagels—but nowhere near enough to satisfy the curiosity of a ten-year-old.

'It's like . . .' Lucian waved his blowtorch expansively later that morning, then set it down. 'I tell you what—I'll show you.'

They were in the workshop, Nou with legs dangling from

the stool beside him, braiding together platinum wires as fine as silver hairs while he soldered them up on the countertop. Captain Whiskers, Lucian's surly lab cat, was snoozing upon the maxed-out weighing scales beside them. The acrid yet somehow intensely satisfying smell of burning metal filled the air.

Rifling one-handed through a drawer, Lucian's fingers closed around something smooth and cool—all he wished to be in life. What he pulled out was a little brass knob for calibrating scales.

'*Gotcha*. All right, this is hydrogen, OK? And hydrogen is element number one—there's just one thing in the centre of your atom'—holding out his palm flat, with the weight right in its centre—'and that thing is called a proton. You add a second proton and you've made a whole new element—called helium— but there's one thing that can rub elbows with your protons and not change the element. And that's called a neutron.'

Rifling again, rifling . . . The pads of his fingers brushed something spiky. He took a chance, and out came a handful of little LED lights. Red, orange, green . . . Lucian tucked one as yellow as a lemon against the brass weight with a thumb.

'So, now our hydrogen has a neutron, too. It's still hydrogen, because there's only one of these'—jiggling the weight—'but it's slightly heavier now, and that means it'll do different things than if it was lighter. Just the same way you and me do, you being a little scrawny thing, and me—'

'Having not missed many meals?' called one of the researchers, Kipini, preferably Kip, grinding ice chips into a piston.

'Retaining your winter coat?' called another, Joules, eyes gleaming wickedly through his glass screen of code. He and Kip were around Lucian's age, both showstopping researchers any lab group would be delighted to have, let alone together. They were both also equally possessed with more triple-distilled, deadpan wit than any two people Lucian had the blessed fortune to know.

104

He glanced over his shoulder as disparagingly as humanly possible.

'I didn't need that, OK? I'm a good person.'

Beside him, Nou's mouth was pulled down in distress, and Lucian quickly explained.

'They're just playing. It's because I was once so excited for a party buffet I broke my toe on the table leg. They wouldn't say it if it was true.'

'Whatever helps you sleep at night, Lu,' called Kip.

Lucian gave an exaggerated eye-roll to Nou.

'But d'you get what I mean? When you've got the extra weight but you're the same element, you're called different isotopes of each other—'

'Here.' Joules had come up behind them; both looked up. 'Try this . . .'

He leant over with a battery pack and a crocodile clip and the lemon light burst into colour, an autumn leaf lit by a shaft of sunlight. Nou stared in open-mouthed wonder.

So, too, did Lucian. Sunlight. Head swivelling across a starry sky. Searching for one star in particular. The sudden pang of loss sank his shoulders with all the force of a centrifuge.

'Cheers, mate,' he murmured, clapping Joules distractedly on the back. 'Man.' He shook himself from the shoulders up. 'You don't see too many warm colours around here.'

'Lucian.'

Lucian jumped at the voice of Halley directly behind him— less gravity, less giveaway noise in footsteps. Then he jumped again at what were clasped between her hands.

'My Hartdegens!'

It was a balancing act for her to hold. Ten books—ten actual, paper, tree-born books—each with bent spines, and dog-eared corners, and the kind of crinkled pages to suggest they had once become acquainted with a bath, probably more than a hundred years ago. Halley raised them higher, in case there could be any doubt why she was there.

'What,' she began, 'are these fire hazards doing in my lab? For that matter, Lucian, what exactly are they doing on Pluto?'

Nou was staring at the books as though they were a whole switchboard of LEDs. And no wonder: the kid probably rarely saw the real things.

Lucian snatched the precious objects into his arms.

'I'll have you know,' he said, protectively stroking the topmost cover, 'that they were part of my *approved* box of personal effects, and that was after the committee decided if they did catch fire, they'd just burn themselves out too fast to spread. It's herd immunity in a non-flammable world.'

'Says the man wielding a blowtorch.' Halley was already turning away, heading back to her workbench. 'But that doesn't explain why your tinderbox anachronisms have to be *right here* cluttering up my lab.'

'Well, it's Hartdegen, innit?' called Kip from somewhere beneath his cylinder. He was a great bear of a man from the Martian north pole, a specialist in ice structural mechanics, and with the frostbite scars to prove both. Right now he was squinting in concentration, screwing something into his experiment. 'Got to be required reading, right?'

'The man is not wrong,' Lucian agreed serenely. 'And everyone loves Elisabeth Hartdegen.' He frowned down at Nou for a moment, who was blinking blankly from the books up to him. 'Maybe they're a bit before your time? They're classics, though, you'd love them. Go ahead, take one.'

With all the caution of reaching for a museum specimen, Nou slid the topmost into her hands.

'The Hartdegen series is where Mortimaeus and the other asteroid names come from,' he told her sagely, as she cracked the battered paperback open.

Mustiness, dustiness, decay; at once he was twelve years old, holding the book up to shield his eyes from the Sun, and his father's voice—'*I'm not going to ask you again*'—more amused than annoyed, was calling him in for tea.

Lucian shook himself a little.

'Mortimaeus is a sort of demigod in that universe,' he told her. 'He's one of the three high Gard Protectors, and the Gard Protectors are the three great overseers of all the gards—and gards are the people who slip between dimensions to watch over humanity.'

He had taken to signing everything he spoke to Nou, even to other people when he forgot himself, but right then both hands were occupied with the books; even so, he could feel his wrists flexing out of habit.

'Every human being who has ever lived has a gard,' he went on luxuriantly. 'They're a special person whose job is to keep you safe—someone who looks out for you—and they normally only appear in times of danger, or distress, or just to make sure you're OK.'

'You might want to mention at some point they're fictional,' Halley pointed out airily from behind them.

Lucian almost dropped the books.

'Halley,' he gasped.

'Yeah, I wouldn't go there.' Kip's head poked up with a grimace.

'Isn't that an Earth thing?' Joules's mouth was curling with a touch of mischief through his screen. 'Not believing in magic?'

'You must have read Elisabeth Hartdegen!' Lucian rushed over to her. Halley was shrugging into a pair of elbow-high gloves, ones that were attached to a sealed glass box taking up half a workbench—the kind that maintained different conditions inside from the rest of the room. 'Didn't you ever have a gard growing up?'

'No,' said Halley, with savage disinterest.

'But didn't you ever pretend—'

'Lucian, do I *look* like I ever played pretend?'

Nou had put the book down: she was at his side signing up at him, movements hesitant, close to her chest. She was signing M-O-R-T-I-M-A-Y-U-S—right pronunciation, wrong spelling—and she was making the word into a question.

Why? she was asking.

Lucian laughed. 'How about we call him Mo from now on, what do you say? Though your letters are just exquisite now. You were asking why call an asteroid after him . . . ?' At her nod he continued. 'I'm getting to that. So, all the gards live in this great big, red hot-air balloon that floats in space but in the dimension next door, just a hair's breadth apart from our own.'

Nou, bless her heart, was watching him with rapt attention. What a novel feeling: even casual fans Kip and Joules would waft their hands over mock-yawns once he got going.

'And here's the absolute *coolest thing* about the gards, you see—they actually live *inside the balloon* itself. Not in the basket—they're right up in the air. They've got rooms and staircases and everything, just like Stern does. It wouldn't make sense in our world, but it does in theirs.'

For just a moment, it seemed to Lucian a dreamy hush fell over the workshop. Kip, Joules, even Halley, all paused in their miscellaneous tasks to listen. Nou was still staring up at him; Captain Whiskers, too, had cracked open an orange eye to watch.

'And because of transdimensional physics, you see,' he surged on, breathless, 'when you work out the mathematics of it, the balloon is always everywhere across the whole Solar System at once, just beside us, waiting . . . So that your gard can appear at a moment's notice when they're most needed—'

Halley shut a drawer with a thump. The soap-bubble spell over the room burst in a shower of fictional foam.

'I've never heard such convoluted claptrap in all my long years in your company,' she announced, 'and please do believe me, Lucian, when I say that's truly saying something.'

'Ah, Halley.' Lucian shrugged good-naturedly. 'You're just upset because you missed out on a childhood's worth of adventures.'

'I'd have rather had a childhood's worth of norovirus. Now, do you want to see this ice block or not, then?'

Lucian's eyes bulged: Halley's gloved hands were inside the box, which he now saw was thickly frost-rinded on its back wall and floor; even her gloves were shimmering with it. And cupped within them, already steaming and slippery, was the ocean ice.

'I've got twenty minutes tops before this whole thing sublimates, so make yourself useful. Nou, girl, grab that camera next to you.'

The ice even looked alien, translucent like frosted glass. Lucian and Nou gathered round and settled in to watch, and Hartdegen, Mortimaeus, and the gards were all quite forgotten.

At least, for the moment. But, naturally, the conversation soon swung back around.

'So wherever you are and whatever you're doing,' Lucian signed and said to Nou and Mallory that afternoon in the hamster wheel of the swimming pool, the water gently whirlpooling around in one unbroken wave, 'if you wish really, really hard for your gard to come, or if they sense you need their help, they can sweep through to our dimension and be by your side in a heartbeat.'

Wow! Nou signed with both hands, treading water to do so. *Wow!*

He'd taught her adjectives at their last chat—good, bad, hot, cold, anything he could think of—and she had all the retention of a magnet among fridges.

'Oh, marvellously phrased.' Mallory, a creature of streamlined grace in a silvered one-piece, took up a polite applause. 'They are such magical stories. My Alexandra adores them.'

'You still need to show me a picture of her.' Lucian kicked his feet to set their raft moving. 'I must have shown you hundreds of my family by now.'

Nou, not to be left out, dived underwater and let her buoyancy fire her on to the remaining third of the float. With all aboard, Lucian kicked harder and their little ship set sail faster than the pool could turn, carrying them up and over like the hand on a clock face.

'Only five minutes to go.' Mallory nodded to one such clock on the wall as they returned level. 'Poor Nou, a swimming lesson now after we've tired you out.'

'Well, good thing they're teaching you early—your kids or grandkids will be out there swimming under the stars if I have my way.' Lucian ducked his head underwater, then shook himself like a dog; the coolness was sweet upon his closed eyelids, the roots of his hair. 'And it's the test tonight, isn't it, Nou? What was it, forward crawl?'

Nou shook her head; drew her hands together and flapped them as though they were taking flight.

Butterfly, she was saying. *Butterfly stroke.* Lucian hadn't taught her that. That was all initiative. Makes-sense signing. Now her hands were turning to form other words: *you*—pointing at him, pointing at Mallory—then indicating around them, at the pool, at the room. *Will you stay?* To make sure he understood, she pointed to her eyes: *watch.*

They weren't standard approved British Sign Language motions, but that didn't matter. Her meaning couldn't be clearer.

Lucian met Mallory's eyes and they shared a smile, like chinking a glass of fizz.

''Course we'll stay,' he assured her. 'Tonight's the one all the parents are coming to, I remember now. Nowhere I'd rather be.'

Other kids were coming out of the woodwork now. Lucian recognised most from that first evening playing magician with the gauntlets. Boys bombing in with hands clasped around their knees; girls diving and handstanding until the pool-wheel turned them the right way up; both belly-flopping on to floats, hurling foam noodles like javelins, splashing, shrieking. Soon the air was thick with water that coalesced and spun in gelatinous dances.

Their teacher was a guitarist from the party—Lucian vaguely recalled she was a mycoprotein cultivator—and now the kids were swimming to the side, their parents merrily waving or calling the most recalcitrant over, many in trunks and costumes themselves.

Lucian, Mallory, and Nou waited until the pool had spun them level with the side before swimming over. He had just placed his palms on the grit-rough tiles, legs drifting clockwise below water, when he saw Nou stop and begin to drift, too. Something in her stillness, and in the stillness of her expression, made him follow her gaze.

The figure made no move to offer a hand, and that was all Lucian needed to know it was Harbour. Edmund Harbour? Here at a kids' swimming lesson? Lucian glanced from the younger Harbour to the older—then, mortified, away as fast. The man was wearing only trunks—not surprising in a pool but more than Lucian wanted to see nonetheless—and some sort of strange stockings that rose above his knees.

'Edmund!' Mallory slipped from the pool in one fluid motion. How utterly remarkable: two people being perfectly civil, each pretending not to notice the other dressed in nothing but water-repellent underwear. 'We weren't expecting you. How are the preparations for next month progressing?'

Lucian surreptitiously stretched an arm back and grabbed

Nou by the wrist as she was slowly sucked past 8 p.m. on the wheel. Though the thought of disappearing up there himself was increasingly appealing.

'I'm well prepared for the expedition, Mallory, thank you,' Harbour returned with a stiff nod. 'I'm also surprised to see you here. As I am you too, Lucian.'

Utmost civility. Utmost courtesy. Like a computer model of human etiquette, poured into the cast of a man. Nou had got her limbs working and reached the side, unmoving in the water with eyes fixed on the hands gripping her in place. The two tools she had to communicate with, both silenced.

Lucian gritted his teeth into something approximating a smile.

'Well, we've been having a right good time, haven't we, Nou?' he managed as he pushed himself out. Water dripped from his wiry curls down his back; exposed skin, exposed vulnerabilities. 'Me and Mallory have been teaching her . . .'

He stopped. At eye level as he pulled himself up, he saw Harbour was not wearing stockings at all. The objects that reached from his toes to his thighs were metal and glass, and through the glass could be discerned illuminated wires. And the floor behind him.

They were his legs.

'Uh . . .' Lucian blinked stupidly. Upright now, eye to eye, he didn't dare let his own so much as flick from Harbour's. 'It's . . . uh. Sign language. We've been teaching her. Right, Nou? And she's getting pretty good. How come . . . How come you're here?'

'You could learn, too, you know,' interjected Mallory, warm and engaging. Thank Earth one of them was functioning. 'Such a fascinating language. And it's all new to me. Lucian is a wonderful teacher.'

'I'm pleased to hear it.' Harbour glanced to Lucian's feet—to Nou, behind him. Then, businesslike, 'I'm here to observe

Nou's swimming progress. You're welcome to join me, unless there was some other reason you were here?'

'Great minds, eh?' Lucian said with forced cheer.

'Or fools, which seldom differ.'

'We'll leave you and your sister together, Edmund, please don't let us keep you.' Mallory was as diplomatic as ever. 'Nou, dear, take care, and we'll see you at Lucian's next session.'

'And, Lucian,' Edmund added, 'if you could arrange for us to speak further about that matter you disclosed to me earlier . . .' His eyes held Lucian's meaningfully. 'That would be most appreciated.'

Ah. That would be the sabotage. Lucian nodded back as seriously and meaningfully as he could in return—but as he did he was wishing he had never said a word at all, wishing he could quietly take this to Halley; bypass anyone he didn't know enough to trust.

'Bye, Nou,' Lucian called and signed as they turned to go, and his heart plummeted at the sight of her. She had no need to move her hands when her eyes spoke for her all too clearly.

He was still dripping onto the tiles as they parted ways, and it was only then he realised what Nou's stillness reminded him of: it was of a kitten, immobilised, as its parent took it by the scruff of its neck between its jaws.

'Flipping *Earth*.' He clapped a hand to his forehead the moment they were out of earshot. 'That might just have been the single most agonising interaction of my whole, good life. Am I still red? I think I'm burning up . . .'

'Why was it agonising?' Mallory was wringing her hair out over one shoulder. 'Edmund hadn't mentioned he was coming, and as far as I know he's not normally the cheerleading type.'

'Absolute agony.' Lucian kneaded his knuckles into his eyes. He wanted to check behind him, but somehow he didn't dare. 'Also, when Halley mentioned the guy had an unfair advantage for running I was picturing some kind of adamantine skeleton, but I don't know why she mentioned a thing.'

'In her defence, I do recall the word *electromechanical* was mentioned at some point,' Mallory conceded. 'They're just exquisite, though, aren't they—the prosthetics? He was a boy when it happened, he told me. And you know Clavius, he brought in the best cyberneticians available. I believe he even created the design.'

'Unlucky family.'

Lucian couldn't say why, but seeing Harbour had riled him, somehow. He still couldn't shake the feeling he shouldn't have let slip to the man about the sabotage hunch. There was something about him that got under his skin—like a cold, metallic, methodical instrument. Lucian tried to comfort himself: Halley would share the information with Harbour regardless of whether he knew already. And he had the base's interest at heart, of course. It was surely better that he knew.

There were communal showers before the changing room doors; the pair stepped inside.

'What's this about an expedition, by the way?' Lucian suddenly remembered. 'You hadn't mentioned anything about an expedition.'

'Hadn't I?' Airflow drew the water down hard as Earthly rainfall upon them. 'There's a heat anomaly over Mikulski Crater on the far side that looks promising.'

'You're going looking for life?'

'Of course, Lucian. It's what xenobiologists do. Edmund asked if he could join Yolanda and me. We'll be back well in time for Mortimaeus. I believe Yolanda has some project she's anxious to resume—'

'But . . .' Lucian stared helplessly at her. 'But that's two months away! Have you told Nou? She'll . . .' He gulped. 'She'll really miss you.'

114

Mallory closed her eyes as water cascaded down her face, one fluid entity wrapping itself around her body. He could have looked anywhere upon her in that one unguarded moment, but found himself captivated by her eyelashes: ensnaring little droplets, one after the other, before they trickled into the flush of her cheeks.

Mallory opened her eyes into his.

'You'll live, Lucian.' And she smiled.

The next day he caught Halley and Harbour for their overdue meeting—and this time it was on his terms. A quiet corner, coffee, cake . . . And the cake was *good*, just like the real thing back when he'd tried it on Earth. This one was a self-assured little lemon sponge, halved with buttercream and coiffed with piercingly sweet curd: all blissful inventions of the matter printers down the hall that Lucian called the Magicians' Kitchens.

Halley set down her fork and swore in the empty space after his words.

'That's a heck of an accusation, kid.'

'I know.'

'First time in human history, on this scale.'

'I know.'

'And it's your best explanation?'

Lucian threw up his hands, scattering crumbs on soaring trajectories. 'I don't know.'

Edmund Harbour had been very quiet. Lucian looked to him now, sitting on the edge of the seminar room desk, elbows on his knees—one of those knees, Lucian could not unsee, being metal. His own cake remained untouched. His eyes were unfocused, and his eyebrows were low.

'Anyway, yeah.' Lucian shrugged. 'At this stage, you know, it's just a hunch. But I figured I'd mention it.'

'We're not a police state,' Edmund said slowly, drawing his

arms across his chest. 'We don't have surveillance, not beyond Gen's structural monitoring, and nor do we have the means of detaining a criminal. We're a scientific base. A research station.'

'There's one way to get more data points here.'

They turned to look at Halley.

'Mortimaeus,' she said mildly. 'Silvasaire. Jovortre. Our gards are heading straight for us as we speak. There's plenty of upcoming occasions for still grander failures.'

Harbour made a strange, unconscious gesture, cut off as he perhaps realised what he was doing. Maybe he, like Lucian, wished to stretch back his collar for air.

'I'll alert Gen,' Harbour said finally. 'There are protocols we can activate, a pattern recognition algorithm it can use to search for anomalous behaviour. No one will see the footage but the computer, and it can report to a set contact.'

'To you?'

The words were out before Lucian knew it, and he regretted them immediately. The cynicism in his voice could not be missed even by his own reddening ears.

'To a working group,' said Harbour with perfect levelness. 'I would suggest the heads of operation for each team to begin with, including the three of us. We can only hope your hunch is false, Lucian. But it would pay to be vigilant.'

Lucian nodded and hid his face behind his mug. The truth was he hadn't stopped to think of the future. He hadn't even considered the possibility of further risk—of further damage. And still, there it was in the back of his mind. The groundless itch that he should have said nothing at all—not to Harbour.

Interlude 2

When Clavius Harbour was a boy, he liked to pretend he was a king.

Not a prince, nor some shining knight; he had no time for pretty princesses or noble quests. As king, he held the maximum capacity for enacting change, and the only limiting factor was his imagination.

He was aged seven when he heard of the terrible tragedy on Mars: a great sun-mirror in the sky cracking and setting whole cities on fire, like a magnifying glass on ants. In his mind, he ordered every mirror in his own kingdom be flown as a fleet to fill their neighbours' sky with reflected light, everything from the hand-held to the gold-gilded, a billion to replace the one. But ordering imaginary people around wasn't much fun, and besides which, no one in the real world had thought up his quite excellent mirror fleet scheme for themselves. How would it be done? he thought. So he taught himself astro-dynamics, and figured it out.

He was aged thirteen when he heard of another tragedy, this time on Mercury: half its first city—a silly, poky thing with an incompetent solar shield—had burned to the ground. In his head, he ordered a special glass be made that regulated its opacity to never let in more light than the brightest noon on Earth. How would it be done? No use ordering the impossible. So he taught himself material chemistry, and figured it out.

(This one turned out to be a quite brilliant idea: one he would enact later.)

But really, he thought, aged sixteen, all of humanity depended upon the Sun. Energy from photovoltaic cells, food from photosynthetic plants. It was a parental hand holding their leash, and independence from its power might prevent future disasters like those on Mars and Mercury. He no longer played children's games of kings and orders, so he sat down and figured out how it could be done. No use planning the impossible. He taught himself nuclear physics—he tweaked the latest model for fusion aged twenty-four, quadrupling its efficiency—but that was not enough. He came to understand that humans *needed*, on some deep-seated level, the sight of the Sun in the sky. But why? Why try to light the Martian sky with dangerous mirrors? Why build a vulnerable structure on the Mercurian surface below its searing heat, and not move sensibly underground?

The Sun, he decided, was a tyrant.

And if his species was ever to become truly independent, invulnerable, interstellar, to him it followed that they must break entirely free of its shackles. And he was going to be the one to prove they could.

By the time he was established in his kingdom of Stern, Clavius Harbour—now aged fifty-four, just over 0.2 Plutonian years—was well on his way to doing so.

Edmund knows all this. He knows because his father has told him. His father has told him everything.

The two figures move in silent unison through the night in leaps from dune crest to dune crest. From the air they might look like a pair of silver leopards catching starlight on their flanks, were their suits not designed specifically for invisibility: no lurid, luminous orange for Clavius and Edmund Harbour. They move fast and they move in single file. They move like creatures at home in the night.

Under any other occasion, Edmund would enjoy the run. He runs every day; it is not something he can ever let himself lapse from. The silence, the stillness, the routine of both every morning: they are to him a held breath, an unlit candle. But this is night-time. This is not routine. The weight of party food and the sugary tang of cocktails fade to memory with the stretch of his thighs and the arcing of his shoulder blades, and the soft methane sand spreads like icing sugar beneath his boots. They keep to the path, following the intermittent footprints that mark this thoroughfare to the bladed mountains of Tartarus Dorsa. More than once Clavius's prints—up ahead of him— entirely smother a far smaller person's.

Edmund keeps slightly to one side.

It isn't far to Pandemonium Promontorium. A half-hour's powerful jog. Maybe an hour for a child. The cliffs named the Cousteau Rupes make up a stretch of shoreline between the sunken Heart and the northern plains of Voyager Terra, bound by the al-Idrises at one end and a little cluster of hills, the Challenger Colles, at the other. They run parallel to that shoreline now, its cliffs scarcely discernible as a strip of starless horizon. The Promontorium sticks out from these some way ahead like a black, grasping arm.

Clavius is humming as he runs; he sounds eager, cheerful. At home among the monochrome twilight of his land.

The headland looms ahead now, ushering them in. Up ahead, Clavius deviates from the Tartarus path bearing right and continues on, keeping to the inter-dune lows where the ice-sand is thinnest, so their footprints might better slip by unnoticed. Details appear in the wall ahead: crags, landslips, strata, all better seen if not looked at directly.

'Hey, Gen?' Edmund hears Clavius murmur to the AI as they draw closer. 'Show me her trail.'

Across Edmund's helmet visor, no doubt Clavius's too, appears a translucent version of the same red-dashed snaking route overlaid upon blue topography, which they had scrutinised back in his office less than an hour ago.

119

'Show my location,' orders Clavius.

A second line appears, white, anastomosing atop the line representing Nou's earlier path. The glowing white dot of Clavius is slightly offset from her furthermost data point.

'Zoom in fifty metres above my location.'

Gen obliges and at once the two dots of interest are spread across their visors. Clavius adjusts his stride as Edmund does. The two dots begin to converge.

They cross several dunes side on. One bound up, one over, one down, and again. Edmund keeps one eye on the ground, one on their relative position. With more and more stars blacked out by the Heart's boundary cliffs to the side and the Promontorium's ahead, he has the feeling of entering a dense forest.

The great wall is directly overhead now. It stretches to the left, to the right, as though it continues forever. The crags he saw from afar are overhanging bulges the size of small hills; the landslips are scree slopes of ice-boulders each the size of his office; the strata are a hundred metres thick. It raises the hairs on Edmund's neck to think of a nine-year-old by herself in such a place.

He can't hold the words in. 'Nou should not be coming here alone.'

Clavius laughs. 'Somehow I knew that was coming. She's resourceful enough.'

Nou's traverse took her closer still to the wall. Edmund and Clavius bound forwards together, closer, until they can each place a gloved hand upon the cliff. Edmund does; the ice is black as obsidian, entirely in shadow, and snatches the warmth from his bones. The stars at its top seem a long, long way away.

'Well, this is it.' Clavius places his hands on his hips like a holidaymaker scouting for a picnic spot. 'What does my resident xenobiologist have to say on the environment?'

'Astrobiologist,' corrects Edmund distractedly. 'Xenobiologists specifically examine non-terrestrials. Astrobiologists focus on the search for that life.'

The map across his helmet visor shows their white dots entirely covering Nou's red. Edmund starts unloading equipment from his backpack: esoteric probes and prongs; myriad instruments with names ending in -ometer or -ograph, each a two-man job under Earth's gravity.

'I was expecting . . . I was hoping,' Edmund corrects himself, 'for something like a cave. A cryo-lava tube, a subglacial tunnel.' He looks up and up at the black, blank wall. He couldn't say if it is disappointment or relief he feels. 'Perhaps we over-interpreted her movements.'

'It's possible we've followed the wrong day,' says Clavius airily. No longer interested in the wall, he turns to take in the dune-swept plains, the tips of the northernmost al-Idrises on the horizon, the base hidden beyond. 'Knowing Nou . . .' he continues, and as he speaks Edmund can bring her image to mind so easily. 'Knowing Nou, she could have found whatever it is weeks ago and sat deliberating it since.'

Edmund sees her in his mind's eye in her room. Tucked up just as they left her under her frayed, planet-studded duvet, face slack in sleep under the rose glow of her halite nightlight. A loving, soft-hearted creature, so readily pleased and so ready to please. Too ready. What had his father once said? *Never mind the old idiom I say 'jump', you say 'how high?'—Nou just goes right ahead, no questions asked.* Too good-natured for her own good.

'You know how she idolises you,' says Edmund neutrally, snapping open a theodolite.

'Oh, yes.'

'It's plausible she wished to convince herself before troubling you.'

That does sound plausible the more Edmund considers it. Nou always has been an uncommonly serious child for her age: even at birth there was an intense sort of look about her, as though beneath that permanently furrowed brow she was concentrating very hard, or determined to puzzle something out. She had grown to become the sort of child whom teachers of a bygone age might have described in school reports as *diligent*, or perhaps *conscientious* for variety. Some found her quiet ways obsequious — an unkind bystander might have said weak — while by those same qualities she endeared herself to others.

Somehow, Edmund can't imagine her sharing her secret without being wholeheartedly certain.

'What are you doing?'

Clavius, interrupting. Edmund does not pause as he clicks open the second theodolite.

'Laser scanning might reveal some details we've missed.' He snaps a lidar detector at its head. 'They have a scanning time of thirty seconds to collect forty thousand data points in a three-sixty radius. They computationally reconstruct the landscape.' He stands beside Clavius and holds a remote before him. 'Please hold still.'

A click, and both theodolite detectors turn slowly in unison. They reach full rotation, then tilt up slightly and begin again. Then again.

'Nifty little things,' Clavius remarks.

'An efficient ratio of time input to data output.' Edmund returns to his bag, searching for his thermal heat-mapper. 'The next step is to—'

'Ed.' Clavius holds up a hand to stop him. 'There's nothing here. We got the day wrong, or the place wrong, or . . . You know what? Probably we just got it wrong taking the word of a kid.'

Again comes that emotion: the one that could have been disappointment or could have been relief. Edmund finds himself nodding.

'All right. Let me talk to her tomorrow. We'll get to the bottom of this.'

'We'd better. Whether my dear daughter's fault or not, I can't especially help my irritation at the best part of two hours taken from me.'

The journey back seems to take longer than the forward one. No planning to plan this time, no wondering to wonder. Edmund runs ahead, wishing to imagine this most unordinary of mornings is entirely his own, any ordinary run with only his own breaths in his ears for company.

They are perhaps halfway home when Clavius calls something—'Wait'—on the intercom. He says it . . . strangely. Something about the one syllable is short, and strangled. Edmund digs his heels enough to grind to a halt.

Behind him perhaps ten metres, Clavius has frozen to complete stillness as though struck by some thought.

'What is it?' Edmund calls, but Clavius does not move. Under the harsh torchlight of his helmet, and even across the distance, his eyes have an unfocused look. He looks utterly transfixed by something.

'What's wrong?' Edmund calls again—and then he hears it, too.

One-two-three.
One-two-three.
One-two-three-four.

The whistles are faint through his intercom but growing louder. They sound almost birdlike . . . almost alarm-like . . . almost human. They sound like nothing he has ever heard before.

The pattern repeats itself. Three short, successive, unchanging notes. A pause. The same three, short notes. Pause. Four notes now, lower in pitch. Fainter. Now a longer pause—has it stopped?—and the whistles begin again.

Edmund is aware of every hair on his body standing on end. He is aware of this only very dimly; his every sense, it feels, is shutting down to better route all power to auditory.

How long the pair remain there he is never able to guess. His fingertips grow chilled, then his whole arms. His eyelids grow heavy. But still he listens. They both listen until the sounds fade away as gradually as they arrived.

Neither speaks for some time. Whether mental echoes or real

ones, reverberating within their ears like a struck tuning fork, neither can say whether the whistles have truly stopped. Edmund's body returns to him in increments of awareness, and each of those increments is frozen to the bone.

Clavius limps over. He looks how Edmund feels.

'Whistles,' Edmund hears himself say. His voice, somehow a thing separate from his body, sounds both numbed and invigorated at once. He goes on urgently, 'Nou said . . .'

His memory from mere hours ago of his sister floods his every thought: Nou in her warm, rose-lit room, tucked under her warm, planet-strewn duvet; Nou saying how her creatures don't talk . . .

They say it together, breathless:

'. . . They whistle.'

The party has long since died down by the time two figures make it through the airlock and into the warm, dark-lit familiarity of Stern, and they are not the same two figures who left earlier. Clavius and Edmund Harbour remove their suits with slow, deliberate movements, without superfluous action or talk. They each shower in the airlock's adjoining cubicle, change into soft, long-sleeved skins, and make themselves their choice of drink. They do not leave Clavius's office; the rest of the base, with its brightness, and its empty bottles, and its cold finger food, cannot understand.

Clavius's office is circular like a castle's tower, with panoramic windows curving on one side and shelves of genuine books on the other. He keeps it warm in colour and soft in furnishings, its patterned rugs luxurious underfoot and its lighting dusky overhead, and he keeps a ring around its edge clear so that he may pace unhindered in endless circles.

They are sitting in silence upon a pair of armchairs, Edmund with the bare soles of his prosthetics pressed flat to the floor as he uploads his lidar data, when Clavius is suddenly on his feet. There does not appear to be an intermediary from seated to standing: he moves in a blur. His Scotch tumbler falls in slow motion under the low gravity, slow enough to catch, but neither of them try. Fumes and tinkling shards rise together.

'Your proximity line.' Clavius speaks clearly and calmly, but there is still something of the high alert in his eyes that holds them too wide in this warm, familiar room. 'How proximate was it, exactly?'

Edmund's heart is a hot weight in his chest as he stares at the other man—this great, imposing figure who fills any room he is in.

'Proximity lines are usually kept at—' He stops dead.

'Tell me.'

Edmund's attention is briefly caught by some change on his screen: the lidar has finished processing. The scene at Pandemonium Promontorium is laid out as though X-rayed. The scene, the stage directions—and the next step in the plot.

'Edmund . . .' Clavius's voice is dangerously low.

Edmund tears his eyes away from his screen. There, hot in his throat like a physical weight, is knowledge.

'I keep mine at forty metres.' He, too, speaks clearly and calmly. His knuckles have gone white around the glasspad. 'I hear any sound sourced within forty metres.'

Clavius holds his gaze for a moment. Then, with unchanged inflection: 'That explains it, then. Why I heard it first. Because mine was set to fifty.'

Silence grows in the hollow left by his words. The room feels brighter—too bright, exposed, a beacon stretching out across the Heart for all to see, and to come to.

Whatever was out there—whatever made the whistles, whatever the whistlers were—it had come within forty metres of them.

Not for the first time in the almost two decades he has called Pluto home, Edmund considers just how very far away five billion kilometres really is.

He pushes the words from his mouth.

'There's something else.'

He turns his screen around. Upon it is the lidar's three-dimensional reconstruction. The black wall is obvious, as are two minute humanoid figures at its base. Edmund uses two fingers to rotate the scene.

'The lidar found crevices our eyes missed,' he says.

Still with the level voice. As though they are acting, just as poorly as possible, to keep the scene from feeling real. He turns the computerised reconstruction and the black wall becomes a line looked down upon.

Clavius squints. 'What am I looking at?'

Two fingers pinch apart to zoom in. And there, perpendicular to the wall and within it, are the beginnings of little veins of pixels disappearing inside.

'They're tunnels.' Edmund can barely hold himself still. He says, breathlessly, 'Around four feet across where they open. The lidar found the entrances to tunnels.'

Clavius says nothing. He looks to be thinking, fusing the facts together in that idiosyncratic way that has made him one of the most powerful men in the Solar System. He brings up his wrist-pad and projects Nou's traverse upon the same wall as earlier. Red sniper dots, cold-blue contours.

Both train their eyes upon the furthermost data point.

'Gen,' Clavius orders. 'Bring up the time stamps for each of these points.'

Gen silently obliges. Red words appear alongside each dot.

07:05 for one. *07:10* for the next. *07:15, 07:20* . . . *07:25* for the furthermost data point . . .

Both men lean forward.

09:05 for the next, for the traverse home.

Edmund stares into the red dot, the furthermost data point, the one that reads more than a full hour after its predecessor. Its red seems to grow in size. Seems to pulse. It pulses in time with the echoes in his mind.

One-two-three. One-two-three . . .

126

'I think . . .' Clavius says slowly. He says the words very deliberately, Edmund thinks, as though he too hopes to drown out the whistling, the whistling he wonders he may never stop hearing. 'I think our little Nou has a big day ahead of her tomorrow.'

Chapter 8

'Nou.'

Edmund's inflectionless voice. Even submerged within her thoughts, that one word wrenched Nou back into the real world.

She blinked at the change. She was in his office—that cold, bare, un-lived-in office that made her shiver—with her legs hanging from the too-high chairs of his teaching table. The other children had their eyes pointedly downcast to its lit surface, where anatomic schematics of some sort awaited annotation.

Edmund was standing beside the glassboard, regarding her levelly.

'Is there something you wish to say?'

No tone was in his voice, nor expression on his face, but neither were needed. He held her gaze with expectation, as though awaiting an answer.

Nou was frozen in the act of spelling the word *cyanobacteria* under the table. She knew the signing alphabet by heart, but the word itself was longer than she ever knew words could be. Memorising it letter by letter, sign by sign, she had been so caught up that she hadn't noticed the class turn towards their worksheets, and their teacher turn towards her.

She knew it now, and her cheeks burned for it.

'In that case,' said Edmund, 'I suggest you join your classmates in labelling the cell structures on the table. In future I will call upon you to contribute through written words. Perhaps that might better occupy your attention.'

Written . . . ?

Nou's eyes bulged. She could write in lessons without a problem, but then having him read it out . . .

Her brother stared at her. 'Proceed at once.'

She couldn't write for him, Nou knew, in thoughts that ran in circles, as she picked up her pen and turned to the table. Around her was the soft chinking of pen on glass as the other children worked—always in silence in Edmund's classes—and above her were his eyes. They rested upon her back like a pair of hands clamped across her shoulders.

Flagellum. She knew that one: the little tail bacteria sometimes had. She raised her pen.

It stayed put in the air.

Cytoplasm. She knew that, too: the jelly inside prokaryotic cells. She brought the pen to the surface and a single computerised dot bloomed.

Edmund's eyes, beneath their heavy, straight brows, watched her every move.

And Nou's pen would not budge.

Chromosomal DNA. Cell wall. Ribosomes. Nou labelled the entire bacterium with her eyes. She heard footfalls to her side and concentrated harder, moving on to the sketch of the Europan creature beside the terrestrial one. Same scale, similar shape—the footfalls stopped and a black wall was to her side—but fundamentally different. No cytoplasm for one, and it wasn't DNA . . . She knew this. Her pen was gathering a little puddle of pixels about its tip. The black wall knelt on its haunches so that a face appeared at eye level. The pen was shaking.

'Look at me,' said Edmund.

Nou looked and let out her breath all at once.

Inside Edmund's eyes were wall beyond wall beyond wall.

'You will read chapter four of the course textbook and write an essay on the arguments for and against native Europan life,' he said. 'You will do this based on a morphologic comparison of cells both terrestrial and Europan, and you will give this to me before next week's lesson. I also suggest you concentrate in future and control your restless fidgeting. Is that understood?'

The other children had their heads bowed and eyes fixed on their work, but no pens moved. Nou knew she would be incapable of nodding for him if she tried until the Sun died.

Edmund rose to his feet. Somebody grabbed her hand beneath the table and squeezed—maybe Allie, a year older, the most fearless of their class, who still pulled Nou into spontaneous hugs. For the rest of the lesson Nou did not look up from her work lest anyone see the eyes she could not keep from filling, and the lips she could not keep from trembling.

It went against her every instinct to remain behind as the other pupils filed out. She stood up and had to grip the back of her chair to keep from fleeing. But it was Thursday afternoon. She waited without moving, keeping herself as small and silent as possible, while Edmund cleared the glassboard and tidied his already immaculate desk. Nou always tried to get a glimpse of that beautiful world through the livestream on his wall, that mythic place somewhere on Earth where there were trees and vast open spaces called fields, but today its blue dome of sky was hidden behind another swollen rainstorm—a scarcely conceivable event where wind tore water from the sky—as it seemed to have been for weeks.

Cyanobacteria. Nou signed each letter in her head. She had just learned how to sign the past tense, too, and went over that: *I was, I did, I learned.*

They walked to the end of the corridor on level −2, Edmund

ahead, Nou following behind. They reached the door and before she was aware, she had her hand raised to hold his own. But he did not see her—and that was as well. She clasped her hands behind her back instead, pretending it was someone else's she held, pretending it wasn't her own pulse stuttering against her fingertips.

The darkened room was lit only by the soft blues of screens and the occasional red or green flash of a button. The desk was gone; the sofas were gone; books, wall art, rugs; personality. There was only the bed, and the scanners, and the drips.

Her dad lay beneath the covers with his eyes closed. His limp head was propped up on a pillow, shaved scalp plastered, lichen-like, with white sensor pads. His bare forearms resting with their palms up held line after line of plugs, and upon almost every thumb and finger was some kind of monitor clip. Wires climbed like ivy on all sides. Far from the polymath who had designed Stern upon a wall in pencil, or the father who had magicked her into the luckiest girl alive just for smiling at her, the King of Pluto was now a silent, skeletal tree, one that stood solitary within the garden of his own creation.

She would say hello first. That was just a wave. *It's good to see you* would come next; that she knew, too. She made the signs behind her back as they approached the bed.

Edmund pulled out a chair and sat down. Nou took his cue and did the same.

Cyanobacteria. She configured the signs in her head. *Today I learned cyanobacteria were one of the first things to live on Earth.*

The room, but for the steady beeps of the heart monitor and the rhythmic breathing from the ventilator, was silent. There were certain places in this room she could never look: the places where tubes disappeared into flesh; where veins bulged out of tissue-paper skin; his face, the face she could never apologise to.

131

Edmund, to her side, had his hands folded in his lap. Nou felt his presence as acutely as if she was standing outside under the stars, and one side of her suit's thermocirculation had failed.

How are you, Dad?

That was what she would say. That was what she knew she could say. But Nou's hands would not move. And she knew, with all the despair of nausea before a night of sickness, that she was incapable of so much as raising her hand.

A windfall came for Nou before the following biology class: Edmund and the two xenobiologists, Mallory and the other one Nou had never spoken to, left ahead of schedule for a planned expedition to the opposite hemisphere. The three of them often took off for the day, sometimes overnighting in one of the little life cabins that dotted the planet for the caught-short traveller, but it sounded like something big was out there that couldn't wait.

Nou did not have to write answers for a class that was now cancelled, but she did have to send over her essay. She took great care with it, drawing deep warmth imagining her brother leaning on his elbow in one of the cabins, glasspad in hand, brows furrowed as he carefully took in her work . . . Even when it was returned to her a day later, a *C*−, she held on to that vision. Maybe he would realise how much he missed her when he was away . . .

'Wait a minute.' Lucian actually set his watchmaker tweezers down. 'You're . . . What, ten, right?'

They were in the terraformers' workshop in what had somewhere along the months since its creation become their default positions: Lucian either designing something, simulating something, or building something, and Nou by his side, helping wherever she could. On this particular day it was getting on for seven in the evening. The lights had slid into warm orange;

the coder Joules—an unsmiling man Nou was too shy to speak to—was working at his desk; Stan and his friend Percy, Parkin's grandson, were discussing something in hushed yet animated voices at the other end of the room; glancing over, Nou could swear they were sticking googly eyes on various lab items. One of Lucian's indie bands from the twenty-first century was entertaining itself in the periphery of hearing, a languorous bass against the heartbeat of a drum.

Nou was working through some fractions on the worktop beside him. She nodded in response to his question; she wouldn't be eleven for another few months.

'And he's giving you graded marks for essays? Hang on . . .' The tweezers, only just retrieved, were set down again. 'You're ten years old and you're being set *essays*?'

Nou didn't know what to say to that. But then, Lucian said and did so many strange things; perhaps the things people said and did on Pluto seemed strange to him. She nodded again.

'*Well*'—he squinted through his magnifying glasses back at his work—'I've been asked to cover those lessons until he gets back, so you can expect *that* to stop.'

Lucian also seemed affected by the biologists' absence. While Nou certainly missed Mallory at their signing sessions—missed her tales of tiny creatures on Europa; missed her pretty hairstyles, plaits like haloes Nou could never reproduce no matter how long she tried; missed how her confiding smile made her feel like someone special, someone let in on a secret—Lucian was positively wistful. He'd taken to staring off into the distance when left unoccupied, sometimes even while occupied. It was nice that he had a friend, Nou thought: nice that he had someone to care about. It must be awfully lonely at first, moving across the whole Solar System.

There was a burst of stars as Lucian delicately soldered a charming green stone to a wire, the sparks dancing against his glasses. They stayed dancing in Nou's eyes, too, if she stared too long, little dots of green and lilac even after she looked away, but she couldn't help but watch.

Across the whole Solar System . . .

She patted the sleeve of his woolly jumper. He set the tweezers and soldering iron down yet again.

Is that what our new sun will look like? she signed. Or at least, that was the essence of it: what her hands actually said was something like *lights-our-sun-same?* but she was growing less disjointed by the day.

Lucian must have caught the gist because he raised his glasses and looked at her for a long moment.

'Haven't I ever shown you what Plutoshine's going to look like?'

Now his hands were free, he also signed the words as well as speaking. Slowly, deliberately, taking care to see she was following. Nou didn't always, but at least in this room, with its singed workbenches and its red toolboxes and its screen after screen of rolling codes, she was starting to get somewhere.

Lucian was waiting patiently for an answer. Their conversations were often slow like this, but he never seemed to mind. It did not occur to her that she was now in fact *answering* on a common basis.

Nou twisted her hand around the panic button at her wrist, collecting herself.

Well, she tried—it was one of her favourite words, giving her a moment to think while acting just like Lucian, who began every other sentence with it—*I don't really know what Plutoshine is.*

The sentence seemed to take forever, especially when she reached 'shine' and, not knowing the sign, spelled it letter by letter.

'*Shine* is like this,' Lucian said, again with such patience, signing the new word with precision. 'Try mouthing the word, too, as you sign it.'

Nou made it with him, committing it to muscle memory. But she was a long way off making even the motions of speaking.

Plutoshine. She asked, *What is Plutoshine?*

Behind them, Percy to Stan: 'You stick them on the front and it becomes predator, you know? Prey have their eyes on the sides, so they can anticipate being eaten, but predators stare right ahead.'

'Plutoshine,' Lucian said and signed, 'is the name for Pluto's long-term terraforming plan. So, way back in the tensies, Clavius Harbour . . . Heck.' He blinked at her. 'I keep forgetting he's your dad. Mad scientist turned mad businessman, builder of brighter futures for all humanity, all that. You might as well say your dad's Albert Einstein or . . . or Mark Alexander.'

Nou only looked at him blankly. Lucian gaped.

'Please, please tell me you've heard of Dignity at All Times? The band? He's the singer.'

Nou hadn't, but that was OK, because apparently she soon would at the next Tombaugh's Day, when Lucian's own band would cover an excessive amount of their hits.

'Anyway, anyway'—he flapped his hands—'about twenty years ago your dad, who is some guy called Clavius Harbour, he decides he wants to build a community on Pluto. Fair do's— he's probably the most powerful maverick in the whole Solar System, he can do whatever he wants. Well. Within the Outer Territories Treaty, of course, but he gets his plan passed no problem. He gets robots to come out here and check things out while he dreams up the base, then him and the terraformers— that's Halley—they start scheming up ideas for making Pluto a little more hospitable. Again, fair do's—I can understand the anti-terraformer protests, but you've got to admit, so long as you're not harming native life, why not engineer a world that's trying to kill you into one that's your friend? And when you think about it, we humans have been engineering nature for thousands of years—terraforming's just that on a whole new level. Think wolves to Border collies.'

Nou was suspended with pencil in hand, homework quite forgotten. She had never heard an adult talk like this: as though she was smart enough to just be told it as it was. As though she was worth the time it took to explain. And hearing him speak of her father—and speak of him so highly—filled her full up with warmth. She concentrated furiously to keep up.

Lucian went on, tucking stray curls that had come free in his excitement behind both ears. He didn't seem to mind the work's halt; his task, too, lay forgotten.

'OK, back to the story. You know that "terraforming" literally means *to make Earth-like*?'

Nou nodded firmly, her mind running to keep up with his. She couldn't follow three-quarters of the signs he was making but that was no matter; she had the suspicion he only signed with his speech to make her less self-conscious when she signed herself.

'So that's the plan, that's the endgame for any terraformer. Clavius was going to bring the Sun to Pluto, either through this colossal fusion reactor idea he abandoned early on, or . . . through a solar mirror.'

He opened the drawer below him in the workbench and there, to Nou's delight, were the gauntlets. She couldn't help herself: she leant forward to better see them again. They were as beautiful as she remembered: filigreed silver wires like fine lace, studded at the joints and knuckles with what could surely only be jewels, deep pink-red for ruby, blue-black for sapphire, green as the Parks' great Atlas cedar for emerald. The pair shone as Lucian turned them under the glow of the evening lights, seeming to catch fire.

'I think I promised you a demonstration months ago,' he said thoughtfully. 'You should have poked me. Just come and poke me any time I don't hold my promises.'

The watchmaker glasses came off, as did the jumper. The sleeves were rolled up, the hair pencilled back, the gauntlets slipped on. The little silver circlet with its round white pads was donned.

Behind them was the raised dais with its three pillars, silent and dormant.

'Earth was the first place to get solar mirrors,' Lucian said as he came to stand before them. 'People wanted to grow crops all year round, and they had their successes and failures with that. Then Mars went to town with the idea and it all went horribly pear-shaped some fifty-odd years ago. Think ants and magnifying glasses. Mirrors went out of fashion a little after that, and they're only just making their comeback. Actually'—he screwed up his face in a wince—'I suppose the same happened to terraforming. People bring up that mirror even now, even after all the asteroid captures, the carbonate mining, the HGWs . . . Hydrocarbon generation windfarms,' he explained, somehow seeing the question in her face even as she hastened to hide it. 'Good stuff happens so slowly people miss it. Bad stuff makes news. Honestly? I reckon another major accident could see terraforming off for good . . .'

Nou flitted to his side between two of the big brushed-metal pillars. Up close they seemed very large indeed, stretching up and up at least twice Lucian's not-inconsiderable height. They grew narrower as they did, exaggerating this towering effect. She shrank a little closer to him.

He followed her eyes.

'These guys are triangulators,' he explained, pointing from one pillar to the next. 'They project things in 3D between them, and the space can be as big as you've got room for. That first night in the Parks was irresistible, so I got a trio of portable versions set up. A little loss of quality but, *man*, all that space. Worth it.'

Nou nodded and nodded. What he spoke of was magic, she knew. He was a real-life magician.

Lucian tapped the circlet at his temples.

'On to the next bit. This thing converts my brain's signals into something readable to the triangulator computers. And these'—holding up both wrists, wires and tiny gemstones winking in the light—'these convert my movements into virtual, then project that in real time where we can watch. Though it looks like someone's been having a go themselves, they're a little tighter than I left them . . .'

He looked ready to clap his hands together, as was his custom, but seemed to remember the delicate gauntlets just in time.

'Plutoshine, yes, right, let's go.'

What should I do? Nou looked up at him.

She saw already he was dropping into that other mode of mind: the one that made him into more than just Lucian. How easy it was to forget, when he was there in his plaid shirt, and his frayed jeans, with that golden locket at his chest. How easy to forget he was here to wake Pluto up again.

All trace of joking and laughter were already being tidied away. His shoulders were settling; his chest rose and fell steadily; his hands were poised as though preparing to catch something. His eyes closed.

Lucian the terraformer said, 'Just stay right where you are.'

And just like that—like magic—there was the mirror, so swiftly and suddenly that she jumped back. The simulated mirror was concave, perfectly circular, and as silver as the Parks' lake in a flat calm. It was also absolutely titanic: Nou could recall Halley once describing its central antenna as the height of Stern, and this she could not even make out. The mirror's total diameter must be . . . Nou tried and failed to reach any plausible estimate.

'Three hundred kilometres,' said Lucian. He looked as happy as a cat being stroked between the ears, eyelids heavy, face relaxed, movements fluid, almost meditative. We went for the bigger design in the end. 'More than twelve per cent of the diameter of the whole planet.'

Nou's mouth fell slack.

'You heard right. This is exactly what our mirror looks like right now, what we've been building in space out of Styx. So, not *quite* finished—you see there's just a few tiles missing at the bottom left?'

The mirror zoomed close with such speed that Nou felt dizziness rock the space between her ears. She couldn't miss them then, little gaps in the silver lake.

'We'll have those fettled just in time for Tombaugh's Day,' Lucian said confidently. He rotated the mirror so it caught the Sun's meagre rays, lighting up like a million crystals. 'If you think of the mirror as turning the heating up, then along come our gard-asteroids—'

Mo, Nou signed with a smile, remembering.

'Mo indeed, and they're the equivalent of tucking you up in nice warm blankets—they give you an atmosphere to trap in the mirror's warmth. You get heat, you get melting of the ground ices, and that pumps more gas into the atmosphere. Thicker and thicker it gets, trapping more heat, melting more ice . . . That's called a positive feedback effect. The cycle keeps going until you start to get to temperatures a little kinder for humans. And there you have it—that's Project Plutoshine. That's your terraforming plan.'

Could Nou have spoken, she would have been speechless. She configured the signs in her head before trying.

Did you design it?

139

'No, no. Just the mirror.' Lucian wiggled his shoulders happily. 'But the gauntlets are a super-convenient way to keep an eye on the gard-asteroids as they get close, so I've been helping Halley out with that. And Joules, he's the master programmer behind them. If any of our gards started to veer off course, I could just pull on these gauntlets, plug myself into these triangulators, and tweak their trajectory faster than a coder would know where to look.'

Nou pondered all this for a moment.

This is a stupid question, but—

'There's no such thing.'

Nou looked up at him.

'As a stupid question.' Lucian held up a hand to still the mirror's gentle rotation, then turned to her quite seriously. 'You knew that, right?'

That patient, level gaze of his. Not a silence-filler question. She was starting to realise everything Lucian said and did was genuine. Nou brought her hands up and found herself quite unable to respond.

'You can ask me why it needs to be so big, or why it's so shiny, or even why I will never, ever grow a beard.'

That made her smile.

Why will you never, ever grow a beard?

Lucian leant closer.

'Because it grows ginger,' he whispered. 'Now'—straightening up, raising his voice—'ask me your not-so-stupid question.'

Nou had so many she didn't know where to begin.

Why does it need to be so big?

'There's two reasons,' he told her. 'If you can guess one I'll tell you the other.'

Nou looked from the shimmering mirror to the tiny pinpricks of light just visible around it. She searched until she found one in particular.

Because we're so far from the Sun? she hazarded.

'Bang on. The second one's a little more complicated, and that's to do with the angle at which the sunlight has to hit the tiles. See the way it's curved? That's called a parabola. We could actually face the Sun just a bit more and harness way more power, except then we'd be at risk of overheating.'

Not good? Nou guessed.

'Not good at all.' Lucian clicked his teeth together. 'Ten out of ten would not want to be around. Magnifying glasses and ants, remember? But it's the angle of the tiles we need, and that's why the bowl-shape has to be so exhaustingly huge.' He grinned at her. 'Ask me another one. I like being asked questions. It makes me actually stop and think, and the strain of such a rare event must be good exercise.'

Nou needed no further encouragement. She was getting good at the signs for questions now, and by the end of their talk could do it far faster and smoother than at its start. Unknown to her, this was also exactly why Lucian had encouraged her.

The terraformer and his small friend passed many an educational evening by the hands of those gauntlets. Lucian showed her their models of the upcoming gard, Mo, or he monitored Styx's robotic sautéing as the mirror's final tiles slotted into place. Some nights one of the other researchers, Kip, asked to see his latest simulation of ice sheet disintegration (though Nou rarely understood what she was looking at), or Lucian would help Stan with a design: gold-coated, silver-coated, things Nou knew no words for. The acronyms they used—like FRPC (*fibre-reinforced polymer composites*) and TRL (*technology readiness level*)—were a fascinating new language she took in as readily as the new signs.

For Lucian's part, it took him perhaps longer than he was proud of to realise that Nou was staying later and later past her bedtime. He would rise at 9 p.m., pulling out his earphones as his mum and sisters goodbyed him in their latest message, and find her still engrossed in some little task he'd set—labelling these wires or calculating those uncertainties or such—with overtired eyes like saucers. More often she would already be fast asleep, her head on the countertop among scorched platinum filaments, or drooped over the SMOD on his glasspad (*Space Mission Operations and Design*, or the *Smible* as he called it). He carried her to her quarters himself those nights, feather-light and boneless as only sleeping children can be, but even when nobody answered the door he never considered she was home alone.

Edmund Harbour was not a cruel man for leaving Nou unsupervised. She wasn't going hungry, or cold, and in the close-knit base it was laughable to think she would be unsafe. But still Lucian's eyes and jaw hardened when he asked her about it and she only shrugged.

I like having the place to myself, she signed in her indifferent, diffident manner. Causing no trouble. Raised that way, he was beginning to think. Raised not to ask questions.

For Nou, the reality was she was happier by an order of magnitude than she had been since the accident. The magnet-meeting-magnet rush of anxiety whenever she entered her quarters—standing still listening before the door; calculating whether he would still be in his lab, still be among his Petri dishes—was gone. So, too, was the hyperconscious scanning of canteen chairs for the back of a sleek dark head, and the jump-start of her heart at the approach of dark trousers and polo neck down the corridor. As the weeks passed she became more open with her signing, stretching her gestures into sweeping ones: the equivalent of raising her voice, speaking more clearly. Her eyes lit up at the thought of her weekly sessions with Lucian, and sometimes Mallory on video: more often than just sitting and signing, they would go swimming, or walk around the lake

142

in the Parks. One time they visited the base's bees; another they made plum jam from the winter harvest, the two of them up to their elbows in the sticky, sweet-smelling pulp, Nou carefully labelling her jar and cherishing it.

For her it was the everyday interactions, the light conversations, the sense of belonging, that kept her practising. Each morning before the dawn lamps rose she would sit in her bubble-pod, cross-legged, and teach herself words, sometimes ones she hadn't even known of to speak. Folks in the lab would sign *Good morning* or *How are you?* when she entered, Joules in particular—the quiet one, the serious and slightly scary one—and Nou wondered whether signing made speaking easier, too, for people who just didn't like to. Stan—another quiet one—signed as well, awkwardly, apologetically, and Nou would nod in encouragement as he tried so very hard, and she thought she would cry at his kindness.

It was for Lucian, though, that she practised. Lucian whom she loved with a fierce, uncomplicated, unconditional devotion—the same way she had once loved her brother, loved her dad. Lucian who didn't pity her, who wasn't trying to fix her, or pretend she wasn't as she was. Lucian was just trying to help. Once as she signed with Stan and Joules she caught his eye over their shoulders, and he gave her two thumbs-ups and a grin. Another time she was signing out number after number, some thirty-digit value from the computer for him to confirm, and he called her a lifesaver. And when she finally understood the difference between mass and weight, and used their signs correctly in a sentence, he placed his hands on her shoulders and told her she was a star. Nou couldn't remember ever being called a star before. It hadn't occurred to her she could be.

News trickled back from Edmund and the xenobiologists as the weeks went by. They were exploring a potential heat anomaly and had come across a network of sub-glacial cavities, perhaps related to a neighbouring cryo-volcanic province. They would be there longer than planned, they said in the video message, the three of them around a dining table in their cabin. It was Mallory who spoke, still with shining hair artfully styled, still with eyes that always seemed to be quietly laughing at something, but Nou kept her own fixed on her brother. She stared at him as though she had never seen him before; as though she could convince herself he was as much a stranger to her as the other biologist, the tall, quiet woman.

But the video came on a Thursday. It was lunchtime, and Nou was sitting among her fellow schoolmates, and as she stared at her brother the stranger, she was quite suddenly unable to touch her cauliflower and mustard soup. That old seizing anxiety was shutting her down as though, in her urge to flee equally in any direction, the forces had cancelled out to root her to the spot.

For the first time she wished she could skip her next lesson. Lucian made biology a game, a story, and sometimes if the other children begged enough he would tell them about the time he lived on Earth: how heavy your feet were; how the sky didn't try to kill you; how life had seeped into every tiniest nook. Or, if they were really lucky, he would don the gauntlets and show them bacteria in three dimensions, wiggling and bursting and monstrously blown-up. They called him *sir*, and they fell silent when he spoke, and it was a widely known fact that he was the coolest teacher in the whole Solar System. But until Edmund's message, Nou had always been too enthralled by these lessons to remember what strictly followed them. She had forgotten her duty.

It went against her every instinct to remain behind as the other pupils filed out. She stood up and had to grip the back of her chair to keep from fleeing. But it was Thursday afternoon.

Lucian was clearing the board. They were in one of the designated seminar rooms, and Nou waited until he saw her.

144

'How's it going?' he said when he did, smiling easily and wiping pixels clear with his hand. He spoke and signed in their secret language: 'Getting excited for Tombaugh's Day? Not long now, and the way you guys go on it must be something special.'

Nou knew what she wanted to ask him, and she knew how to sign it, but shyness ducked her head and held her hands.

Would you . . . ? she began.

It was the custom when signing to make eye contact, but she found herself instead preoccupied with the Stern Base patch on his crookedly knitted jumper. QUICQUID CAPIT, the stitching read. It meant *Whatever it takes*, and it was what lovers of Pluto had been saying to one another for hundreds of years, before Stern, way back before the *New Horizons* mission even had a name.

Nou tried again. *Would you . . . ?*

It was no good. But she had prepared for this eventuality, so she handed him the note instead. When he was done reading, he looked back at her with sober eyes.

'Of course,' he said quietly. 'We'll go right now if you want.'

And though Nou's heartbeat quickened to do so and her every instinct said not to, she knew she had taken a step towards something good. She had asked someone to do something for her. Her body had grown just a little into what little space it occupied in the world.

They walked to the end of the corridor on level −2, side by side. They reached the door and, before she was aware, she had her hand raised to hold his own. She hesitated—electricity jumped within her wrists and charged the very roots of her hair—then clasped his hand tightly, for the very first time. Lucian squeezed her own in response. His palm was hot and she could feel his pulse fast against her fingertips.

The same darkened room. The same beeps of the heart monitor. Rhythmic breathing from the ventilator. Just as they had been for more than a year.

She felt Lucian tense as he saw the bed. Knowing it was one thing; seeing was another.

It was Nou's turn to squeeze Lucian's hand now, her turn to reassure him, before letting go and approaching the bed. Her hands shook but she held the words firmly in her mind as she signed:

Hello, Dad.

She breathed in slowly, pretending she was Lucian. Always calm, always steady. She continued: *It's good to see you.*

And it was. It was scary, seeing him like this. Her dad was someone who was never still, never sick, never silent. He was never supposed to be any of those things; a year ago she would have sworn he couldn't be. Her dad was unstoppable. But the man on the bed was still her father. She would always love him beyond her ability to prove it.

A hand upon her shoulder. As she looked up, Lucian bent down to whisper in her ear.

'Would you like me to translate for you? So he can hear?'

His voice was so quiet she could barely make the words out. But she shook her head.

He will hear, she signed firmly. *He knows.* She took his hand in hers and led him to the bedside. *This is Lucian,* she told her father. *He's the terraformer you invited.*

Lucian began signing, too, slowly, simply, so she could follow: *It's an honour to meet you, sir.*

He turned to Nou. *Shall we sit?* he signed.

Up until then he had always spoken with the matching gestures, and his silence in this place was full of respect. More than ever it seemed they shared a secret language, one that could perhaps reach her father through some magic of their own making.

The pair pulled out a chair each and sat at Clavius Harbour's bedside.

Cyanobacteria. Nou made the signs in her head. *Today I learned that cyanobacteria were one of the first things to live on Earth.*

Lucian gave her a small nod of encouragement. Steadying her breath, she turned to her father, and she began.

Chapter 9

The last weeks in the run-up to Tombaugh's Day were more exciting than Nou could ever remember them being, even after a childhood's wide-eyed anticipation that returned each year. It was through no coincidence that the celebration of both Pluto's discovery and its settlement was about to collect another anniversary: the arrival of Mo, the first gard, and the first test of Lucian's solar mirror. Project Plutoshine was in full swing.

On the morning of the day itself, Nou woke up cocooned within her pod in her fleece-lined nightdress, warmer and more comfortable than she had ever known it was possible to be. She had no memory of falling into bed the night before: she'd been helping Stan quadruple-test the germanium-charged ceramic he'd invented to coat the mirror's solar cells, and she could just about remember Lucian, Kip, and Joules coming back from band practice.

'Dinghy at All Times. No, wait! Dignity Under No Circumstances,' she'd heard Kip say. He was a rosy-cheeked, burly man who frequently made her almost laugh out loud, who was some kind of interplanetary-grade ice specialist.

'All right, mate'—the drily amused voice of Joules, who really wasn't so serious and scary once Nou had come to understand his mannerisms—'only problem is, we're not actually a Dignity tribute band.'

'We might as well be. OK then, *the Mortimaeusians*.'

'The *what*?'

'No, no, wait, I've got it!' Lucian, dramatically: '*The Minus Kelvins*.'

Kip had burst out laughing. 'You idiot, there's no such thing as a minus Kelvin!'

'But, Kip, that's why it's so brilliant!'

Nou had fallen into the habit of falling asleep in the workshop come hustle-and-bustle or quiet concentration. She had even taken up Halley's wry (sarcastic?) suggestion of coming down ready-dressed in pyjamas.

Why, exactly, she found the workshop so conducive for sleep was hard to put her finger on. It was hardly a peaceful place: there was always the whirr of some furnace or vacuum pump on the go, or banter between the lads and even the scary and elusive professor Halley, and every so often there might be an unexplained *bang* followed by a curse, followed by an apology for cursing. But somehow she managed, and somehow most mornings she awoke tucked within her bubble-pod, slippers neatly by its side, with no memory of climbing in.

She wondered whether it was magic at first, because if there was one thing for sure about the workshop, it was the magic within it. The Plutonians had nicknamed it the Terramancers' Lair and with good reason: it was a place where an opened drawer might reveal row after row of tiny glass jars with handwritten labels, or loose gemstones rattling among silver screws the size of peas; where a 3D-printed human skull (known as Keith) gazed languidly from his shelf within a feather boa; where sheets of gold foil were folded exquisitely into chains of origami cranes. Magic, alchemy, enchantment: they seemed crafted into the workshop's very walls.

But as a child raised by scientists, this explanation of magic only remained satisfactory for so long. Nou knew what *method* meant—following a series of tasks to do something—and she had just learnt what a *hypothesis* was—having an inkling of an explanation and setting up a method to test it—so she put both to use. Her hypothesis: not magic. Her method: lie in wait, pretend to sleep, and see what happened.

What happened was Lucian scooped her up and, almost one-handedly, carried her to bed. It was all Nou could do to keep her breathing deep and steady and her eyelids still. The moment he left, her eyes had opened as round as any of the planets on her duvet, and she had stayed that way, in the dim glow of her rose-hued nightlight, for some time.

And so on the morning of Tombaugh's Day it was no mystery how she came to wake up, cocooned within her pod in her fleece-lined nightdress, with no memory of falling into bed the night before. Her hypothesis had been proven *null*, as the scientists would say: it really was magic that carried her home, and it really was true that somebody—she would hug her hands to her chest and spin on the spot with happiness at the thought—somebody cared.

Presently Nou got to her feet and stretched her arms high above her, feeling happiness light stars behind her closed eyes and tingle right through to her fingers and toes. She spun on the spot, flaring out the gown, spiralling the fairy lights on her walls into long lines of peaches and violets.

A quick shower, a quick dress, then she'd head down to breakfast . . . She opened her bedroom door, already lost in blissful thoughts. To breakfast, where Parkin would wave at her, and Kip would call her *kiddo*, and Stan would give her a warm smile, and Halley would move over to let her sit, and Lucian would brightly sign her a good morning, and she would sign back . . .

'Good morning, Nou.'

Nou stopped dead in her doorway.

Edmund was at the countertop holding a cafetière. He was dressed straight from her memories—black polo neck, black trousers, black expression—but the pallor of his skin was new: the half-moon shadows below each eye; the bloodlessness of his lips.

'I trust you are well?'

Edmund's face was unreadable as he plunged the filter to the depths of his coffee. He had been gone for more than two months.

Nou remained helplessly where she stood. Her nightdress was soft pink with stars and planets etched in Earth-sky blue, and as her brother poured the steaming black liquid she thought she had never felt so small or so ridiculous in all her life.

But she managed a nod. Later, when she recalled that moment—the shine of her brother's immaculate hair; the acrid, wet-bark smell of the coffee; his gaze resting coolly upon the glittery butterfly at the end of her plait—she couldn't ever say where she found the courage to do so.

Edmund only inclined his head; returning her nod.

'And do you . . . speak yet?' he asked stiffly.

Were Nou ever to experience drowning, she knew, it would feel exactly like this. To open her mouth would be to swallow water, and to die. She tried to shake her head . . . She couldn't think . . . She was nodding when she meant to shake . . .

'Don't.' Edmund held up a hand and looked away. 'You don't have to upset yourself. I understand.'

Nou could not bear to meet his eyes. She couldn't bear to see disappointment again. It seemed a lifetime since she had felt like a disappointment.

Edmund raised his coffee, nodded curtly, and turned to leave.

A surge of recollection hit Nou as though her ears had been boxed by thunder.

Wait!

The sign was out before she knew it. Edmund—knowing nothing of her progress, nothing of the language—stared at her with open bewilderment.

Nou felt her cheeks glow like the Betelgeuse supergiant. She held up a shaking finger. *One minute.*

In two bounds she was in her room, on her desk, stretching high up past the fairy lights and the Sun hologram and the lovingly coloured paint-your-own-Solar-System model, and wrapping both hands around a piece of treasure. The cool of its hexagonal glass pushed memories into her fingertips: a day of other people's laughter, of messy craftwork, of carefully, painstakingly writing the label in her best cursive handwriting, her tongue sticking out to do it . . .

In the kitchenette Edmund had not moved. Nou couldn't meet his eyes as she sidled forward and thrust the jar of plum jam into his hand.

Even focusing on his hands, she couldn't miss the flinch as she did, nor the raising of eyebrows, the slight widening of eyes. She jumped back the moment its weight left her hands. Her gaze was on his shoes—his black, flawless, mirror-polished Oxfords—so that she couldn't see his face at all as he twisted the tissue-paper lid around to read its tag: *Welcome home Edmund.*

She wished she could read it aloud for him. But then, if she could speak (as he continued to stare at the label), that would mean they were any normal little sister and big brother. And then what would she say? (As he turned the jar in his hands, its froth of golden ribbon catching the light.) Or would she just run up to him like she used to? Would he hoist her up into his arms and kiss her forehead, like he used to . . . ?

'Thank you,' said Edmund, and there was something in his voice that made her look up. He sounded *startled.* Unguarded. And just for a moment, like a pool reaching perfect stillness and seeing with unbroken clarity the pebbles below, she saw startled and unguarded right there in his expression, too.

'Thank you, Nou,' he said again. 'This is . . . very thoughtful.'

(He used to lift her underneath the arms and hold her against his hip, one-handed, as though she weighed nothing at all . . .)

He was still looking at the little jar.

(He used to make her tell him about her day. He used to tell her to talk slower, and talk clearer, and he would teach her new words—jewels of words like *sastrugi* and *komorebi*—words she would tuck away and cherish and whisper like mantras . . .)

Nou didn't dare move.

(He used to sit in the tasselled chair by her bed and read to her. Some nights he would make her read the book set by the teacher, but some he would cave at her pleading and breathe life into fictional worlds with every word, and when she fell asleep it was his warm voice narrating her dreams until morning . . .)

Edmund picked up his coffee with his free hand.

'I . . . ah.'

(He used to. He used to. He used to.)

'I won't keep you from your breakfast.'

With that he raised a hand in parting—the one with the jar—and left. The entire interaction had taken less than five minutes.

It was only then, with the silence ringing in her ears and the thumping of her heart slowing, a heart too big in a chest too small, that she realised she hadn't thought to ask whether he had found life.

There was no school on Tombaugh's Day. No work, no duties. The people of Pluto were both host and guest to this most anticipated of days: they chipped in together to decorate the base; they arranged wreaths for every surface; they hosted board games and guessing games and shout-the-fastest games; they concocted drinks; they played music; they served lunchtime spreads of steaming bread rolls, quiches, pies, pasties filled with spiced nut-roast and sweet tomato and curried apricots; later there was an evening buffet of hot stew, followed by sour cherry trifle and banana-cream profiteroles and chocolate tarts that oozed caramel. On a world where everything held so little weight, every person pulled their own.

The base was already a hive of activity when Nou emerged. Everyone had a job to do and was going about it: the corridors were full of passers-by, some carrying tanks of oxygen to the main airlock or sacks of potatoes to the galley, others on errands with a skip in their step, all calling *Good morning!* or *Happy Tombaugh's Day!* with smiles thrown over shoulders or hands briefly clasped in passing. Feeling her heart skip a little despite itself—and how could it not on such a day?—Nou ducked behind a chain of people linked by silvery bunting and followed in their wake.

'You don't have to play it if you don't want to,' Stan was saying when Nou saw them, as he and Lucian carried what would on Earth have been excruciatingly heavy amps under each arm. 'If the rest of your songs are there for a bit of a dance then maybe it won't fit right with the mood.'

'*Stanisław.*' Lucian squeezed his eyes shut. 'We've been through this. We're playing it, they're going to love it, and yes it will fit, but if you keep this up then you'll never get to hear it, because I am going to throw you in the asher.'

'What's the asher?'

'It burns things. Now come on, *scoot.*'

'Perhaps you could sing it instead? Please, could you?'

'Stan, have you ever heard roasted aubergine sing? Because let me tell you, if roasted aubergine could sing . . . and look, even if I sang like Mr Alexander himself, you've got to do this, mate, if nothing else it's another feather to your boa.'

154

'If only I wore feather boas.'

'You should try it some time. Hey!'

The pair caught sight of her, and Nou's heart sang at the genuine smile in Lucian's eyes. She waved and rushed over.

Happy Tombaugh's Day! she signed. She knew the alphabet so well now that there was no need to plan all those letters for the name.

'Happy Tombaugh's Day!' Lucian and Stan chorused back.

Both looked exceptionally dapper, Stan dashing in a shirt that shone like oyster silk, Lucian snug in a maroon jumper twined with gold thread. Lucian beamed at her.

'How are you on this fine morning, young lady? And aren't you just the belle of the base in that dress! Would you call that cerulean? Listen, we're heading to the hall to get set up, but come find me later, OK? I've got something for you.'

OK, she signed with a nod. *Can I help?*

'Yes! Halley was desperate for a second pair of hands in the galley. Come find us for lunch, we're going to decorate the sequoias.'

See you later, she waved as they rounded a corner.

'Do you know,' said Halley ten minutes later, as they chopped parsnips side by side over a massive sink, 'that when I first categorised Asteroid one-nine-seven-seven-oh-four-three as a potential target for Plutoshine's atmospheric grazing sub-project, the last place I expected to be upon its arrival was up to my elbows in root vegetables?'

Meanwhile Lucian and Stan had reached level 0, where the plaza had been transmogrified into a snow globe. Lights wrapped in coloured tissue paper were draped down every vaguely vertical surface; tables were laid with silver cloths and wreaths of crocuses and daffodils; and the hall, through its great double doors, was the dance floor.

Kip had already set up the stage and was rolling out his drum kit. Vasily, the Russian of few words, was tuning up his guitar in short twangs that echoed around the empty room. Their other electric guitarist was hanging up disco lights from atop an enormous ladder. Parkin's saxophone already lay polished to perfection at the stage's side. Though the overhead lamps still blazed, and the galley hatch was still piled with trays, no imagination was needed to picture the absolute knees-up this place would contain come evening.

'We come bearing gifts,' Lucian called, setting the amps down with a commensurate number of thumps. 'I promised our dear chef I'd make my courgette moussaka again, but point where we can help and we'll do our utmost.'

'Ooh, you couldn't get us all a tea, could you?' someone called over.

'No tea.' Vasily stopped strumming and pointed his plectrum at Lucian. 'You and I must retrieve the last of the damson gin.'

Damson was fabulously easy to grow, and the pair had combined Lucian's micro-brewery hobby with Vasily's exquisitely honed palate to produce surely the finest (first) gin Pluto had ever tasted.

'We need a name, my friend,' Vasily pointed out as they unboxed their hand-blown bottles at the plaza's makeshift bar ten minutes later.

'"Damn, Son",' Lucian said without looking up. His thoughts had been stuck as much on band names as solar mirror contingencies; today he was on fire.

Vasily was shaking his head. 'That is too good a name. It is almost certainly already taken by some Martian bestseller.'

'Yeah, but'—balancing several crates in one hand and managing to shrug at the same time—'by the time the copyright lawyers get here, Vasya, they just won't care any more.'

'We will make them forget to.'

'That we will. Cheers.'

The gin was delivered, as was the tea. Errands were run, sound-checks were checked, and jumpers and dresses and wrist-warmers with subtle sparkles were adorned by all. By now the base was really coming to life, and when Lucian later passed through the plaza he found it thronged with the sounds of laughter and light conversation.

He was tying his hair back with a string of violently purple sequins, bending to admire the effect in a silvered balloon, when another face slipped beside his own. Burnished sunlight for hair. Eyes scintillating with wit drier than bitter-lemon vermouth. Mallory Madoc, arms bare, in more sequins than he, reaching up to take both his shoulders from behind and lean in, and kiss him on the cheek.

'Hello, you,' she said to the Lucian in the balloon.

It was all Lucian could do not to spin on the spot and pull her into his arms and kiss her right there.

He opted for the respectable option—just the first two—and she laughed as he hugged her close. The nape of her neck smelt of the unmistakable astringency of new plastic, spacesuit fibres rubbing into skin week after week.

'I had no idea you were back,' he managed as they drew space between them. 'Did you . . . ? Are you'—there was something important to ask her, but he couldn't remember what—'find well? I mean, are you well? Did you find life?'

Mallory still had her hand on his upper arm. She was still smiling at him in that way that made his stomach momentarily forget that gravity was indeed a thing.

'You're supposed to ask first whether I'd like a drink,' she said, and there was mischief and reproach together in the curve of her mouth. 'I love the jumper, by the way. It's very Mark Alexander.'

And what exactly did people do on Tombaugh's Day? Only

157

what people always did on public holidays: they ate a bit too much; they drank a lot too much; they laughed just as much as they ought to. People stole into beanbag-filled corners to catch up with friends; people helped themselves to chocolate hearts the size of almonds; people were run off their feet making soufflés rise and frisbees soar; the unlikeliest of people could be found in merry conversation over a glass of damson gin and ginger ale.

As the hour grew later, the music grew louder. The ceilidh was tradition: group dances with stamping feet and clapping hands and chorusing cheers, guitar and sax and fiddle and pipes and drums and voice, songs it seemed the whole base knew by muscle memory.

On bass, Lucian was just grateful for the excuse to conceal his gracelessness when dancing, which was on a par with that of an airborne octopus. Halley was also absent, but with her own excuse: she'd be there in the darkened control room from now until the time, checking and rechecking the entire sequence from mirror switch-on to total asteroid annihilation. And not without reason, Lucian knew: after Styx—after sharing his hunch with her—none of them could afford to be complacent.

At least, not until the band was over. Then Lucian would be right there with her.

Edmund Harbour had unfortunately returned alongside Mallory, and didn't dance either, it seemed. He stood at the side and sipped his drink—was that coffee?—and conversed with the many folk who came up to presumably ask after his trip and his health. The latter of which didn't look so good, Lucian couldn't help but think: even under whirling rainbow lights and from across the room, those gouged hollows below his eyes couldn't be missed.

Nou, meanwhile, was nowhere to be seen. But then, dancing was its own form of communication: one of the boldest and the simplest. He would search for her afterwards.

158

As the evening drew yet later, the lights drew lower. Then came the hour for the most banging tunes: covers from the electro-punk of Caloris Crater, to two hundred years of the cheesiest pop from Earth, and now to the jovial anything-and-everything that were the Minus Kelvins of Sputnik Planitia. They played local classics that had been around since the days of the first villagers: songs about the *Mayflower*; about Scott and Amundsen; about the pale blue dot; about firsts and failures and carrying on regardless; about why we try in the first place. The dancers waved their hands in the air, one thumb tucked against their palm. *Nine.* Historically the Solar System's ninth planet, and now its ninth inhabited world. Because whether formally designated as a *planet* or not, there could be no doubt about it: Pluto was a *world*.

And what were they celebrating? What was Tombaugh's Day *for*? The anniversary of the day their world came into human knowledge—yes. The anniversary of the day their world became *theirs*—yes. But this year was different. This year would become a new anniversary.

Stan sang a new song for the final tune of the night. He sang of an old war general in the 1900s who, in the final years of his life, learnt of a vast, bygone cedar forest that had once carpeted the mountains of his outpost. The old man drew his men to him and ordered the forest be replanted at once.

But, the men objected, *such trees grow by the millennium.*

The general only gave them a stern look.

That, gentlemen, he said, *is why we shall start immediately.*

Plutoshine was not going to happen overnight. It was not going to happen in a human lifetime; perhaps none of the people celebrating that night would ever live to see its benefits. But that was not what terraforming was about. And—as Stan's old general knew—that was not what planting forests was about, either.

'Nou. Wake up, Nou, it's time.'

Nou's eyelids weighed surely as much as they would on Jupiter. She blinked them apart but was still on Pluto; still in her fairytale dancing dress, still in sparkly buckle-up shoes, curled up under the guardianship of the sequoia grove in the Parks. There was a carpet of soft grass like sheepskin beneath her cheek, and all around was the drifting perfume of spring flowers.

It was Lucian who had nudged her awake. His hair was back to its wild self, and there was glitter in it that caught the low lighting like tiny stars. A reddish mark like rubbed lipstick lit the five o'clock shadow on his jaw.

Is it sunrise yet? Nou asked. Her arms felt heavy, too.

'Just about,' Lucian whispered. 'There's still time to get in your suit and go outside. I've got to stay in the control room, but I'll come find you after.'

OK, she tried to sign, but her hand went to her mouth instead to cover a huge yawn.

'Come on, then. Up you get.'

He held out a hand and she took it, letting herself be lifted to her feet and taken into his arms. She weighed nothing under Pluto's gravity but she was getting too big to be carried, and in that sleepy, simple moment she wished the world could stand still just the way it was: that she would never grow bigger; that Edmund would never look at her in disappointment again; that her dad would never awaken; that Lucian would always look after her even though she wasn't clever like Stan, or pretty like Mallory, or accomplished like Halley.

You never told me why Mo is called Mo, she signed with her eyes closed, her head safe on his shoulder.

'Didn't I, now?' Lucian said musingly, and she felt his words as much as heard them through the deep humming in his chest.

His jumper smelt of rich food, and burned metals, and of the oils he cleaned his tools with. 'Well, of the three great Gard Protectors, our friend Mortimaeus is the one who keeps everything running. He's the balloonist—he flies the big red hot-air balloon. So he's the asteroid that comes first, because without him none of the gards would ever get anywhere. That's the job of a gard. To be there for their wards, and to be there exactly when they're needed.'

Do you really believe they're real? Nou had her eyes open now, watching him.

'Not in this universe,' Lucian said, with an easy shrug that jostled her. 'In our universe they're just fiction. But I believe in parallel universes because I can follow the scientific evidence for them. And who knows? Maybe there's a parallel universe where we're the fiction. Maybe there's one where gards are real.'

Nou gave this some thought.

Can anything cross over from parallel universes?

'You'd have to ask a quantum physicist to know for sure. I'd certainly like to know. Here we are.'

They were nearing the airlock. The plaza was all quiet now, only lone figures or intimate couples conversing among the tables' empty wine glasses and pecked cheeseboards. Faint music still emerged from the hall but it was playing to itself: anyone lively enough to dance was outside, waiting for a dawn such as their world had never seen.

Lucian set Nou on her feet.

'You'll be wide awake in no time. Find yourself the best spot, OK?'

Nou nodded, then remembered something.

What did you want to give me? She felt wider awake with every word. *You said earlier. You said to find you.*

Lucian snapped his fingers. 'Yes, I did!'

And he took her by the shoulders and directed her to one of

the velvet-wrapped chairs around a table. Settling before her on his knees, they were eye to eye under the glow of the fairy lights.

'Something every sign language course will teach you eventually,' he said, signing along with care, 'is that names are an utter nuisance. Spelling anything out is too clunky to bother with. Which is why it's a rite of passage in most classes to christen each other with your own *sign names*.'

Nou's lips parted in a silent *oh!*

'What do you think?' Lucian was already grinning, as though encouraged by her response. 'Until you can speak again?'

He said the words so easily. So confidently. As though there was no question about it—just a matter of time. It was belief in his words, whole and unconditional.

How do we do it? was her first question. *Can it be anything at all?*

'Anything in all the worlds.' Lucian nodded. 'And it's entirely your choice. Want to go first, pick for me?'

Nou's eyebrows came down as she thought.

'Could be the first thing that comes into your head,' he suggested. 'Maybe that's the best way to do it. The simplest word to sum me right up.'

Nou signed the first word that came into her head. Up came her hand to her face, where she opened it like a flower turning to the sky.

Lucian laughed, a real bark of a laugh. 'Sunny. I like that a lot.'

You're very happy, she explained, ducking her head as her cheeks flared. *You're always happy.*

'And I'm building you all a sun, let's not forget that, too. All right, my turn . . .'

Nou knew he was thinking about her then as his eyebrows twisted into parentheses. His eyes darted to hers—and Nou wondered, wondered how he thought of her—then away again as they flew to the ceiling.

A strange concept: she existed to this man. She was a character in his head. Someone he had an evolving view of, someone he might think about at times. She was real to him. Did she occupy just the smallest corner of this man's thoughts? How easily and wholly she loved him for his kindness and his care. Was she lovable in turn?

'Spark.'

Nou blinked back to attention. Lucian was pointing a finger at her.

'Spark. Because you're very little, but very lively.'

Now it was Nou's turn to laugh. Silently, silently, but with all her teeth. It felt good to laugh like that.

Lucian was signing it now: a squiggle of the finger upwards, then out burst the hand as wide as it would go. *Spark*. There was something dazzling about it. As though real sparks were raining down and coming to settle in both their eyes.

Lucian put a hand on her shoulder and gave it a squeeze.

'Go find the best spot.'

I will, she promised. *You don't need to be scared, by the way.*

'Scared?' He looked alarmed.

Of what's going to happen. The mirror.

'Oh, well, I'm . . .' An attempted shrug; an attempted crooked smile. 'You know, it's . . . Well. I'm a little nervous. But it'll be fine, I know.'

You're the smartest person in the whole Solar System after my dad, and maybe my brother. And Halley. It was perhaps the longest sentence she had ever signed, and she felt herself going redder and redder the longer it went on. *You don't need to be scared.*

Lucian was watching her very intently. Quite suddenly he leant forward and kissed her, earnestly, on the forehead.

'Your dad must be so proud of you,' he said. 'Now go on. Get outside. Find somewhere good.'

Minutes later, as she suited up in the airlock antechamber, Nou tested his words on the tip of her mind. Her dad . . . proud of her? One year without a father was a long time for a ten-year-old. Remembering him—remembering him with her—was like tapping on ice where once had stood a lake, and trying to summon up the feel of water. It was difficult to imagine it had ever existed at all.

Atop a methane dune, a little apart from the anonymous cluster of suits beyond the glow of the base's light, Nou folded her arms around her knees and craned her neck back to look at the sky. It wasn't black, as expected, but deep, velvet blue, melding to violet where sky became ice. White and red and blue pinpricks—more and more as she blinked herself awake and let her eyes adjust—freckled the surface of the universe like snowfall.

There was barely a sound across the communal channels now. Never had she seen so many people outside at once, little figures casting shadows in no particular direction, some holding hands, some with arms around shoulders, some linked. Stern on its hill at the foot of the al-Idrises was a lighthouse, waiting to guide them home.

Nou returned her gaze to the sky. Wide awake now, numb in fingers and feet. She sighted along her arm in that age-old ritual. Connect the starry dots, star by star. Search with cross-eyed concentration until you find it. Now that she was older she knew the ritual was unnecessary, the Sun clearly brighter than its neighbours, but still she followed it. She followed it like she would the trail on a treasure map, past the volcanoes and the quicksand and the pirates, to the spot marked with the x.

She took a breath. Her world was as still as the silence between heartbeats. Particles of nitrogen dust, so fine they hung in perfect suspension, caught the milky starlight like diamond chips. If she imagined hard enough, if she kept still enough, she could almost believe they stirred with her breath.

'We are T-minus five minutes to Asteroid Mortimaeus' atmospheric entry and the test run of solar mirror Plutoshine.'

Halley, over the public line, at her tersest and finest. Nou felt her heart jump to attention.

'Initiating nominal mirror operation. Stand by for momentum wheel repositioning.'

Inside the darkened mission operations centre, beneath the blue lights of scrolling code, Halley would be in the role the fearless professor had surely been born for. Nou had seen her while the band was playing: headset firmly affixed, hair a neat line down her back, eyes and voice sharp and clear. Nou knew Halley could translate code as fast as it came, and surely return commands as fast as thought.

'Momentum wheel undocking. Alignment looks good.'

Lucian would be at Halley's side, anxiously following the sequence with eyebrows low and breaths resolvedly calm, like Nou had seen him when executing the most important simulations of his own. Headset pushing his hair back, feet tap-tapping, maybe running his thumbs up and down the locket clasped between his hands—the one whose insides she longed more and more to see with each glint of its gold. Ready to dive in at a half-second's notice.

'Asteroid Mortimaeus is T-minus two minutes from atmospheric entry.'

Stan would be standing behind, probably with knees a little weak, knuckles a little white atop his mentor's chair. Head full of equations, full of songs, eyes torn from the screens to the sky, the sky where, just like Nou, he would see a dark patch of cleared stars, growing closer . . .

'Torque rods in position. Mirror membrane unfolding.'

165

Edmund would be behind them all, of course. Watching. Scanning. Following the code with intense concentration, back to the window, no distractions, no compromise to his duty.

'Membrane deployed. Moving into position.'

Her dad would have his eyes closed, heartbeat steady, and maybe he would be listening, listening . . .

'Initiating thruster burn. Minus twenty degrees to position.'

The Plutonians before her, waiting, waiting upon their Heart, in hushed anticipation.

'Asteroid entry and mirror alignment in T-minus fifteen seconds.'

Breath loud in Nou's helmet.

'Ten.'

Heart seizing.

'Five.'

All eyes on the sky.

'*One . . . !*'

A blinding flash. A *crack* that seemed to reverberate through suit electronics, a crack from *outside*. Cries rose across Pluto like the flight of a thousand wings. A white fireball hanging in the sky, sparking and spitting, a billion sparklers, igniting through the atmosphere as though down a trail of gunpowder. Gard Mortimaeus was ninety per cent ice and it was boiling, vaporising, water and methane and ammonia burning up in an incandescent streak that cut the sky clean in two.

And behind it, haloing it, lighting it from the inside out, was the Sun.

A cloth drawn back. A blindness lifted. A world on fire.

Like an old photograph restored, like watching the first ever sunrise, out of the greys and the blacks and the sepias of Pluto's icescapes erupted flaming scarlet, liquid gold, iridescent violet as Lucian's mirror ignited. The Heart was a kaleidoscope of dancing colours, deep blue sky meeting ruby-red mountains, and the light between was like the rising of dawn mist. Over ice and cloud the light rained, etching shadows where none had ever lain and rainbows where none had ever shone. Nou raised her hands and caught sunspots of green, purple, colour under bare stars as she had never known it could be. For the first time, Pluto had light. For the first time, her world was in colour. Nou spun and she spun and she spun, dancing with her shadow, hiccuping with laughter, feet stirring up a flurry of diamond dust lit from within, arms outstretched to the sky and its hanging chain of fire and the white disc the size of her thumbnail.

A hand on her shoulder: Lucian. Nou leapt up and threw her arms around him. She was 0.04 years old, almost eleven by Earth's calendar, and as the ice glittered and the sky shone and the mist rose, she was the happiest being on all of Pluto.

Phase 3

Chapter 10

Midnight. Both for humans on Earth-time and for Pluto on its own.

Stern Base was at its quietest. No pitter-patter of fingertips on screens in common room nooks. No feather-light footsteps whispering down low-lit corridors. After all the excitement of the last month, and all the bustle and action in its anticipation, the one hundred and seven inhabitants of humanity's loneliest outpost were presently as collectively calm and quiet as they would ever be.

All, that was, except one.

The room known as the Terramancers' Lair was bathed from floor to ceiling in light the colour of a forest fire. Too bright to look at, too bright to look anywhere. The light was fickle, flickering and flaring. A scalding backhand slap one moment, a velvet caress the next. The Sun in the centre of the raised dais was its source, and the silhouette at its feet was caught in the flames. A figure still dressed for daytime with scrunched shoulders. Unmoving. Unblinking.

Lucian stared into the heart of the Sun with red-raw eyes opened wide. His hands in his gauntlets were fists at his sides. The tracks down his cheeks shone as white as liquid metal.

Lucian knew he was not well. For week after week since the

switch-on he'd lied to himself; thrown himself into anything. Band practice. Frisbee. Helping out at the greenhouses, the kitchen. Simulating and re-simulating the mirror. Latching on to projects, not letting himself hold still. Not letting himself think. And still he saw it every time he closed his eyes. Phase Two, executed flawlessly. He saw the light in the sky. He saw the Plutonian night illuminated, as though just for one moment he really had brought this tiny world into the centre of their Solar System.

Silence, despite the hiss of electromagnetic waves, like wind through trees. Stillness, despite the seething mass before him, bubbling like boiling oil, pulsing in time with his own heart-beat. Sunspots catching fire with each hitch in his breath. Charged particles soaring along parabolas with each broken thought. The Sun in front of him seemed to move before he did; the puppet master now become puppet, jerking at the end of his own strings. The hideous thing was swollen to its maximum extent, distended between the triple pillars, a blistering, roiling ball that seemed to rush forward without ever growing. It was engorged, grotesque. Monstrous. Godlike.

Home.

Lucian stared and he stared, and as his skull throbbed for staring and his chest convulsed he saw the scene blur and move, and it was only when his forehead touched the floor that he knew he had fallen to his knees. His hands came up to cross against his chest and grip his shoulders. His lungs came togeth-er to breathe, only to crack and to tremble.

Teaching Nou; maybe that, all along, was why he had adopted her project so fiercely. The purpose of *helping*, like his mum did, and of having someone to help, like his sister, little damaged Fliss, all grown up now. A sense of place, of home. He was a selfish creature all along. He knew that now. And it hadn't even worked. He was still here. He was still on the floor.

Lucian the Sunbringer felt his Sun warm the crown of his head and his arms as he tried to hold the pieces of himself together. He pressed his forehead hard into the cool metal floor, harder, and there he sobbed like a child.

It wasn't just Lucian. In the months that followed the mirror's ten-minute flash-test, a sickness started to sweep through Pluto's newcomers as sure as spores carried on the wind. Some it barely grazed; others—others like Lucian—it brought to the ground.

The symptoms were the same. It began, simply, as a tug in the chest. A sort of nausea of the heart that, from this foothold, sent coldness to the tip of every limb. Appetite decreased, or increased; time asleep decreased, or increased. Either way, a hunger and a tiredness grew that no food or rest could sate. The coldness spread until movements became stiff and slow, and thoughts became trudges up spiral staircases. Emptiness took a form of its own and filled the hollows it carved. Breathing became a chore. Action became inaction. In its most advanced stages, the afflicted were almost incapable of coherent thought.

The Plutonians knew this sickness well. Many of the oldest villagers—those born in sunlight—had endured it. On Earth, it was called seasonal affective disorder. On Pluto, they called it solar deficiency disorder. They called it *sunsickness*.

Chapter 11

To Nou, the concept of debilitating homesickness in inverse proportion to stellar proximity seemed so foreign a concept as to be utterly mystifying. It was as though the Sunbringers had each left behind the same beloved friend, and only upon seeing his picture had they remembered all at once how much they missed him.

To Nou, those first days following the arrival of Gard Mortimaeus and the mirror test seemed normal. To her, still dancing in sunlight in her mind, they appeared a joy for all. Mo had completely disintegrated in a blazing success, skidding down the atmosphere in a shower of sparks that circumnavigated the globe. Each of those sparks, she fancied, was a seed, and from each seed bloomed blue sky that spread and coalesced with other seeds' pieces of sky, until the very air above was a forest's canopy of interlocking blueness. She could see it when she closed her eyes: the new constellations they made, new stars to join the dots between. You couldn't quite tell it was happening with your own eyes—so she signed in earnest each night when she ran outside to check, dragging Lucian or Stan or Mallory by the hand, turning in circles upon the ice—but she knew it was.

What Nou didn't know was that the volatilised methane and ammonia and water vapour released by Gard Mortimaeus—ten billion tonnes of it, the object 2.6 kilometres in length—had only increased the atmospheric weight by six per cent, and the global temperature by 5 °C. Impressive for Earth or Mars, perhaps, but not much for a world with only scant microbars of an atmosphere to begin with. Certainly not enough to produce tangible changes in sky colour; those would come later, with the arrival of Mortimaeus' superiors.

But Nou didn't know that.

What she did know was that Lucian was in trouble. She knew the magic that once seemed to light the workshop up like a storm of fireflies was back in its jar, on a high shelf, with a child-proof lock. She knew there was no more music: no indie bands over the speakers, no toe-tapping from their admirer in time to his guitar. Nor was there what the team called *banter*: the light teasing, the exchange of in-jokes like their own language, the to-ing and fro-ing of playful retorts. Stillness was settling inside the workshop like dust.

Nou found her friend that morning in the telescope room. It was a place she rarely ventured: a grand, glass-domed place dominated by its floor-to-ceiling telescope. Set around the room were other treasures: a hardware spare from the *New Horizons* mission; a frost-shattered radio transceiver from Pluto's first crewed, ill-fated *Beacon* mission; two framed postage stamps side by side, the first a hazy sketch of Pluto with the caption *Not Yet Explored*, the second of *New Horizons* itself, released to commemorate that first exploration. And at the foot of the telescope, a small, lonely figure beneath the stars, was Lucian.

He straightened up heavily from its eyepiece as she entered, looking so thoroughly woebegone sitting there all alone that she flew over at once and wrapped her arms around his neck.

'Hey, Spark,' he croaked from her shoulder.

Nou pulled away to free her hands. Concern drew her signs in anxious jerks.

175

Mallory said you're sick. Does it hurt? Are you going to be OK?

Lucian smiled at her, but it was a lacklustre one, an unLucian one, too weak to reach his eyes.

'I'm not sick, Nou, but that's very sweet of you to worry. I'm . . .' There was a dimple in his cheek, as though he was biting its inside. Something inside his eyes seemed to open up wide. 'I'm just . . . a bit sad. For home. I, uh, hadn't really realised just how far away home is. I'm feeling it badly right now.'

Nou had never seen Lucian down, ever, before this sun-sickness. Slumping when his paper was rejected from some scientific journal; sitting quietly, a little misty-eyed, watching and re-watching a family message on his glasspad; no matter— he would shrug himself together with a clap of his hands. She knew it was possible, adults being sad—she had seen the base's reaction after That Day, as she thought of it, the day her family had broken apart—but that was more like observing the storm in Edmund's livestream, something happening through a filter far, far away. Edmund's own grief had never been publicly visible: he had put up walls nested within walls, and painted them all in grey. Now, though, for the first time Nou was up close to the storm, inside it, within someone's walls. It might have scared her—if the storm wasn't her best friend.

So, not knowing what else to do, she did what she wished her loved ones would do for her when she was sad, and she hugged him again. Lucian was so warm as to be roasting in his tickling woolly jumper, his arms across her back two hot-water bottles, and he held her as tightly as she held him. Pulling away was harder this time; she even found her mouth opening as though to speak, rather than lose that contact to raise her hands.

Were you looking at the Sun? Glancing from him to the telescope.

The un-smile again. 'Ah, not quite. Take a look for yourself.'

He scooted over on the little bench to make room for her.

Nou leant forward and let her eyes adjust.

A white, featureless disc just about filling the view. The Sun, surely? Nou frowned in concentration. It had to be. Nothing else was so big and so close.

'You can't see my home from here.' Lucian's voice was nonchalant, but there was a faraway look in his eyes. 'It's too small. But it's there.' Nodding at the eyepiece, swallowing hard.

Nou looked up at him. Up close he was unshaven, and his pulled-back hair was disordered frizz. That little golden locket she always tried to catch glimpses of was exposed between an open button, catching the telescope's silvered shine.

Her eyes jumped back to his as he went on.

'On Mercury, in daytime the Sun fills the entire sky. Plus four hundred degrees at noon, minus two hundred at night. You can feel how baked the ground is when you're out walking. You feel it resist, then crumble to pieces as you go. You look up . . .' Breathing in, eyes raised as though he could really see it. 'You look up and it's like the entire universe is on fire. And you're right in the middle of it. You get to *touch it*. And you know . . .' Nodding now, nodding to himself. 'You know exactly where you belong. You know humans were made for this.'

No gauntlet simulation could have more effectively flooded that room than the Sunbringer's words. Nou sat transfixed, wide-eyed, staring at him. It was love in his eyes, and she recognised it at once: Lucian loved his Mercury just as she loved her Pluto.

'They used to worship the Sun on Earth, you know. Ancient people.' Lucian pressed his lips together, his expression somehow peaceful and troubled at once. Quieter, then: 'You start to really see where they were coming from. I came here . . . Well. I came here wanting to bring something like that to you. Some noble philanthropy, I suppose.' His shoulders sank. 'Seems stupid now.'

The vision from his words still hung, dreamlike, in the air. She hesitated in raising her hands in case it dispelled before them like smoke.

Will you show me some day?

Lucian looked down at her. 'With the gauntlets, you mean?'

Nou shook her head firmly.

Will you take me there?

He laughed. It was short—it was more of a surprised cough— but she knew it was a laugh because in its wake was something of that Lucian-smile again, and his eyes looked a bit like morning frost softening to dew.

Lucian smiled at her as he nodded, then shook his head, as though to himself.

'Yeah, OK then, sure. Why not?'

Nou got to her feet in one quick motion. She held out her hand. Lucian looked at her with eyebrows raised in surprise.

Come on, she signed, then gave the hand a wiggle.

'Why?' Lucian took it, but his voice was wary.

Nou tugged and tugged until, bewildered, he was on his feet.

Because I'm going to show you my Pluto the way you'll show me your Mercury, she told him, and in her words—she almost thought *in her voice*, but the two seemed the same now—was a determination she wasn't sure she had ever seen before.

I'm going to make you love my world just as much as you love yours. And we're going to go right now.

Every child, no matter whether they grow up among corrugated-iron shanties, pine forests rooted in pale sand, or icebergs the size of mountains, knows where their world's magic places are. They don't have to be beautiful—they don't have to be grand— but what they do have to be is secret. And a place known to many can still be a secret, much like keeping quiet on the day of your birthday: walking through a crowd with a knowing smile,

178

anonymous, with no one in on the secret that, just for today, you are special.

'Silvasaire is our next gard because he's sort of the deputy headmaster of it all.'

Lucian answered her question one fine, starlit day as the pair bobbed together atop one such special place: the crest of Wright Mons, a great ring-shaped mountain a good hour's flight to the south of the Heart.

'Silvasaire is this . . . this celestial accountant whose job is to run the whole gard operation. It's also been hinted he's the one who assigns which gard looks after which ward.'

Lucian was a patient teacher, if a distracted one who tended towards the over-explaining, and there was no topic he loved better to explain than the Hartdegen universe— which was why Nou asked. To kindle that spark back in his eyes. To make him sound more like his old self. Besides, the slumbering ice-volcano of Wright Mons made for a beautiful day out: rolling fields of black water-ice, frosted puddles of crimson tholins, all abutting a horizon not so much a line as a scrawl.

Do gards have only one ward? she asked as they bobbed, her gestures exaggerated to compensate for the bulkiness of her gloved hands. *Or can they have a few?*

'Huh,' Lucian said, without interest. It was hard to tell if his eyes were taking anything in from this angle. 'That is a good question.'

There must be a lot of gards, then, if there's so many people?

'Well, the balloon is . . . a whole lot of balloon, I suppose . . .'

Lucian seemed to be doing better lately: he still *looked* wan, and Nou knew he still felt it, but he was acting it less. He was finding it in him to try.

She needed it to not be an act.

Would they know to come and find us on Pluto? she signed

179

now; if left in long silences, she found he tended back towards the melancholy. *Do gards ever get lost?*

'I . . . I don't . . .' Lucian was trying to shrug and shake his head at the same time. 'Well, it's a magic balloon, isn't it? And I think Mo is very good at flying it.'

Nou kept trying. *Does your gard just appear when you're born? How do they know to come when you need them? What if they don't come?*

'Nou!' he cried, rounding on her, and that was something. 'It's all online. People have written literal theses about this stuff.'

But I'm on book three and there's no mention of Mo or Silvasaire—she signed Silvasaire 'silver-s-air', having never seen it written down—*or anyone.*

'That's because they got their own spin-off series, they come later.' Lucian was staring at her. 'I've created a monster. I tried to get you to talk, and now I can't get you to stop.'

But could we ask her? Nou pressed.

She was pushing her luck, she knew—pushing his buttons—but if she could just get that spark again, in amusement, in annoyance, she didn't care.

Lucian blew out a breath. With it, out went the embers she had been so furiously fanning.

'Well yeah, we could,' he said, as his eyes became inanimate objects, 'if she hadn't inconveniently died two hundred years ago.'

Nou bowed her head. She would have to keep trying.

Will you please tell me about Mercury? she asked one late morning.

They were walking at the foot of the active glaciers on the Heart's eastern edge, cracked, misty-white plains glowing underfoot, and the sky was at its bluest: the richest navy and *deep*, somehow, as though you might fall upwards to land with a splash, and set all the stars above rippling. It was still the same old sky she had grown up with: the mirror had functioned perfectly as planned, but for now it had to remain safely dormant. As Halley explained one evening seminar, under the present atmosphere the mirror's light would be a dangerously focused beam; there were still several months before the forthcoming gards could cause sufficient scattering for that light's safe and even distribution.

Nou went on, skipping to Lucian's side: *Is it like Stern? Do you have to wear sunglasses all the time? Are you always really hot?*

'Nou Harbour,' came the reply in her ear, two-dimensional through the earpiece, 'are you getting me to talk about my beloved homeworld, the one I am desperately, achingly yearning for, just when I'm trying to forget about it?'

Well, yes! Arms swinging, boots kicking up flecks of frost. *Because if you can only think about it and be sad, then you'll just be sad every time you think about it.*

Lucian brought his gloved hand up to the bubble of his helmet visor, as though to stroke his chin.

'Ok . . .'

So if you think about it now, when you're not so sad, you'll feel less sad about missing it.

Nou was breathless, as though she was speaking the words as fast as she signed them. And how fast she could sign now! Her hands were a blur as they struggled to keep pace with the symbols in her mind.

'Do you know, Nou,' said Lucian, and he too signed so fast now that her eyes watered to keep up, 'that sounds just about ridiculous enough to have a little truth in it. Have you been speaking to Mallory, by any chance? I heard she's been reading up on psychology on my behalf—'

Is Mallory your girlfriend?

181

'My—!' Lucian almost tripped over his feet. He rounded on her but she only blinked up at him, all innocence.

You're always together. Kip said he saw you holding hands.

That last one wasn't quite true, but Kip did say he had seen him breathing in the perfume on a long-fingered glove—and Nou was feeling uncharacteristically mischievous.

'We do not—!' Lucian seemed to recover himself. With measured dignity he strode ahead. 'Kip is . . . deranged . . .'

Nou found her hand coming up to her visor, as though to muffle the giggle she could almost hear.

Do you want to kiss her? Are you going to marry her?

'All right, you!' Whirling around, coming at her with arms outstretched. 'Do you know what I do to nosy little girls who know more than's good for them?'

No!

Nou laughed—the silent laugh, the breathless one—dodging out of the way, trying to run . . .

'I throw them straight down the nearest crevasse!'

And she squealed then, an actual, physical cry, her first, enough to jolt her eyes into circles, but still the laughter burst from her in gasps as he scooped her up and pinwheeled her round and around, sweeping away the world and pouring in that ocean-sky to fill every crater and every crevice with the hungriest blue.

Quite unprompted, later that day as they flew home in the Sadge, he told her. His hometown was a world bathed in warmth and orange through domes of photovoltaic glass, he said, crossing his feet on the dashboard as they soared through the haze. The glass was extremely clever, one of Clavius Harbour's earliest works: it tinted all by itself depending on the hour of the day, never letting in more than a fixed, sub-decimal-place percentage of the Sun's power. Bulsara the Third was its name, and it shone like kidney-ore hematite under the Sun as though it had grown, cactus-like, from the very ground.

Bulsara was a beautiful word, and even as Lucian spoke Nou began spelling it out to herself, silhouetting her hands under the flicker of the green and red and blue controls. Why 'the Third', though?

'It's all part of our history now,' Lucian said mildly, around a bite of jalapeño sourdough. 'We lost the first in a structural failure something like forty years ago. Then twenty years ago there was an explosion in one of the generators. Ruptured the main dome.'

Nou was suddenly acutely aware that Stern was still far ahead of them now as they crossed the ice sheet. She fought the urge to grab the pair of binoculars and find it, safe, waiting.

'I must have been your age or so,' Lucian went on easily. 'A lot of people died. Decent folk, you know? Good people. But we all came through for each other. They wanted us all rehomed—they wanted to write the whole planet off—but we fought to stay. We all wanted it to be worth something. Here . . .'

And to Nou's surprise and delight, he was reaching inside his suit's chest and recovering the little golden locket, catching the reds and the greens and the blues down its oval frame. He snapped it open with a click and Nou leant forward eagerly as two improbably tiny screens flickered to life in each half.

'My dad.' Lucian pointed to the laughing man in a video on one side. 'Carrington. He didn't make it.'

Carrington was a fine man, somehow both rugged and boyish together, and it was clear at once that Lucian had inherited his toothy smile. Some memory bobbed to the surface of her mind then, tales told when she was very small: of blinded astronomers in ancient history; of giant mirrors cracking and melting Mars; of fried pioneers on Mercury . . .

Nou bowed her head. *I'm sorry.*

'Ah, it wasn't for nothing.' Lucian pulled his lips taut in a smile, the kind you both know is just for show. He twisted the locket between his fingers so it turned green one moment, red the next. 'My mum took in a load of the kids who had nobody left, and that's how we found Joy and Fliss—these two sisters who turned out to be such a pain we couldn't get rid of them.' He grinned at her, then seemed to turn inwards and smile at himself. 'Fliss was pretty badly injured. She was lucky she didn't lose more than her hearing.' He let the locket fall against his chest as he signed alongside the words: 'And that's how I get to chat with you.'

Nou thought about this Mercurian girl, this stranger who through a coincidental chain of events was the reason she, Nou, was slowly becoming herself again.

She would just have to meet her one day.

What about the other side? She pointed to the side opposite Lucian's father, where pictures and videos of different faces seemed to change with each second. *Are they your family, too?*

Lucian brought the little oval between his fingers again.

'They're the people who died for science.' He idly flicked the screen and faces flashed past in sepia, colour, video, too fast to catch. 'You could say it's my morbid hobby—collecting the ones who do. Like Dad—he was one of the engineers who went into the dome instead of out. Trying to save it.' The stream paused on a woman's greyscale portrait, grim-faced but doe-eyed, somehow sad. 'Here's one of the most famous—she's Marie Curie. She was the first to discover radioactivity, and it got her in the end. It was no way to go. But perhaps there are worse ways to die than for science.' More flicking. 'And this guy. He's called Robert Landsburg.'

The man in this photograph was also greyscale but more modern: he was smiling, for one, the kind you'd pull for a camera but as though he was caught having a good time. The thought of this happy, balding man dying earlier than his time was suddenly deeply, unbearably sad.

Who was he? Nou tore her eyes away.

'Photographer, way back in the twentieth century,' Lucian said. 'He was buried under ash when a volcano called Mount St Helens blew up. From the looks of things he realised he couldn't outrun it, so he stood his ground and filmed right up till the last moment. Then he stowed the camera safe and lay on top of it. Most of his pictures survived.'

Nou peered into the smiling eyes of Robert Landsburg, the man who stood his ground as his world upended.

Would you do it? she signed as she did. *Would you give your life . . .?*

But when she glanced up Lucian wasn't looking, and she thought perhaps it better not to ask again.

'Are you telling me,' gasped Lucian, his heavy breaths a tide rolling in and out of her earpiece, 'that you do this by yourself, and you do this often?'

Yep! Nou signed in great sweeps from some ten metres above, the sign equivalent of shouting. She leapt from foot to foot as though there was wind in her hair, though she was a child who had never known the touch of a breeze; she leapt as though she was in a dream, the kind where you take a breath, let your heart catch, and up you go like a hot-air balloon to the sky. *It's fine, really! It's about jumping with the gravity. I can get to the top in a day if I start early enough.*

'In a—! Nou, Nou, slow down, kid, we don't have much topography on Mercury . . .'

Bent over, hands on knees, cheeks two beacons even through his helmet. It would be sunrise soon—for what that was worth.

'*Hiking,*' she heard him mutter under his breath, as though the word was some bodily affliction. Which, perhaps, was not far from the truth: while Nou's limbs sang with the climb, and her fingers and toes glowed with warmth, Lucian the sprinter, the pilferer of second desserts, was a little past glowing.

'How high is Krimigis again?'

They were nearing the crest of one of the al-Idrisi Montes: that great cluster of mountain-sized icebergs that had long ago ground their way across the Heart. Looking over from their vantage point, Nou could almost imagine they had been swept to shore by some long-dead wind, flotsam-like, and cemented there in that frozen sea.

It isn't too big, she signed. *It's about four kilometres above Stern. Can you see it, down below?*

'And you're telling me that you regularly hike four kilometres in elevation—in a day—*on your own?*'

Lucian was catching up to her now, close enough to see his gaze through the rictus of his grimace. There was something in his eyes that made her insides feel a little odd. That made her feel guilty.

Plutonians like hiking, she fumbled—like mumbling.

'But what about your brother?' Lucian persisted. Closer still, so his face was nearing hers up the slope. 'Doesn't he worry?'

Closer. Leveller. Earnest blue eyes. Nou's hands forgot what they were meant to do.

Cabin. Configuring the signs in her head. *There's a life cabin. I radio home from there. It's fine*, she added. *He doesn't* . . . Her hands hung in mid-air. Why did he have to look at her like that? So worriedly? *Come on.* Turning away. Her toes were getting cold. *We're almost there.*

Krimigis wasn't as big as its neighbour to the north, or as strenuous as the one next door, or filled with ribbonlike bands of every blue like some were, but what it did have was Stern sheltered at its base the way a child shelters between its parents' knees. It had the same view as her bedroom window, but better: it had the great Sputnik Planitia ice sheet clinging to the curve of the planet. It had the misty bluish haze below her, not above.

An anticipatory thrill ran through her from head to toe as she looked down and across it, same as every time.

'OK.' Lucian was gasping between gulps of air from behind her. 'I get it now. Why you come up here.' Hands on hips, one knee braced atop the frosted summit. 'This is really something.'

Nou's heart was beginning to pound.

It's even better during the descent, she told him. Her hands shook to do it.

'Oh, Earth, not yet, not yet.' Both Lucian's hands came up in protest. 'Let's just . . . Let's just go and find this cabin of yours and we'll have our nice flask of lentil soup, and you can show me where you stay, we can put our feet up . . .'

We'll have lunch on the ground. Nou could feel her pupils dilating; the world grew more colourful for it. *And I don't spend the night there.*

Her breaths were so loud she was sure he could hear them. Finally, he noticed her.

'What do you mean, you don't stay there?' He forgot to sign along to his words. 'You said it takes you a day just to reach the top.'

I did. Nou nodded, and at the sight of his still-uncomprehending face she could hold it no longer, and a smile broke across her own. *But it only takes two minutes to get down.*

Realisation dawning on his face was as brilliant to witness as the monochrome dawning of the Sun just behind him.

'Oh, no,' said Lucian. 'Oh, no. Nope. No, I'm not. I'm not—'

I do it all the time! Nou told him, and though she didn't realise it she was mouthing the words; imitating him in his soothing way of opening his eyes wide, pouring expressiveness into every sign. *The gravity's so low, and the air's only getting thicker.*

'But the Sadge—'

It's got auto-homing, hasn't it?

'Yes, but . . .' Lucian had his hands clamped on either side of his helmet. 'But . . . If gravity here's point six two . . . and—how high's this mountain?—call it four thousand metres—'

See you on the other side!

'No! Nou, wait—you'll hit the ground at . . . at . . . two hundred and fifty kilometres an hour!'

That's what the extra air tank is for!

'Retro-propulsion? Are you *kidding me*?'

But by then Nou was running, leaping, legs taking her faster than her body could keep up, unthinking, feeling only the chill of each step and the burst of each breath and her pulse at her temples, seeing flashes of blue-white at her feet, the line below her where blue-white became cream-crimson, the wall of adrenaline where solid ground became nothingness, where feather-light Nou came just for a moment to perfect, floating, feather-light stillness . . .

Sublime happiness. Euphoria. Her world came into crystal clarity.

Then up came her stomach, up came her heart, up came her arms, and she was falling. No air resistance to buffet her, no hungry jerking of gravity to tug her down. Nou heard Lucian swear in her ear—actually swear!—heard the hitch in his breath, heard him cry out in one long, protracted wail, like a ball of wool whose end was left knotted at the summit. Then he was laughing and laughing like she hadn't heard in months.

'This . . . is . . . *amaaaaaaziiiiiiiiing!*'

And Nou laughed, too, for the second time, a laugh she heard as much as felt in the warmth of her toes and in the burst of her breaths, a laugh that became a shriek of delight to harmonise with his own as the pair of them fell to her world.

*

The dream goes like this. Nou and Lucian are out walking on the ice, or in opposite armchairs, or he is sitting behind her father's desk—it varies. But every time they're just talking. They talk about things so ordinary its content dissipates like clouds of breath when she wakes, but that's it: just talk. They laugh a lot, too. They laugh as much as Lucian does in real life now, and in the dream it's the same sunny smiles she sees when awake. And it's only when Nou wakes up, not quite able to shake the feeling that something wasn't right, something was more than ordinary, that she realises by talking she was *talking*.

Riding pillion on a snowmobile over crashing waves of methane sand. Dozing under the warmth of a woolly jumper as the Sadge circled for landing. Signing together over her father's unconscious form; sometimes forgetting where she was as she did. Soldering the last of the peridot gems behind enormous blackglass goggles as Lucian's hands directed hers on the instrument.

Distractions. Wonders. Company. Lucian was an extrovert; extroverts feel drained the longer they stay on their own. For Nou—the introvert—the opposite was true, but that didn't stop there being exceptions. She and her best friend Allie before the accident, scattering baked pumpkin seeds then passing the binoculars back and forth, watching the robins and the nuthatches and the peacock as they feasted. She and Edmund back before the accident, opposite each other in his wing-backed armchairs beside the window to Earth, glasspads in laps, her legs tucked beneath her and his crossed before him.

Nou loved Lucian enough to love his company more than her own. She loved him—it was very simple.

She wanted the words to be the first she would say out loud. She wanted to tell him that parallel universes did exist, and that things could cross between them, because he was her gard. She wanted to tell him everything, she wanted to tell him . . .

'Can you guess what they are yet?'

Lucian, holding up the wire meshes they'd been working on for weeks. Several sparkled now as he turned them, their gem-stones winking at her. Nou's eyes lit up as the filigree lacework and the coloured stones and the linked cylinders all welded together in her head.

Gauntlets! Mouthing the word, clapping her hands with delight. *They're so beautiful.*

'Oh, but what they create will be the real beauties. Humanity's first night school for simulated terraforming begins ASAP.'

Will you teach me? Can I come?

'You'd better come'—with a nod at the pair still on the work-bench—'because you've been working on your own all day. Now . . .' He rose to his feet and shooed her away. 'Off with you, Spark, you're going to be late for kitchen duty.'

'Lucian?' Stan's tenor and Kip's baritone in unison, rounding the corner.

Stan called, 'This simulation's saying the Heart will completely melt within twenty minutes of mirror switch-on, which we're going out on a limb to say is a bit off.'

'A bloody big pond, that we do want, but this is a little much.' Kip. 'Bit of help, Lu?'

'Did you activate the dispersal of nitrogen ice-clouds?' About to stride off, placing his hands on Nou's shoulders, 'Catch you later, kid.'

Nou, already bounding off, thoughts alight with the worlds she would create, with sharing kitchen duty with cheery Percy, with the twinkling peridot crystals, waved goodbye as she danced off and called over her shoulder, 'Yep, catch you later!'

As she made it out through the door she noticed her throat felt odd. A little scratched. There was a strange taste in her mouth. A dryness.

190

Nou stopped where she stood. Her hand came, very slowly, to her lips.

She turned around but he was already there. Stan, Kip, Joules, too, but Nou didn't see them. She only saw the look on Lucian's face.

He took her into his arms and there, her face pressed into his chest, eleven-year-old Nou Harbour cried as though she would never find it in herself to stop.

Chapter 12

'It's remarkable,' the doctor was saying while Nou forced her gaze away, staring at blue-lit touchscreens, the roll of the light over Edmund's shoes, the zipping heart monitor. 'He's responding shockingly well to the treatment at a rate none of the previous tests have shown.'

Shadows crooked their long fingers in the peripheries of her vision. Red lights were watchers with unblinking eyes. Flickering eyelids. Tapping fingers. Signs of *life*. Her father's mind was alive.

Edmund had his hands clasped before him. His knuckles were white.

'This is . . . better than we had hoped for,' he said slowly. His face looked pallid in the anaemic light. It looked pallid full stop these days: there was a hollowness to his cheeks, and his eyes had taken on a perpetual sunken quality. 'I speak for everyone in the base when I say we cannot thank you enough for your continued perseverance. Especially as we approach the two-year anniversary.'

The anniversary. Nou knew this was the deadline, the one no one liked to talk about: no improvement after two years and all life support would be stopped. Or so the extended family back on Earth had agreed, her only blood relatives: not real Harbours but distant cousins, the Whittaker-Harbours. For some reason these strangers had more of a say than Clavius's own children: it seemed, when it came to someone as important as her dad, it took a whole committee to decide when he was allowed to die.

The doctor spoke as coolly and efficiently as Edmund: 'I will alert the family to these developments, see that the anniversary agreement is renegotiated. And you are still keen to employ the terraforming gauntlets to attempt communication?'

Nou had heard Lucian mention this new idea—give her father the gauntlets and the circlet—plug him into a computer instead of a dais with three pillars—see if his brain's activity could be translated to words. She had needed sign language to talk again; perhaps her father needed a machine's. If her father could hear them but not respond (and they weren't sure, but they thought so), then perhaps he could *think* his response and the words translate to a computer. He might be able to think his words into reality. They would connect Gen right up to him, too: the AI whose algorithms would dim the lights if blinks surpassed an individually tailored heaviness; who would remind you where you left your slippers if you turned on the spot, barefoot, first thing in the morning. Gen mapped humans better than orbital dynamicists mapped meteor storms; if anyone could detect patterns in a brain's electrochemistry, Gen could.

The whole thing was Mallory's idea, of all people. But then, Nou understood well how it could take an outsider's input for true insight.

'I am ready to enact that plan, yes,' Edmund responded levelly. 'The terraformers have agreed to custom-fit the equipment and have it operational within a few days. What, may I ask, is your medical opinion of the likely outcome?'

Flickering, flickering. Bloodless fingertips twitching against sheets. A dragon in its lair, hoarding syringes and drips and antiseptic gloves. Nou, imperceptibly, shrank closer to her brother's side. Her dad had looked scary the moment she had first seen him like this—the moment she had first made him like this. But now there was the chance for his other version to return. The one that wasn't still, or sick, or silent.

What would she say to her father if he could reply?

Her father, talking again. *There* again.

Do you love me now? she would ask him.

Nou's empty hand twitched by her side. Edmund's own was within reach. She sneaked a glance; only a palm's width of space to cross . . .

Stay asleep. That's what she would say to him. *Stay asleep, Dad, so I don't ever need to find out.*

'Good.' Edmund's voice snapped her to her senses, and in came her nails to gouge four crescents into her palm. 'Thank you again, Doctor. Please keep me updated with any developments.'

The cue to leave. The doctor knew it, too, and left with a nod, but as Nou turned to scurry after her Edmund held up a hand.

She almost walked right in to it. For a moment she could only stare at that upturned palm—wishing she had—before slowly, heavily raising her eyes to his.

It was a kind of despair she felt every time she did. *I'm not good enough*, her eyes told his; and every time his own would silently reply *I know*.

Edmund joined his hands behind his back as he addressed her.

'I heard you . . . ah . . .' He pressed his lips together and looked resolutely to one side. 'I heard you are . . . *talking* . . . again.'

It looked almost as difficult for him to speak as it was for her. A strange concept: to share an emotion with this stranger. Nou kept her breaths shallow and slow, staring fixedly at the fine stitching at the end of his trousers.

But she managed a nod back. *Communication.* Even that was more than they had had in months.

Edmund did not immediately respond. When Nou risked a glance up, his eyes were upon the button at her wrist—long ago had she stopped thinking of it as a panic button—taking in the little golden stars and silver leaves she had painted, intertwined, around its face.

'I hope I don't need to remind you,' Edmund continued carefully, deliberately, and Nou hurriedly cast her eyes to the floor as his own narrowed back on her, 'that there are some matters about which you *cannot* speak. About which you must never speak. Do you know which matters I am referring to?'

His every word was distinct, slow, as though she was somebody slow.

Nou nodded again. She did know. And she did not need to be reminded.

Edmund stared hard at her. Then, with a curt nod he turned, and he left. And though the blinking red sensors and the sickly sheen of her father's skin turned every shadow into a coiled menace, for some time Nou could only stand where he had left her, eyes fixed on the painted button at her wrist.

Nou signed, *There's something I want to show you.*

'What was that?' Lucian, the crooked hitch of a grin on his face, arms swinging by his sides as he bobbed along. 'I didn't quite hear that. You'll have to speak up.'

Heat rushed to Nou's cheeks.

I will, I promise. Just not right now.

'Ah, you can keep saying that,' said Lucian cheerfully. 'I'm starting to think I imagined the whole thing.'

Lucian was almost always cheerful these days. He had responded well to the prescribed treatment: working set hours in the greenhouses; taking communal saunas under special sorts of lights; taking on the classes that sprung up in boxing, baking, cocktail making; his own in gauntlet wielding. Throwing himself with renewed vigour into Plutoshine. Shouldering new responsibility, honing fresh focus, finding meaning again. And it worked. Most of the others afflicted were similar: time, friends, encouragement, and the base's slow slide into summertime were for many all the subtle nudge needed to regain their equilibrium.

The pair of them were following the foot of the cliff edge that embayed the Heart, keeping in the wan starlight just to pretend it felt a little warmer. Lucian kept deliberately ahead, refusing to turn around, meaning she had to catch up every time she wanted to sign. And he moved fast: sure-footed upon the ice, still a little clumsy, but now only within standard deviation—as he would say—of average. He looked in his element. He looked like a native.

He wasn't going to make silence easy any more.

Nou stared at the back of his fluorescent orange helmet, already ahead of her again. Swallowing her pride, she pushed on ahead.

If I can show you this one last place, then I'll talk.

Bobbing along beside him, almost running to keep up.

'You mean you haven't shown me all of Pluto yet?' Lucian gasped, his grin teasing. 'I feel cheated.'

He no longer signed with his words and the loss was a bittersweet one, their secret language no longer needed, like a hand holding hers high above her, teaching her to walk on the wobbling soles of her boots. Her palms stung in the coldness of that absence.

Onwards they sprang, for the most part in a silence uncharacteristic of the two. Lucian held his own like a ransom: waiting for her to make the first move, to admit it, to prove everyone wrong who ever said she wouldn't. Nou was less holding hers than being held by it. The right word would come to her head, only for her to say its antonym. She would think *Kip* and say *Joules*; she would say *yes* and mean *no*. Or the word would be there in her head, but . . . *just* . . . wouldn't come out. It was there: she could see it in her mind, spell it, taste the coarseness or the silkiness of its syllables, but there it stayed. And the harder she pulled, the harder it gripped.

It was stage fright, of a sort: the stares of Stan and Joules and Kip, then of Percy—who learnt it through Stan—then of Parkin—who learnt it through Percy—then of Mallory and Halley and Vasily and the chef and the gardener, who learnt of it from Parkin, from Allie, from Lucian . . .

Does everyone know?

Her signs were doing that thing where they felt *sticky*, somehow; each stuck to the one before it as though glazed in setting glue; as though the words were sorted in unlabelled drawers and she was rifling through them for the next. It used to happen when austere Halley would try to sign at her . . . or when Lucian would ask her to—*quick!*—read out those numbers, he needed them right now . . . or Edmund would look at her and she would forget left from right . . .

Edmund. He was why she was here, right now, with Lucian. Edmund, who had told her never to tell. Though Nou could not articulate why, and though she had known she would show Lucian before her first words even left her mouth, somehow Edmund's warning was the catalyst for today.

Edmund had told her not to *tell*. But to show?

That he had not specified.

'I think the whole base knows, Spark,' Lucian told her, but gently. He slowed his pace to more of an amble. 'Pluto's a small town for big news.'

I'm not big news, she fumbled back. *I don't want people to look at me.*

197

'They'll forget it soon enough. Silvasaire's only a month away. And they all mean well.' He had a very easy, unequivocal way of saying things that left no room for doubt. 'They're all just happy for you, Nou.'

I only did it once. All her fears seemed to rush into the light at that moment, laid raw with names clearly legible. *What if I can't do it again?*

Lucian fixed her with that long, level look of his.

'Do you feel you could do it again?'

More honesty. Candid and non-judgemental and steadfast. Not coddling her like another adult might do; no blind reassurance. Lucian never lied.

So she showed him the same regard.

Calling the word to mind. The same sticky *stuckness*—the words were *there*, just shying away, just lagging behind, not aligning right—don't think about it too hard—here is the word, just say it—just say it, just say it, just say it . . .

'Yes.'

She made herself jump as much as he did. Then, simultaneously, both broke into enormous smiles.

He thumped a hand on her shoulder. Nou looked first to his helmet clasp, the edge of his balaclava, the lone mole on his left cheek, before meeting his eyes.

'You,' Lucian said, with precision, 'are a star. And that's all I'm going to say about it. But you'd better not forget you are one. OK?'

Nou nodded and nodded. *OK*, she thought. Maybe she could say it if she tried. Don't focus too hard, that's the word, just let it happen . . .

'OK.' A whisper.

A roar of triumph between her ears. Twice in one minute. She blushed so fiercely the roots of her hair tingled.

They bobbed on, lighter now, Nou's heart still hammering, her eyes still alight with his words going around her head. *You are a star . . . You'd better not forget you are one . . .*

But it wasn't long before her heart beat to a different tune. They'd walked for an hour now. Not much further. Already her feet were arcing a loop of their own accord, the long way round, keeping their distance from the one place she never let herself think about . . .

'So has Edmund said anything to you?'

Nou's footing slipped down the lee of a dune.

I haven't really seen him. Too distracted to think of speaking—especially about this. Edmund never came up in their conversations. *He gets up before me and comes home after bedtime. I think he's been in the lab.*

There was the wall now, she saw with a stumble of her breath.

'You know, I've been here for—How long is it? A year?—and I still couldn't tell you what your brother actually *does*. He's a biologist, I get that, some kind of xenobiology, but what exactly does he *do* all day?'

Starless sky up ahead, out of which would soon emerge crags, strata, notches . . . Like the creases of a face she couldn't decide if she never wanted to see again, or missed so dearly she couldn't bear to think of.

'Mallory's work I get, that's microscopes and ice samples and stuff. But I can never understand a word of our great leader's research.'

It took a moment for Nou to realise she was meant to reply.

He's a genetic engineer, she signed uncertainly; she had no idea how to spell either word. Talking about Edmund was like rubbing sandpaper down her skin in this place; even his name was a form of his presence.

'He doesn't look like you, you know.'

Another stumble. There were still footprints in the methane sand, she saw as she looked down. Many of them. Running back the way they had come.

I think, she tried but it was hard: the footprints were deep, and still fresh out here where nothing changed fast, the sand below sprayed around each like impact ejecta blankets. *I think we have different mothers. He's twenty years older than me.*

It was something she'd never really thought about. Her mother had left on the first ship she could after Nou was born, so her father told her. She'd had a very pretty name, a name Nou cherished like a ruby tucked in a velvet-lined box—Maiv—which meant she must have been a very pretty lady. Her father said she couldn't stand motherhood—yes, those were his words, and when she was little, Nou had always imagined this beautiful, faceless woman being unable to stand under the weight of something. The weight of her.

'There's a life cabin not far from here.' Lucian was looking at a map on his wrist-pad and did not see her freeze where she stood. 'Yeah, not two kilometres west. We could stop if you fancied? I brought flapjack—'

No.

Nou cleaved the air with her sign as she tensed all over. She tried to speak it out loud but found herself too seized up to so much as open her mouth.

Lucian turned to look at her. There was confusion in his face, a question.

No, she signed again. Her suit gloves just about masked the shake of her hands. *Please.*

She had given herself away now, surely. Lucian would want answers—he would want a series of words she would be incapable of even signing. But perhaps something about her gave him pause, because he did not press the moment, and Nou turned so he would not see her relief.

200

They kept close together now. The wall was clear for both to see, rising, now at eye level, now towering above, now climbing ever higher, pushing up the stars like a hand sweeping back dust. Abruptly it occurred to her: this day, what she was about to do, had been her hope and her plan for months. A year. Back when she had decided to tell; back when the Sunbringers had been one homogenous group of strangers—and it had to be a stranger, it had to be someone post-*That Day*. Back when she hadn't known which she would choose.

'Is this the place?' Lucian's voice was hushed.

Details were emerging in the cliff. Nou knew them like knowing freckles, creases in the corners of eyes, the tiny nicks of scars. Gnarled knots like the burls of trees, bulging out towards them.

Pandemonium Promontorium. They came to a halt. Nou hesitated for half a beat—a learned habit she still had to break past—then took Lucian's hand in hers.

'Do . . . ?' she began. She steadied herself. (*Don't think about it too hard.*) 'Do . . . you . . . you . . . trust me?'

Lucian looked down at her. Candid, non-judgemental, steady.

Ready, Nou hoped.

He gave her a single, sincere nod.

Nou nodded back once. Then she pulled him by the hand, bent her head, and together they disappeared into the wall.

The blackness inside was total. Outside of helmet-light aureoles was nothingness so wide it could have been the absence of existence itself.

Nou had tight hold of his hand. She led the way before him, agile and sure-footed. For Lucian, the tunnel was at times so narrow and so twisting his arm had to twist, too, into painful contortions not to lose her. The ice was bitterly cold when he touched it, like grazing a boiling pan.

He wasn't afraid. He should have been, by all accounts. He should have been filled with a creeping, sickening dread.

But when Nou had asked if he trusted her, he hadn't hesitated. Lucian had grown up with children his whole life: he'd been dad, brother, and son after the second Bulsara disaster, when his mum took in the kids left with no one. Someday he knew— he hoped—he'd have his own family. He'd like that. Someday he'd marry and give a home to a couple of kids from Earth: the ones who didn't have houses, let alone homes. He'd be a good dad. He'd be like his own dad.

In the meantime, if Nou asked to show him the very centre of Pluto itself, he would hold her small hand inside his own and tell her to lead the way.

Down the pair went. Their crevasse-crack narrowed further, scraping ice against arms, torso, the crown of helmet. Flashes of whiteness before the torch, flashes of blackness, each as blinding. Nou's hand in his, seeming to know exactly where it was going.

Then, quite suddenly, the walls were gone. Lucian blinked. Not gone—just further than an arm's stretch away. Nou dropped his hand. He raised his eyes and saw a little cavity, maybe the volume of the seminar room where he'd not that morning laid out gauntlets for his class. The walls were smooth like calved glaciers, the light a bluish-green that ticked his heat-pumps harder just for looking.

Nou was standing on the cavity's far side, looking back to him with hands by her sides. Beside her was a patch of darkness their helmet lights could not penetrate.

A hole. Lucian bobbed closer and peered down. His lights caught more bluish-green ice, then more, until he could lean no further. It showed no sign of ending.

Nou was kneeling at the edge.

Not much further, she signed.

He could hear her breath in his earpiece, deep, level. Her pupils in his torchlight were two black buttons. Nimbly, with knees then elbows on the sides, she lowered herself in.

Lucian brought his arms up and simulated dropping something from above his head; sign language for *falling*. He raised his brows as he mouthed the word, making it a question: *falling?* Somehow in this place he couldn't bring himself to break the silence, either.

Nou nodded and lifted a hand. *Not far*, she told him.

Lucian drew in a breath. Falling off the edge of the al-Idrises hadn't been so bad; what else was trust for?

Slowly, aware of every part of his body, he lowered himself in after her. Elbows upon the sides, as though at the edge of a swimming pool.

Nou hung by her fingertips over the abyss. She couldn't sign, but her eyes and the incline of her head spoke clearly enough:

Follow me.

Falling, falling like feathers. Falling feet first. Arms wrapped tight away from the sides. Legs together, feet braced for the unknown—for the touch of a surface at any moment. They fell side by side, the crevasse plunging straight down, the walls all around that same bluish-green glow, lightening as they sank deeper. Lightening to . . . Lucian looked closer . . .

White. White as Halley's sawtoothed block. As an ice cube. He wheeled his helmet's torchlight round. This deepest part was cut through water-ice, the very bedrock of Pluto.

Not far below, where the planet's heat and crushing pressure grew stronger, this ice would be liquid. Not far below was a buried, planet-wide ocean.

Abruptly his world had dimensions again: Nou, a little way below, stopped first before his own feet met ground. But the tunnel did not end there. Their fracture cut horizontally now, too low to stand. Nou led the way, ducking her head as Lucian crawled along on his knees.

A second fracture overhead, barely wide enough to fit him. Now they climbed upwards, the ice coarse enough to grip, the fracture slanted enough to brace a foot on its opposite side and climb. Neither spoke. Lucian kept his thoughts on a tight leash. Where to grip . . . Where to place his foot . . . Where Nou's own were above him. Think of nothing else. There was madness down in this labyrinth. A twinge of fear could spark headless panic. He knew this objectively, but all he felt was that same calmness. The cloudless quiet of faith.

All at once it was over. Lucian's hands gripped a flat surface— bluish-green—nitrogen-ice again; they must be straddling the very base of the Heart. He hoisted himself over it and sat with his feet hanging over the edge, letting his heaving pulse catch up and his eyes fall shut. He could never remember shutting his eyes in dreams, which seemed a key indicator that this was real.

Nou was already on her feet when Lucian found his. They stood there staring at one another, their faces . . . Well. Lucian couldn't imagine how his looked. Nou's eyes were wide and clear, and in her expression was something older than herself. A neutral certainty. Like hands spread bare with the truth held between them, offered up.

'This,' she whispered, quiet as breath, 'is it.'

Lucian lifted his eyes. Wherever they were, however deep below ground, the cavern walls were too distant for their feeble lights to touch. There was an industrial-grade lamp in his utility belt, but as he reached for it Nou held out a hand to stop him. Holding his eyes, she raised the control pad on her wrist and, one by one, shut down each light on her suit.

And Lucian, unquestioningly, as though acquiescing to some sacred custom, followed her lead.

Blackness. Blindness. No hands before his face, nor feet on

the floor. Sight was a dream slipping between his fingers. Breath in his ears. His own and Nou's beside him, each as deep and as steady. Both kept very still.

A flicker of colour up ahead. Higher than head height. A sparkler of scarlet. Lucian heard Nou's breath hitch, or it might have been his own.

There was another, to the side. Like a shot of electricity, dendritic tendrils shooting out in a half-second's brilliance before vanishing. And another. Closer. Bright enough to leave an after-image.

Then Nou moved her feet, and Lucian knew this because the glow was beneath her. A moment later it was beneath him, too.

They were beneath him. A network like the filigree threads between cells, between cities. Red light, pulsing now in rings at their feet. Constructive feedback where his and Nou's over-lapped. And Lucian realised all at once that the lights were not the *They* themselves. The lights were only made by them. The *They* were everywhere all at once. Beneath the ice and within it, saturating it, blood vessels through tissue, tiny capillaries fine as gossamer.

And now, as the glow spread across the ice, then up distant walls to climb, and keep climbing, Lucian's senses of space and time came trickling back. A great chamber as vast as a cathedral; a ring of openings like their own entrance around the walls; openings encircling a grove . . .

Lucian felt his throat choke up as the sight became inescapably clear.

A grove of pillars stood as still as sentinels in a circle about the chamber. Each was at least his height in width, the tallest surely twenty, thirty metres high, grazing the high-vaulted ceiling, six of them spaced evenly apart. As the light faded from crimson to soft white, he saw each bore subtly different colours that melded into the floor like roots: moonlight-silver, ice-blue, chrysoprase-green, steel-grey, faintest teal, the indigo of the horizon on a clear Plutonian day.

How did it feel the moment you discovered the Europans? His own voice inside his head, a world away, a lifetime ago.

They weren't ice. They weren't metallic but they were smooth, seamless.

Can you guess how people imagine it felt? Mallory's mellifluous voice. All that time ago on his first morning.

But they weren't pillars.

Euphoria, he'd said. *Vertigo . . . Awe . . .*

They weren't trees.

Lucian, eyes burning, mind on a pendulum . . .

It was euphoria. Mallory, smiling with all the sphinx's secrets. That one word in his head. *Euphoria.*

They were Plutonian.

Lucian gasped in a breath and he tasted it then, vertigo distorting gravity, upending it.

Euphoria. One clear word among the tumult. *It is euphoria after all.*

As he thought it there came through his earpiece one long, high, musical whistle. Not quite human. Not quite birdlike. Like wind through ice, through leaves, through keyholes.

One-two-three, sang the whistles. *One-two-three.*

Hello, Lucian thought back.

He looked to his side: there was Nou, watching him the entire time, and she was smiling. Her eyes were bright and clear.

He brought his lips together, miming the shape made to whistle back. She nodded and nodded.

Lucian smiled back at her as widely as he knew how, brought his lips together in a tight *o*, and whistled right back to them.

Chapter 13

You can't tell anyone.

Nou, signing fervently back out on the surface, blinking in the starlight.

You've got to promise. You've got to.

Lucian's head was stuck on that moment. The whole day he would play over and over, etching pathways in his head ever deeper that he would slip into, every detail traced and retraced. But more than the sight of the pillars, or the firework filaments of the lights, he kept coming back to Nou.

He'd asked her why—why could anyone possibly want to keep such a discovery secret?—but she had only shaken her head.

Please, Nou had signed, and that was all the reason he was going to get. *Please, please don't tell. Not yet.*

The real question he should be asking was, if those life forms were Nou's secret, and he had been let in, then why was he still left with so many questions?

He didn't *think* she could have found it recently. He saw too much of her. He'd have noticed, surely, if she'd come to the workshop one day, breathless, zoned out, picking things up, putting them down again, tripping over things. Or maybe that was just him. And—OK—he'd cried a bit, too. He was a damn softie at the best of times and held no shame about it. But that first night after Nou's revelation he'd slipped into his quarters, past Halley, past Stan, and he'd shut his bedroom door and stylistically explored the definition of caterwauling.

He could just ask her. He should just ask her. Except, every time he had the chance, something held him back.

And it was that above anything that made him start surreptitiously watching the only other person she might have told: Edmund Harbour.

The gauntlet classes were growing so popular Lucian was thinking of splitting the group up and running separate sessions. He was working flat out, putting together more gauntlets in between simulating Silvasaire's upcoming arrival next month. Which at least kept him from obsessing over this new conspiracy of his. And keeping an eye on twenty gauntlet-wielding amateurs felt a little like watching twenty frying pans at once.

'No, no, *gently*, just slowly, OK?' he said coaxingly to Halley, who was attempting to levitate a simulated boulder, movements stiff with leopard-like dignity, the force of her concentration severe to behold. 'Small movements. Like you're windsurfing.'

'That's it, yeah!' Smiling encouragingly up at Yolanda Moreno, rolling her boulder through the hoop of a mousetrap obstacle course as though her life depended upon it. 'Now just relax your arms a little, relax them—No—*relax* . . .'

'Small movements . . .' To Vasily, whose tight-set mouth had disappeared into his beard.

'I don't know why I'm pretending to be any kind of expert on this thing,' Lucian sighed to Captain Whiskers when he had a minute, hoisting the humongous mass into his arms, 'when everyone here knows you're the real mastermind.'

Captain Whiskers stretched back his great neck at Lucian's scratching and offered nothing remotely helpful in return.

'Yes, you are the mastermind,' Lucian crooned, as ten tiny needles sank into his chest, 'even if you do refuse to use the ingenious anti-depressurisation cat flap I designed especially for you, and just sit inside my bubble-pod and yowl like death is imminent.'

'Well, at least you herded the cat—if no one else,' said a warm, female voice a head's turn away.

And there was Mallory and her fusion-powered smile, leaning back on the countertop. Lucian's thoughts scrambled for something witty or charming to say and came up just scrambled.

He nodded as casually as he could to the scene of general entropy before them.

'Seems to be going OK. Most've got their head round holding an object now, so we've progressed on to moving things this week. Some are better than others—Percy's well ahead of the curve, thanks to Stan, and your Yolanda's got a real flair for this.'

'You're very creative.' Mallory was still watching him with that smile. 'I love the obstacle course. It's a three-dimensional board game of sorts, yes?'

'That was the idea.'

The Captain had given up expressing his distaste at being held via gouging, and was now holding up a paw every time Lucian tried to pet him. *No*, the paw said. *Oh no you don't.* Lucian planted a kiss on top of his head.

'You must explain it to me better,' said Mallory. 'It operates as a type of virtual reality, I gather.'

'Eh.' Lucian wiggled his neck in lieu of his better-occupied hands. 'Sort of. It's like VR without the goggles. It's VR but inside the real world, instead of being in its own. I'd get out my portable triangulators and show you up close, but they've gone wandering, I'm afraid.'

He nodded at the raised dais with its three pillars, which had never known more company or activity in its life. Surrounding it on all sides were clustered the dozen or so couples, each sharing a pair of gauntlets: Parkin and his wife; Percy and Stan; Halley and Nou, of all people; Edmund and Vasily. Others, too: colleagues, friends, familiar faces—chatting, laughing, concentrating. In a base in recovery from sunsickness, where many present might still secretly be hurting, or might unknowingly be helping, the sight of so many people in such spirits was its own kind of sunlight. And among it all, between their outstretched hands, was the magic of their own creation.

'Watch Stan now, watch.' Lucian pointed with one of the Captain's paws.

His student was teaching Percy, and it was like watching the demo for a textbook he hadn't written yet. Percy was a rosy-cheeked lad of perhaps twenty—a little younger than Stan and a little rounder—with an easy laugh from his grandad Parkin and a kind of wild, ceaseless happiness that was all his own. He'd been known to leave Lucian incapacitated with hysterics on multiple occasions, and he was the best possible friend and influence for demure, studious Stan.

Presently Stan had his hands right up beside Percy's gauntlet-meshed ones, and Percy was miming his steady, careful movements, raising and turning and manoeuvring his simulated boulder with eye-watering concentration. They moved so closely that, if Lucian didn't know better, he couldn't have said who was leading whom.

'The kid's a natural,' he told Mallory in awe, as much as himself. 'One day it'll be me working for him. Look how he moves all his fingers in together. Man. It's like he's closing a rose. I didn't teach him that.'

But then Vasily was poking his head round to look, too, curling his own gauntlet-clad fingers the same way, and they were talking, and Edmund was joining in—had he and Stan ever spoken before? They must have, they'd been here more than a year now, but nonetheless the sudden protective surge took Lucian by surprise. He didn't want the man who would turn Nou white by walking into the room anywhere near his other apprentice.

'What's Harbour's story anyway?' he said, with a little more savagery than intended. At Mallory's questioning glance, he elaborated: 'I mean'—lightening his expression, nonchalantly folding his arms as the Captain jumped free—'you've been here longer than me. Has he always been so . . .' *Cold, nasty, aggravating.* '. . . serious?'

'Edmund?' Mallory followed his gaze, to where Stan was now adjusting Vasily's position while Edmund nodded along with brows furrowed, arms also folded. 'He's such a darling, isn't he?'

Lucian blinked. 'Oh, well, he's—'

'He was as knowledgeable as any of us on the expedition.' She was referring to that life hunt to the far side, months ago now. 'A genetic engineer, you know, but just a marvel in our mobile laboratory. His work on bacterial resequencing has no parallel. I dare say he was the most tireless of us at all hours— his *stamina* . . .'

Stan glanced over and threw a grin—then, eyebrows plummeting, signed *Everything all right?* Lucian shook the scowl off his face with a start.

'His science is truly pioneering.' Mallory was still, regrettably, talking. 'Just last week he was first author on a paper in *Terraforming Advances* . . .'

Lucian had seen it, and really wished he hadn't. The journal published nothing less than the furthest-reaching research in his field, and—in his impartial opinion—was overzealous in its rejections.

He unground his teeth to say, 'Busy guy, eh.'

'He's the best of us. He was so strong after his father's . . . Well.' Mallory delicately tucked a stray fringe into her fishtail plait. 'We were all very shaken up, afterwards. I had only been here a year at the time, but we've all noticed such a change in him.'

'So what happened that day?' Lucian pressed suddenly. 'I know we talked about this ages and ages ago, but, I mean, what *exactly* happened?'

He'd tried asking a few times: the lab lads; his friends around the base, like Vasily and the chef and the gardener; Mallory herself, once or twice. People gave him the same answer every time: they didn't really know, but here's what the rumours said. And the rumours differed each time. It hadn't taken him long to realise that discussing—or rather, not discussing—what had happened *that day*, as people tended to refer to it, was a matter of etiquette, discretion. People shied away from it. If people did know, they also knew not to talk about it.

Somehow to actually ask Nou herself, and all those other people on her behalf, felt invasive. Dredging up old shipwrecks from settled silt. But tonight, Lucian wasn't going to take *I'm not entirely sure* for an answer. Right now there was mutiny strumming his heart a pulse faster. Perhaps it was the cocktail-party hum of laughter and raised voices tricking him into living the courage of a cold beer; perhaps it was the touch of cold he could feel in his eyes, a veneer of something hard that was unwilling to compromise—something he knew Mallory could see, too. Either way, as Lucian leant forward, and as Mallory caught his eye in something like warning, then looked about her and leant forward too, he felt he had finally passed some sort of test. He was about to be let in on the shared secret.

'It was the morning after the Tombaugh's Day before you got here,' Mallory murmured, slipping closer. 'I saw them all at breakfast. Clavius, Edmund, Nou. They went out for a walk. They were gone maybe . . . maybe two hours. No one knows where they went. And I do mean that,' she added in answer to Lucian's arching eyebrows. 'Clavius and I were . . . close.' A shadow settled over her eyes. 'I asked Gen, but he—she, *it*, I never know—won't answer to me. Edmund won't answer to anyone. And everyone knows Nou answers only to you.'

There was a moment's quiet while Lucian considered this new information. In spite of himself, his pulse was jumping at his wrists.

'And what happened when they came back? Or . . . or did they make it back?'

'It was Nou who called the mayday.'

'Nou?' Lucian's eyes jumped across the room to her in horror: a tiny, furious force of concentration, lips pressed together, a pursed spring with all that potential energy going nowhere.

Loosen up, loosen up, he thought, and the instinct to rush over and correct her taut grip and tell her to bend her knees a little might have got the better of him, had Halley not taken her hand and done just that.

He shook his head and bit back a curse.

'It's easy to make this into a story in my head, you know? Forget there were real people involved.'

'I was in the Parks clearing up with a few others.' Mallory went on as though he had not spoken. 'We saw someone running past, *sprinting*—how often do you see someone running like that? We called and he stopped long enough to say . . .'

She took a breath. Lucian realised he was leaning forward, so close he could see a clearing of palest blue in the overcast skies of her eyes.

'He told us, "The Harbours are in trouble,"' Mallory said. 'Just that.'

A tickling sensation on his forearms; the fine hairs there were standing on end.

'We all dropped everything and ran with him. Parkin was calling for order in the plaza. He was wonderful. No time wasted—you, you, and you take the Virgo, you and you prepare the medical unit, such forth. The most important thing he did was keep the rest of us occupied.'

Lucian listened around the thumping of his heart, keeping his eyes on her, not quite able to defocus from the two Harbours on the periphery of his vision.

'They found them out on the plains,' Mallory continued. 'I wasn't there, but I heard Clavius was already unconscious. It was a ruptured airpipe—'

'What, like on his suit?'

'I would presume so.'

'How? How did it rupture?'

'Well . . .' Mallory had to think. 'General poor maintenance, I believe. Edmund said they were running and it seemed to snap. I read the report very thoroughly, there were of course so many questions—'

'And Nou? What did Nou say?'

'She . . .' Mallory threw up her hands. 'Well, she stopped talking, didn't she? Edmund refused to discuss that day after the official inquiry, and no one heard Nou's side before she went quiet.'

'Why did she stop talking?' Lucian had lost all pretence of casual interest now. He was standing up straight and he was staring at her, hard. 'You said she was the one to radio in. So it wasn't the trauma of seeing the accident that did it.'

Mallory had been gazing somewhere away from him—Nou and Edmund's direction—but now she turned her head very slowly to meet his eyes. Within her own was all the calm of revelation.

'I hadn't thought of that,' she said softly.

Lucian stared at her.

'The accident was one of the biggest things to happen on this rock for the last two years, and no one—*no one*—thought to stop and reconstruct exactly what happened to traumatise Clavius's kid into a kid-shaped shell?'

Mallory didn't have an answer. Lucian nodded to himself.

'So something happened after,' he said grimly. 'Something that made her stop talking.'

Nou was handing her gauntlets over to Halley now, and she was smiling—she held herself with pride—and Halley had her eyebrows raised at her as though in question.

'Coffee?'

Mallory must have opened her little flask; Lucian could smell it, that familiar earthy bitterness. He blinked out of his reverie, pulled a polite smile—pulled them both out of their trance— and reached for her proffered cup.

'Hang on,' he murmured.

A lingering sweetness in the aroma of the coffee, just on the edge of each inhale. Like honey, or cantaloupe.

Right before answering Halley, just for the half-moment it took to raise one's eyes and bring them back again, Lucian saw Nou's flash to her brother. In a half-moment the act was only imagination; her eyes were back again. But now Lucian was remembering.

'Mallory, didn't you say . . . ?' His hands came up, as though to grasp that first conversation so long ago. 'When we met that first morning after I arrived, when I had *g*-lag . . .'

Nou, Edmund, the cantaloupe-and-coffee scent of that first conversation: they were fusing together inside his head in a rain of crimson sparks. Lucian blinked, dazed by his own memory.

'. . . Didn't you say you reckoned Nou had already found life?'

215

'Yes, I did,' Mallory began, surprised. 'I'm not one for eaves-dropping, but I overheard her at breakfast—'

Lucian snapped his fingers.

'Yes . . . Yes, Nou was saying she'd found life . . . and she was going to show it to her dad and brother . . .'

And that would mean . . . Lucian felt his world do a little flip.

'Wouldn't that mean Edmund Harbour has known all along where to find life?'

And wouldn't that mean, Lucian didn't say, *that he, too, would have seen the whistling pillars under the ice?*

'I know.' Mallory raised her eyes with a self-deprecating sigh, and Lucian stared. 'So much for that hypothesis. I asked him all about that while we were away together.'

Lucian fought to control himself. Lightly, lightly. Casual conversation.

'I must have misheard, I'm afraid,' Mallory went on. 'It was the first Edmund knew of it when I asked.' She lifted her shoulders in an elegant shrug. 'Alexandra is forever admonishing me for conduiting unverified whispers. So that scuppers my little theory.'

Lucian looked back to Nou: now she was saying something to Halley. Just look at that: actually speaking. It was painful to watch. Nou still spoke as though each word was a line she was fighting to recall before everyone's parents at the school play. Her hands at her sides looked closed taut with the effort, her eyes resolutely on the Stern Base logo at Halley's top pocket. But still she spoke. In the several months since she'd begun to, the act was no less startling each time.

But that half-moment glance was enough. There was only one person left to talk to now, and that person was Nou.

He went to the music room that night. The Minus Kelvins still met up weekly to jam, but sometimes a terraformer just needed to plug in to some bass and get off the path: improvise without caring what he sounded like; jam with Mark Alexander and his boys. It was strange: before the sunsickness he'd have baulked at the thought of hanging out on his own, but these days that was exactly what it felt like. As though he was checking up on himself; as though he was flopping down and saying 'So, how's it going, mate?'

It was getting late, and Lucian knew from experience that most folk would be reading in the common room by this time, or tucking their kids up, or in their rooms generally winding down. Nonetheless, for a base of one hundred he was disappointed but unsurprised as he approached the door to hear the muffled crests and falls of a piano—and one very nicely engaged.

He crept closer.

The door was closed, as was protocol, but pressing his ear against it coursed the melody through as though he stood right beside its source.

Melody was too soft a word. This close, the piano was a storm. Every key seemed to have its turn, the thunderous lows shadowing a high, sweet, summer downpour of a tune. The music was a dancer leaping between raindrops, bursts of sunlight piercing tumbling, sweeping cumuli far above. Higher the highs lofted and lower the lows plunged, until from horizon to horizon Lucian's head crackled with energy, caught in the pure joy of the sound.

The player stumbled once, just catching a slightly off note. The music halted. Then came a few slow notes—tentative, testing—before repeating the passage, and again. There was something endearing about the error: the humility in its careful correction; the punctilious repetition. Still a learner, imperfect but trying, maybe practising for one of the upper grades. Then the pianist was off again, the storm resumed, and the skies took flight once more.

217

Lucian had never heard anything like it on Stern. Percy could belt a few toe-tappers on the thing, and he'd heard it rumoured Yolanda Moreno was a demon on some kind of instrument—though the memory called to mind a cornet, or some other esoteric brass thing like a serpent. And he'd heard Mallory attempt to regain her youth's training once or twice to a dexterity somewhat diminished compared to this.

With two fingers on the control pad, Lucian silently, inchingly slid the door open.

The man had his back to the door, both hands a frenzy over the ivories before him. He had sleek hair, and wore a stiff shirt rolled up to expose bare forearms, and as he played his shoulder blades shifted to sculpt a figure lean and agile.

As quietly as he could, Lucian slipped the door shut and left the pianist to his practice. It was, he thought, just one more thing he hadn't known or guessed about Edmund Harbour.

Chapter 14

There was something odd going on with Silvasaire.

Feet apart. Bottle-green jumper pricking sweat at his clavicles. Concentration contracting his eyebrows together. Toes right pressed against the edge of the raised dais. Lucian squinted at the jetpack-propelled rock between his three pillars and reran the simulation with a twirl of his finger.

Really, though, he was only half-concentrating. It was a bit silly, he knew, to be distracted by thoughts of sabotage when running an anti-sabotage simulation. And on the day of their second gard's arrival, too. But once he'd opened his mind's window to the *why*—why go about destroying good things? *Cool* things, life quality-improving things—a whole horde of potential *why*s had swarmed in, moth-like. And just when he thought he'd shooed the last out, another would start flittering overhead.

There it was again in his simulation. A wobble. Just as it started to get close. A wobble that grew until Silvasaire was knocked off course, either into space, or into Pluto. He rewound the sequence. Played it again.

There were people against terraforming, sure, and Lucian had listened to their arguments. Native life kept popping out of the ground in unexpected places, with surely more jump-scares to come. Terraforming also went wrong sometimes, and quite horribly so when it did. And did we have the right to mould a world to our will? What if in ten years, fifty years—like the old anthropologists, picking up fallen henges, blundering all chance of true reconstruction—we realised we had made irreparable errors?

Or—and Clavius Harbour himself even used to point this one out before switching sides—what if we were wasting our energy, our potential, renovating worlds never meant for us? What if we were too preoccupied with recreating parent Earth underfoot to remember the waiting stars overhead?

Lucian's attention nosedived back to Pluto: the Silvasaire simulation had flown perfectly this time. Flawless atmospheric entry. Flawless disintegration. Its firefly embers braided luminous rings around the worldlet, once, twice, three times, white-gold lighting his raised palms as though before fire. Then . . . gone, faded. Another successful annihilation.

He ran it again.

So a person, or persons, could have their reasons for sabotage. Got it. And what was sabotage for? Sabotage in itself delayed or stopped a scheme you weren't happy about. Very simple. But— and now Lucian was burrowing head first after his thoughts, wriggling to keep their whirling sparks in sight—something else it did, which a saboteur would just love, was highlight how dangerous the whole business was to begin with. And after the mirrors of Mars, and what he could only describe as a growing *unsureness* from the general public, terraforming couldn't afford another failure.

Lucian blinked, momentarily blinded by his mental light bulb. He'd said as much to Nou once—how had he phrased it? *Honestly? I reckon another major accident could see terraforming off for good.* But thoughts were like things: they weighed more under heavier gravity.

220

This wasn't just Plutoshine at stake. If Plutoshine failed, this could spell the end of the very art of terraforming itself.

'Lucian.'

The gard-asteroid jumped as Lucian did, crashing just due west of Stern.

'Halley.' The gauntlets fell to his side. 'I was away with the stars then, sorry. What's . . .?'

He stopped: something was missing in the master terraformer's eyes. Something he couldn't place.

'Uh, Halley? Is everything . . .?'

Halley stared past him to the looped simulation. Like Mortimaeus, like Styx, Silvasaire was bloody crimson in colour and so peppered with craters as to appear sponge-like. It wobbled now like a top—if that top was hurtling towards them at the speed of a comet—but again disintegrated as planned.

'What's wrong with it?' Halley asked quietly. 'Our gard looks like it's about to keel over.'

Lucian looked from her, to the crater, then back again before deciding to drop it.

'Ah, it's not so bad.' He spun back to the simulation and rewound it with a gesture. 'This shimmy's started up, but there's still a tonne of ways I haven't tried yet to set it straight. I'll keep working on it a bit longer, it's probably the gauntlet settings—I think someone's been tinkering with them again.'

'Do,' Halley agreed, 'but . . . don't miss the celebrations.'

Lucian stared at her.

'You've got to make time,' she said, with a tight nod, 'to be proud.'

'Halley.' Lucian took a step towards her. 'Is everything, uh, everything OK? You don't seem—'

'It's what I would tell myself.' Halley was backing away now, still with her strangely flat eyes, eyes that reacted a half-second too slow to the world around them. 'We'll talk after Silvasaire, all right?'

'Halley, is something—?'

'Not wrong, no. Not wrong. But it can wait. It will wait.'

Just as Mortimaeus' arrival coincided not by coincidence with the anniversary for Clyde Tombaugh first sighting a world beyond Neptune, so Silvasaire, too, was meticulously timed for another occasion. *New Horizons'* Passage was not a whole day like Tombaugh's: much like clock-watching on New Year's Eve, the Passage was an event. At almost ten minutes to midday precisely by Greenwich Mean Time, on 14 July 2015, the *New Horizons* spacecraft had made its closest approach. The point of light named Pluto had been its destination for nine years as it crossed interplanetary space—and twenty-six years since its first conception on the back of a napkin in a restaurant, on the back of a pale blue dot at the end of Pluto's strongest telescopes.

The Passage was a day of quiet reflection. From a point of light in 1930, to an unimaginable winter's microcosm in 2015, and now to a home.

It was presently 10.49 a.m.; one hour exactly to the Passage, both historically for *New Horizons*, and what would become historically for Silvasaire.

A shame the thing hadn't flown past in the p.m.; that way a drink or two might have been acceptable. And the closer it got, the more Lucian could have done with one.

'Lucian? Lucian, hey.'

'Ngh.' Lucian waved a hand. A glance up at the curving metal of the telescope revealed the intruder's identity. 'Unless that's a beer you're holding, Stan, I'm busy.'

'It is, actually,' said the young not-quite-doctor, beaming with a cheerful ease that was all Percy's influence, 'but it's mine.

222

I'm forcibly removing you from your station, and you've got to get your own yourself.'

'Mutiny and morning alcohol,' Lucian murmured, already returning to his eyepiece. 'Sounds like the name of a Dignity song.'

'It is, isn't it? That one that goes, *oh, oh, smells like integrity* . . .'

'Voice of an angel, Stan, what I've been saying all along. Look . . .' Lucian spun to face the interruption, 'I know Mortimaeus was no trouble, and I know we've run our simulations a million million times, but I just want to watch it come in. Just in case. That way if there's any problem—'

'Halley will catch it in the control room.' Stan shrugged his folded arms, a feat of dexterity with the beer. 'Then Joules will fix it with his code. We're a flawless team. Best in the Solar System.'

Lucian raked his fingers through his hair, which subsequently decided the laws of gravity were optional.

'You take a look.' He pushed back the bench and hopped to his feet. 'If there's nothing weird in ten minutes, the thing'll be too close to move, anyway.'

Stan eagerly took his place.

'Can you see any colour? Can you make out any detail?'

'Just after Styx, you know?' Lucian took a pace, throwing up his hands in agitation.

'Ooh, I've got it now, I see it.'

'Mo was all clear, but with Styx . . . Man, I don't think I even told you, but I had this hunch, you know, and after Mo was fine I tried to forget it but—'

'Lucian?'

Something in Stan's voice stopped Lucian with one foot in the air.

'It's not . . . It's not supposed to be sort of . . . *tumbling*, is it?'

223

Lucian dived on the eyepiece as Stan dodged to the side. It took him a precious second to see straight, get the centre right—then there could be no mistaking it.

Lucian leapt to his feet and was running before he could register the direction.

'Stan, go find Halley and Joules, get them on to the code!' he yelled over his shoulder. 'I'll get the gauntlets, we might be able to realign it faster!'

Bashing hard into a corner; scattering a gaggle of startled acquaintances; Lucian couldn't even feel his legs, no straining, no aching. The base the size of a university department had stretched into a whole campus. He skidded into the workshop, crashing into a singed armchair in lieu of brakes, and lunged at the drawer where he kept his gauntlets.

The tray was empty. Lucian stared as though it was a magic eye illusion, and at any second a three-dimensional latticework would jump out at him.

The training gauntlets: he had a cabinet full of twenty pairs. At once he was movement again.

Another illusion. Another empty drawer. And the one below it, and the one below that.

'Lucian! Lucian!'

The clatter of footsteps behind him. The voice that followed them, breathless, was Stan's.

'Halley's working on the code but I couldn't find Joules,' he gasped. 'You said the gauntlets would be faster, though. We can dual-wield, just tell me what to do—'

'Stan.' Lucian took him by both shoulders. 'Do you remember a week or so ago, I asked if you'd seen my remote triangulators?'

'Well, yes, but . . . but why do you need them? We've got the big one—'

'All the gauntlets are gone.' Lucian strode past him and broke off running again, Stan hot on his heels. 'If someone's taken them, and if they've got the triangulators, that means they can control Silvasaire from anywhere and we can't.'

'But . . . Wait, you mean *stolen*? But *who*?' Stan was aghast. '*Why*?'

'The same person who did for Styx,' Lucian told him as they reached the darkened control room, all blue-lit screens of code and bustling activity; it looked as though word had got out. 'I knew I'd left them right where I left them,' he hissed, more to himself. 'Someone had stuck googly eyes on them, I remember the light catching them as I closed the drawer . . .'

'Lucian!' Halley was marching over, face like a winter storm. Lucian had only ever known her in two modes of operation: silent, absorbed, obsessed; or spitting acid. One lived in interesting times to see the latter. 'Gauntlets on, *now*. We've got fifty minutes till this thing makes landfall. Joules is here but there's some corruption in the code.'

'Halley, the gauntlets are gone.' Lucian wasted no time. 'Someone's taken them, and my remote triangulators—someone who knows how to use them.'

'The saboteur.' Halley's eyes were two chips of her ocean ice. How Lucian wished he could feel more anger like her, and less fear like him.

'If someone's controlling Silvasaire remotely they'll need somewhere they won't be disturbed,' Stan said, voice a squeak but level. 'An office, maybe? A meeting room? Can anyone think where they'd go?'

'Let's be systematic.' Parkin strode in, astonishingly speedy for the base's oldest resident. 'The music and seminar rooms aren't likely—too communal.'

'And offices are too small for the proper set-up, if they're anything like mine,' Lucian said in thought, 'though maybe the bigger ones—'

'This is ridiculous,' Halley burst out, 'they could be any-where! By the time we search the base—'

'The life cabins!' called a new voice: Joules through the glass of his screen, fingertips a blur on the touchscreen desk. Lucian hadn't even noticed him. 'You know, those huts they space on the plains, in case you're stranded? You'd be well out of the way.'

'Out of the way, yeah.' Lucian was thinking fast. 'Good chance you'd not be disturbed.'

'They're certainly sufficiently sizeable,' added Parkin.

'No one's going to notice one more person slipping out when everyone's on the plains,' Stan said in a single breath.

'All right.' Halley held up her hands for silence. 'We've got forty-five minutes. Lucian, Stan, fly out to the two nearest cabins, get someone to join you if there's more candidates. I'll get Harbour in here and have the base checked out, too.'

'Do we . . . do we need to evacuate?' Stan's voice contracted in fear. 'Do we know where Silvasaire might hit, if it does?'

'Still sputtering around, too mental to tell,' called Joules. His eyes never left his screen, and his hands were working furi-ously. 'One in ten chance, maybe. It's looking like the northern lats, more like Voyager Terra. We should be OK.'

'You tell me if that changes,' Halley said severely. Then, to Lucian and Stan, 'You two, go!'

They ran. Lucian called Gen up as they did: prepare his Sadge, one for Stan too; get up a map of the nearest life cabins. Manning the Sadge in blue jeans and pointed boots felt tanta-mount to nakedness after the bulk of his accustomed suit, but there was no time to change. He'd just have to hope he wouldn't need that protection.

'Stan, this is Lucian,' he called to the other ship as the pair took off. Even the touchscreen buttons felt foreign beneath his gloveless fingers. 'You take the ten-kilometre one on the Heart, I'll go for the forty by Cousteau Rupes.'

'Forty kilometres?' Stan's one-dimensional voice over the radio. Lucian punched off the autopilot as he reached minimum altitude. 'Bit far for someone on foot, don't you think? And Gen says none of the craft are missing.'

'My triangulators disappeared at least a week ago. That gives him plenty of time to amble back and forth with a pillar under each arm.'

What was that beeping? Oh! Seatbelt. Lucian clicked it in, then pressed his joystick flat; there was a mechanical roar, a brief tunnelling of his vision as the *g*-force tried to weld him to his seat, then he and his ship became a shooting star.

'If I was him,' he panted around gritted teeth, the acceleration only climbing hotter, 'or her, I'd choose the further one. Less obvious. More time before they catch you.'

If I was who?

Lucian had never read mystery thrillers. He was more of a rom-com kind of guy, where the highest stakes were heartbreak. Someone who understood the gauntlets . . . He'd bet his arm it wasn't a terramancer: Kip and Joules were his brothers, and Stan was too pure, still running on passion and ideals. There were others, the twenty in his classes, but they needed more skill, not to mention motive—and Plutoshine had been voted in unanimously by the Plutonians. Motive, gauntlet skills, knowledge of the project . . .

'What if it's a bluff?'

The acceleration was easing; Lucian had crossed thirty kilometres in under three minutes.

'*crrrk* . . . Lucian? I'm docking now. What if it's a bluff and they didn't go for the further one?'

There below him: a little toy hut all alone on the ice, a fleck of black upon criss-cross crevasses of white.

Anyone could be inside. Or nobody.

'Stay on the line,' Lucian told him. 'Go inside now, and if they're there I'll come to you.'

Motive, gauntlet skills, Plutoshine knowledge. Parkin was going blind, he was a hazard to himself in lessons. Halley had dedicated her career to Plutoshine, she had no motive . . . Harbour . . .

'Lucian? Lucian!'

Lucian snapped to attention. 'I'm here, Stan, I'm right here, what's happening?'

Harbour was at the lessons. Harbour knew all there was to know about Plutoshine.

'You were right,' said Stan. 'There's no one here. I'm coming to you, OK? Please, please wait for me, I'll come as fast as I can.'

Harbour had the huge office overlooking the Heart. And Harbour hadn't been in the control room.

'Stan, look, it's OK,' Lucian began as he levelled the Sadge against one of two docking stations.

Up close the cabin was bigger than he'd realised, and with enough windows for anyone inside to see his arrival. That was, if there was anyone inside at all. That was, if the saboteur wasn't back in his office in Stern.

'*Earth*,' he muttered. What if he'd been lured out here, out of the action? 'I'm going in, Stan, all right? I'm opening a line on my wrist-pad, I'll keep you in the loop.'

He hadn't even grabbed a jumper before take-off; with only the thin Sadge airlock between him and death, Lucian couldn't help but think the indigo horizon had never looked so bone-breakingly cold.

The airlock beyond hissed. He hadn't thought to bring in any kind of weapon—but what was he going to do? He'd never started a fight in his life (who had?). And if there was no one there . . . The airlock was at seventy per cent . . . Harbour had the skills and the knowledge, but did he have motive? Airlock at eighty per cent . . .

'I'm five minutes away, Lucian, can you see anyone?'

Harbour was Clavius's kid. He'd be sabotaging his inheritance . . . Ninety per cent.

'Just . . . Just be ready to turn around at my word, Stan, OK?'

'*Turn around?*'

And still . . . Still Lucian could never shake that gut feeling about the guy, that hunch, like Styx . . . One hundred.

'I'm going in. I'm going in, OK? I'm . . .'

The airlock door began to slide open. He'd have a quick glance, then dive back on the ship. Lucian took one step forward—and his face met a fist.

Knuckles crunched into cheekbone with blinding force, erupting pain down every nerve in his skull. The power of it was unbelievable—like being hit by a comet. A half-second later came new pain: a sickening crack to the head, then shoulders, as he slammed into the airlock wall and crumpled with limbs askew to the floor.

Weight across his torso—a knee, jammed in hard—then hands, gauntleted hands, seized him by the jumper. Lucian caught a glimpse through his uninjured eye of his attacker, of the saboteur, before Yolanda Moreno pulled back her fist to strike again.

The force of her attack was incredible. Up close, the woman was narrow-boned but pure muscle, sculpted and sinewed, at least a foot taller than him. Lucian thrust his neck to the side and the blow just missed, smashing the floor instead; thunder howled inside his clipped ear. One of his arms was unpinned as Moreno shook her bleeding hand within the gauntlet and Lucian lunged, seizing her by the shoulder and tumbling them both into the cabin.

It had been so long since Lucian had thrown a punch that he made that fatal error and tucked his thumb inside his fist; he almost keeled over as he felt it snap. Moreno's cry was muffled

229

as the hit took her square on the mouth, knocking the circlet from her head to spin across the room. Lucian caught a flash of bared teeth before a knee jabbed him in the kidneys, two hands whipped around his own, and then wrapped themselves around his throat.

The attack hurled Lucian on his back hard enough to slam the wind from him. Moreno was straddling him, long legs snaked over each of Lucian's own, locking him in place, while her hands . . .

Oh shit, Lucian had the flash of coherency to think, *she's actually going to kill me.*

Moreno's gauntlet wires ground into his flesh. Her eyes were wider than Lucian knew was possible, a ring of white around each wild centre. Looking into them was like staring into an empty vortex.

Lucian tried to raise his arms but they were cold, savaged by pins and needles, and only flopped uselessly. His whole world was turning the same crimson of his killer's torn mouth. Something hot was running down the back of his throat.

Moreno leant forward, so close their noses touched, then pressed, then flattened enough to hurt. Her bloodied teeth were gritted in what could surely only be hatred, and now those teeth were parting . . .

'*Fuck you, terraformer,*' she hissed.

Lucian tried to kick his legs but they were locked tight. A black ring was tunnelling his vision from the outside in.

'This isn't your planet,' spat the saboteur, and hot blood sprayed across Lucian's cheeks. 'None of them are. You have *no—fucking—right.*'

Someone dived on Moreno from behind, hard enough to slam her flat on Lucian before ripping her off, tearing that murderous grip away, and air flooded his lungs with a lusty, grating, drawn-out gasp that sounded barely human and exploded a stellar nursery of stars across his eyes.

Behind him came groaning, banging. There was a crash, as of steel meeting steel, and someone howled like an animal.

On trembling arms Lucian twisted on to his front: there up ahead were his triangulators, extendable pillars spread equidistantly in a bunk-bed-lined dormitory—and between them, spinning in mid-air like a tumbleweed, was the crimson behemoth of Silvasaire. At its feet was another tumbling mass: that of two figures entwined.

Lucian struck out a hand and almost fainted as he hit his snapped thumb. It was maybe a second, maybe a minute or more, before he came to and felt what the hand had met, something cool to the touch: *the circlet.* He rammed it on and shoved himself upright through a vision that lurched.

Stan was scuffling between the long limbs of Moreno, both hands wrapped around a gauntlet, shoulders and elbows and feet jabbing her torso as he tried to tug it free. Lucian hurtled into the fray, grabbing Moreno by one wrist with his good hand as Stan wrestled with the other, forcing open fingers, all three of them flicking floating crimson droplets from brow, mouth, knuckle as they fought. Stan wrenched one gauntlet free with a roar from Moreno, but it was the wrong one—the ruined one, the one that had crumpled—and now she curled the remaining one into her chest, under her body weight, and with strength Lucian would never have guessed her muscles were locked solid.

Lucian got one wrist. Stan got the other. Moreno bared her teeth and held tight, veins protruding down forehead and forearms, then struck out, gauntleted hand scrabbling and flailing, scraping down Stan's cheek, Lucian's neck, a blur of mesh and crystal . . .

Stan lunged faster and truer than Lucian had thought possible. With both hands he ripped the gauntlet loose, and Lucian saw blooms of red as the hand within was near-skinned. Stan propelled himself back with a kick, right below the projection of Silvasaire that spun like a spinning top upon a spinning plate, and tugged the mesh up to his forearms.

'Stan!'

Lucian tore off his circlet and frisbeed the thing in a sweet, clear arc. Stan snatched it from the air, swung it on his head, and stretched out his gauntleted fingers. His chest rose and fell, in and out. He closed his eyes and all his features relaxed.

Silvasaire obliged.

Chapter 15

The cure stung decidedly worse than the blow; Lucian hissed through clenched teeth as the iodine bit through his split temple. The cloth was saturated, and amber-coloured liquid was slowly dribbling through his fingers and up his sleeves. Wriggling the jumper back one-handedly revealed the greenish ring of a bruise, complete with . . . he leant closer . . . *teeth marks*. From actual teeth. Sunk into his arm. Lucian had no recollection of the bite, but the sight seemed perfectly reasonable after the morning's adventure. What was a little nibble to being clobbered off his feet and half-strangled to death, anyway?

'. . . hardly designed with the intention of housing a criminal, Professor, never mind an infiltrated anti-terraforming radical . . .'

Lucian pushed himself to his feet with a grimace as Harbour, Halley, and Parkin rounded the corner, walking fast and talking faster.

'The officers from Titan won't be here for another six months,' Harbour was saying, 'and we have no precedent for an investigation or trial, not even the means. Such a situation was never anticipated for a scientific base. Drunks, violent altercations, a crime of passion at most—but this is into the realms of the pathological.'

'How's Stan? He still in the medical bay?' Lucian fell into a hobbling step with them. 'You've questioned him? How's he looking?'

'*Earth*, Lucian, didn't they give you stitches?' Halley frowned at him. 'Stan's fine. He's a resilient kid.'

'He's a hero.' Parkin thumped a hand on Lucian's shoulder. 'You make sure you tell him, same as we did.'

'His story checks out, same as yours,' Halley added. 'Now we've just one more version to hear.'

Yolanda Moreno, saboteur and terrorist extraordinaire, was detained within the music room. Drum kit, grand piano, guitar stands: all had been swept away to leave a windowless box—a box with a glass divider, one that created a separate room accessible only by an outside door. Who would have thought a recording studio would make such an effective interrogation room?

Moreno was pacing beneath incongruously jazzy mood lighting when her questioners entered. The studio on the other side of the glass wall quickly became crowded, with Vasily the base manager already in one corner with arms folded, heavy brows fixed on the saboteur.

Who immediately strode forward and slapped both palms on the glass. Lucian instinctively stepped back, but he was the only one who did.

'Do you know what we call you?'

Moreno's stare seared each of them in turn. Nobody had cleaned her up, or perhaps nobody could get near: crusts like old wine stains stretched around a black eye, and it was a wonder she could speak at all around that lip. Lucian stared at the battered face and wondered if he ought to feel guilt or satisfaction. Neither were forthcoming.

Not waiting for an answer, Moreno went on.

'*Terrorformers*. That's what we call you. Because you shape terror and tyranny out of worlds that were never yours to touch.'

'Nice line,' Halley deadpanned. 'Though no points for originality, and next time work on the overacting. So who's "we"?'

'You imagined it was just me?' Teeth were exposed in a smile that reached no further than those split lips. 'Did you really think, arrogant even as you are, that the whole Solar System was falling at your feet in gratitude? That there might not be some of us who treasure the wilderness, who have dedicated our lives to protecting it?'

'Ah. Wilderness first, people second, the usual rhetoric. Let me guess—humans were the virus all along.'

'Your people have taken more than your share of a Solar System probably teeming with life,' Moreno hurled back. 'Earth is still limping through ruin and already you locusts are infesting the next world, and the next—'

'We're not having this debate.' Harbour held up a hand and—incredibly—she fell silent.

Only when she had did Lucian realise how his muscles had been pulling tighter with her every syllable.

Harbour folded his arms. His eyes were two perfect discs, so lifeless as to appear entirely inanimate, and under the magentas and cyans and shadows of the spotlights, the resemblance to something metallic was so uncanny as to raise a chill.

Those flat eyes had hold of Moreno.

'Who employed you?'

The saboteur pushed herself back from the glass. For the first time, there was something uncertain in the demeanour of her position in the little room's centre: something tense in the slight bend of the knees, the hunch of her shoulders.

'We employed us,' she said.

'Yolanda.' Parkin's voice was soft—the carrot to Halley and Harbour's sticks, perhaps. 'Your operation required funds,

235

inside information, planning, possibly from Plutoshine's start. No organisation like that is an island.'

'And wouldn't you just love to know?'

'If you tell us who you're working with—if there's someone here in Stern . . .'

'I'm not sure there is,' Lucian murmured, making himself start a little; he had not meant to speak out loud. Five faces rounded upon him. He met their enquiring eyes and took a breath. 'Well, it's like . . . Styx had sabotage written all over it, and I'll go out on a limb here and say Silvasaire, too. But why not Mortimaeus?'

There was a moment's beat.

'Because she was away for Mortimaeus,' Halley said softly.

'Right, exactly. She and Mallory were stuck out on the plains until the very last minute.' Lucian drew himself up and turned to Moreno. A strange feeling: speaking civilly to a person whose teeth imprints were going black on your skin. 'So, uh, hi again. You got here a year before me and the terraformers, and then you had plenty of time to set up Styx. Right?'

Moreno only stared in sullen silence. Probably wishing she'd bitten harder. Lucian went on.

'But it looks like you needed us to know how to hack the gards. And you weren't back in time to get it done.'

'So if there were accomplices'—Halley was putting it together—'they would have set up Mortimaeus in her absence. It's a possibility.'

'That may be.' Harbour was frowning. 'However, someone must have got you access to Stern. Bypassed security checks, released confidential documents. *Someone* was on your side.'

Lucian kept his expression neutral. Even with the culprit caged and his own knuckles bruised, it was not easy to forget the feel of seizing conviction: so sure he'd be flying back to Stern at full speed; so sure of what he'd find in Harbour's office.

So sure had he been that he could see it all in his mind like a memory, like a film. He couldn't brush it clear. It was like trying to incriminate someone based on a dream.

And, said that voice from the film, overlaid across memories that didn't exist, *Harbour, too, was away for Mortimaeus.*

Lucian tried to shake himself while holding entirely still. No motive. The guy had no motive. Lucian just found him shifty because of how he treated Nou. People could be terrible human beings without being terrorists.

'Whatever you tell us, Yolanda,' Parkin said, 'we can protect you in exchange for information. We are required by law to treat you fairly in the event of a wider operation beginning with your help. We can contact Interplanetary Investigations. Have them assure you a shorter sentence.'

'No.' Something bled from Moreno with the word. Something that ran down her skin with all her contempt and her pride. All of a sudden Yolanda Moreno looked human, and for one stomach-churning moment Lucian thought she was welling up. 'No, I can't do that.'

'Why can't you?' Harbour, each syllable tight.

Lucian was watching Moreno's eyes. It was something he tended not to do with people—afraid of what he might see, perhaps, if he looked too close. Afraid of seeing another human within them, just like him, looking back. Except now he wanted to understand. Now he wanted to see what this woman saw: a woman whose deepest desire was to ruin what Lucian's own was to build.

Moreno locked her eyes on Harbour's. Stepped forward until she was so close to the glass Lucian saw more reflection than person.

'Because,' Moreno said, and her voice was so low it was barely there at all, 'I wouldn't live to serve it.'

*

237

Lucian huffed out a breath as they filed outside.

'So what'll you do with her? Has any other base dealt with this?'

'They had anti-terraforming radicals on Mars when I was a lad,' Parkin said thoughtfully, 'and we have protocols, of course. The Outer Territories office has already been notified and a team dispatched.'

'We'll strip her quarters down,' said Harbour. He stood a little away from the group, as though ready to shoot off. 'She'll have her own room, bathroom, living space.'

'That we can keep locked down until law enforcement arrives from Titan,' added Vasily. 'Six months. It can be done.'

'Six months?' Halley, Lucian was relieved to hear, seemed to know as little as he did in this situation. 'That's the Outer Territories' solution?'

'Yes,' Harbour said, as though that was perfectly reasonable—and Lucian supposed it was. What else could they do? 'We're not an island nation—we answer to their government. Not every scientific party can be expected to run its own police force. And Moreno will only receive here what she will on Titan.'

Halley came up to Lucian as the others slipped away.

'You holding up OK, lad?'

Lucian raised his eyebrows at her.

'If by "holding up" you mean is my face still one unified piece, then yes, just about, I think so.'

'I should have sent people out with you.'

'What, like an armed contingent?'

'You and Stan could have been shredded more than you already were. He's a good kid, Lucian. You tell him that was some serious gauntlet-wielding.'

'Through a broken nose to boot,' he agreed. 'I'll tell him. And, uh, it's called terramancing. That's what I'm calling it.'

'That will never catch on. Tell him now, and get yourself some stitches while you're there.'

'Righto, yeah, on it.'

Lucian moved one way as Halley moved the same; the awkward dance ended only when Halley took him by both shoulders and forcibly moved him to one side.

'Sorry, sorry,' he cringed—then stopped and turned. 'Wait. Halley?'

She looked over her shoulder.

'What was it you wanted to tell me?' Lucian asked. 'This morning, when you looked . . . distracted. Was everything OK?'

He was expecting a quick answer, maybe an *I'll tell you later* or *Oh, it was nothing*. But Halley stared at him for a moment, and when she blinked it was as though she was waking up.

'I almost forgot about that,' she murmured. 'The ice. The ocean ice. I got the isotopes back.'

Lucian's eyes widened. '*Oh*. I can't believe *I* forgot. You've been working on that all these months?'

'In between bringing a planet to life, not to mention a mass spectrometer.'

The words sounded like Halley, but the voice didn't. The voice sounded as hesitant as it had that morning.

'After all the commotion it hardly seems . . . It's more of a scientific curiosity, but . . .' She drew her hands together. 'The isotope ratios. They're off the charts.'

Lucian rummaged among his memory for a translation and came up empty-handed.

'And that means . . .?'

'Different planetary bodies have their own isotopic signature,' Halley told him, visibly slipping into lecturer mode. 'Like a fingerprint. A slightly different blend. That's how they confirmed Martian meteorites were from Mars—from the isotopes. Pluto has its own signature, like Earth, like Mercury, like

239

everywhere else. But the stuff from the ocean ice . . . it doesn't line up. Not with the rest of Pluto. Not with the rest of . . .' She shook herself. '*Anything.*'

Ocean ice. Lucian recalled that day out in the canyon with Halley and Harbour. A vein of water-ice, migrated up from an ocean. An ocean beneath the Heart. Mid-breath, he went very still as what Halley was talking about finally clicked.

Beneath the Heart. White walls in a cavern of ice. Pillars as thick as sequoias. Roots of light that flowed and sparked. Whistling, whistling, as though carried on a wind. He'd been inside that ocean: somewhere near its surface, hollowed out from the space where it was still frozen.

'When you say "off the charts",' Lucian began slowly, slow enough to think, to consider that being mauled by a respectable colleague might only be the second strangest thing to happen to him that day, 'just what exactly do you mean?'

News of Moreno travelled fast. *Drama this big for a planet that small*, as Halley once said; she knew what she was talking about. For days after the last Silvasaire embers had faded from the insides of eyelids, people had only to catch each other's gaze or blow out a breath for someone to curse with a shake of their head. That Silvasaire had disintegrated as completely and spectacularly as its junior, Mortimaeus, was of second-rate interest: the phrase *anti-terraforming radicals* was passed from gossip to gossip like something delicious and exotic to be savoured.

But news like Halley's could only be kept from the people of Pluto for so long. Lucian wondered if she had thought of Clyde Tombaugh as the mass spectrometer's data had come through. Whether she had thought how a farmer's boy, sat in a draughty old observatory, flicking between photograph after photograph of stars, was for half an hour in 1930 the only person in existence to know of a new world.

And Lucian also wondered, when the news was out, who else would realise exactly what it meant.

Nou knew what *interstellar* meant. *Inter* meant *between*, and *stellar* meant *stars*. Between the stars.

Something on Pluto had arrived from outside their Solar System. Professor Halley stood before them all in the hall, tawny hair loose and settling past her shoulders, and told them of things called interstellar asteroids, tiny worlds that travelled from other solar systems; of rogue planets, or *orphan planets*, worlds that were unloved by their parent star and sent wandering through the space between spaces, searching for a foster family. Of the evidence suggesting such a thing had once hit Pluto hard enough to penetrate its surface, to mix with its ocean. It was the only rational explanation, Halley said, to explain that ocean's alien isotope medley.

The room filled with murmurs ranging from the interested to the excited as Halley finished, but Nou's heart was pounding as though she was about to take the stage. Something from another solar system. Something below the surface. *Near the ocean.*

She raised her eyes to Lucian across the room. Lucian was a scientist; he would make the connection, she knew he would. But Lucian was not looking at either her or Halley. He was looking—Nou followed his gaze—straight and unwaveringly at Edmund.

Edmund was watching Halley, but it was only through noting Lucian's absorption that Nou saw more: arms folded as usual, expression neutral as usual . . . except, it wasn't. It was a moment before she noticed.

Edmund wasn't blinking. He wasn't nodding with interest, or turning to catch his colleagues' eyes. He was perfectly still; as composed as a cut-out version of himself.

Nou's thoughts hurtled to supply an explanation. Had Halley

already told him, and this blank reaction was from spending his emotion earlier? But no, that wasn't right. He was feeling *something*: the muscles of his jaw were taut; his eyes were flat; and although it was hard to tell—he hadn't looked well for some time now—his skin was a nasty pale. But why? She raised her eyes back to Lucian . . .

And almost gasped aloud with fright. Lucian was looking straight at her: looking at her with cold calculation identical to the stare he had given Edmund. When Halley's brief was over he strode straight for her, and then—she stood immobilised to the spot—straight past. But there was enough time to catch his sign:

My office. Now.

Lucian never used his office. Too isolating, he said, too small. But the cubbyhole, when she found it, wasn't quite empty: coffee rings and scribbled notes dotted the glass desktop, and on the glass wall were blown-up pages from books with titles like *Solar Architecture* and *Twelve Rules for Post-Fusion Space-flight*. It looked as though Stan was using the place to write up his thesis.

Lucian wiped the desk clean with a hand and leant against it to face her. He was unsmiling.

Now, he began, the sign itself brusque in a way Nou had never seen before, and she felt herself shrink at the look in his eyes. *I need you to be as honest and clear with me as you possibly can.*

Why are we signing? Her own were very small.

Lucian signed, *Humour me.* That humourless expression adults used, the one that meant *no comment.* He went on with exacting precision:

I need you to tell me who else knows about the creatures beneath the Heart.

To her horror, Nou felt her eyes fill. Her hands fumbled together but every word short-circuited.

Lucian went on in short, jagged strokes.

242

We're not just talking about a fourth, maybe fifth emergence of life here any more. We're not even talking about the first multicellular. For all we know from just looking, they might be the first intelligent life.

I know. Nou's signs blurred before her as her tears grew fast. *I know.*

All at once the walls in his eyes fell down. Bending so he reached her height, he took her by both shoulders before releasing her. He signed, *Nou, if Halley is right, those creatures might be life from somewhere else in our galaxy.*

Nou couldn't have said why she was crying. She nodded and nodded.

I know, she managed again, head bent to the ground, hair shielding her face.

A hand beneath her chin, firm but gentle. Raising her eyes. *I need you to tell me, Nou.*

He stood with his hands on his thighs at her eye level. His eyebrows were raised in something like a question, or maybe a plea. Asking her for truth. For trust.

Nou felt herself slacken. Sudden exhaustion—or maybe release, maybe both—sunk her shoulders low enough to hurt.

Lucian pulled up two chairs.

Will you sign it for me, Nou? he said in their secret language, lowering himself into one, looking up at her. *Can you do that for me? So no one hears but us?*

Shame and relief together. The urge to run, both from the room and into his arms. The desire to hold herself tall and strong and grown-up, and to curl up as small and inconsequential as possible.

Taking the other chair met these in the middle. Her feet touched the floor as she sat; she was getting big now. She would be twelve soon.

She looked into Lucian's eyes and she began her story.

243

Interlude 3

Edmund thinks he may never sleep again but his body has other ideas when, at four or so that morning, it finds itself curled tight on its side between the bedcovers. Leaden arms, muscles, even lips, too leaden to call for the blinds to close, so that silvery starlight and Heartshine lance through the long windows. The joins between his prosthetics and his thighs ache as they have not in more than a decade, the kind of ache the doctors used to say was only limbic. He keeps them attached—there is a nakedness, helplessness, to being without them that he cannot bear tonight. His dreams have no picture, and only one sound.

He doesn't eat much that breakfast. He sips his coffee; he rolls up the sleeves of his skins; he rolls them down again. He listens with all his attention to Nou, sitting beside him happily spearing black cherries on her fork, chattering away about school, about Plutoshine, about her life forms—just as the new xenobiologist Mallory Madoc places her tray opposite them, and by the slight freezing of her polite smile, Edmund can't say for sure if he changed the topic fast enough.

Clavius, to his other side, makes up for him in appetite. Garlic pesto slathered on crusty, steaming bread; wonders from the green-houses like meaty, juicy olives and sweet yellow tomatoes; thick pancake stacks with honey and almond cream and sliced mango. All the leftovers from yesterday as a second feast; the thought makes Edmund slightly nauseous, and the wafting tang of the garlic is not helping. Clavius, though, has second helpings of everything. He downs his first cream coffee between accepting congratulations from the head electrician on his dance moves; he jiggles the base's newest-born member on his knee while her mother, his comms officer, excitedly reads out an article on more life found on Mars; he jokes how none of them, Martians nor Plutonians, are really in the right genre for an alien attack.

And no matter how hard Edmund tries, pulling facsimiles of smiles for his sister, nodding in what he hopes are the right places, he can't tune out that laughing confidence beside him.

'Ed, Nou,' Clavius says within the hour as breakfast winds down, 'why don't we all go for a family walk? Just the three of us. Stretch our legs after yesterday, hm?'

The men's eyes meet.

'Could I show you my friends?'

Nou. The emotion Edmund felt under the shadow of Pandemonium Promontorium, the one that was either disappointment or relief: he now knows it was relief. It had to be—because this is its opposite.

'There's an idea,' says Clavius brightly. 'Not a half-bad way to kill a morning. And if you have found us life, Nou, I hope you know I'm going to be pretty damn impressed.'

Clavius knows perfectly well what he is doing—and he knows how to do it perfectly. Nou's face is the definition of joy. Her eyes shine with it. And Edmund knows from his own experience: he knows that right now Nou feels like the most special person that ever lived.

'Ed, do you reckon she's old enough to see our secret entrance?'

'A secret entrance?' Nou looks from Clavius to Edmund. 'Can I? Please?'

Nou doesn't get to come into Clavius's office much—like the old pubs or school staffrooms, he keeps it adult-only—and she looks all around her with swivelling eyes when they enter ten minutes later.

She approaches with birdlike caution the square desk with its four panes of smartglass, scribbled equations and shorthand cast in cold blue across her face.

'You get changed first, Ed,' Clavius calls. 'I'll be right in.'

Edmund glances back as he turns into the adjoining room. Nou is holding her suit against her in one hand, helmet in the other, and Clavius is watching her with arms folded across his chest.

'What do they mean?' She means the equations; Edmund has been teaching her the simpler rules of algebra all month. 'Are they to do with Plutoshine?'

He ducks into the changing room and just catches his father's reply around the door:

'You know the score, kid—I'll tell you when you're older.'

Edmund strips down and pulls on his suit in record time, dressed head to toe in the brilliant orange of the standard spacesuit—no need for secrecy today, not with their cover story.

There, hanging limp on its stand, is Clavius's own suit.

Edmund has practised enough on his own suit to know exactly what he is looking for. It won't take a moment—but Clavius could enter at any time. He lunges towards it before he can lose his nerve—like leaping from a great height—then grabs the pipework snaking up its back—fingers jerking in discrete executions—and the task is complete. Scant heartbeats have passed.

'The kid's like you.' Edmund jumps back as Clavius lopes into the room, stripping off his T-shirt over his head. 'Question after question after question. Poor sod seems to be taking after you.'

Edmund cannot think of anything to stay to this, and so does not. He is just clipping his helmet in place inside the airlock when Nou peeks around the door frame, all buttoned up in airtight fluorescence.

'Did you do the checks, Nou?' he asks out of habit over the comms, running his hands across his own.

Clavius laughs as he clips his own helmet in place.

'If you can't sort out your own suit by now, that's got to just be natural selection.' When she continues to stand there, he adds, 'Not gonna bite, you know.'

Nou hurries inside the airlock and he seals it with a click. The lights turn red as depressurisation begins its hiss.

There is a pause where all is quiet. Edmund knows it is too good to last—and it is.

'You know,' says Clavius with bland cheeriness as the air thins, 'you'd better be telling the truth.'

He's talking to Nou. Edmund feels coldness trickle through him as the all too familiar powerlessness takes hold.

Clavius hitches his lips up in a smile and raises his brows.

'You are, aren't you?'

Edmund's heart is sinking through his chest as though through soft mud. That's just the thing with their father and his praise, the part Nou has yet to figure out: that while Clavius can turn night to day and sweep every last star down to flood her nightlight, he can just as thoughtlessly cast every one of them right back. And he does. Every time.

Nou's eyes are on the floor and her mouth is a tight, unhappy line.

'I always tell the truth.'

'Bit of eye contact would be nice when you're making claims like that, pickle.'

It seems to take Nou an age to do so, raising them in distinct increments as though lifting some great weight. The airlock has reached forty per cent by the time they've climbed to her father's own.

'I'm not lying.' Her voice is very small.

'I hope for your sake you're right.' Clavius pops his eyes a little as he smiles again. 'This airlock's a bit magic, you see. It'll let you out, but if you've ever told a lie . . .' He breaks off with a shrug. 'It knows. And we don't like liars in Stern.'

It took Edmund years, but he finally realised that what Clavius wanted were backups. Carbon-based copies to finish his work, should anything happen to him: a second pair of eyes as an extension of his own. With Edmund, his technique was simple: give him reason to be grateful, to idolise him—but that was only effective until Edmund figured him out.

Nou's body seems to be growing as small as her voice. Hunched shoulders. Lowered gaze. Arms held tight at her sides. It physically hurts to watch, every time like the last: a sharp pull somewhere inside his chest too deep to press.

'What will it do?' She's barely whispering now. Any lower and she would disappear entirely.

Nou. With her birth Clavius then had two backups—and furthermore he had the long-term means of keeping Edmund under his control. Edmund, who would do anything to keep her safe.

Clavius places his hands on his knees and bends down. Edmund sees Nou flinch back, her eyes fixed on his boots.

'It locks you out,' he murmurs. 'And it's no use going to the front door, either, because Ed went and programmed that to lock you out, too. Ed can't stand liars any more than I can. Especially not ones who are silly little girls.'

Two wills, one thumb. How simple Clavius must think humans are, compared to his nuclear physics.

Edmund can't say anything. He knows he can't. He is too close.

Nou draws in a breath and it is a sniff.

'I promise I'm not lying,' she squeaks.

'Hey, no use telling me that.' Clavius holds up his hands and catches Edmund's eye—inviting him to share in this humorous carry-on. 'No one's died on Pluto since the *Beacon* expedition, so I don't even know how it would happen. Maybe your oxygen would go first and you'd suffocate. Or maybe your power would die and you'd freeze to death. Or you might die of thirst if they both held. Fuck'—he laughs—'if that was me I'd just cut my pipes first chance I got and have done with it. Get me out of my misery. So. Let me ask again. Are you lying to me?'

'The . . . airlock.' Edmund can't help himself: Nou is crying now. She's trying to wipe her face and meeting only helmet. 'The airlock, it's . . . finished . . .'

'I'm waiting, pickle.'

Nou sniffs. Her arms look as though they don't know what to do with themselves: unable to clean her face, or hide it, they settle for hugging around her.

'I promise,' she sniffs again. 'I'll take you right there.'

'Well, that's all right then!' Clavius claps her on the back so hard she stumbles; Edmund jerks to catch her and has to stop himself. 'What are you worrying about? If you're telling the truth there's no problem at all. No use getting all worked up about it.'

The airlock light is flashing green for go, but something else is flashing on Clavius's suit—something that makes him pause. Something orange, or maybe red, gone too fast to catch.

And Edmund thinks, *Not now. It's too soon . . .*

Clavius hums to himself.

'What is it?' Edmund barely breathes.

Clavius pats the front of his suit—checking a connection here, a valve there. He glances at the control panel at his wrist.

'I was having trouble with the thermocirculation a few months back. Ought to get it looked over again.' Then he shrugs. 'All nominal now.' He claps his hands together; a curiously muffled sound through the comms. 'OK. Off you go, kid.'

And it is only when both have turned, and Edmund knows he will not be seen, that he allows himself the luxury of closing his eyes— even if it is only for a moment.

The same soft, icing sugar sand. The same sinuous streams of footprints. The same star-punctured Plutonian night, midnight now, three Earth-days into the darkness.

Nou leads the way. She's fast: there's an unconscious efficiency to the angles of her lightest of footsteps, propelling her forward as though in seven-league boots. A winking orange speck in a world of greyscale, just to remind him that colour still exists.

Edmund is not far behind her. He keeps between them both, each footstep hurling up floury ejecta on all sides. Clavius's heavy breathing obscures any hope of hearing Nou's—but at least he can see her.

They bear left now, diverging from the Tartarus Dorsa path. The misty arm of the Milky Way, skimming the sky like water in the wake of a skipping stone, spearing overhead to guide the way. A wall of black to one side: Cousteau Rupes, the north-western edge of the Heart. Silvery light saturating all, thief of bronze and gold and burnished crimson.

The base of Pandemonium Promontorium slides into view as they crest another dune. Nou calls, on a gasp:

'This is it.'

The three of them line up barely feet beside Edmund's theodolite marks, but this passes unheeded by Nou: her eyes are fixed at the foot of the cliffs. And there, following her line of sight, is what was entirely invisible without her: a shade of black darker than elsewhere; a little notch at the lowest stratum; a shadow that disappears out of sight . . . that disappears *inside.*

They duck inside at the exact point Edmund's lidar found. The tunnel is of carved ice and it is marred by the ages: walls stained by methane seeps, their edges smoothed by the indescribably unhurried pace of some steady chemical weathering. They creep further and deeper within these unmapped depths of claustrophobia. Perhaps twenty minutes pass with nothing more than one another's breathing and the white-black-white-black flashes of ice and tunnel under headlamp.

Then they all hear it. A sound that stops them dead where they stand.

One-two-three.

For Edmund, the sound is like hearing the song he used as his alarm tone twenty years ago—like jerking awake when he hadn't realised he was asleep.

But Nou's face, when she turns, is rapturous.

'That's them!' she whispers, and her eyes are two stars. 'They're saying hello!'

And she brings her lips together and whistles back—the sound just like the Whistlers', so human, so light, so eerie coming from that face, that both men flinch.

'Stop, Nou, stop!' Edmund feels his eyes go wide in alarm. 'You don't know what you're saying!'

Nou stops. The Whistlers don't, and continue on all sides like a half-remembered lullaby.

'They know we can't understand them,' she says very matter-of-factly. 'So it's only polite to answer back, isn't it?'

Clavius laughs. 'She's got you there.' And he whistles too: *One-two-three. One-two-three.*

'Lighten up,' he adds to Edmund over their personal line, and laughs again as his son jumps at the hand slapped on his shoulder.

'You seem a little anxious considering we're about to have tea with a couple of bacteria.'

Edmund has his back to Clavius in the tight confines of the tunnel, but he turns as he says, rigidly: 'Bacteria don't whistle.' He looks up—looks into Clavius's eyes—and wills his own into walls. 'Your mistake is to assume this is another Europa or Enceladus. We have *no idea* what we are dealing with.'

He turns back around.

'Hey.' Clavius takes Edmund's shoulder and pulls him close, as though—in a gesture that makes no sense out here—to whisper in his ear.

'We stick to the plan,' he murmurs. 'Search and destroy. All right?'

Edmund is watching Nou, blowing whistles and receiving them in turn. She is almost laughing with delight.

They push on. In time the whistles fade—or perhaps they become

251

white noise, same as the humming of the heat packs or the hiss of the oxygen flow. They must be very deep now. They must be below the Heart itself.

'We're here.' Nou's whisper comes in the blackness, and Edmund's heart seems to surge forward. 'Turn your lights off.'

In a click she has hers off and so does Edmund. But Clavius points his forward. Up ahead, their tunnel opens up into nothing but a blackness so vast his torch can't pierce it.

'Quick, Dad!' Nou cries. 'Please!'

'I need to see this,' says Clavius, eyes dead ahead.

'Just . . .' Edmund can't help himself. 'Just do as she says—'

The series of three short, high, piercing whistles, then again. Like a bird call, or an SOS. The pattern is familiar now, and the three figures listen for the sequence's final part: *one-two-three-four*, lower in pitch, the cycle then repeating itself. But it is faster in tempo now. There's something like an urgency to it.

Their breaths are short and close in the confines of their helmets. They say nothing. Out there, under the black of the ice and far from the comfort of the stars, one thing is certain: this is no bird call, and if it is an SOS, it is the most distant ever heard by humanity.

A shot of red in the torchlight, gone as fast as it appears. Edmund feels his eyes bulge.

The colour red floods their vision. Floods—like a burst blood vessel.

The walls are lit scarlet from the inside, and within them are ripples of light writhing as air bubbles do within frozen ponds. The walls behind them, in front of them, everything red, red, out into a void no torchlight can touch . . . *A chasm.*

'Well,' says Clavius. He says it all wrong: calm, cool, blithe. 'This changes everything.'

With a snap he shuts off the torch and strides forward past Nou and Edmund, where the tunnel widens just enough to squeeze through. Edmund is torn: there is something sacrilegious about pushing onwards with such haste, but it is worse, far worse, to leave Clavius alone with whatever resides inside. The decision is made for him: Nou bounces after her father, still weightless with delight, still shining, still unheeding, and Edmund follows at her heels.

Then stops at once.

His suit is red. His hand before him is red. The domed walls, the rough-hewn floor, and beyond—to a grove—to pillars—to—to . . .

They reach as high as the cavern, stretching up like trees in search of sunlight, and they are almost as wide as he is tall. They have the proportions of sequoias but the morphology is all wrong: their surface (their hide?) is texturally smooth to beyond the scale of Edmund's perception, and there is no anabranching of additional limbs with their climbing height. Cryophilic? Yes. Chemoautotrophic? Perhaps. Xenobiological . . . Edmund turns and turns where he stands, thinking of all the other words from his textbooks, all the -*philes* and the -*morphs* and the -*ites*, until he runs out. The cavern before him is lit red with the bioluminescence of non-terrestrial life forms.

There's a slight shift in his head, somehow. Edmund tries to regain some focus, to pinpoint what it is. Dizziness, perhaps. He then realises it is the new perspective that has come with his world, and their world, being changed forever.

Nou's whisper makes him turn around.

'What do you think?'

There's a light in her eyes but she's a little hunched now, twisting her gloved hands before her, like she gets when she is anxious. She is anxious to hear what he thinks.

Edmund stares at her. His lips part, then close, seeking words and finding none.

'It . . . Nou, it's . . .'

'It's a heck of a finding.'

Just for a moment, Edmund had forgotten his father existed. Clavius is lumbering over, jerking a thumb behind him at the grove.

'So, what do we reckon these things are, then?'

253

Edmund looks up all around him and only shakes his head. Nou hovers between the two on the balls of her feet, looking from one to the other.

'Alive?' Clavius prompts. 'Made by life? Some crazy, as yet undocumented cryological phenomenon?'

'I . . . I call the biggest one Tag,' offers Nou in a very small voice.

Both men stare at her.

'It's Morse code,' she explains. 'I looked it up. He spells the letters *tag* a lot.'

'Pickle.' Clavius draws his hands together, as though with great patience. 'Are you trying to tell me that these giant *things*, whatever they are, are speaking to you in a technological human language that's been extinct for centuries?'

'There's no sign in Morse for the four-note segment we hear repeated.' Edmund is thinking it through. Then, a little sharply as the implication sinks in: 'You're saying the creatures communicate more to you than the three-piece song?'

'Sometimes.' Nou stares up at the pillars with awe, and something like love. 'I think he wants to talk.'

Talk. Edmund repeats the word in his head. But another one is stranger still: *he.*

Clavius catches his eyes and raises his eyebrows at him. The eyebrows say, *This is getting better and better, isn't it?* He bends down then, sits back on his haunches; stares at the swirling redness underfoot.

Edmund, too, is drawn to look closer. Is the redness within the ice? Beneath it? The thing—things?—move like smoke behind frosted glass, like threadbare lightning. A different species from the pillars? Or part of the same? Which are the Whistlers, or are both?

It is a feeling like nausea sliding over his insides as he realises how close the moment is now. It is coming. The decision, long ago made. All that is left is its execution.

'We should . . .' he starts, but he can't get the words out. 'We

254

should . . . study them. I have the facilities in my lab. I could conduct a thorough investigation within several months.'

Clavius trails his finger atop the ice and watches as the lights— creatures?—follow his movements. They seem to grow brighter.

'Sure.' He shrugs. 'Knock yourself out. Let's chisel out some ice. Chip off a piece. Nou'—he turns to her—'where's softest in here? These . . . these *poles*'—waving vaguely behind him—'you ever tried cutting them? Looks like titanium . . .'

He's drawing his ice-axe from his utility belt when Edmund moves faster than he thought possible. Within the space of two pulses there are hands around Clavius's arm. Four of them.

'Don't.' Edmund's voice is a whisper. A plea. A threat.

'Please don't hurt them.' Nou has her hands either side of Edmund's.

Clavius flicks his wrist to swat them off; Nou flies back but Edmund grips tighter. Clavius looks from those hands to their owner.

'I won't let you hurt them.' Edmund hears the words, feels them leave him. Neither convince him this is real—not after years, after a decade, of waiting for this, dreaming for it, dreading it. He has practised his next words so often they cannot help but feel like those of an actor: 'And I won't let you hurt her any more, either.'

Clavius barks out a laugh. Each syllable of it is distinct, falling flat across the helmet intercom.

'You don't think there's enough life in this Solar System as it is? You know, when we've got *other things to be doing* with this particular planet?'

A flash of torchlight in motion and he has one hand over Edmund's, and with it has twisted himself free. Nou is within reach; he grabs both her shoulders.

She squeaks in alarm and struggles—Edmund's voice is hoarse as he cries *'Don't!'*—then the pair of them go still.

Clavius follows their eyes to his feet.

A tiny nick has formed in the ice beneath the toe of his left boot.

Out of it, for all the world like blood from a wound, is pouring that glowing, swirling, sparking redness.

Clavius leaps back, relinquishing Nou, as Edmund's heart thumps so hard his fingertips hurt.

'It's OK, it's OK!' cries Nou breathlessly. 'They did this to me once. It's how they say hello. They want to feel you!'

Clavius backs away but the redness underfoot follows. Edmund is frozen in place, eyes fixed on the bleeding ice.

'What's it doing?' Clavius says, and his voice is too flat—too controlled. 'Get them to stop, Nou, get them to stop *now.*'

'Dad, it's OK!' Nou rushes forward, but Edmund locks her in place by both shoulders. 'Please, Dad, it's fine.'

The creatures touch Clavius's boots. Edmund only stares as they begin to flow up his father's ankles, up his legs.

Clavius cries out wordlessly. There is no pretence of control now. No confidence.

'Nou, stop them, stop them now—'

Swarming, seeping, one amorphous, translucent mass as though that light is within them and only appears red for passing through some capillary-lined outer skin. It reaches up to his torso.

Clavius jerks his upper body—as though trying to run—but his lower half is locked in place.

The creatures climb higher.

'Nou, what's happening?' Edmund cries.

'I don't know!' Nou sounds frightened, confused.

Up his arms, up his back, the creatures climb and flow and spread, and now Edmund picks up a sound he wishes he had not: that of his father's ragged breaths, gasps punctured and throttled, each tighter than the last.

And as he does, he also tunes in to something else: a flashing in Clavius's helmet. Red like the creatures but distinct; not unknown like them but known, a warning—a warning all trained spacefarers know by instinct.

256

It would have happened whether the redness had touched him or not. It would have happened because Edmund had planned it to.

The lights signify a paper-cut fracture somewhere, a leak, a rupture, and now Clavius is breathing too fast—the creatures washing up his helmet—*Warning*, the red lights cry—redness sealing him shut . . .

A choked gasp, half-throttled. Another.

The rupture ruptures. The leak leaks. The man they call the King of Pluto gasps again for air—and finds none. There is none left.

Over the comms there is silence.

'Dad!' Nou screams. '*Dad!*'

Edmund lets her go and she rushes over. Clavius Harbour is face down before she can open her arms to catch him.

257

Chapter 16

Lucian listened without moving or interrupting as Nou told her story. Her signs were at first short and disjointed—like when she spoke, unable to find and connect the right words—before she forgot she was translating from mind to hands at all as she submerged herself in the memories.

The pair sat in silence when she finished. The cyclical hum of air flow was soporific in its rhythm.

You hadn't been back? Lucian signed eventually. *Not since you showed me?*

It was a moment before Nou could respond; telling the story was one thing, but discussing it—answering specific, incisive questions about it—was a sort of interrogation. Like having her diary entries scrutinised for consistency.

She wrung her twisting hands apart.

I couldn't find them, she managed in tight angles. *They went away. I thought they didn't want to see me, so I stopped looking. Then I went back before I showed you and they were there. We—* She stopped herself; collected her thoughts. *I knew I could show you, then,* she finished faintly, hands trailing off before falling back to her lap, two empty puppets.

Lucian sat in silence. Then:

We've got to tell the Interplanetary Astronomical Union. If this gets out, the Court of Planetary Protection will try all of us for withholding this—you, me, your brother . . . even your dad, if he comes round.

Nou stared unhappily at her hands as though they could sweep back up all the words they had said.

They won't, she told him. *Because the life forms are from Earth.*

'From . . . ?' Lucian spluttered out loud.

He was staring at her, but Nou could not bring herself to look up at his expression. He leant forward and began to sign precisely in sharp angles.

What exactly are you on about?

They're—Nou had to line up the letters in her head just like the old days. *They're Earth contamination*—

Now that sounds like exactly the kind of thing your brother *would say!*

The sign struck the air with enough force to make her flinch. Lucian was on his feet.

Am I wrong? Is that what he told you?

He's got a PhD in genetic engineering, Nou tried, but she had no idea how to spell the words, and she couldn't have told him what a PhD was if all the worlds depended upon it.

He could have a PhD analysing Hartdegen-inspired transformative novellas for all it would matter. He's not blind!

They were at an impasse. Lucian and his reason; Nou and her loyalty.

Why are you so afraid of him?

Nou's eyes flew to his, then away as fast.

Did he hurt you? Lucian's signs were tight. *Did he . . . ? Did that . . . ? If he hurt you*—

No, Lucian, no. Nou shook her head vehemently back and forth. *Never ever.*

She didn't mean to lie. It was only after she signed that she remembered. But Lucian was already signing back:

Then why are you so afraid? He's your brother. If he's not hurt you, then . . . has he threatened to? Or someone else?

Nou wished she could press her hands into her eyes and rub so hard she could rub herself out like scribbles on a glassboard.

Opposite her, Lucian folded his arms and waited. Nou shut her eyes so she wouldn't have to see her own signs:

He doesn't like me.

The lump in her throat came from nowhere. So too did the tears: from zero to one hundred per cent, from both her eyes, rolling too fast to catch down her cheeks. Mortified, she staunched the flow with the backs of her hands.

I don't know what I did wrong. He won't even look at me. Not since that day. I'm trying as hard as I can.

Lucian unfolded his arms and made to move forward, but stopped as she went on.

It's not him I'm scared of. I'm scared we'll never be close again. I don't know how to make it better.

Lucian's hands clasped and unclasped into fists before he signed:

I don't know what his problem is, Nou, but it's not you. He's a . . . And here he used a sign Nou didn't recognise, and he made no move to explain. *Do you really believe him? That those creatures aren't alien life? Halley's isotopes can't lie.*

He wouldn't lie to me. Nou kept her signs small. Her mouth was set in a tight line. *Edmund wouldn't lie to me.*

Wouldn't he?

She knew from his face that Lucian wished the words back into his hands. But he hadn't given them in spite, or provocation. He was, as always, only being honest.

He slumped down opposite her.

We have to tell someone, Nou. You asked me to keep your secret and I promised I would. But this is too big now. He leant forward. *We could tell Halley. She's the best person in the whole*

Solar System to tell. She'd be on your side. And—he threw up his hands—*from the sound of things she's pretty close to figuring it out anyway. This could well get out whether you want it to or not.*

Nou followed his hands with increasing misery. *But . . .*

She stopped herself. Lucian only watched in silence as she wrestled her feelings into something describable. Any time she almost caught sense of them they pricked her—they *hurt*—and she dropped them, shied away, started again.

Don't think too hard. Don't look at the words. Just *see*.

Nausea. That's what she felt. A nausea of the mind. She didn't want to look any closer because then she would have to admit it. That she had always known they weren't from Earth. That if Lucian wasn't lying, and if Lucian saw it, too, and if Halley and her science were proving it, then that meant her Edmund . . .

Why would he lie?

She watched the signs as she formed them; watched the air they cleared. Her defeat hung in the spaces left behind.

Why would he lie to me?

Lucian shifted where he sat.

We should at least let Halley and the xenobiologists look. Get their take on it. And Mallory's our friend. What do you reckon?

He was asking for her permission. Even with the stakes so high. He needed her to be OK with it.

Please, she began. *Could you . . . ? Could you not tell Edmund just yet? That you know?*

Lucian closed his eyes for a moment in an emotion Nou couldn't place, then nodded. Still with his eyes closed, he signed, *All right. We'll wait until after Plutoshine.* He opened them and raked his fingers through his hair. *I suppose there's enough going on right now. Pluto doesn't need any more drama.*

He was right about that. But that had never held it at bay in the past.

261

Chapter 17

Jovortre's disintegration was simulated to be the most spectacular of all the gards' put together, but that was one of scant few facts known about the thing. It was significantly larger than its predecessors, that was well defined—bordering the size of the smallest of the Plutonian moons—and of course its bulk composition had been confirmed by the remote sensing surveys and drilling campaign. But that was about as far as scientific characterisation had ever got, hence its name: no one knew anything about Hartdegen's Jovortre, either.

It was the evening before its arrival, and Lucian had his ankles crossed beneath the chair at Clavius Harbour's bedside. It was late summer, by the weather sim: the room's cool felt good on his bare forearms, and Nou had brought string-tied crocosmia and set them on the bedside table. At some point, in the quiet since she left, he had unconsciously aligned his breathing to match the taps of the heart monitor.

The blank screen behind the flowers had a little flickering tick mark, luminous cyan against black. Lucian couldn't help but watch, waiting—even knowing it was like picking a star in the sky and waiting for it to go supernova.

But there were the gauntlets at the wrists. There was the circlet upon the crown. And there beneath that crown, so the doctor said, were strengthening signs of life.

'They're good fun, you know,' Lucian murmured—the sound startling him as though another had spoken. 'And I'd really recommend talking—your kid barely stops these days and I think she enjoys it. Maybe you would, too. We've even got Gen right in there with you. Gen can do all the hard work. Isn't that right, my friend?'

'Certainly so,' came the familiar, serene voice, as was customary from everywhere all at once.

'How's the weather in there, Gen?'

'Blue skies, Lucian. Clear, calm, and quite beautiful.'

'Like anything could happen, eh?'

'If you like.'

Clavius Harbour wasn't really a handsome man, Lucian supposed—but then, great men didn't need to be. Lucian kept his eyes mostly averted from the bed, the same way he wouldn't watch someone sleep, but the dim lighting kept tricking him into thinking the lips were hitching, or the eyes winking.

Suddenly he could contain himself no longer.

'You know I could really use your advice,' he blurted out.

The heart monitor beeped. The computerised tick ticked. Clavius Harbour did nothing. Even Gen seemed to know this wasn't the time.

'Sorry.' Ruffling his hair. 'Earth, *agh*, you don't even know me, I'm sorry. I know I shouldn't even be here on my own. But. I just.'

He'd been out by the lake in the Parks earlier. There was a light rain puncturing tiny impact craters, there and gone in seconds, on the lake water. He'd had his arms around his knees, socks pressed to the cool, damp grass under the shelter of the canopy. He was wondering, as he watched the lake, if this was how Pluto's first years would have looked, were an onlooker to speed up a billion years of footage. Impact after impact bombarded the surface, excavating, rebounding, recurring, as though in slow motion under the half-hearted gravity.

'Sorry,' Lucian said again. His locket had slipped between his open shirt collar; he tucked it back beneath the plaid. 'I just don't know what to do. You know? I mean . . . You don't know, you don't know what I'm talking about, and that's fine, I'm not expecting an answer . . .'

When he had stood in the Parks at the end of his first full day, casting stars and worlds above the children's heads, were the Whistlers in that timeline just slipping in unnoticed? Did they bury themselves below the proto-Pluto surface, safe from the onslaught, or were they but seeds at the time, calculatedly dormant? Or were they seeded much later?

'See, my dad, he used to . . . He was always . . . I could go to him for anything, you know? He was kind of like you. He could solve anything.'

Whistling. He'd whistled to them and they'd whistled right back. Could perhaps he just—there, opposite Clavius Harbour, Lucian shook his head to himself and chafed both hands against his forehead—*ask them?* Could he ask them what they were, ask them what he should do?

'And I can't go to Halley, I promised I wouldn't, and I'm not really expecting an answer from you right now.'

Ask them, ask the creatures? Ridiculous. Besides, soon it would all be out of his hands. Once Jovortre had disintegrated they would get the mirror switched on, then Project Plutoshine would be complete. He and Nou were agreed: they had to tell someone. They had to tell everyone. Then Lucian knew what would happen. The Court of Planetary Protection would order a lockdown on the site. Mallory and her team would take over the analyses—probably Harbour, too, whatever kind of biologist he was. Nou's Whistlers would be picked apart for their secrets, probably literally. The grove and its light show would be sprawled across every glasspad on every inhabited world, and Plutoshine—his beloved Plutoshine—would be . . .

Lucian squeezed his eyes shut.

For a moment—just a moment—he let himself consider just doing nothing. Sat there by Clavius Harbour's side, listening to the ticks of the life support, his hand—he realised—still around his father's locket. Nou could keep her secret. Her creatures could stay free from probing examinations. Humanity could carry on as normal, never knowing otherwise.

'I wish you could talk, is all. Yeah. I suppose that's all I wanted to say. I wish you could talk.'

How he missed sunlight. Under the full blast of the Sun all was laid bare, and the Mercurian people took that way of life to heart. There could be no secrets on a world without shadows. Even now, even months after his sunsickness, such thoughts could still burn his mind like icy hands before fire, unable to bear the touch of what once was warmth and comfort.

The heart monitor continued to beep. The computerised tick continued to tick. It was some time before Lucian rose and, later that night, some time more before his pod carried him to the next morning.

He rose at the simulation of daybreak. Stan was already up in their kitchenette, toasting pikelets and setting the table with almond butter and damson jam, hair standing on end with sleep. Nou and Mallory arrived, already in silvery skinsuits like two soft-bodied creatures outside their exoskeletons, and the four set off to the aircraft hangar.

As they took off they saw Halley, or at least presumably it was Halley, out for her morning run; rising higher and they saw the xenobiologists' latest camp, some fifty kilometres west of the base, their great drill and platform dwarfed to inch-long toys.

They got ready, Lucian with his portable gauntlet set-up, Stan with his multiple glasspads and their sweeping lines of code, Nou helping where she could, Mallory . . . Lucian ducked his head to catch a surreptitious glance.

It had been a while since they had seen each other. At least, *seen* seen each other, not just in passing between dinner tables or down different rows at evening seminars. Nou, of course, had asked to come the moment she learned of the plan to monitor Jovortre from space, and when Percy turned down Stan's offer of the other seat on the Sadge, Lucian had sought out Mallory instead. As one last try.

Her hair was tied back and floating behind her as she moved, and so graceful were her movements that his glance became a gaze as the moment became a minute. Somewhere along the last nearly two years something had stalled between them. It was hard to say what, because if he knew he would have taken that problem straight to his workshop and fixed it up until it shone. Back when Nou was their shared project they had been a team: they had schemed together over coffee by day and, in no time at all, gin and tonic by night. To Lucian, their small charge had been an excuse to hang out, to learn what made each other laugh. To Mallory, though—he glanced up again and there she was, tucking stray side-fringe behind her ears; seeing his look this time; offering a bland smile—perhaps she had grown bored of them both.

'Everything well?' she asked, but she said it wrong: she said it quickly, politely, expecting a quick answer.

Lucian knew his lines.

'Mm? Oh, yeah, I'm good. Just thinking about . . . trying not to think about . . ah . . . Silvasaire. That's all.'

'I thought the code all checked out, didn't it?' Stan swung himself in one dexterous movement to their eye level, long-limbed in his skins. 'Didn't Gen give the all-clear? Nothing out of the ordinary this time?'

266

'Yeah, but there's a reason Gen's on his side of the table and we're on ours,' Lucian pointed out. Like the rest, he, too, wore his skinsuit, which called for rather more body confidence than he possessed. 'Sometimes each of us misses things. As Gen did with Silvasaire.'

'Could—Could—' Nou, drifting over, and Lucian still felt a beat of pride hearing that determined stammer, 'Could it happen—again?'

'You mean could my esteemed colleague Yolanda have hidden code to attack Jovortre, too?'

Mallory smiled at her, but Lucian caught the sadness in her eyes. *Guilt by association*, she had told him not long after the arrest. *Xenophobia for xenobiologists. I won't be surprised if no one looks at me the same.*

'Well, that's why we've got Gen checking the sequence ten thousand times a second.' Lucian shrugged as casually as he could. 'But it'd be sensible to be on our guard.'

'We'll stick with the plan, then?' Stan looked up at him.

'Yep!' Clapping his hands together, injecting some level of the party atmosphere no doubt already budding on the ground below. 'I'll rock the gauntlets and monitor its progress in real time against the sim. Stan, you keep the code up and rolling and read out any space oddities. Nou, you keep your binoculars on total lockdown once you catch sight of this thing. And Mallory'—Lucian stumbled for a moment; the old thrill of saying her name was still there—'would you stay next to comms ready to update them on anything that comes up?'

'You're in full battle mode, Lucian.' Mallory smiled. 'I don't think I've seen you as serious about anything that isn't your latest cross-stitching design.'

'Hey'—he pointed a finger at her—'one wrong thread and weeks of work is a goner, and that is nothing to joke about.'

Down on Pluto Halley, Harbour, Parkin, Parkin's engineers,

and Halley's terraformers would all be assembled in the control room on standby for the countdown initiation. Jovortre's trajectory for atmospheric entry was all computationally calculated and cross-checked, then meticulously translated into code and executed directly by the asteroid's thrusters. The correct sequence of firing the thrusters for course correction—called burns—had all been successfully completed months prior, and telemetry returned by its onboard computer showed this course was still perfect to several sub-degree orders. The disintegration of Plutoshine's last gard was good to go.

And who, exactly, was Jovortre? Lucian's guess was as good as any. Gard Protector Jovortre was master of the gards—Jovortre was the inventor of trans-dimensional travel—Jovortre was a man, a being in the shape of a man, a formless, eldritch consciousness who existed at untold points in space and time. Jovortre was Hartdegen's greatest mystery, one she had remained vigilantly reticent about until her end.

It was Nou who saw it first. Nou with her binoculars, and with her quiet concentration, and with a chirrup of excitement.

'Here! *There!*'

The ship erupted in response.

'You've got it? You see it?' Lucian, hovering before his portable triangulators, gauntlets taut across his wrists.

'Where? Point to it!' Mallory, swinging herself over, grabbing a pair herself.

'Visual confirmed!' Stan, at his station, myriad glasspad screens firing update after update. 'AOCS is saying we're still on for an eleven forty-nine atmospheric entry. The signal's been strong the whole time, too—the Silvasaire resonance was well under way by this point.'

'So we're out of the uncertainty zone?' Mallory looked from Lucian to his student.

Stan looked at Lucian.

Lucian looked at his simulation. Held in place by his outstretched hands was Jovortre: tholin-red, split into two distinct lobes—a contact binary—strangely smoothed but for the occasional chain of endogenic sublimation pits. There was no unusual outgassing; no fluctuations in thruster output; no wobbling deviation from its intended beeline. The simulation hadn't so much as tugged at his hands: it was stable.

He hesitated. 'Well . . .' he began.

He felt the tug the exact moment he heard Nou's cry.

'It's—It's—*moving*—' came her gasp—right before the simulated Jovortre was dragged from his grasp and he was hurled off balance.

'The trajectory!' Stan exclaimed. 'The ETA, the angle of entry, they've all . . . They're recalculating . . . They're not settling!'

Lucian got a grip on a railing and propelled himself to where his simulation was careering wildly from boundary to boundary of the triangulators.

'Right'—in a snap he had his hair wound up—'the resonance is back, and it's worse, and we'd better get it under control before our aerobraking asteroid becomes a lithobraking one.' He seized Jovortre between his gauntlets once more. 'Stan, bring up the code for the thrusters.'

'What do you mean, *lithobraking*?' Mallory had pulled herself to his side, her eyes wide. 'What's happening? Tell me fast.'

'*Aero*, air—*litho*, ground.' Lucian tried to say the words calmly but each one attached itself to the thud of a heartbeat. 'Should be *cryo*, I suppose. Ice-brake.' He turned to look her in the eye. 'Jovortre has to skid through the atmosphere at a very specific angle, otherwise it will just pierce straight through. Like Chicxulub did.'

'Chic—?'

'The impactor that saw to the dinosaurs.'

'Getting the code.' Stan, voice firm as a grip. 'Can we shut off two of the thrusters and power up the other, make it change direction?'

'We could—could—' Nou was saying on repeat, the words coming round and around again like a pulsar.

'Use the gauntlets!' Mallory pushed herself in the direction of the dashboard. 'You controlled Silvasaire last time.'

'—could—could—' Nou, almost crying with frustration.

'It's got too much momentum, there's nothing to slow it down!' Lucian had the gard gripped in one hand, his other racing through Stan's code projected by its side. 'And it's too close now, I couldn't shift it enough to escape Pluto's radius. Stan, did you lock down this subsection?'

'No! Why would I do that?'

'It's . . .' Lucian bit down the coldness at the base of his throat. 'It's not letting me alter the sequence. It's read-only.'

'Read . . . ?'

'That's for every user. It's requesting some kind of master code.' It took Lucian a moment to place the coolness in his palms as the outbreak of sweat. 'I'll keep . . . I can try backtracking into the creator source . . . Stan, can you bring up my workbench remotely, maybe if I try from the original router . . .'

'Halley's phoning in,' called Mallory from the dashboard. 'What do I tell her?'

'Could we somehow *deflect* it?' Stan was rifling through his code.

Nou propelled herself to Lucian's side with enough force to bounce off the wall behind him.

'*Nix!*' she cried. 'Nix—not Nix . . . The other—other—St—St—'

Lucian's eyes widened as he translated her.

'Styx!' His body fizzed right through to his fingertips as the revelation bolted down every limb. 'Of *course*, Styx!'

'Lucian!' Mallory's voice. 'Halley needs you to talk to her *right now.*'

'What, Styx, what?' Stan was pulling himself over with a handrail.

'Stan,' Lucian turned to him. 'I need you to bring up Styx's orbit for me right now, and I need you to get Jovortre's projected path up as well.'

Stan's eyes bulged with understanding. 'Give me two minutes.'

Lucian turned to their smallest member.

'Nou, keep watch on the binoculars just on the wildest off chance our gard gets back to normal, OK?'

Nou retook her position with a look of utmost determination as he clapped her on the back.

'Mallory'—he turned to her—'tell Halley we're going to Styx. We don't have time to wait and see if the code lets us in. We might be able to stop Jovortre another way.'

'What other way?' Mallory's head spun so fast her plait came around and slapped her across the cheek. 'You said you can't use the gauntlets, you can't slow it, can't stop it—'

'I didn't say we can't stop it. Right now Jovortre is too close. Even if we could tweak its propellant it won't clear Pluto's radius. But . . .' He slung himself into the pilot's seat. 'If we can't get Jovortre to move itself, it's possible that . . . we might just . . . maybe we can get something else to do it for us.'

'*What?*' She grabbed him by the shoulder as he set both hands on the joysticks. 'What do I tell Halley? What are we doing?'

Stan called, 'Styx and Jovortre are going to get within max two thousand kilometres of each other if Jovortre's trajectory holds steady.' Damn, the kid was fast. 'It's set to impact east Cthulhu Regio for the moment, but I'll let you know if that changes.'

'Great, perfect!' Lucian pulled the engines out of stasis. 'We can do that, that's doable . . .'

271

'I'll get Parkin on the line, get the reactor specs.'

'That's my man.' He turned to Mallory, who was dragging herself into the co-pilot seat. 'Put Halley on speaker. She's not going to like this.'

'I heard the whole thing, kid,' said the driest voice known to humanity from overhead. 'Mallory was way ahead of you.'

'Halley!'

Funny old world, when it's the sudden, disembodied appearance of your old mentor that sets off your mind's high-intensity-threat-leitmotif, more than the asteroid thundering your way at fifty kilometres per second.

'Look'—dry mouth, thoughts bashing into one another in multi-word pile-ups—'we've got forty minutes until this thing hits Pluto one way or another . . .'

'Just put it in plain language so we've got you on record when someone gets arrested for this.'

'We can't alter the thrusters on Jovortre,' Lucian told her, turning the ship on its way. 'I don't know why. And I'm going to put it right here on your record that I can only say they've been tampered with. Like Silvasaire. Like Styx. If we can't get back into Jovortre it's going to create a crater the size of Wales uncomfortably close to Stern in'—he checked—'thirty-eight minutes. I can't say for sure it's not going to hit Stern, either.'

Estimated time of arrival to Styx: eleven minutes. He winced to himself. This whole thing was going to be close.

'But if I can get us to Styx,' he continued, 'if we can get the fusion reactor to . . . to . . .' He couldn't say *meltdown*; what was this, a bad film? 'If I can get it to act like a thruster for Styx,' he settled, 'then there's a chance we can make it knock our gard off course.'

'Lucian!'

The panicked voice made him turn.

'It's—' Nou was fighting to say, 'it's not—it's moving—'

Jovortre's trajectory was changing again. Lucian was out of his chair as fast as his arms could pull him free.

'Mallory—take over—talk to Halley—'

'It sped up,' Nou gasped. 'I can't—keep hold of it—'

She sounded just like him when she talked. What an absurdly incongruous observation to make—but now he had noticed it was unmistakable: the slight exaggeration of the *o* sounds; something intangible in the twang of the sentence ends that was pure Mercurian.

Lucian mentally shook himself to sense. How far had Jovortre deviated? What was the estimated time of arrival now? Diving past Nou, he brought up a screen and ransacked through the code.

'Got it!' Stan, not triumphant, but with success. 'If we blow the plant we get enough velocity and then some to intercept Jovortre. We can get them both straight out of the Pluto system with no problem, and we've got a thirty-one-minute window to do it.'

Scrolling, scrolling. *There.* Pausing. Reading.

'Stan'—swallowing—'would you run that calculation again? This time with a Jovortre to Pluto ETA not in thirty-eight minutes, but twenty-four?'

Stan looked up at him. He wasted only half a second to do so, but it felt like a dozen.

Five minutes to Styx. Five minutes to get inside and figure out how the heck to destroy a fail-safe nuclear fusion reactor. Five minutes to get the absolute flipping Earth as far away from Styx as possible. Five minutes for Styx to reach Jovortre and blast the pair of them on a one-way ticket to interstellar space. Five minutes to spare in case any of those took longer than five minutes.

He'd look good when he went grey over this, Lucian promised himself. It went with the learned scholar look.

273

He heard himself speak as though reading from a book.

'We've got to go. *Now*. Mallory, ignite the fusion drive.'

'This thing has a *fusion drive*?'

'Left panel under the auto-homer, touch the dial image with your finger and spin it counter-clockwise. It's just a tiny one.' Without even thinking, his hand was in his hair only to find it already tied. He pulled himself across the ship to the airlock—then, gripped by a kind of momentary mania, recited straight out of a Hartdegen: 'Keep on target at full speed!'

The fusion drive kicked in with a spasm of vibration, then anything and anyone not fastened down was sucked to the back of the ship. Lucian screwed his eyes shut in time for the crack of his skull on the windowpane, Stan pinned beside him like a taxidermised butterfly.

Somewhere a female voice was crying out, more likely Mallory than Nou, but Lucian could no more call to her than he could raise a finger: on top of his chest was the whole Earth. He couldn't see: his eyeballs were being thumbed to the back of his skull, his vision vignetting to a tunnel as his corneas warped.

Air returned and filled him to bursting as the acceleration ended. Blood burned down his frozen fingertips enough to prick tears. He and Stan drifted free, each clutching their chest.

'Everyone OK?' Lucian gasped. 'Nou?' Tugging himself over, legs kicking behind as though to swim. 'Nou, hey, you're OK? A little bumped, OK, that's fine . . .'

There, out of the window, was Styx. Not Styx the minor gap in the stars, but Styx the size of a mountain. They had jumped right in front of it; the moon's deep-red craters filled the cockpit's windscreens.

And right there, out of the window, was the mooring line, the single strand of hair connecting the reactor to Condatis Crater.

Lucian drew his watch before his face: they were ten seconds into his *blow up Styx* time.

'I'll be right back.'

He clipped on his helmet as he stowed into the Sadge's slim airlock—just on the chance the docking would go wrong, or the pressurisation monitors were faulty, or who knew what else. He was not a man either self-absorbed or fanciful enough for paranoia, but it was fair to say he was having something of an off day.

'Just wait here, OK?' Catching Stan's eyes, catching Nou's eyes, holding them, promising them. 'Be two seconds.'

The airlock closed; the Styx–Sadge docking clicked home; the adaptor trilled and whirred into action. With no air to pump in or out, Lucian was soon free to leap aboard. White padded corridors, bright spotlights, silvered handrails to propel himself down with both arms . . .

But where exactly was he heading? To the big red button marked *Self-destruct*?

All at once, Lucian felt himself grow cold in places where he knew his thermocirculation was functioning just fine.

'Easy, now.' The murmur was down the radio waves before he registered he had spoken aloud. But the spreading coldness did not stop. 'Easy, easy, easy . . .'

Doesn't it all sound so plausible when you're out in your spaceship with your mates? I'll just land on this moon, snip the blue wire or the red wire, save the world, wait five years until they make a film out of my autobiography . . .

In the control room now, and there was Parkin in his ear, the scene reversed to all that time long ago when it was Parkin and Halley here in this room, and Lucian outside in their ears.

'The only thing that comes to mind is somehow distorting the magnetic fields, then focusing the resulting plasma anomaly on to one side of the torus,' Parkin was saying, his deep,

275

slow voice switched for once into one deep and slightly faster. 'But . . . ah!' There was a bang like a hand slapped on a table. 'We have fail-safes for each series of fail-safes written into the very *foundations* of this machine! By sheer necessity, a fusion reactor is the most over-engineered object of creation in the known universe!'

Lucian's five minutes were leaking through his fingers like cupped water. In desperation he threw his eyes over each touch-glass panel—but he was an engineer—on to the next—his job was to *build things*—back to the first—his job was to *fix* things—scrabbling for any scrap of inspiration—he'd once been here to *fix* this station, and he'd been doing a good job until the moment it blew right up in his face—backlit screens of controls in blue and red and green . . .

He halted in his tracks. Stood there blinking in the electric glow.

He was an engineer. He'd once been here to fix things. And now the scene was in reverse.

'Lucian!' Stan's voice over the comms. 'I think I've got it. If you can destabilise the magnetic fields you can get the whole toroidal unit to—'

'Stan, it's OK!' Lucian was already propelling himself back down the corridor as fast as his arms could swing him. 'Get the ship back, OK? *Get it back* and get it out of your projected trajectory for Styx.' He reached the gear room, grabbed what he was after, clipped them to his belt, then raced onwards to the airlock. 'I'm going outside and I'm going to do this as fast as I can, but if our blow-up-Styx five minutes are up then this is going to eat into our get-the-heck-away-from-Styx time, so I need you guys to do that in parallel to me blowing up this reactor, OK?'

There was a half-second beat before Stan said something Lucian never thought he was capable of.

'Oh *shit!*' The young scientist pulled himself together. 'OK. OK. Tell me what you need. Mallory will move the ship. We'll rendezvous with you after you've . . . you've . . .'

'Argon pipes.'

Lucian was in the airlock, tapping his toes inside his boots, tapping his fingers on the railings, tapping to the second-by-wasted-second countdown to depressurisation. Eighteen minutes, seven seconds to go, his wrist-pad flashed. How bad could opening the door be at this stage? There were only thirty seconds to go. No, no, his mum always told him, you open an airlock early and you end your life early . . .

His *mum*. His sisters. He'd left a video for them this morning; it wouldn't even have arrived yet. If he didn't come back they would be waiting for news, waiting as normal, thinking nothing was amiss.

The airlock was clear. Spinning the handle loose, pressing forward . . . straight into the raw, open space between spaces.

'Do you remember, Stan?' Leaping into it, fearless along his tether, the lamp-like orb of Pluto there above, then gone with the turn of his head. 'Remember the day the simulation caught fire, so we flew up here?'

Lucian did. Lucian remembered the exact pipe that had malfunctioned. The one that had started spewing coolant as ice crystals into space at a rate of two cubic metres per minute. The one that—if the malfunction was severe enough—turned his simulation into a fireball.

Adrenaline, Lucian had the rush of coherency to think, was to him as bathtubs were to Archimedes. He pulled himself further down the cord connecting the station to the crater and Stan was saying something—Mallory was saying something—Halley, Parkin, even Nou—but their cries and orders and pleading were only background ambience to the sharpest focus Lucian thought he had ever felt in his life.

He needed level 505. He was at 233. And he had—a glance—fifteen minutes, twenty-seven seconds until it was too late to try.

'Stan, exactly how long will it take Styx to reach Jovortre at closest approach?'

Level 278.

'Halley, can you get up Styx's rotation and tell me how long I'll have facing the exact right way?'

Level 359.

'Parkin, could you get up the blueprints and tell me how long the tokamak can hold without its coolant?'

Time, time, time. Lucian glanced at his wrist-pad; thirteen minutes, forty seconds. It must be nearly 11 a.m. Nearly biscuit o'clock. More to the point, his five-minutes-to-blow-up-Styx were ancient history and he was now halfway into his get-the-heck-as-far-away-from-Styx time. That extra-five-minutes-in-case-anything-goes-wrong time was going to be a necessity.

Level 490 . . . 502 . . . *Got it.*

Lucian pulled himself level with the pipe and whipped out a powersaw from his utility belt. The pipe was as thick as his outstretched arms, seamlessly welded, fortified and refortified after the sabotage so long ago.

'Lucian!' Stan was first, naturally. 'If the station blows at full power and intersects Jovortre at the planned angle of seventy-two degrees due south-west'—he gasped in a breath—'they'll collide two minutes, forty-six seconds after ignition.'

Some good news! That gave him one minute, fourteen seconds more than calculated. The covering panel came loose; he chucked it over his shoulder.

'Lucian'—Halley, a beat behind, tones clipped—'there's some leeway with the angle you can use to intercept Jovortre, given their masses, so your window to blow this thing is open for five minutes, nine seconds.'

Lucian checked: he had ten minutes, fourteen seconds until Jovortre reached Pluto. An iota of the tension stiffening his limbs let up. He might actually be able to make this.

'When does that window open?'

The cord's interior was laid bare before him, not so much wires to snip as gargantuan arteries, the largest as thick as his waist. He could have sabotaged the pipe anywhere, but right here was that pre-existing weakness. Now where was it exactly?

'Halley?' he called; she hadn't answered. Maybe he'd been concentrating so hard he'd blocked her out.

'Lucian.'

Just that word. She spoke it tonelessly, as though exhausted.

'That's right now. You've got four minutes, fifty-seven seconds until the window closes.'

Lucian felt his world physically contract. In his half-second of mental processing there were no thoughts, no consideration whether to swear, to cleverly figure out some loophole. He pressed his saw against the argon pipe, right along its scar, and made sparks fly with the perfect focus of a dream.

'Parkin, talk to me. Last piece of the puzzle. If I cut this thing in two, how long do I have till it blows?'

'Oh, so you're not actively suicidal, then?' Halley, incisive, an octave higher than usual. 'You'll have to excuse us if that didn't appear immediately apparent.'

'Am I *chuff*, I've got so much to live for!' Lucian was getting a little breathless now; the adrenaline curdling to something like fear, or whatever this affliction was that shook his hands and dried his mouth. 'They're bringing out a Dignity's greatest hits compilation next week and there's going to be a livestreamed gig, it's their twentieth anniversary . . .'

'Lucian.' Parkin, finally. 'You will have one minute to move once you cut it. I can't get the timing more accurate than that— too much comes down to the toroidal plasma fluid dynamics—I would need to model it—but that is the rough figure.'

Lucian glanced at his wrist-pad amid the flaring, floating sparks and did the maths. His window to blow up Styx closed in three minutes, thirty-two seconds. If the reactor took one minute to blow once he shut off the argon, that cut his time down by one minute. Meaning he had two minutes, thirty-two seconds to cut this pipe.

The sparks spat around him like fireworks in a snow globe, little stars within arm's reach for split seconds before quenching and vanishing. His saw met a loss of resistance—he was through the wall, he was inside the pipe—before mounting again, slowing his progress as he cut his way to the other side. How long? Glancing at the time. One minute, fifty-eight seconds.

Once on the other side he pulled out, shifted the saw a hand's breadth, then started again. He would cut the chunk out—the argon would freeze solid—the reactor would lose its coolant—*boom*. Straight-talking physics.

(One minute, twenty-five seconds.)

He pressed harder and harder into the pipe, one hand anchoring him in place. He'd taken more than a minute to saw the first section; he had to be . . . Had to be . . .

(One minute, two seconds.)

Would they name the crater after him if he died trying to stop it?

(Fifty seconds.)

His saw lost resistance, already inside the pipe.

(Forty seconds.)

'Lucian!'

(Thirty seconds.)

'I know, I can do this!' he called. 'I'm almost there, I can make it!'

(Twenty seconds.)

'No, Lu—cian'—that was Nou—'behind you!'

(Ten seconds.)

Resistance mounting. He was in the final wall. Fingers convulsing with cramp. He could make it . . .

(Five seconds.)

He was through! Chucking the saw away—he'd buy the base a new one—grabbing the pipe chunk with both hands—(two seconds)—tearing it free—molten argon flash-freezing in place too fast to change shape—solid-white like a freezer in need of defrosting . . .

He saw it all in under a second before he unhooked his tether, pressed his feet against the pipe, and backflipped from the tower straight into open space. Soaring, now spinning, now tumbling out of control—no thought for where he was heading beside what he was leaving—breath gasping, ragged, loud enough to hurt—he would never get far enough—it would be over fast—stars streaking—he had so much to *do*—Pluto whirling overhead, a lighthouse flash—he didn't want it to end . . .

He had a second to register an object, gone then back in the next revolution—bigger now—closer—cutting off the wheeling stars—before he cracked straight into it. Bouncing, tumbling again, but the object drew alongside him—*the Sadge drew alongside him*—and Lucian was grabbed by an arm and swept to a stop and pulled inside by a hand, an arm, a face— Stan's face, disembodied in his helmet, grimacing with effort. Lucian grabbed him back, scrabbling at all sides, so fired up he barely knew left from right, as the door sealed and the hiss of air filled his ears the same moment as the voices:

'Have we got him?' Mallory.

'Have you got him!' Halley.

'We've got him!' Stan.

'You've got me!' Lucian yelled. 'Now for Earth's sake, *go!*'

The rush of speed shoved him into the airlock walls and smacked his head either side of his helmet. Parkin had said about a minute, but what was an order of magnitude among friends? As the airlock repressurised and as he burst inside the ship, there was Styx in the rear window, already so small it could barely be distinguished between the stars, and there was Nou strung around his middle and Stan hanging off his shoulders, both clutching him so hard he'd have been pummelled silly in his normal knitwear, and why was Styx not on fire? Why was Styx not a comet? Surely a minute had passed . . .

The flash was so bright he saw it all, even through eyelids that screwed instantly shut. Survival instinct kicked in the next moment: he threw himself and his companions to the floor, covering Nou's and Stan's faces beneath his body, shielding his own around the bubble of his helmet.

The blindness was over as soon as it came: just like that, Styx was gone. Mallory cut the engine and the four of them clambered to their feet, then flung themselves to the windows.

A hundred kilometres away, now two hundred, Styx was a star blazing across the crescent moon of Pluto. Four hundred kilometres away, now three hundred, Jovortre was straight in its path.

And what could be made out of Jovortre? No one in the Sadge was close enough to see its scarlet-flecked coat; its jagged, contorted, cratered bulk; its engines converting raw ice to ammonia gas that hissed behind it in a discrete white finger, as though a disembodied hand was powering it inexorably onwards.

But no one in the Sadge, and no one in Stern in the darkness below, could miss it when the two collided.

It was a sight straight from the birth of the Solar System. It was an event life forms had never evolved to process: one that meant death, and the end of evolution. When the asteroids collided most of their matter converted instantly to energy, light and heat, in an explosion that knifed down the atmosphere and burned itself on to the retinas of all witnesses. A fan of debris scorched in the wake of the two wrestling titans, each ripping chunks off the other the size of mountains that spat and skittered and effervesced, all the while growing smaller, smaller, dimmer, dimmer, wrapping around the planet, now fully encircling it, now cutting across the equator before clearing its second lap then, finally, breaking up and scattering like bonfire sparks caught in the wind.

Lucian, Mallory, Stan, and Nou, gripped in place at the windows, bodies free-floating behind them, were silent. Lime-green coronae across their visions rendered them as blind as they were dumbstruck. For a moment it was all any of them could do to blink.

'Well,' Lucian heard himself say, 'I suppose I owe you all a new moon.'

Phase 4

Interlude 4

Nou had sat down and told Lucian of the day of the accident. She had told him of Edmund's presence; of her father's incapacitation; of the Whistlers' behaviour.

That was as far as Nou told him. But that was not where the story ended.

Edmund has their father over his shoulder. The Whistlers let him go—they dissipated into the ice the moment he dropped in slow motion to the ground—but Nou can't tell if her father is conscious, is breathing, is alive. His suit lights are off—darkness inside as much as out, an empty shell. She doesn't know what they have done to him. She can't draw a full breath, hiccuping in air as fast and as shallow as her pulse, too scared to ask.

Edmund runs with their father over his shoulder through the labyrinth of cracks that lead to the surface. Nou runs behind, one hand feeling in the dark, one hand clasped to the side of her helmet as though to clamp it across her mouth or wipe her streaming eyes.

Neither speaks. The journey up is full of sharp shadows, blinding flashes of helmet-light against ice. Nou keeps trying to say something but every time she opens her mouth her chest starts spasming. Two sets of breath puncture the otherwise silence: Edmund's deep, cyclic, steady; each of hers the hitch of a swallowed sob. But even straining to hear, Nou cannot make out a third. She stumbles and bashes and scrapes her way up, limbs aching and throbbing to keep up with her brother's tireless sprint.

They burst onto the surface. The return of space beyond her hands, and light beyond her torch, gives knee-weakening relief that neither wastes time to savour. As Edmund lays their father down, Nou calls home on every frequency she knows.

'*Help!*' she cries, her voice breaking. Instinctively she looks towards the horizon as she does it, towards home, as though the words will carry. 'Help us, please—my dad's hurt—'

'Nou,' Edmund says.

'Is anybody there, *help*—!'

'*Nou.*'

Nou stops. Edmund is on the ground, leaning over their father's darkened suit. While she almost convulses with adrenaline, her brother sits as still as the body.

'There're no signs,' he says calmly. 'There's no heartbeat. The suit is offline.'

Edmund's expression makes no sense. While Nou can't hold herself still enough to concentrate, Edmund's eyes blaze like morning stars. They blaze with something unplaceable, like triumph. For a moment, they share a silence.

Then both hear it together. The rasp of breath. A third breath.

The lights of Clavius Harbour's suit flicker on. Off. On. Edmund whirls his head around. Blue-white light floods the face of their father. The gasping face. The contorted face. The silently screaming face.

Then no longer silent.

Over Nou's radio comes another sound:

'*crrrrk . . . Nou Harbour, we read you, this is Vasily Voronov at Stern Base. Can you tell me what's happening?*'

In no time the ice is a whirlwind of action. Nou stands to one side, forgotten, as the medics and Edmund lift the body into a ship that hovers rather than lands, a ship that within minutes of arriving is up again with acceleration enough to knock them off their feet. Nou pushes herself into the least occupied corner and grips the handholds, wishing she could stop staring, wishing she could pretend it is someone's hand she holds, wishing she had never showed them, that she had got up that morning and gone skating on Alcyonia Lacus with Allie and the other children . . .

They rush her father away the moment Stern's airlock stabilises, still in suits, others joining in work clothes, all asking questions, all shouting unfamiliar words in medical short-term, the stretcher parting the crowd as the bow of a ship parts the waves. Edmund sweeps away with them, balaclava tugged off, and Nou takes one step to start after him—but as he turns, something in the whites of his eyes and the wildness of his disarranged hair stops her where she stands.

Over his shoulder he points a finger at her.

'*Go to your room and stay there.*'

In seconds he is carried away by the tide and Nou can't help herself: she throws her face in her hands and bursts into tears. It takes a good thirty seconds to bring herself under control. When she does she scrubs her face clean, and there is resolve set in her eyes.

The crowds have thinned now. She hasn't been ignored: Vasily asked what happened and checked she was OK, but once it was clear she was unhurt all attention shifted to their valiant leader. No one is aware of her now. No one would notice if she were to slip away.

She crosses the room to the airlock. Slips inside. Clips her helmet back on. Each thud of her heart presses her determination home.

Out she leaps into the night. If she pushes, she can be at the Promontorium in thirty minutes. She pays no heed to the gelatinous tremble of her legs as she runs, nor the gauge of her oxygen tanks as it ticks, ticks lower with each footfall.

Edmund backs away through the medical bay door and holds himself very still. The corridor is empty: anyone who can be of use is inside, shouting instructions, rushing for equipment, following the doctor's curt orders. All sound, movement and coherent thought centre upon that room.

Pressure against his back—a wall. The sweat at his temples has dried cold but his limbs won't stop shaking. His heart still thinks his body is running.

Clavius Harbour isn't dead. The suit was dead but the body wasn't; Edmund ran with him, holding the illusion of urgency, when in truth he ran for joy. *He was dead. The suit was dead.* Until it wasn't. Until he wasn't. Until Nou broadcast their location to every soul within a billion-mile radius, and the rescue teams came.

Edmund eases his shaking knuckles between his teeth and bites, hard.

He should have severed the pipes deeper. There had been time: he had been alone in the dressing room. Or could he not have stumbled in the passage up? *Why*—he bit harder with each thought—had he not wrenched the loosened pipe free?

Or perhaps he didn't have it in him after all? Did he not have the courage to take a life when the moment came, even knowing the consequences of inaction?

He had had his logic. Killing Clavius Harbour was not an evil: to stand by and let him live was. To let him live would be to accept the bruises never visible on his sister's heart; a heart looking only for love from the man who was supposed to protect her. It would be to deal those bruises himself.

The issue with logic, though, was how easily the head could accept it. The issue was to assume the rest of the body had, too. And now he was living the consequence.

He could have delayed Nou calling the base. That much was blindingly clear in hindsight. They were too close to the entrance—how could he have not thought it through? Regardless of Clavius's fate, there would be an investigation—the site would be upturned—there would be questions—if the grove was found . . .

290

Edmund feels his pupils dilate in urgent, seizing dread.

If the grove was found.

Clavius's intentions were clear for a decade, kept between the two of them: if we find life we hide it, or destroy it. Humanity doesn't need another Europa, another Enceladus, but our people need a Pluto. We keep Plutoshine going. Whatever it takes.

'Is he stable—?'

'. . . looks like he's stabilising . . .'

'. . . stable heart rate, pulse holding steady . . .'

'. . . breathing stabilising . . .'

That one word, jumping out of the maelstrom.

'He's stable. Mr Harbour, sir, can you hear me?'

Edmund's feet stride of their own accord as his mind races to catch up. Before he knows what he's doing—before he knows what he will do—he is in his office. Packing items in his suit's pack; he can't say what he will reach for next until his hands are doing it, but he and Clavius prepared for this eventuality. His hands find all they need. Scant minutes later he is at the −3 airlock, the deserted back door he uses each day for running, and he is slipping unnoticed inside. Barely has the chamber purged when he is sprinting off into the night.

Nou is catching her breath at the edge of the grove. She barely waits for the Whistlers to rouse, lighting the chamber to the tips of its great domed ceiling, before running into its centre.

Nou Harbour.

It is not a word Nou hears, even inside her head. The Whistlers have no need for language: they have no need for that intermediary, that translation of meaning from one mind to another. Not when they can bypass mouths or hands or facial expressions all together and deliver comprehension directly. It is the creatures' innermost secret, one Nou was holding out to share—bursting to share—just waiting for the right moment.

The Whistlers go on.

You are back.

It is not words Nou hears, even inside her head, but she *understands*. The running monologue humans narrate their lives with is by no means the foundation of thought: you know you are hungry before you can think the sentence *I'm starving*; you remember where your keys are before you can think *I left them in the kitchen*. So it is with the Whistlers, sweeping aside gesture and spoken word, tapping into the one truly universal language of sentient beings: that of consciousness itself.

It took her months to hold back the urge to nod or speak in response; even training herself out of thinking in sentences took its own months. Nou quiets her mind as she conjures up her response: a clear affirmative only in meaning, wordless both inside and out.

At once the tallest of the tree-like columns, whose smoothed surface shines as though in silver moonlight, begins to move. There is nothing slow or subtle in this: the great pillar bends itself fluidly in half as though made of wire. Within seconds its towering height halves as it draws itself before Nou, just above head height, so its featureless crest is at something like an adult's eye level.

You should not have come, Tag conveys. In his meaning, clear as reading a tone of voice, there is uneasiness.

I needed to, Nou tells him, and were anyone to enter now they might scarcely notice her: one sapling among a ring of giants. *My dad is hurt. I need to know . . .*

But what she needs to know, she cannot formulate. She isn't sure herself. Tag uses the moment of quiet—the Whistlers never interrupt—to correct her.

You should not have come at all. It was a mistake to bring your family. We saw them inside you. We thought they were benevolent. But you are only a juvenile—your perceptions of them are incomplete.

Nou absorbs this in silence—no words or voices in her head, just new information. She cannot choose when to respond, just as she

292

cannot control her thoughts; she cannot hide the question that rises within her.

Did you mean to hurt him?

Nou looks at her feet. She hadn't meant to ask it like that—accusatorially. But, of course, the Whistlers have understood her intentions: her unease is as clear to them as the question itself. Deception is impossible here.

You shouldn't have come, Tag conveys again, and were he able to move—were he anything like her father, Nou thinks—he would be pacing this cavern.

We are nothing like your father.

The meaning is sharp as a spoken word across Nou's mind. Never before has Nou had reason to fear Tag and the other Whistlers—nor does she now. And yet, creeping up her spine, pooling cold sweat in her gloved palms, something starts to feel deeply wrong.

We looked inside your kin, Tag speaks into her mind again, *and we did not see peace. We did not see co-operation.*

No. Nou is shaking her head. A soft *beep* from somewhere makes her jump, but it is only something on her suit. *My dad's been searching for native life for years—*

We are not native.

But Nou is frowning now, thinking hard.

He wanted to make sure nothing would get hurt by his plan.

You are almost right—Nou looks back up into the featureless crown of her friend—*Clavius Harbour did not want anything to hurt his plans.*

Is that why you hurt him?

Movement to one side jerks her limbs in alarm; another Whistler is stirring. Under the wan light she sees its magnificent ice-blue body twist. Then, all about the chamber the rest stir, too. Chrysoprase-green, steel-grey, faintest teal, the indigo of the horizon . . . Nou's head swivels from side to side as the giants awaken. This has never happened before; it is like watching the spike-shaped mountains of Tartarus Dorsa start talking to each other.

293

What's happening?

You must understand, Nou Harbour, that violence of any kind is not in our nature. Somehow Nou knows it is still Tag inside her head, even as the others continue to twist on the spot like sequoias in a gale. *Violence to our kind is as abominable as murder appears to yours—which is a concept scarcely within our ability to understand. How could we ever end the life of another, when we are one? You who walk singularly seem unfettered by such notions. We saw so in Clavius Harbour today, and we could not stand by.*

The cavern is writhing with movement now, and glancing to her sides Nou can make out the Whistlers rocking back and forth, bulging the ice that encloses their bases, cracks rifting apart under the strain.

We cannot stay, Nou Harbour. You must understand.

No. Nou thinks the thought as much as feels it. A rush shoots along her limbs and she finds her face moving from Whistler to Whistler, from blankness into blankness. *No.*

We sought synergy. We sought mutual curiosity, and benevolence, and wonder. These we have not received.

Let me bring them back. Nou's heart is beating very fast. *I'll bring them again and we can all talk. I can teach them to talk to you. Let me teach them—*

But could you teach them to listen?

Pure red floods the chamber and everything in it. If Nou were to look at her feet, she would see the life forms swirling below her like kelp in a sea storm, dragged back and forth with the columns' writhing. Now only Tag remains motionless.

I can teach him. Nou barely breathes. *My brother can, too. We'll all come back . . . Please . . .*

We will come back. We will try once more—and here Nou cannot translate their exact meaning—*generation*, or *lifetime*—a word that to them denotes some significant length of time—*but it is not now.*

294

At this, as though by some signal, the five other columns begin moving as one. They curl themselves back, away from Nou, out to the chamber walls, where they bow together behind Tag. Some ten metres above the floor they join together like knotting string—they twine together, still attached to the ground—then, seamlessly, soundlessly, the five columns begin to disappear into the base of the wall.

Nou lets out a strangled cry.

'No! Wait!'—*Wait! You can't leave!*—'Please!'

Goodbye, Nou Harbour.

No! She stumbles forward—her feet are numbed, her legs leaden—as Tag, too, begins to turn. Her father's empty, unconscious face swims before her eyes—*Don't leave me!*—then the alien coldness of her brother today—*Don't leave me, too!*

But the crown of Tag's great crest has bent to disappear after the rest, and as he does the columns uproot themselves seemingly as one. Adrenaline jerks Nou's eyes between each slender limb slipping out of the fractured ice, not silver, not blue, not green, but red, red, red . . .

Her hands are on the empty ice—she must have fallen—and her arms tremble as she pushes herself to her feet, feet that already move with dreamlike heaviness after them. If her body goes slowly her mind is the opposite, shot through with a power overload. Thoughts burst and spark as her face turns feverishly, her eyes jerking from the base of each column, now knotted together, now vanishing like tentacles into the wall. The creatures that produce the lights are following them—or part of them?—and now the cavern grows darker, red fading to black.

Nou doesn't think. She runs after them.

Chapter 18

Lucian looked up as Nou entered the control room.

'Hey,' he said warmly, setting down the battered book he was reading. 'All excited for tonight? Got your viewing spot sorted?'

By *tonight* he meant the moment they finally turned on the mirror, and by *view* he meant sunrise. Just the very word in Nou's head was like watching golden light pour over the horizon.

Encouraged, she came inside with a nod.

If the terraformers' workshop was a classroom, their control room was the staffroom: a place Nou had never needed to be told was off-limits, and a place she had never been inside before. The mission operations centre made a kind of crescent moon around the Heart-facing front of the base. Looking across it were sweeping touchscreen panels, some flashing, some steady, others switching from electric blue to red to green and back again.

It was at one of these panels that Lucian sat, the mirror unfolding sequence looping on one of the screens. He already wore his hair tied back, ready for business.

Nou pulled herself into the swivel chair beside him. She spoke slowly to disguise the pauses between each word; in the months since she had found her voice, the stammer had refused to budge.

'They said—there's a new plan?'

'Yeah. We're tightening security.' Lucian tried for his usual beam but forgot to include his eyes. 'Halley suggested we seal off the code and control the mirror manually'—he pointed sky-wards—'from up there.'

'From space?'

'Mm.' Lucian nodded somewhat regretfully. 'It's possible there was a malware injection—a bug, a virus—for someone to get to Jovortre. You know, like it was hacked or something. Or maybe Moreno sabotaged the code in advance. Either way, can't be too careful. There's a little module attached to it up there, a super-cosy one-person space station you can operate it manually from, with Gen's help. Never thought I'd actually use it. Only added it for a funding loophole . . .'

He motioned around the empty room.

'We'll get all the team stationed in here to monitor the switch-on from every angle we've got, but Halley will be in full control. I'd have gone,' he added, 'but our chief Sunbringer says up there's the most dangerous place to be if anything happens, and she wouldn't hear of anyone else going. I reckon she was having us on. Just wants the best viewpoint.'

But Nou knew he didn't really think that. He was unchar-acteristically restless, tapping his knees, glancing with every other blink at the screens. He gave the nearest one a gentle rap with a knuckle: the mirror was folding itself out, flower-like, individual panes slotting into place to form a perfect, slightly concave circle like the enormous satellite dishes that made up Stern's comms. As she watched it began turning until it was almost side on to the Sun; a moment later a white flash an-nounced its rays had glanced off the first of the tiles.

'See how the Sun only needs to touch the tiniest little bit?'

Lucian murmured, tracing his hand lovingly above the screen. 'That's because the light gets swept inwards and instantly reflected into every panel. Then *that* is what gets shone down to Pluto. We built the mirror far away enough for the light beam to spread out, and that's why the whole planet gets slightly brighter. Never been done before, that. Not for a whole planet.'

'I thought—Mars had one?'

'Just a patch over Deuteronilus,' said Lucian absently. 'Hm. I bet they'll be wanting one for Titan next. Of course, their methane is already liquid. Come to think about it'—he was speaking musingly now, more to himself—'the temperature gap to melt Titan's water-ice is roughly the same as Pluto's methane-nitrogen mix. Huh.'

Nou glanced at the book Lucian had set down: one from the *Gards and Wards* series, past where she was up to.

'. . . and with an atmosphere already in place, of course, a Titan-wide ocean would be relatively easy to maintain—'

'Ocean?' It was a strange word, a stranger still concept, and one she rarely had need to speak out loud. 'Where does an ocean come in?'

'Mm?' Lucian seemed to have forgotten her. 'Oh . . . oceans are the end goal for a lot of terraforming projects. You can get feedback cycles of all sorts going then—heat sinks, greenhouse gas build-up, atmospheric exchange. The Martian one is coming along beautifully, and the surface temperatures are shooting up every year for it. Pluto's, though, that'll need all the help it can get. The Heart forms the perfect natural basin for one, but the heat flux right now is still way too short—'

'Pluto's what?' Nou had gone very still. 'Pluto's ocean?'

'Mm-hm. Not for a long time, you've got to go through several phase changes of nitrogen and methane before you get anywhere close to human-viable temperatures . . . Nou?'

There was a roaring, rushing tide in Nou's ears. The world

seemed to have turned very still. The blue and red and green lights of the control panels dimmed, then, one by one, began folding in on themselves.

'Nou,' said Lucian's voice from far away, 'it's not for years and years, you know. The ocean. It's probably centuries away . . .'

The mountains of her home, pouring through her fingers. The Heart, a rapid tugging at her throat. The Whistlers, flailing in unison. Thrashing to keep afloat. Drowning.

'Nou, look at me.'

Nou choked on a breath that scraped. The kaleidoscope tunnel of the world pulled back. Background sounds returned.

Lucian was still talking.

'I thought you knew. I thought . . . We all . . . The end goal, the plan all along. We mention it all the time.'

Lucian had his hands in a vice around her shoulders. She could see her reflection filling his eyes.

'We'll have helped them by then. Your Whistlers. We're going to, right after the mirror today. You can't think . . . You know I'd never let—'

But what Lucian would never let happen, Nou couldn't hear. She pulled out of his arms and stumbled back. She had never realised it could physically hurt to look at a person. With her dad it never hurt like this. Not even with her brother. The pain from her chest was as real as a slap.

Lucian rose to his feet.

'Nou, talk to me—'

Talk. Nou felt herself go cold at the word. Lucian had earned her voice as he had earned her trust. She had trusted him. She had trusted him with the Whistlers.

She turned where she stood, and she fled.

'Nou! Nou, wait!'

But Nou, smaller, faster, had already sped through the corridor beyond and was out of earshot of his pleas.

Where to? She willed her thoughts to run as fast as her feet. She had to stop it. Stop Plutoshine. To do so meant telling someone, telling everyone, about the Whistlers. She could tell Parkin, but Parkin's allegiance was with the people, and everyone knew he was Plutoshine's strongest advocate. She could tell Halley, but Halley was chief terraformer; she, too, would want to see the plan through. She could go to . . .

No. She couldn't.

Stan was her friend, but what could Stan do? No one offworld could help, severed by light-hours' delay—and who did she know to call anyway? Who would believe her?

Nou skidded to a halt outside a door so fast she had to grab its frame to keep from toppling. There, at eye level, was an embossed silver plate:

DR MALLORY H. H. MADOC
and
DR YOLANDA J. MORENO

PLUTONIAN LABORATORY FOR XENOBIOLOGY

Nou didn't think twice. She knocked—no hurry could push aside deep-seated manners—and stepped at once inside.

Four faces looked up as she did, from microscope, weighing scales, fume hood, a rack of tiny glass vials, all wearing identical white coats and yellow-rimmed goggles. They were people she knew by sight (how could you not on Pluto?) but no names followed this information. Nou stood in a kind of airlock before an array of brightly coloured clogs and hooks bearing more white coats. The room beyond was entirely silent.

One of them set down her chinking vials, scraped back her chair, and pulled open the door with a hiss of inrushing air.

'Yes?'

300

Her voice was neither patient nor impatient, but probably keen to return to work. Nou, put on the spot, floundered. It seemed suddenly absurd that, in two years of knowing the other half of Lucian's sign language duo, Nou had never been to Mallory's workspace before.

'Is—Is—Is Mallory here?'

'Who wants to see me?' said a rich voice, and Nou pulled in a breath.

Mallory had emerged from an antechamber, snapping off purple plastic gloves, sliding up her goggles into a hairband. Nou had learnt all about the concept of royalty in her History and Culture lessons, and every time she saw the xenobiologist she couldn't help but wonder from which of the great empires Mallory was descended. And whether one day she could ever emulate such grace herself.

Mallory caught sight of her in the doorway.

'Oh, hello, Nou. It's been some time. How are you doing, dear?'

Nou rallied her thoughts but could feel the all too familiar heat creeping up her neck. The worst part of getting her voice back was the attention: few people were insensitive enough to outright ask *Say something!* but the murmurs and well-intentioned congratulations and renewed interest only rammed the spotlight down harder. Stan had got it right: Stan, who had only silently hugged her, and never said a word on the matter, and treated her just the same . . .

Her thoughts stopped dead. Had Stan always known? All those hours in the workshop teaching him to sign, folding golden origami crane after crane, keeping him company as he wrote his thesis, and he, too, had never thought to mention the Heart's eventual fate.

Nou quailed.

'It's—It's—' Round and around, OK. She could do this. Next

word, what's the next word? 'It's—about—about—'

'How about some coffee, my office?' Mallory interjected smoothly. 'Come along, through here.'

The office was through a glass divide, regimentally separated from other desks outside; as Nou sat she had the feeling of being mounted on display. There was no such space in Lucian's workshop: there his crew worked elbow to elbow, or commandeered corners. The space before her in xenobiology seemed very neat and very quiet.

Mallory rustled somewhere behind her before producing two steaming, acrid-smelling cups and setting them on her vast touchscreen desk.

Nou knew what was polite: she took the drink between her hands. Then she blurted out, before she could lose her nerve: 'I found life.'

Mallory stopped with her hand suspended before her drink.

'On Pluto,' she added. Every word was an uphill struggle. 'I need—your help. They need—protection.'

'Where?'

Mallory's expression was odd, somehow. Not surprised, not happy. She was frozen, staring at Nou unblinkingly.

Nou found she could not look away.

'They're—under the Heart.' Heat crept up her neck, and something else: something uneasy. 'There's a cavern. Can you— stop Plutoshine? The mirror—'

'Of course,' Mallory breathed, her eyes boring straight through Nou's own. 'I always knew you had found it. I was right all along. I knew I was right.'

Nou was clutching her cup so hard her fingers were burning.

'Do you—' she tried again, breathing heavily now, words entirely disjointed. 'Do you have a way—of stopping—the mirror—if you found life?'

'Who else knows?' Mallory ignored her, and Nou was powerless in the face of her interrogation.

'L-Lucian,' she heard herself squeak. 'Just—Lucian.'

Mallory's pale eyes seemed to engorge.

'*Lucian*,' she said, almost *purred*, and Nou felt her chest constrict in something like fear—except there was no reason to be afraid. Then reason came all at once and she jumped in her seat: Mallory had let out a short, high laugh.

'All this time. All this time I thought he was such a sweetheart looking after you, but he was just following my advice.' She laughed again, fuller, and there was nothing happy about the sound. 'Oh, he *is* a dark horse, isn't he? I ought to be angry but I can't help it, I'm too impressed . . .'

Nou had the distinct thought that whatever Mallory was talking about, it could not be anything good.

'What do you mean?' she asked quietly. She had forgotten her urgency, forgotten the mirror—forgotten even her life forms. 'What do you mean?'

'It was *me* who first told Lucian, for goodness sake. You, life—that was the rumour, and I gave it readily as a piece of gossip. Well, that's certainly made the fool of me . . .'

The roaring was back in Nou's ears. For the second time in ten minutes, her world had upended. It couldn't be true. Had Lucian—her honest, genuine Lucian—only befriended her to find out what she knew? Had he been using her this whole time?

'You must take me there at once.' Mallory was imperious once more. 'How long has Lucian known?'

Nou could barely think, let alone speak. How long ago had they ventured across the ice together, just after he helped her find her voice? Helped, Nou realised in a rush of breath as though punctured, because he knew there were secrets she would not release without trusting him. Without loving him.

Lucian, the only one not impatient, or irritated, or bored by her silence. The only one to care. A complete stranger, taking her under his wing—why? What had he stood to gain by helping a broken little girl? He was not her father. Not her brother. He had no reason to care. None except for his own gain.

And Mallory, too. Mallory, who had never seemed to pick up the sign language. Who had barely spoken to her since the lessons stopped. She, too, had been after the glory of life . . .

'M-months,' Nou whispered. 'Half—Half a—year . . .'

'And does no one else know?' The gleam in Mallory's eyes could only be described as hunger now, obsession, and Nou sensed a palpable change in the room: the time for talking was over. 'No analyses have been conducted, no samples collected? Have any specimens—?'

'They are not'—Nou was on her feet—'*specimens*. They are *people.*'

Never before had she thought the words, but it was only now she knew them to be true. The Whistlers were not human, but they were *people*, like all the people she had ever known and ever loved and ever feared. And they needed her help.

She had no options remaining. Mallory wouldn't care for the future of the Whistlers, only her own fame.

There was just one person left.

For the second time that day, Nou turned on her heel and fled, ignoring Mallory's indignant cries, ignoring the startled stares of the scientists, out into the corridor and back on the run with renewed urgency. This time she knew where she was going, and when she reached the door, she didn't pause to knock.

'Nou!'

Edmund looked up sharply from his desk as she burst into his office. It was the first time she could ever remember entering unannounced, and from his expression there was clear reason for this. The glass screen between them cleared instantly; Nou caught a glimpse of the mirror unfolding sequence before it slid into the wall, and there sat her brother before her.

For a moment they stared at each other, the man caught unawares, the girl trying to gather her thoughts as fast as her breath. Edmund had not heard Nou speak for years; he was the last before she went silent. For a moment Nou was blinded by memory at the thought, hurtled back there with him—frozen, oxygen-starved, barely conscious—before she drew up all her courage.

'Edmund,' she said, and though her voice audibly shook and her hands too, she was *speaking* to him. 'You have—to help. Please.'

If Edmund felt anything hearing her speak, he did not show it. Up close he was almost grey, and Nou had never seen anyone with such bruise-like half-moons under their eyes.

Edmund regarded her inscrutably. 'Help with what?'

Nou took a breath.

'The—terraformers—want—to—to—'

No, Nou begged herself, not now, not in front of him. Next word, what's the next word? They want to freeze—melt, *melt*, the Heart—she hadn't muddled her antonyms for weeks—what if she stopped talking altogether? Her mind felt like an overloaded glasspad, freezing, crashing, reopening with data lost. She found herself incapable of stringing any two thoughts together.

'—to— m-melt the—Heart. They want to—make—an ocean.'

The effort blurred her vision in and out of focus. Only then did she take in his expression, and only then did she see it had not changed.

'Yes,' said Edmund coolly, 'I know.'

'Then—Then you've stopped them?' Relief coursed through her limbs. 'You've told them—to stop?'

Edmund watched her with aquiline eyes. He inclined his head slightly.

305

'Why?'

It took her a moment; she could not make sense of the word in its context. Then, like the delay before a snowflake melts on skin, cold seeped in.

'No,' she breathed. 'Edmund . . .'

'A surface ocean is the final stage of the Plutoshine master plan. That goal is decades away, perhaps centuries, but when the mirror turns on it will become inevitable.'

'No, please—'

'*Think*, child.' Abruptly he lost patience. 'What happens when solid-state nitrogen is heated from nearly absolute zero by fifty degrees? What, exactly, did you expect would happen?'

Nou realised the question was not rhetorical. Her brother was staring at her and there was incredulity sparking below the hoods of his eyes. Of all the times she had strained to stir some emotion in him, and this here—his utter disbelief—was the best she could do.

'Your classes ought to have equipped you with more than the necessary knowledge to piece this together yourself, if your immoderate time with the terraformers had not,' Edmund said coldly. 'Then again, perhaps if you spent less time making a nuisance of yourself to our scientists, you would not be the last person on all Pluto to open your eyes.'

Open your eyes. Something in those words triggered a memory, breaching the surface of her mind like a buoyant iceberg: the two of them at the shoreline where their mountains met the ice, looking back at the base. She couldn't have been more than four Earth-years old.

Her brother was talking to her, and rewritten by time her memory made him distant and towering overhead, untouchable as the stars.

A billion billion of them were above her. Little bright lights.

Some red, some blue, most white as the ice below. Edmund was pointing to one in particular. A particularly bright one. The brightest.

'*That's* our *star*,' he said. '*We call it the Sun. And one day that Sun is going to change the face of our world.*'

Nou blinked back to the present as the words surged over her and she realised the truth: that she was the last to know.

'Everything has been prepared for,' Edmund said now, face ageing as the memory sank. 'Pluto's future is set.'

In desperation, she tried again. 'But the Whistlers—'

'I have sufficient genetic variety of the xenocryophiles to continue my research on the species.'

It took a second to register. Then, were the very spin of the world to halt, or gravity to upend them into vacuum, Nou would have had no awareness.

'You knew all along.' Her lips could barely part to speak the words. 'That they're not from Earth.'

'Of course.'

Nou felt as though her head had been severed from her body and was a balloon slowly rising to space.

'The day I showed you and you said . . .' She had to squeeze her throat shut to swallow the burning lump. 'You said afterwards they were contamination.'

Edmund regarded her expressionlessly. 'Even you, a child, could see they were not. I extracted research samples that same day.'

Samples of her Whistlers? *Research?*

'But you'll still destroy their home?' Now it was her turn for incredulity. She wasn't aware that her voice was no longer shaking, her words no longer sticking. 'You'll still let them *die?*'

'I have all I need to continue my study. The others are, under the circumstances, superfluous.'

'But they're still life!' To Nou's shame, her last dregs of pride

307

were spent and she felt wetness spill down her cheeks. 'They're still going to die!'

'Calm yourself.' His words were a slap, and she felt herself recoil into submission. His fist was curled tight on the table. 'You embarrass both of us. We are discussing an event that will happen in more than a hundred years' time. You also forget that we have indulged the protection of multiple enclaves of xenoforms across the Solar System at the expense of human expansion. Clavius Harbour was always very clear where our loyalties lay should such a species be discovered on Pluto.'

Nou barely paid attention to the strangely detached use of their father's name. Never had a conversation had the power to so cleanly destroy her.

'But—' she began, as Edmund snapped, '*Enough!*'

He did not raise his voice, but he did not have to. It was more than disappointment weighing his eyebrows down like that; she was beyond disappointment, into something like disgust.

'You are dismissed,' he said quietly. 'I will not have decades of planning and research questioned by a child who will not listen to reason. Run along and watch the sunrise with your classmates.'

With that, he returned his eyes to his desk and Nou felt herself slide into non-existence. Panic rose in her throat. The terraformers, the xenobiologists, and now Stern's head . . . All her allies were adversaries and all her secrets were spent, and still nobody would listen.

She was numbed to the spot, caught somewhere between opening her mouth and moving her feet, managing neither. Then something shining caught her eye on the shelves behind her brother's desk.

A tissue-paper lid. A froth of golden ribbon. Cursive handwriting on a little tag. *Welcome home Edmund*. The plum jam was unopened, pushed to the corner of the highest shelf. Gathering dust.

Nou's world grew very quiet then. A happy day, peeling off skins and squeezing up the soft flesh inside; a thrill, kept close to her heart, knowing just who to surprise with it; practising the message in her best glitter ink.

Something strange swelled in her chest as she stared at the jar. She was helpless, and she was alone, but now—something new—she was furious. Yes: she realised with a jolt that the heat in her fingers and the red surge behind her eyes was fury. For nearly three years she had strived her utmost to win the heart of this stranger, the one who had replaced her best friend, who wore his face but not his smile. She had followed his every order with unfaltering obedience, emulated his every habit with unquestioning adoration. And why? To wear every day his disdain like a stained dress, and feel smaller in it than anything else.

Now, finally, she was furious with him. Even then, in that blackest hour, the freedom of it tasted like euphoria.

Nou didn't waste another moment. She turned her back on the stranger who was once her brother and she ran, and she did not look back.

Interlude 5

Edmund's breath is steady when he reaches the Promontorium. He doesn't know how long he has: until his absence is noticed, until they search this place, until his oxygen runs out. He moves briskly, stripping off his pack, deftly retrieving the equipment. Not scientific tonight. He glances up at that towering, rough-hewn cliff. No, Edmund thinks bitterly. This equipment is the exact opposite. How proud Clavius would be if he could see him.

The plan all along. Search and destroy.

3D printers don't just print bombs if you ask them to—the same way you can't print viruses or reactors. What you *can* make are the raw materials. And taking together the biochemist with a penchant for mechanical engineering, and the polymath who cracked efficient fusion as a side project, Edmund and Clavius have put together something of an arsenal.

The remote detonators Edmund now carefully removes from their casing are all he requires. This isn't his plan. This is his father's, his employer's. His master's. Edmund should be planning a funeral, planning public grief, planning a new life—taking Nou to Earth, to his homeworld, to his snow-swept peaks by the sides of lakes. Starting again. Starting free.

If he takes Nou and runs now, and Clavius wakes, they'll be hunted. What kind of bounty can the richest man in the Solar System brand on your forehead? Edmund already knows: he saw it when Maiv got out. He knows it is an indefatigable one. It is one whose jaw must be cut from its body after biting.

If he unveils the creatures to humanity and Clavius wakes, Clavius will punish him. There are many ways he could, but Edmund knows the most effective. Maiv had her reasons for having Nou, but Clavius had his own for letting her: letting her create something lovable, something breakable. Something that could be taken away. If Edmund unveils Nou's creatures and Clavius wakes, Edmund knows exactly what will happen.

But if he goes along with the plan and Clavius wakes—if he performs exactly as expected, behaves as programmed—then Edmund will have proven himself. He will be trusted. When you are trusted, you become invisible. And when you are invisible, you can try again.

And if Clavius doesn't wake? Edmund cannot bear the touch of the thought. He cannot bear hope.

The stars are at their brightest. The Milky Way is a streak gouging the Promontorium, and it strikes Edmund quite suddenly how that misty band is made of places. The planets he cannot see, no, but for every star without them are two that possess ten apiece. Innumerable places. Places like Earth. Like Pluto.

Is anything—anyone—looking back at his star and wondering the same thing?

Edmund drags his face down. His musing has cost him three seconds. The passageway into the heart of the Heart is as unforthcoming as ever, but he remembers the way.

Without glancing back, without glancing again at the stars, he disappears inside.

Nou's shoulders buffet the sides of the crevasse as she scrambles, half-slipping, half-running, through a world that exists only in the bubble of her helmet light. The light is white but there is red ahead— she is sure of it, just around the corner of her vision. She can catch it.

A persistent beeping from somewhere is pleading for attention, but Nou doesn't want to see a maintenance reminder, or a message from Stern. She has to keep going.

She stumbles again; her legs are rubber beneath her and so battered they must be blue all over. She scrabbles for some hold and her helmet bashes the ceiling. The loud scraping sound . . . the wild flare of her lights . . . the rattling of her head on her shoulders . . . For a moment she is too disorientated to tell up from down.

She hurtles onwards. They are just ahead of her. She knows it.

The incendiary devices are pocket-sized and adhere easily to the crevasse walls. Four evenly spaced will do; just the one at the entrance would have sufficed, but Edmund is a careful man, and he does not underestimate that the xenobiologists will be careful, too. The collapse should be deep and it should be thorough, sealing the entry for a good hundred metres. As Clavius wished: search and destroy. Or, better: search and *hide*.

The collapse will not hurt them. The creatures are located too deep. On the contrary—he almost halts, so powerful is the thought—by some adventitious stroke he may be executing the best course of action. Hiding them might be the only way to save them. Keep them from the reach of his father.

He runs onwards. For good or ill, the course is set.

The beeping has become a voice. Nou can't hear what it is saying—her breathing is heavy now, and short—but it isn't happy. Nou tries to focus on the words as *Caution* seeps through, but it's so hard to pull apart one sound from the tinny whine in her head, the pounding of her own blood at her ears, the heaving breaths that racket around her fishbowl world. The tips of her fingers are tingling as though they've been sat on. Are the lights dimming or is she having trouble seeing?

Low power mode. Low power mode.

The words flash across the inside of her helmet. She fumbles on, gulping for each breath now, and there's something familiar to the feeling. Yes: it's the same she gets hiding under the bedcovers at night, when her brother has kissed her to sleep only for her to open up her glasspad in secret, face lit by glowing pages on hydrothermal vents and the vast ecosystems they nourish. She'll pull back the covers with a gasp—then, oxygen circulating freely, cover herself again and continue.

Here, there are no bedcovers to throw back. There is no oxygen to circulate. Dreamily, lids heavy, Nou draws up her wrist and reads the words there just as the voice kicks its way to her senses:

Caution: oxygen at three per cent.

Chapter 19

Hours had passed. Lucian had untied his hair; it now stuck in every direction, inflicting the appearance of one mildly electrically shocked.

'She didn't know, Halley, she didn't know!' he burst, not for the first time that evening. 'It's pretty obvious, isn't it? You heat up an iceball and it's going to melt, right?'

'Perhaps the boy from Mercury is forgetting we weren't all raised beneath the dictatorship of a gargantuan ball of *plasmatic death*.' Halley was shrugging on the screen, rotating inside the mirror's tiny hab. 'It's been two E-years out here and already I'm forgetting the feel of sunlight on skin.'

'Besides, did we ever *explicitly* say it?' Kip's head appeared above the Environment control panel a row over. 'None of us will live to see the ocean. We're just here for the fireworks and the history books.'

'And the money,' pointed out Joules, over at Mechanical. 'Some of us have plans that don't involve changing sky colours for the rest of our lives.'

Kip raised his brows in interest. 'Care to share?'

'Llama farm in Suriname.'

'Joules, you dark horse. Dark llama. Where the heck is Suriname? Is that the Asteroid Belt?'

'She'll turn up, Lucian,' murmured Stan from where the pair of them sat at the Instruments sub-system; he was at the helm this time, leaving Lucian free to keep an eye on things. 'She's just upset. I get it,' Stan added. 'If someone told me they were going to dry up Kraken Mare or . . . or dam its neck or something, I'd be broken up about it.'

'Yeah, I know,' Lucian conceded wretchedly. 'But she was so excited for today.'

'She's probably on the ice right now,' said Stan bracingly. 'I would be. I don't think any of us know what to expect today.' He gave Lucian a quick glance. 'Anything, er, out of the ordinary on the gauntlets?'

'There never was with Silvasaire and Jovortre,' Lucian pointed out, 'but thanks for shoving my mind on to something worse.'

'I can do one better—I've got my methods chapter for you to read.'

Lucian groaned.

'Twenty thousand words,' said Stan with savage pleasure, 'and it's as mind-bleachingly boring as you said it should be.'

'I knew there was a catch to having a minion do all your dirty work.'

'You forgot the biggest—I'll be your direct competitor soon.'

'Nah, I'm prepared for that. Joules has his llamas, I've got my unemployment fund.'

'OK, people,' Halley's voice called across the room and from every screen before them. 'Countdown to Phase Four is at T-minus ten minutes. Everyone at their stations and prepare to talk science to me.'

Lucian briefly laid a hand on Stan's shoulder before rising and pulling on his headset. Looking around the low-lit blues of the control room he saw every one of the terraformers; all of Parkin's engineering team; faces he knew well and liked;

there was Edmund Harbour at the back of the room, expression almost uncivilly emotionless; there was Vasily to his side, who gave Lucian a wink; there were base co-ordinators; base communicators; some of the older students; there was Percy catching Stan's eye and giving a little wave.

She was outside, Lucian told himself. Out on the ice, atop the land he'd condemned to death, waiting with the hundred others to shout and cheer. He wasn't worried for the Whistlers—after all, it would be decades, if not centuries, before Pluto's graceful arc into summer would affect them, and by then they'd have a proper plan in place. Long before then. But he would have to find Nou the first moment he could. He would have to make her understand that.

And the land wasn't *condemned*—any more than a block of marble is condemned to the sculpture.

No, Lucian thought to himself, Nou, Pluto, the Whistlers, they'd all be fine. It would all work out. In fact—the plan came to him as though he'd intended it all along—he'd go to Harbour the moment the mirror was stable. Halley, too; Earth only knew those isotopes of hers were days away from pointing the finger at biology. Halley would have contacts off world, and in any case—Lucian ran a finger across his lips in thought—Harbour already knew. The guy must have reasons for keeping quiet— reasons he'd also want to keep quiet. Bypassing him entirely in all this seemed instinctively a bad move, but certainly the guy couldn't be trusted to handle it on his own.

All right. That was the plan. In an hour, maybe two, he'd tell Harbour what was beneath the ice. Tell Halley when she was back on the ground. No more secrets in this tiny base. No more shadows. It would be his apology to Nou.

'Mechanical?'

Lucian's concentration jumped back; Halley had already started the call. Time to do his job.

'Go.'

'Comms?'

'Go.'

'Power?'

'Go!'

And with Stan's reminder of the calm before Silvasaire and Jovortre, flicking into the mode of Lucian the terraformer came with all the immediacy of hurtling into a freezing pool.

'Telemetry?'

'Go.'

'AOCS?'

'Go!'

Lucian paced the room, glasspad in hand, feeling his heart rate jump to attention as each successive voice rang clear.

'Structure?'

'Go.'

'Environment?'

'Go!'

'Instruments?'

'Go!' called Stan.

'Systems?'

'Go!'

'PI?'

Principal investigator: that was Lucian. Without his gauntlets he felt powerless, a civilian. And he was. He could no more control what would happen now than Captain Whiskers.

He opened his mouth to speak, and hesitated.

All systems looked good. There was nothing out of the ordinary; the sequence was computationally flawless. The program had been kept in an offline system since his final check yesterday evening and, even now, was held in that state in orbit. Nothing could have possibly got into the code this time.

And still . . .

Some of the best PIs in history, for missions far greater than this one, had called it off at the last minute for threats less tangible than this. *New Horizons* itself had been one of them on its second attempt at launch. But the map of Pluto was scattered with the names of missions that perhaps ought to have called it and didn't: *Challenger*; *Columbia*; *Beacon*, and with it Pluto's first humans. With *Columbia* they'd known the risks and had no choice but to try; with Plutoshine, did they have to?

'Go,' Lucian breathed.

On his screen, Halley was looking straight at him—no, looking straight into the camera, the same camera watched by twenty others.

'Copy that.' Halley dragged herself into position off-screen. 'Initiating nominal mirror operation. Stand by for momentum wheel repositioning.'

Lucian felt as though his every nerve had been electrified. He glanced at the faces around him: some calm, some frowning in concentration, others with set determination. How could they stand this, watching and waiting?

'Momentum wheel undocking. Alignment looks good.'

He ought to have brought his gauntlets. Monitored the simulation in real time, checked for new bugs. At least he could have stilled his hands, pretended he had purpose.

'Torque rods in position. Mirror membrane unfolding . . . Ten per cent.'

Halley was her usual efficiency, no word more than needed. But where everyone else was watching the blueprint simulation, Lucian was staring at her face.

'We are at fifty per cent,' said Halley. 'Mechanical, confirm.'

Lucian raised his glasspad higher. Her grim expression filled his vision.

'Fifty per cent confirmed,' called Joules. 'All systems nominal.'

'Copy that. We are at eighty per cent.'

She looked . . . *trepidatious*. That was the word. It was dread in his old mentor's eyes, in the tightness of her mouth, too subtle perhaps for anyone to pick up but him: the one student who had been alongside her for mission after mission. Halley, for the first time Lucian could remember, looked afraid.

'Membrane deployed to one hundred per cent. Preparing to move into position. Power, what's your reading on the thrusters?'

'We are go for ignition,' called one of Parkin's engineers.

The thrusters. The controlled release of xenon propellant into two streams. A controlled explosion, and Halley was strapped to it.

'Initiating thruster burn on my mark in three, two, one . . .'

On Lucian's glasspad the sequence for the auxiliary drive systems showed ignition: the boosters propelled themselves off the mirror's perimeter exactly as instructed, setting the mirror on a slow course of rotation before counter-burns would return its velocity to zero.

He steadied his breath. That was a part he had simulated and re-simulated. But his head couldn't quiet his heart. Not until Halley called home. It would be any second now.

His glasspad slipped an inch between his fingers. Any second . . .

'Comms,' he called hoarsely, 'what's happening? Can we boost our sig—'

'Auxiliary thrusters successful.' Halley's voice rang through the control room to applause and a lone whoop. 'Mirror rotating at expected velocity of point two metres per second. We are minus sixty degrees to position.'

Lucian neither thought it through nor recalled thinking it. He pulled up the mirror's private messaging service and began typing, his hands writing even as his mind caught up:

319

Halley, this needs to stop. Before anyone gets hurt.

On his screen, Halley gave no sign that the message had been received but for the slightest flick of her eyes. She said, 'Minus fifty to position,' then Lucian received her response:

You're the PI on this, lad. You make the call.

Maybe it was because she held them before twenty onlookers, but Lucian saw none of the harshness of her words in her eyes. She was looking directly into the camera, her gaze steady, and although Power announced the successful firing of the retrograde thrusters and although AOCS confirmed the loss of acceleration, for a moment the two of them were alone.

Lucian typed back:

I don't have any evidence. It's not scientific. It's a hunch. I can't say 'no go' on a hunch.

'Minus forty degrees to position,' Halley said, then, glancing down once, twice, taking time enough that 'Minus thirty to position' filled the room as her words appeared:

A hunch is the amalgamation of a brain's observations that are so many decimal places from one they individually round to zero. But cumulatively, if you take those values together, they make positive data. It is scientific.

Lucian lifted his eyes to hers. There was quiet determination there, meant only for him. When he looked back down there was more:

It's your call. But I wouldn't be up here if I had doubts. Know that whatever happens, I will do all in my power to keep this ship sailing.

'Minus twenty degrees to position,' she said softly.

Time to be a responsible adult. Make decisions and face the consequences. Face whatever comes.

Lucian typed back one word, his hand steady:

OK.

He met Halley's eyes and, not knowing whether she would

see it, gave her the smallest nod. She returned it, then blinked and the connection was broken.

'Minus ten degrees to position. I can confirm visual on sunlight entering the disc . . .'

More cheers, this time more pronounced.

'Optimal mirror configuration in T-minus thirty seconds.'

Lucian was going to crick his neck looking between the glasspad's code and the window's view. Was he imagining it, or was it already getting lighter . . . ?

'Twenty seconds.'

People were on their feet now. Lighting a whole planet had never been done in human history, not for more than the Mortimaeus test.

'Fifteen seconds.'

Ten years of planning. The realisation came to him with a jolt. This was what it all came down to.

'Ten.'

Every cell in his being wanted to run to the windows.

'Five.'

Gripping the glasspad with both hands.

'Four.'

Feet apart.

'Three.'

Face the consequences. Face whatever comes.

'Two.'

Whatever it takes.

'*One—!*'

The room erupted as though ignited. Every person at every station leapt in the air as one. The noise was incredible. All around people were shaking hands, high-fiving, hugging, some in tears. Someone grabbed Lucian's shoulders and vigorously shook them while another slapped him on the back; Stan jumped up and ran to him, face beatific, and threw his arms around him; Kip started up a chant of 'SUN-BRING-ERS, SUN-BRING-ERS' that swept across the room; Lucian kissed Stan on the temple as someone else kissed his hair—and where was his glasspad? It must have fallen through his fingers . . . He ducked under the crowd and found it narrowly escaping half a dozen feet. He raised it to eye level and there was Halley, grinning from ear to ear at him—no, at the camera—and Lucian found himself grinning back, found every tensed-up muscle in his body relaxing; found his eyes drawn over the tops of waving arms and bobbing heads to the windows—to the view beyond; to the rich, indigo sky; to its winking stars; to the sparkling Heart; to all the colours of a world entering summer.

The ice was glittering. Sunlight was splitting it into greens, purples. Dazzling, mesmerising.

The ice was melting. Only slowly—only over decades, centuries—but it was melting. And it was the most beautiful thing Nou had ever seen.

She spurred herself onwards. She could not look back.

Chapter 20

'Hey, Halley.'

Lucian was breathless, light-headed, his cheeks radiating heat. He had Captain Whiskers scooped in his arms, and he wasn't sure he would ever remember how to stop smiling.

Halley just shook her head at the sight of him, but all the creases of her face were lost beneath her own smile.

'Hello, Lucian.'

She was still in orbit, holding herself one-handed before the camera, body floating behind in the kitchenette-sized hab. And the view behind her . . . If Pluto before was an overcast winter's day, now it was still winter, but the Sun had come out. There were colours on the little world's surface that kept dragging Lucian's attention away: *scarlet* over Cthulhu Regio, and the al-Idrises sheltering Stern were no longer dishwater-grey but the gleaming whites of marble chips.

'Thank you,' Lucian said to her, with feeling. 'For making the right call. For keeping my head for me.'

Halley just shrugged; a strangely elegant move in zero gravity.

'You made the call. Save the maudlin for the media.'

'You got it.' Lucian nodded. 'But thank you for—'

'Look.' Halley's eyes grimaced shut. 'I get you're pleased,

but my sentimentality allowances will only stretch so far—'

'. . . thank you for believing in me . . .'

'For *Earth's sake!*'

'. . . and for giving me the chance to come here . . .'

'I'll disconnect the server, I swear.'

'. . . just, yeah,' he finished on a mumble. His cheeks flared hotter still as he dared look back at his dear mentor. 'I don't know where I'd be without you.'

'Are you *drunk?*' Halley stared. 'If you're not, then get out of here and get started. At least then I'll have an excuse to knock you about the head.'

'OK, OK! I'm out of here, I swear. I've, uh. I've got to go talk to Harbour now anyhow.'

'Edmund?' Lucian didn't miss Halley's rising eyebrows. 'What for?'

'It's . . .' He hesitated. Someone pushed a martini glass into his hand; he jiggled the Captain to accept it. 'Cheers, Vasya. I'll tell you soon. I promise.'

'All right.' Halley let it go. 'Keep your secrets. I'll be on the ground in an hour.' She looked to one side, her eyes drawn by something off camera—one of the myriad flashing screens and control panels identical in all but function to those behind her. 'Just got a couple of odd jobs to sort.'

'Really?' Now it was Lucian's turn to twist his brows. 'But isn't it all . . . ? I mean, we automated it all, right?'

'Just about.' Halley was tinkering with something now, shoulders manoeuvring as her arms worked off-camera. 'Two ticks and I'll fly back to join in the revelry. Looks like the power command unit's a little confused.'

An intermittent green flashing caught Lucian's eye on a panel behind her; part of the power unit, too. That ought to be dormant now, as instructed. A good job she had spotted it:

324

the mirror needed to run at maximum efficiency to achieve its expected lifetime.

'OK.' He shrugged. 'Don't be a while. I can only guard the cocktails for so long.' Then, with the sort of lurch that suggested his stomach had discovered a non-negligible void directly beneath it and subsequently fallen through: 'Actually, Halley? You can have this one. I've just spotted the very man I'm after . . .'

Thoughts of downing the martini for courage were dismissed: he needed what limited wits he had about him. Eyes on his mark, Lucian hovered, then hesitated, then surged forward, wedging open the window of opportunity. Any moment he feared his nerve might disappear back through it.

'Uh . . . Edmund?'

Edmund Harbour turned. He was walking away from the control room; Lucian had staked him out until he was alone, much like he used to with eminent scientists at conferences. At least today he wouldn't be stammering how much he admired his latest paper. He was hoping Captain Whiskers might help.

'Hi.' Lucian tried for an easy smile as he caught up.

'Hello, Lucian,' said Harbour, with what Lucian could only think of as wariness. 'You must be very proud after the day's success.'

His slight bow, his words, all were perfectly courteous, but there was that filter again over his eyes: the one that let light in and let nothing out.

'Yeah, you might say I'm having a pretty good day. Look'— Lucian skipped the preamble—'I need to talk to you in private. It's . . . about Nou.'

He realised at once that this was the wrong thing to say. Harbour's eyes perceptively narrowed.

'What about her?'

'Can we, er, just nip into my office?' Lucian glanced anxiously around, unwittingly catching eyes and forcing smiles in response. 'It's just down the hall, I've got mint-chocolate tiffin—'

'I'm afraid I don't have time,' Harbour interrupted. 'I have to send several messages to the inner Solar System and I'm about to intercept a response from our security advisers, but perhaps Vasily can book you an appointment.'

Lucian shot a look behind him, tightened his arms around the cat, and leapt.

'I know about the life forms.'

His wrist-pad vibrated—one of the automated updates to all mirror personnel. Lucian glanced at it and caught snippets of some kind of code: *At 1709 . . . if x at 94 and y and z at 32 . . . thruster burn for 024 to 112 for x . . .*

Some kind of a vector? Only, Halley had the sequence locked down. According to the code Lucian had written, movement in any dimension was now only historically possible.

At 1709 . . . He glanced at the time just above the code. It was six minutes past five.

But now Edmund Harbour had stopped dead, and Lucian felt his every sense focus as though doused in cold water. The mask of Harbour's face slipped, just for a moment, and revealed something raw. At once the man was a decade younger, and Lucian remembered there were only scant years between them in age.

The look was gone as soon as it came.

'So Nou told you her hypothesis, did she?' said Harbour quietly.

For a moment, Lucian understood that flash of fear Nou got in her eyes at any mention of her brother. The man before him seemed suddenly in sharper focus, the whites of the corridor vignetted, the revels of passers-by dimmed.

'She didn't tell me anything.' Lucian kept his voice equally low. They were both leaning in. 'She showed me.'

'That is not possible.' Harbour's nostrils flared.

'She showed me their grove. Under the Heart, under Pandemonium Prom—'

'You're describing what she told you,' Harbour hissed. 'What you, like others, sought to ease or trick or force from my sister.'

'I know there's six pillars,' Lucian breathed. 'They're smooth and metal-looking, like . . . like wires, thick as you're tall. I know the lights under the ice will whistle back if you whistle at them, and I know they live under the Heart—somewhere the ice sheet touches the water-ice bedrock. I know they're probably not from our Solar System, and I'm pretty sure you know that, too.' He took a breath. 'That enough to convince you? Wait . . .' Something had just registered. 'What did you mean about the others? What others?'

Another buzz at his wrist; Halley had typed something in response. When Lucian glanced at it he read *Cancel all*.

'So you got it out of her,' said Harbour, with dangerous calmness. 'Where others before you failed. Yes, there have been others. Good people line up to do ill acts for Clavius Harbour.' Contempt burned in his eyes. 'What glory do you imagine there is in staking claim to the discovery of life when you stole it from a little girl?'

'Glory?' Alarm bells rang in Lucian's mind. There was another buzz at his wrist, but he paid it no heed. 'Hang on, I think you've got the wrong end of the—'

'Everyone else said you were so *kind*'—Harbour's voice was a growl now, his hands clenched into fists—'taking her in the way you did. Coaxing her to talk again. You're patient, Lucian, and you're smart, but I saw right through you from the start. I knew exactly what you were after—you and half the people in this base. You even told me yourself.'

Lucian could have squeezed his eyes shut at his own stupidity.

He *had* told Harbour as much: all that time ago when he invited him to help with the sign language. What was it he'd said? *I heard she knows something about native life around here.* Lucian had been so incredulous, so *reckless*, that he'd lied just to see what reaction he sparked.

'It was clever of you to get Mallory on board.' Abruptly Harbour was calm again. 'She was just like you. The moment she got here she was willing to try anything to be the one who found life. She would use anything, anyone. She even—' He broke off, and there was disgust in the flints of his eyes, or perhaps shame. 'I held her off Nou as long as I could after the accident, but you found a way to exploit that, too.'

'Mallory had her own reasons for wanting to help Nou.' Lucian shook his head in earnest. 'Her daughter. Alexandra.'

'Her daughter?' For the first time—and it was unnerving to witness—Harbour's lips twitched. But his eyes remained hard, flat, and within them was something like pity. 'Is that what she told you?'

'Yes.' Lucian stared at the other man. 'She didn't want to bring her to Pluto. She'd just started high school. Why? Is . . . ? What of it?'

Harbour paused, apparently in thought. Lucian used the split second to grab a glance down: Halley's code had responded with *Access denied*. Not alarming in and of itself, but anything unexpected with Plutoshine had good reason to feel worth turning upside down. He shot a look at the time: it was eight minutes past five. He would call her at that nine minutes past marker, Lucian told himself. Just one more minute with Harbour, now he had him talking . . .

'Mallory is very inventive,' Harbour said eventually. 'She never tried that one with me.'

Lucian opened his mouth, then closed it again. Creeping up the ladder of his memory was the time he had showed Mallory little video clips of his sisters waving on the Mercurian surface; the time he opened up his locket—talking about his dad and his mum and the day everything changed. He hadn't been able to hold it in. He had wanted to share them, all of them. Only now did Lucian realise never once had Mallory shown her family in return.

'Edmund,' he said very quietly, 'where is Nou? How about we go and find her, and you two can talk? I swear on this cat'—he half-raised his arms in case there was any doubt which he meant—'I'll leave you to it. I mean, you've really got to tell Halley, and there really needs to be some kind of plan, and we'll have to be systematic about toning Plutoshine down or something, but . . . but . . .' He pulled himself together. 'You two need to talk first, and I'll leave you to it.' He locked his eyes on to Harbour's own, willing him to see the truth there. 'All I ever wanted was for her to be OK. This whole time. Compared to that, I want nothing to do with what's under that ice. That's between you and her.

'I don't even need to come with you,' he added. 'You've no reason to trust me, I get it. Just . . . tell her we've talked. Do you know where she is?'

Harbour's eyes were downcast. Lucian had to keep a grip on himself not to bend to see what expression they held. Whatever it was, the cold fury that had seemed to light his skin from the inside had receded.

'I haven't seen Nou for several hours,' Harbour said eventually. 'I presumed she was outside with the others.'

'I thought the same,' Lucian admitted. 'They've all come back in now, maybe we could check the airlock register—'

He broke off at the same time Harbour craned his neck. There were raised voices in the control room. In Lucian's arms, the cat's ears flattened before he wriggled himself free.

'What's . . . ?' He turned around.

People were running to the windows. They were pointing up at something in alarm. Others were running to their stations, shouting statuses. And was it his imagination, or was the world beyond growing . . . *brighter*?

Lucian and Harbour ran over together, Lucian grabbing his glasspad from the side.

Halley's face was on his screen and everything was in motion: her eyes leapt in time with her hands; her ponytail swung as she moved in a deluge of activity. The background behind her was on a merry-go-round.

On a—?

'Everyone to your stations!' Lucian roared. He found his headset and rammed it on, holding down the *transmit all* switch. 'All mirror personnel, back to control *immediately*. Power, what's your reading?'

'Unauthorised manoeuvre in change!' cried the engineer, eyes racing across the screens. 'It's in the code, it's . . . It *was* authorised—'

'It's a sleeper code!' gasped Stan.

He must have set off running the moment he heard trouble; he was breathless and ruffled at his station. Lucian spun to face him; Stan explained before he had to ask.

'Remains dormant and split as individual characters across a thousand million lines.' Stan was scrolling through four screens of code. 'Easily missed or passed as typos, spliced together moments before execution. Almost impossible to detect. It's the simplest explanation.'

People were running to their controls on all sides, some still with drinks in their hands.

'What will it do?' Harbour's voice cut clean through the confusion. He had pulled on a headset of his own and was staring at Lucian's screen in intense concentration. 'How much time do we have?'

'Halley . . . Control.' Lucian turned to her live feed. 'Talk to us. What's happening up there?'

Halley did not give Lucian or the camera a glance. Her voice was clipped and her face taut as she hauled herself from station to station.

'Pluto, this is Control.' Her voice rang across the room. 'We're turned too far to the Sun . . . We were never designed to take this much power . . . Everything's overheating . . . short-circuiting . . .'

Lucian followed the eyes of everyone not occupied with the computerised equivalent on screen: there in the sky, as big and as bright as Venus on a clear Earth dawn, was his mirror.

For a half-second he was overcome with sheer incredulity at the sight: the most luminous, most beautiful evenstar Pluto had ever known. Even to the naked eye the star glowed fiercer by the second, already a greenish blotch across his retinas, brighter still as it narrowed to a crescent as though in an eclipse.

And Pluto was responding: just as Lucian had intended, only chillingly distorted, the world outside the window lightening, lightening by the second, so fast it was as though by dimmer switch . . .

'Environment,' he called, 'what's our temperature outside?'

He had phrased it to Nou once, hadn't he? What would happen were the mirror to overload. *Ten out of ten would not want to be around . . . Magnifying glasses and ants . . .*

'We're at minus two-forty Celsius and still climbing,' Kip shouted, 'but that's only within this longitude, the rest of Pluto's dropping . . .'

'Most of Pluto's gone dark,' Halley confirmed. 'There's a slit getting the full blast—Sputnik, east Cthulhu, Voyager. You guys are smack in the middle of it.'

'Not by coincidence.' Lucian knew it was true the moment he said it. 'Just like Styx. Just like Silvasaire and Jovortre.'

331

'I'm running every counter-command I can think of but there's a lockdown, everything's frozen, it's like a remote operation—'

She broke off with a muffled cry. There was movement too fast to catch.

'Halley?' Lucian gripped the glass with both hands. '*Halley!*'

The screen flickered, then froze over the last recorded image, displaying the words GRACE HALLEY: CONNECTION LOST.

'Talk to me, people!' Lucian cried. 'Comms, get that connection back online. Power, what's the status of the mirror? Environment, are we still . . . ?'

But he did not need to ask Environment to know, nor to understand why at that moment the room ignited in cries: the world outside his window was ablaze. For a staggering moment Lucian was crippled with déjà vu: he was on Earth, under a full noon sky, under a dome of clearest cornflower blue.

And now he understood the loss of comms, because up there, for all the world like the Sun shone on Earth, was the fire that was his mirror.

Interlude 6

Edmund holds the detonator steady. A tiny thing—but then, he has always known the smallest things are capable of so much damage.

He lays his gloved thumb upon the first switch. He stands well back. Perhaps his eyes have adjusted, or the starlight is just right, but the Promontorium is no longer shadow-shrouded greys. Instead, the ice cliff is every shade of blue and green, in parts almost indigo. Layers upon layers in colours which, though dim and darkened, he rarely sees outside of his livestream. Colours he saw when he last stood upon that place within it—when he was last home.

The switch for the first incendiary is pressed against his finger. He glances up once more, but all colour has gone again.

He tenses his thumb . . .

'*crrrk* . . . Harbour? Edmund, come in, it's Voronov . . .'

Edmund deliberates, then lowers the control and presses the transmitter on his wrist. Confusion raises his voice an octave in question.

'Vasily?'

'They can't find Nou.' Vasily speaks in his usual heavy, unhurried accent, but there is a tightness to his words. 'They've searched. I have searched also. She is not in the base.'

'Nou?'

'Is she with you?'

'No.' Edmund's eyebrows draw together. 'I haven't seen her since . . . I told her . . .'

He trails off. He stares at the cliffs of Pandemonium Promontorium.

'They're sending out a team to where they found you—Parkin is playing forensics. You need to be here, my friend, they are asking questions. I will accompany them and do what I can, but . . .'

'How long?' Edmund pushes each word out on a heartbeat. 'How long until they get here?'

'They just set off.'

The hand holding the controller falls to his side.

Caution: oxygen at two per cent.

There is a roaring in Nou's ears that rocks her where she stands. Nausea parts her lips as though to empty her body of it. Then the panic hits.

She bursts into a sprint back the way she came. Her feet are in darkness and she dare not glance down. Her outstretched hands hit ice as she stumbles once, twice, frenziedly dragging herself up, hurtling onwards. Light, darkness, the flashes between the two as her helmet whips up, down—

CRACK.

Nou is flat on her back too fast to process how it happened, helmet bulb ringing like struck glass. She makes to gasp in a breath—and can't. Heaving now, hoarsely, as though choking, the air comes in stunted drags too slow to quell the sparks that burst across her vision. One hand presses down—where is the other? *There*—both press down, both push her head upright . . .

Dizziness sucks between her ears and she collapses back. She gasps again, dragging each breath as deeply as she can, unable to fill her burning lungs fast enough.

With a moan she tries again. Both hands down. Both hands pushing. The world lurches below . . .

Crying out, this time in triumph, grasping the walls, feet apart.

334

Then a hand reaches inside her ribcage and closes around her heart.

The crevasse disappears out of sight in each direction. The problem is, Nou cannot remember from which way she came.

A hunch, a memory, a plea—Nou knows not. She chooses left, raising foot after numbed foot in a run, but either way would have sufficed: she doesn't make it five metres before the fall comes, dreamlike, as perhaps her deadened feet trip over themselves; as perhaps her oxygen-starved legs give way; as perhaps the blood rush blackens her sight.

Nou falls upon the chasm floor. Lights grows dim; the flashing warnings say her suit's power, too, is shutting down. Perhaps her eyelids have given up.

Each breath is water upon fire. Nou gulps, and gasps, lying on her side, as piece by piece her body ignites.

'Edmund.' She feels herself say it as she hears it, but the two are disconnected. 'Edmund, help . . .'

One last, feeble push, but she only rolls on to her back.

'Edmund!'

Louder, hoarser.

'Edmund, I'm here!'

It's not logical. He can't possibly hear. He can't possibly find her. But still she calls. Edmund always comes.

'Edmund.'

The cold has reached her lips. The convulsion of a shudder ripples down her spine, but her body does not have the energy to execute it.

'Ed . . . Here . . .'

The black of the chasm rushes down to meet her.

Chapter 21

Lucian was halfway out of the control room before his feet knew what they were doing. He heard his name—he ignored it—then a hand grabbed his shoulder and spun him round.

'*Lucian!*' It was Harbour. 'What are you doing?'

'Going after Halley,' Lucian replied without pausing.

'*Stop*, Lucian, and think!' It was not so much a request as a *command*, and the authority of that voice momentarily knocked some sense into him. 'You have responsibilities. Send someone else and do it right now, I agree, but do your duty first.'

Harbour was still gripping his shoulder. The two men were so close Lucian could discern individual spokes in each iris, their backdrop the improbable reddish-brown of light through black tea. Alongside one eye was a small mole; there was something humanising about the detail.

Harbour released him and pulled up his wrist-pad. He spoke into it directly, his voice projected across the room, down every corridor, in every headphone:

'This is Edmund Harbour. All personnel excepting those on the mirror response team are to return to base and proceed immediately to the plaza at their designated emergency meeting points. Register yourselves as present and report anyone missing from your prearranged group.'

Lucian hesitated—one foot pointed in each direction—then strode back to the control room.

'All right, I need volunteers at once to fly Sagittarii to Halley and get her out of there. Everyone else, give me reports.'

A kind of wild energy coursed through him with every word, barely contained, with all the force he could trust himself with. He had to keep moving, keep talking, or it would rip him apart.

Sabotage, he was thinking. *Sabotage again, in a sabotage-proofed plan. And this time they've really done it.*

'Systems, what's our overall status?'

'We are still online, but barely,' Parkin reported. 'Every system is displaying heat stress, but the integrity of the hab itself appears to be holding.'

Relief took the form of dizziness so severe it momentarily blackened Lucian's sight. He gripped a control unit until it passed. Halley might still be . . .

'Life Support, what's the weather in the hab? Oxygen, temperature?'

'Oxygen to fifteen per cent and falling. Temperature is thirty-five Celsius and rising.'

Keep moving, keep talking, do your duty. But what Lucian was thinking was: *An accomplice. Moreno had to have had an accomplice after all. She could have figured how to plan Jovortre in advance, but not this.*

'Comms,' he ordered, 'keep attempting to regain contact, that's all we can do until the Sadges arrive.'

Or maybe not an accomplice—maybe an employer. Here on Pluto. The one Moreno wouldn't talk about.

'*Power*'—Lucian rounded on the room with unintended fierceness, grasping every last straw he could get his hands on—'get me a projection of the expected energy output over the next two hours. I want to see how long we've got until the mirror gives out under the present conditions. AOCS, get our orbital trajectory up and see how we're holding. Are we stable or are we still rotating? Structure . . .'

But what could they do? They had rescinded all control to the mirror with the exact aim of preventing this. All they could do was watch in horror as, beyond their window, Pluto blazed.

Stop the saboteur. Find him, or her, and fast.

'Lucian.'

Harbour. Behind him. Close enough to see the mole.

'Whether there's a second saboteur or whether this was pre-programmed, someone has to speak to Moreno.' Harbour spoke fast and he spoke without wasting a syllable—and he spoke precisely Lucian's own thoughts. 'I'll go to her and find out what I can. I'll be in contact. Keep me informed of any developments here.'

There was such authority in his voice, such assurance, that Lucian found himself already nodding in agreement. Then he blinked himself to his senses.

'No . . . Wait . . . Hang on.'

Harbour had already turned away but Lucian ploughed on. If this really did have anything to do with Harbour—and what was it Halley had said about a hunch?—then he couldn't go talk to his potential accomplice alone.

'Shouldn't, uh, someone go with you?' As Harbour stared in open impatience, like disbelief, Lucian floundered. 'As in . . . As in, is it safe? Why don't you take . . . ?' Glancing around: Kip, Kip was a big strong guy, but he was needed at his station. . . 'Vasily—take Vasily with you, or let me—'

Lucian broke off in that moment: something was happening. There was a rumble beneath his feet, beneath everyone's feet. A hush fell across the room like thick smoke.

Everyone was facing the window, so everyone saw it. One moment the Heart was a smooth disc, glittering with a skin of melting nitrogen that instantly sublimed to form a gathering mist.

338

The next, something white and gargantuan, the size of a mountain, was crumpling into it. One of the al-Idrises was toppling into the Heart, broken free of its weakened cement, an entire mountain twisting loose. For a terrible second the behemoth hung suspended in the arc of its fall. Then it slammed into the Heart, billowing out plumes of ice and dust, scattering diamond shards of frost high into the atmosphere.

The response of Stern itself drowned, then silenced, all others: a horrific, metallic groaning, like an ancient tree contorting in the wind, coming from the very floors and walls itself. Stern was *howling*.

Every person inside felt it simultaneously: a drop in the pits of their stomachs, gone as fast as it came. *The base was moving.*

'*Everyone out!*' Harbour shouted, then again into his wrist, the words ringing through every hall as the room erupted in cries and activity. A piercing alarm joined the cacophony overhead: the one Lucian on the induction day had thought of as the whooping of some terrified bird, the *base incident alarm.* 'To your evacuation positions! Suits on, possessions behind. You have trained for this, *go!*'

Airtight doors rushed down and red lights flashed overhead. The base was in emergency lockdown as had only ever been simulated. Lucian sprang into action but tripped on his first footfall: the floor was tilted, and tilting further.

'Edmund!' He tore off his headset, rushing sidelong through the mass of faces all either dear or familiar running for the exits, but it was like fighting an upstream flow. 'Edmund, listen, you stay here—'

'. . . list of any personnel missing, everyone but the mirror team should already be at the airlocks now.'

In a room that was a blizzard of commotion, the base's leader looked every inch of his assumed role, a fixed centre around which all else spun. He spoke into his raised wrist-pad and that

339

sounded like Vasily distorted at the other end, but he looked up as Lucian skidded to a stop.

'Edmund!' Lucian had to yell to be heard. 'I'll go to Moreno, you stay and get everyone out. Leave it to me, OK?'

Harbour glanced up, but before he could speak Vasily's tinny voice was reporting:

'We've got two names still missing. One is Mallory, Mallory Madoc—'

'Try every name in her lab group,' Harbour said without a beat. 'Have Gen get a visual on the xenobiology labs and offices.'

'The second . . . Edmund, it's Nou. She's not here.'

The two men stared at the screen. Lucian had never realised it was possible to physically feel yourself go pale.

'I'll find her,' said Harbour at once. He had gone very still. 'This is my fault. I should never have—'

'No.' Lucian shook his head fiercely. He was the exact opposite: he thought he would explode if he did not move, and fast. 'You get everyone out. It's my fault she's gone. And I know where she'll be,' he added as the realisation struck.

There was only one place she would go. Hope, *hope*, a sunbeam. Then fear seized his insides. Nou, out there alone, among overturning mountains.

She won't be alone.

Lucian knew he was right. He knew where to find her.

Harbour nodded once. 'Go find her. Vasily will get everyone out. I'll find Moreno. I'll stop this.'

'No.' Lucian stared at him. 'No, look, I'll get Kip or someone, you're needed here—!'

'Lucian!' Both were yelling to be heard, and the longer the conversation continued the more absurd it seemed to be standing still. 'Lucian, we've never had reason to trust each other, but I need you to trust me . . . as I am trusting you, with my sister's life.'

340

The two men stared at each other amid the wheeling of the sirens and the flashing of the emergency lights. And though it was not scientific—it was not based on fact—it was not based on his head—Lucian found himself doing as Edmund asked. The look they shared could only have been a second, but that was all it took.

Lucian nodded to Edmund. And Edmund nodded in return to Lucian.

Then each turned, and each ran.

Lucian ran straight for his Sadge. Blood-red light drenched the base in circling flares; the alarms wailing overhead matched the exact thump of his heart; every depressurisation-proof door he waited to open was agony.

The aircraft hangar was packed with people piling into the evacuation ships, but he forced his way through. Inside the Sadge he set the autopilot for take-off while he yanked on a skinsuit, then atop it a proper, bulky spacesuit. He clipped on his helmet last and did the checks. He would be going outside tonight, no matter what.

Edmund ran the opposite way. He spilled from the control room and sped across the plaza at full sprint, past the suited people rushing against him. His training snapped into place with iron coldness: morning after morning, year after year, running on the stillness and silence of the ice. This was why.

Another lurch in his stomach told him the base was still on the move. The *New Horizons* replica in the dome was swinging at an angle. Trees lining the plaza squeaked and bent. Depressurisation could come at any moment but there was no time to stop . . .

Cries billowed behind him and Edmund saw their cause in a glance over his shoulder: another titan-sized al-Idrisi, falling against the sunburned sky, so colossal his mind could only

341

perceive its movement in snapshots. There was nothing to hold on to, nothing to brace himself against, as the shock wave shot through the ice, hit the base and hurled him into the air. He fell dreamlike in the low gravity, finding his feet before the quaking floor could whisk them away, then he was running again, scrabbling on all fours, then upright, sprinting through the whirling of the lights and the clamouring of the sirens and the *crack-crack-crack*ing of raining ice pelting the dome.

He reached the spiral stairs and leapt clear over their railing. The jump was perfectly angled as only years of knowing a place could hone; grabbing the ledge of the floor, he swung clear onto the level below.

He kept running until he was before the sign that read DR YOLANDA J. MORENO. AUTHORISED PERSONNEL ONLY.

The door slid back with a hiss and Edmund swept inside. Excepting the lock on the door, the standard living space was barely changed by its repurposing to a prison cell: the surprisingly tidy white kitchenette, breakfast bar, and corner sofa all matched Edmund's own. Moreno was already on her feet, pacing by the Heart-facing window. Clearly there was no need to fill her in.

Nevertheless she said, with a note of hysteria, 'You'd better be here to tell me what the *fuck is going on out there*!'

Edmund stood before the open doorway. It was not necessary to close it: he would not be there long.

'I'm here to oversee your evacuation. Providing you answer several questions as succinctly as possible.'

'What questions?'

Moreno stared at him and there was raw, unguarded fear in her eyes: the fear of a caged animal on a sinking ship. On cue there came another distant rumble deep below their feet, the sickening squeal of straining metal being forced in ways it should not. Moreno jumped in alarm; Edmund took particular care to remain as still as possible even as his heart thudded straight to his throat. Then, very deliberately, he took a step closer.

Moreno stepped back.

'Your confederate,' Edmund said quietly. 'Tell me their name.'

Pluto's surface was undergoing more change than it had known in over four billion years. Collisions both glancing and catastrophic; seasons of atmospheric freezing and thawing; convection cells churning and turning ice the mass of continents: these the little world knew well. These it had endured for time inconceivable before the world had become a home. But never before had Pluto known the inexorable force that was sunlight.

From space the Heart-side was a crescent of scorching white, all else in darkness. The crescent was lit to a scalding −200 °C: straight down the middle of the hairline zone where nitrogen and carbon monoxide exist as liquid. And the Heart was responding: were it not for the ice-crystal mist that clung to it, its topmost millimetres would be seen from space as stippled with a million silver pools like the inverse of the stars.

Yet despite this carnage, beneath the molten skin all else was calm. While the feet of the al-Idrises rocked, and the boundary scarp calved, and the glaciers creaked and cracked, the world away from light was as decoupled from the chaos as a parallel universe.

Nou was in this universe. Nou had reached the Promontorium just as the new star had ignited, before the first nitrogen rain had fallen, and she had drawn the darkness of its tunnels over herself like a hood.

All six Whistler pillars were bent at their middles and suspended scarcely a metre above Nou's face. She could have touched them. She had never done so in all their friendship, and she wondered now whether their surfaces were as velvet-smooth

343

as they looked, glossy as petals in the white light of their own making.

Presently they were conveying the concept of more than four billion years' stasis, and Nou almost reached for them just to steady herself.

Do you understand now? they asked when they were done.

It occurred to Nou that, now they were all leaning forward and active, she couldn't possibly say which had spoken. Tag was the tallest one, the moonlight-silver one, but were they *all* Tag? Perhaps they were all an *it*, one individual being, like the colonial aspen sprouting tree after cloned tree from interconnected roots in the Parks. Perhaps humans had no name for what Tag was.

She tried to tell them—it—she understood, but she did not, and so she could not. She shook her head in frustration.

It's too much.

There was a hum like understanding, or perhaps sympathy, in her head.

Your kind is not evolved to comprehend such vastness, Tag agreed. *You have never had need to. Especially for one so young. What is a thousand years to us? We can wait, as we always have. We will wait.*

Was that *we* a *we* or an *I*? Nou realised she couldn't say; all this time she had only assumed the translation. She ploughed on:

If you show yourselves now, you can stop it before it's too late. They won't listen to me. They will have to stop when they see you.

The pillars twitched.

We have survived worse. We were here when the binary body you call Charon cleanly skinned our crust. We were here when the impactor that formed this basin ejected half our roots to space. This, too, we shall outlast.

But you don't have to, Nou persisted.

344

How difficult it was to speak persuasively without moving her hands! Without making her eyes wide and trusting, without pouring as much belief into her words as she could. But how very human these desires were: how easily faked, or misinterpreted. The Whistlers had no need for them. She pushed herself into thinking all those things instead of gesturing them, just as hard as she could.

My people want to meet you. We can work together.

Tag—the Whistlers—the Whistler—was silent inside her head for several seconds. Then:

Do you believe your father loves you?

Nou was speechless. All thought felt knocked from her head as keenly as from a blow. She shook herself to attention.

Yes. She couldn't have said why her heart beat faster. She waited for them—it, him—to go on, but he did not. *Why?*

The pillars became still. Nou had the self-conscious feeling of being analysed inside and out from all sides.

From what you have told us, Tag went on, *a parent is both genetic contributor but also a figure of guardianship. One who protects his young while they outgrow their vulnerability.*

Nou's heart thumped harder. She could feel herself shrinking, the sensation all too familiar, with each passing moment.

When Tag next spoke, there was a quiet behind his touch in her head like gentleness.

You have never spoken of how he hurt you.

'Your confederate,' repeated Edmund expressionlessly. 'I want their name, now.'

'What?'

There was something odd about Moreno's tone. Like the fear on her face, the confusion in her voice sounded genuine.

Edmund took another step closer. Moreno took another step back.

'Let me ask again. Your accomplice. Who are they? You could have pre-programmed Jovortre, but not this.'

'I don't want to play games any more.' Moreno shook her head, backing further away even as Edmund closed the space again. 'Please. I won't be any trouble. I don't want to cause trouble.'

'You're causing me trouble.' Edmund's voice lowered further. 'The other saboteur. I want their name. Now.'

'Please.' Moreno shut her eyes, then squeezed them to slits. 'Why are you doing this? Please leave me alone.'

'Tell me.'

'I'll do my time.' There was a childlike pleading in the voice now. Her head was bowed, limbs huddled. 'I won't say anything to anyone, I swear. You know I won't say anything—'

'Say it to *me*!'

'I messed up!' Moreno cried, and Edmund masked his amazement at the sight of reddened, watery eyes. 'I know I messed up. You know I tried, please, you know I won't tell anyone . . .'

Something was wrong: there was no explanation for this much fear. The sneering, sanctimonious zealot from the day of Silvasaire's thwarting was another person, and Edmund had the feeling the explanation could mean nothing good.

'You are not making sense,' he said quietly. 'Explain yourself, and fast.'

Moreno stared at him through eyes like fresh wounds. Edmund held himself very still and let her. Let her see only truth, and the search for it. Somewhere in the distance, a new siren joined the others beyond the open door.

Moreno's lips parted as she kept on staring. Down came her eyebrows, even as her eyes widened. Confusion and revelation. Terror and relief. It didn't matter how long Edmund looked back: there could be no fathoming what such a tangle of emotions could mean.

'You really don't know?' Moreno said, her voice turned to a whisper under the din. Her eyes were widening and widening. 'He really didn't tell you, did he?'

The Sadge's protests were high-pitched keens but Lucian only pushed harder; this was no time for autopilot. He flew across the blinding crescent of sunlight, beneath the glittering clouds, so low he was level with the boundary cliffs. Below, fifty kilometres wide and two thousand long, was a lake.

Nou wasn't answering. That meant she was either underground—which he hoped, which *he hoped*, she surely was —or . . . or she was not answering.

His ship's reflection darted in tandem with him, then shuddered and broke apart as another cliff knifed into the Heart.

Ten minutes to the Promontorium. He called her suit again: still nothing. Be underground, he pleaded, be unreachable . . .

He could use the panic button.

The solution was so simple he wasted a whole second blinking in incredulity. Then he dived upon his glove compartment. How could he have forgotten the panic button? The one he had given the shy, silent, scared Nou the first time he took her to space, all that time ago back when Styx existed; the one that could record her location back when she was so young she probably shouldn't have been up there at all. Of course he had forgotten the panic button: it hadn't been used since that fateful day. There was a chance. If she was wearing it . . .

Lucian rifled one-handed among butterscotch sweets, the spare gauntlets he'd monitored Jovortre with, an unravelled ball of wool, until his hands closed around the edges of a wrist strap and he pulled his half of the panic button free.

It was a sort of oversized watch, except in place of a face was, in Lucian's case, a screen where Nou's held the button. It blinked to life at his tap.

'Find Nou,' he told it.

Its response was immediate:

No signal, and Lucian nodded with grim satisfaction. She was underground. There was still a chance. He set the device on the dashboard and powered onwards. He was almost there.

Edmund brought his wrist-pad down. Vasily was on his way; he would oversee Moreno's evacuation.

He felt clammy, inside and out, as though something cold and membranous had slid through his skin. Inside Moreno's eyes there had been only truth; Edmund knew this as much as he knew there was no surprise in his own. He had not come there for answers, he realised. He had come in denial.

He broke into a run. Walls lit scarlet in the circling pulsars of alarms. Head aching, ears aching, sirens scraping at the skin inside. An acrid smell, something like plastic, itching his nose. The depressurisation door to the main hallway was down; it hissed open at his touch and he hurled himself once more over the banister and straight under to the floor below.

Another door, another hiss, another run. By the time the stench of burning carbon hit his nostrils, and the wall of heat registered on his skin, and the sneering orange flames unpeeled themselves from the flashing red, the door had already snapped shut behind him.

You have never spoken of how he hurt you, said the Whistler, and Nou felt heat creep up her neck. It took her a moment to place the emotion as shame. The omission had not been deliberate, or to deceive, but nonetheless she felt all the guilt of one caught in a lie.

It's normal, she told the Whistler with as much nonchalance as she could push into the thought. *It's what parents are like.* But other thoughts were cross-cutting her, and here all thoughts were bared. *But Lucian isn't like that. Lucian would never hurt me. And Edmund . . .*

But Edmund *had* hurt her. And so had Lucian.

Tag's thoughts flooded across her own:

Does he love you? And yes, he went on, in response to Nou's flashing thought, *we too feel and understand love. To do so represents the foundation of consciousness itself.*

Silence, for a moment unchecked by time.

Yes, Nou answered again, but the thought felt all too like pleading. She tried for stronger, but there was no hiding the desperation as she did. *He* must *love me. He's my dad. He* has *to.*

Try as she could, she couldn't help her thoughts rise up in response to that, thoughts she could no more hide from Tag than she could her filling eyes: *I thought, if I found him life, he might love me. If I was better, if I was cleverer, he might love me. He's my dad. If he can't love me, why would anyone else?*

You are *loved, Nou Harbour.* Tag was cool water on the rawness of her thoughts. She raised her face into his many ones. *We see this clearly. We remember them. . .*

Nou stiffened: It was not names she saw in her head: as they appeared, filling her mind's eye. Edmund and Lucian, as the Whistler had known them. Lucian from only months ago, his eyes a child's, two wonder struck lanterns. Edmund from those years ago, and it was only for seeing him through Tag that Nou realised now how much he had aged in so little time. How much sadder he now looked.

She focused on one, then the other. To her horror, the wall of pressure behind her anger for them began to bleed away. It collected at the base of her throat, somewhere too deep to swallow, a lump large enough to hurt.

Tag continued.

We feel your betrayal. We feel your grief. But they acted how they saw best. We saw this. They acted for you, Nou.

349

Nou nodded with a sniff. Her vision grew too blurred to see, but that did not matter. Inside she saw Lucian's lantern-eyes, and the young Edmund's own. Both the same. Both wonder struck.

Then the vision changed. Another face replaced their own.

We saw inside your father, said Tag, as Nou stared at the man she tried never to think about. *For two individuals of the same species, you could hardly be more different. Clavius Harbour intended to detect, then dispose of, any life that threatened this Plutoshine you speak of.*

Is that why you hurt him?

She had not meant to ask; were she to experience a lifetime of this communication, she knew she would never master its utter transparency. But it had been years of wondering. If she did not ask now, she would never know.

There was a silence in her mind Nou could only describe as thoughtful. Keeping her own thoughts from rushing to fill it required all her concentration.

We intended only to re-equilibrate him, the Whistler said eventually. *For his intents, and for his treatment of you. We could not stand by in the face of these. What we must ask of you is, if your own father would not listen, what makes you think your species will?*

They're not all like him. Nou poured her heart into the thought. In her mind's eye she saw wonder struck eyes, and she knew Tag could see them too. *You met Lucian. He wants us to tell people. He's going to do it soon, after tonight. And they found life on the moons of other planets and it's protected, it's loved—*

But we are not akin to those creatures, said Tag. *We are an ancient being who wandered far from our home. We grew from a single seed, one of millions cast upon stellar winds, to seek fellow sparks of consciousness where we rooted. You were our first such spark. There is no precedent in your species' history for such a meeting.*

'But there's *me*!' Nou blurted the words aloud. 'You *have* met my species, and you *don't* need to hide any more!'

Fire. The one nightmare in a sealed base that throttles all others to silence.

The flames coated the corridor wall and licked across the ceiling, spewing thick smoke and melting plastic to curls as they went. The stench was overpowering. Humans could live on Earth, on Pluto, on Proxima Centauri b and beyond, but never could they escape the horror hard-wired to their bones at the sight.

That, and the awe. It had been decades since he had seen real fire, back on the only known planet where it could form on its own. The fire before him now was a living thing, a spirit, a deity. It was a piece of the Earth, a piece of human history, something inconceivable spliced into this place and time. It was more beauty than a man could bear.

Edmund moved too fast for thought. The heat opened every pore.

'Gen!' he shouted, shielding his mouth and nose as he dived on a panel of filter-masks. 'Gen, are you there?' He snapped one on and sucked in a breath. His eyes stung. 'Gen, answer me!'

Hissing, rushing, sputtering. No answer.

'*Gen!*'

Stern Base was fire-resistant to its foundations, had automatic water jets, could suck the oxygen from a sealed room. All these had failed in a day of fail-safe after fail-safe breaking down. And now so had its brain.

The malware was not only up there on the mirror. It was right here. It was running through the veins of Stern itself.

Beneath Edmund's feet: thunder. Vibrations shot up his legs, then whole tremors. Something fell with an explosive smash behind him, then he, too, was hurtled to the floor, both knee-caps cracking on contact with pain that blinded.

Something hot tickled his leg.

Fire tickled his leg.

Edmund surged to push himself up but was unable to support his own weight; the room was still shaking him to the
point of spasming, his head spinning as though hurled from
a centrifuge. It was then he realised it was not only the floor
on the move: something was happening inside the hardware
of his prosthetics. A kind of muscular convulsion, contraction,
tighter and tighter—some kind of nervous storm shuddering
them beyond his control. Scrabbling at the wall, he dragged
himself upright—just as the floor fell beneath him and the base
plunged into free-fall.

The grove rang with silence. Nou stared at each faceless pillar
and waited. Her thoughts were impossible to control, every
smallest and most tedious and most childish idea echoing high
to the vaulted ceiling for all to hear.

What must we do?

Nou, automatically, looked to the moonlight-silver pillar. For
a moment, disbelief stunted her thoughts as they rose.

You'll do it? You'll come with me?

Tag's every pillar held still in the air before her.

Our outposts—and Nou saw in her mind they referred to
other pillars, the same as themselves but different, encircling
and interconnected beneath all of Pluto, further, deeper, *more*,
than she had ever thought to imagine—*Our outposts have confirmed the severity of this warming project. And we trust you, Nou
Harbour. Yes. Let us work together. Let our species work together.*

Warmth coursed down Nou's every limb. Her chest filled as
though she had swallowed a balloon. Everything, she knew to
the depths of her bones, was going to be all right.

I'll go and get Edmund and Lucian, she told Tag on thoughts
that leapt together with joy. *I'll be right back.*

She could have kissed him; she could have thrown her arms around the moonlight-silver pillar. Edmund and Lucian . . . Even minutes ago the last two people she would have trusted, who had each betrayed her, who had each hurt her . . . But together they would know what to do. Together they would understand, and both of them would see how truly special the Whistler was. She would share her friend with Pluto, with the rest of her species. It would be a second chance to do so, when her first had gone so horribly awry. It would reconcile her with Edmund, she knew it would. They would be a family again.

She looked over her shoulder at the straightening pillars as she reached the crevasse opening and waved goodbye. In action they were a sight to behold, like watching skyscrapers she had seen in pictures bend at the waist. As they pulled themselves upright she could almost convince herself they were waving back.

Up the winding dark of the crevasse. Flashes of light and black with each turn of her head. A feather-light heart, a gait that danced. Nou Harbour did not run through that passageway: she soared.

She soared until she slipped. Something slick beneath her foot ran away with her balance and she gripped the walls, breathless, turning to light the source.

And at once jerked back her foot in alarm: rolling down the path in lobes was a silvery fluid thick-skinned with frost, a skin that tore as the rivulet flowed on, oozed more fluid, then frosted again in skin that wrinkled even as it set.

Cryo-lava. Ice-lava. Like on Wright Mons, the ancient ring-shaped caldera. But no: there were no known hotspots nearby, none of the thermal anomalies they'd covered in her geography lessons.

Nou ran. The silvery fluid slipped beneath her like both ice and water together and she skidded to keep her balance,

353

half-pulling herself up the crevasse. But something was wrong: there was light ahead of her now, as strong as her torch, so fierce she had to shield her eyes.

Nou burst to the surface and sucked in a gasp that tore her chest in two.

The star at the centre of the Solar System was hanging above her head. Not the spark she could blot out with her outstretched thumb, not the beacon of Lucian's mirror: the Sun itself had come to her, and it stretched from horizon to horizon.

Nou stood below it, ankle deep in steaming liquid nitrogen. Humans knew no word for the sight. It was not despair that crumpled her shoulders down, nor terror that drained all feeling from the backs of her knees, nor panic that set her every thought to the sky in flight. The last of the great dinosaurs must have known it, too, their eyes raised to the sky in confusion and fright; the people caught before that Earth volcano St Helens; those first, doomed humans on the *Beacon* mission. They, too, must have felt that quietening of the mind as their world up-ended. They, too, must have felt their end with acceptance.

A slab of ice the full height of the Promontorium calved, then toppled forwards, seeming to hang in the air before slamming down with enough force to rock the cliffs behind her. Another broke free in its wake, collapsing straight down in a torrent of ice shards. All along the cliffs, entire segments were giving way.

Thoughts of crying, of running, of calling for help: these were all choices—all of which she dismissed faster than the thoughts could form. But she could warn Tag. That was something she could do.

Lucian saw it before Gen could alert him: Nou's location had come online. Nou was alive, and she was on the ice, and he was four minutes away.

He could make that two.

354

He lunged the Sadge below the cliff tops and shot directly for the flashing red data point, swerving to avoid a sheet of falling ice. He was almost there. He drew lower now, hunting for the Promontorium by sight but it was gone, entire stretches all gone.

It was over before Edmund could throw out his hands: his cheek smacked the ground and shot daggers into his skull.

Stern Base was listing, a sinking ship. The walls were creaking like grinding ice. The precise moment he realised the fire was eating a blackened hole into the wall was the moment he realised it was the other way around: the fire had come from within the wall. The fire was in the very marrow of Stern's bones.

He was on his feet faster than the blood rush could catch him, faster than the prosthetic spasms could knock him back down. He was running, limping, leaping, before he could register whether the direction was the right one.

He slammed into the next dividing door. It hissed open at his touch, then he was running again.

Sparks rained across his shoulders. Smoke dispersed at his feet. Stern was being torn apart.

He was almost there.

Nou was back inside the crevasse when the whole of Pluto broke apart. There could be no other explanation: crack after crack knocked her to her knees, a giant hand swatting her flat. Pressure on her legs, her sides, her arms, a heaviness that was a burning, searing cold—whole blocks of ice sluicing down around her. The ceiling was falling in. The blackness was alive.

Go.

That one thought, over and over and over.

Go, Nou called to the Whistler, not just her own in that

familiar cavern but across the planet, all those other pillars, other outposts, wherever they were.

Maybe it was dreaming, or maybe it really was something, something tangible, but Nou knew they heard. The information was there in her mind, sure as truth.

Piercing screeches rent the walls apart. Nou clung to the memories of wonder struck eyes as she was shaken into senselessness.

His whole being centred on the lost shoreline, Lucian didn't see the cliff collapsing beside him until his wing fell down with it, hacked clean off. There was no time or thought to scream: he was spinning, and he was nose-diving, and the sunspots flooding his vision could have been the Sun-filled sky from the surface of Mercury.

Nou pushed a hand against a surface—floor, ceiling, wall, there was no *down* to tell—but no part of her body was able to respond. She was pinned. She was buried.

She wouldn't have become a terraformer like Lucian. She'd have studied the life of Europa, of Enceladus, of home. She would have been a xenobiologist.

There are worse ways to die than for science, Lucian had once said.

Did this count? Would she fill a frame in his locket of lost scientists, the side opposite his smiling family?

How she longed to unclip her helmet. To unclasp her gloves. The man she'd seen in the locket, the volcano photographer who was buried alive. He had had that, at least: he had felt his world between his fingers, in the end.

Nou shut her eyes as another crash rocked her hollow. Red lights flickered at the corners of her vision.

There were worse ways to die.

Edmund crashed through the last door just as the second wave of tremors hit, catapulting him into the air. He landed on one shoulder, hard, before sliding across the floor to split his crown against something cold and hard that showered him with steel instruments. For a moment even the hissing sparks and screeching sirens were muffled as he stumbled down the thread between conscious and not.

A rhythmic *click-click-click*ing dragged him back. An insect-ile whine.

He cracked open an eye.

Red and blue and green buttons, flashing on touchscreen monitors. Wires creeping like vines, up into wrists and chest and mind. A figure, unmoving, supine upon the bed.

Edmund's every nerve spiked in anticipation.

Clavius Harbour, on his throne. Right where he had left him.

Interlude 7

What does it feel like to drown?

On the cavern floor, with the *bleep-bleep-bleep* of the oxygen alarm a far-off pulse, with the tunnel disappearing into identical darkness left or right, Nou's lungs are sinking in on themselves. Her whole body is slowly, slowly imploding.

Drowning feels like delirium. Trapped in your own body with knives that breed at a touch beneath your skin. Drowning leaves no room for reason.

Edmund.

She calls with her mind. As the Whistlers taught her. Not the word: the meaning. Family. Protection. Arms that will close around her whole body. Keep her safe. Arms that will reach for anything beyond the reach of her own.

Edmund.

Nine-year-old Nou Harbour squeezes her eyes shut, rattles in a scrap of breath, and loses all ability to think.

Something broad and strong and solid wraps itself around her chest. It holds her tight enough to hurt. The sight of white walls rush past the slit between her eyelids now as something moves her, rolling her on her side, prodding something, pulling something that pulls her with it. And then, like being born again, air floods her lungs. Sparks explode across her vision. Pain that feels somehow like bright tightness stretches her skull to its seams. Something that scalds like heat and burns like ice scorches down every limb. When she next blinks her eyes apart, she squeezes them shut right away: the world is on a pendulum, colours pricking the blackness until it bleeds. Feeling returns and she wishes it wouldn't: not pins and needles but daggers, not chilblains but shrapnel spurting from the walls of her veins, and she thrashes and convulses, spluttering, backwards and forwards across the line between coherent and delirious.

Arms grip her. Arms raise her. Arms hold her fast, then strong legs kick into a run. There is an urgency to them; Nou feels this abstractedly, but any reason why is beyond her. The concept of *why* is beyond her. A *who*? Him. It is him, she knows. She clings to him as hard as she clings to consciousness.

Caution: oxygen at one per cent.

Edmund cannot feel his limbs. His thighs and prosthetics are both stone; the arms clutching his sister are only a concept. His vision is a twilit sky. One breath in, one breath out. One leg forward, other leg forward. Now out of the crevasse, now out across the plain.

Caution, his suit says. *Caution. Caution. Caution.*

His legs are airborne. The plain is airborne. The fall comes in discrete flashes. Nou is on the ground beneath his body. His faceplate is pressed into the methane sand.

Caution, his suit says. *Oxygen at one per cent.*

Edmund drags himself upright. He drags himself to his feet. He drags his disconnected air siphon out of the ice grains and back into Nou's side. He drags the two of them onwards.

Caution. Caution. Caution.

He drags in a breath.

Caution.

He drags them both up the steps of the life cabin.

Caution.

Airlock door. Open. Closed. Nou tumbles from his arms. Edmund is on his knees. The button, the pressurisation button, is above him. It is at the top of the stars.

Caution. Oxygen at zero—

He smacks the button down.

Nou is motionless across from him. There is a discordant humming in his helmet. Sound returns as air floods the tiny cubicle, a rising hiss. His vision is blackening from the outside in. He waits until the pressure reaches ninety per cent. Then, gloved hands a pair of paperweights, he unclips Nou's helmet. Unclips his own. Nou's vital signs suggest she is alive. Edmund is not so sure about his own.

The humming is still emanating from the helmet in his hands. It focuses into a voice as the dizziness abates. He catches sounds that could be words—then a name.

'Edmund? Edmund?'

Vasily.

'Edmund, we are at the site. Where are you? They are searching. Taking photographs. You must tell me what is going on—'

Edmund's hand rises slowly, dreamlike, and reaches inside to sever the connection.

Think. He has to keep thinking. The problem is, he is unable to think straight.

The Promontorium is overrun. He had his chance, the chance to destroy, but now that future is closed. What next? Pray they don't find the tunnel. Or—he cannot think—did he press the button to detonate? If they do find it, take Nou and run. Make for Earth, lose themselves, await the bounty hunters. Like Maiv did, before they got her. Better hunted than executed.

And if they don't find it? If he destroyed it?

Think straight, think straight. But Edmund is falling apart.

If they don't find it, no one needs to know life exists at all. Not the right thing, but the safe thing. The only halfway sane future left. Clavius would awake to everything as he left it, none the wiser to his

360

own attempted murder. No one else needs to know life exists at all. There is still a chance.

Sane? Halfway sane? *Neither*. Falling apart. Wildness, madness, closing in on every future. His options are crumbling. Edmund can't think straight.

The safe thing. Still a chance. Except . . .

He looks across from him. The world screeches back into the present. Mere seconds have passed.

. . . Except there is one loose end.

There, across from him, is Nou. Barely nine years old. How do you tell a nine-year-old her father would murder them both for telling the truth?

Still a chance.

The answer? *You don't*.

There, across from him, is Nou. And Edmund knows what he must do.

When consciousness returns, Nou is in her brother's arms and being swept into a small room. She cracks open an eye against the assault of light, but before she can adjust abrupt hands wrench her off and hurl her to the ground. She can't help herself: she cries out in shock. No sooner has she landed and silenced her tongue when she cries again: Edmund has grabbed her wrist and, twisting so hard tears spring to her eyes, he is dragging her further into the room. A glance up tells her she is in one of the life cabins, those bunker-sized refuges for the stranded traveller full of air and warmth, but when she turns around both leave her body at once.

For as long as Nou can remember, everything about Edmund has been controlled. His creaseless clothes, his clean-shaven jaw, his voice level, his presence one of calm and reason. She has seen Edmund angry before—even in anger calm, reasonable—but never like this. Never has she experienced fire.

Edmund's eyes are black but they shine, they *spark*. His mouth is a thin line, jaw tight, and this close she can see the individual beads of sweat on his cheeks, see the muscles there twitching, see her own reflection staring back at her, fishbowled, within his black irises. He looks wild, mad, and Nou shrinks in a terror she has never before felt in his presence as he reaches for her.

'Edmund—!'

Edmund wrenches her to her feet and throws her back down with force enough to shove her face against the slick-smooth floor with a sickening crack. Nou can scarcely believe the raw sting of her cheek. When she pulls herself up there is a line of blood dribbling between her and the ground.

Edmund bends down and Nou can't help herself: she flinches back.

'Don't you *ever*,' he shouts, the whites of his eyes livid, 'defy me *ever again*!'

'I'm sorry, Edmund.' Nou is sobbing, cowering, whimpering. 'I'm sorry—'

'Get to your feet!'

Nou scrabbles to find her footing but her legs are jelly beneath her, and in her fear all co-ordination flees. Edmund seizes her by the wrist and yanks her half-suspended before him. In one swift sharp movement he has drawn his hand back and he moves so fast, as though to strike her. Nou cries out in pure panic and feels sudden spreading warmth as her bladder gives.

But Edmund only shakes a finger before her face.

'Your creatures are *contamination*, they are from *Earth*, and now your father might *die* for your stupidity.' His eyes are wide, flat, and staring. 'Did you not think to check, before you brought us? Did you not *think*?'

Nou's eyes cross as she stares and stares at his raised hand as though it is made of fire.

'*Answer me, child!*'

But she is limp in his grip now, the world a haze of sparks and blackness, and Edmund lets her go in disgust. Nou knows she will never forget the way he looks at her in that moment. Towering above her, motionless and absolute, a stranger's mask set upon a face as impassive as the Whistlers'. The disdain that curls his lips could crush hearts far stronger than Nou Harbour's.

The man who only hours ago was her brother turns and walks away. Nou stares at the empty space he leaves.

'Vasily will be here shortly,' she hears him say. 'Do as he asks and be a good girl. You will not discuss this with anyone, do you understand me? You will never speak of this day.'

Nou does not answer. Footsteps, fading away; the click of a seal, the hiss of air; silence, silence. *Silence.* She cannot say how much time elapses between Edmund's leaving and Vasily Voronov's arrival. The gruff, bear-like man finds her lying on her side with her legs drawn up, barely conscious, and kneels down beside her.

'Nou?' he says quietly. 'Nou, can you hear me?'

Nou breaks her eyelids apart.

'Nou?'

Nou opens her mouth to speak. Her lips move silently, more of a tremble, but no sound comes out. She tries to find her voice—but there is nothing there. Nou can no more speak than she can bring her family back together.

Chapter 22

Edmund sucked in a breath through his mask. The room was swollen with sound, a swarm of hands thumbing into his skull, his ears, his eyes, but he would swear he heard the breath clear as a call.

Across the darkness lay the man called Clavius Harbour. Like a fixed point in the universe, even as the base fell apart around him Clavius was the same as ever. Wan skin tinged blue. Limp, shaved head glistening. Eyelids flickering within purplish hollows. There was the same beeping of the heart monitor. The same rhythmic breathing from the ventilator. The same aura of power and control.

There, set upon his head in place of a crown, was a shining white circlet. And there, covering the drips pin-cushioning his forearms, were the filigree meshes of the gauntlets.

The doctor's new treatment had been working too well. When the gauntlet suggestion was made, Edmund had jumped at the chance to know what was happening. Being brain-dead was too much to hope for, but to gauge movements—plans, an expected time of revival, whether hope existed for its opposite—for that there was a chance. Lucian was drawing words from his silent sister; could the terraformer do the same for his father?

The circlet had been snapped against clammy forehead; the

gauntlets pulled over punctured wrists; the system connected to the base supercomputer, sharing a home with Gen.

All this time Edmund had been waiting for the computer to translate, for the scans to say something, and all this time the patient had been playing him. Using the gauntlets for his own ends. With access to Gen he didn't need a body, didn't need Moreno to hack Jovortre; plugged into Gen, he was right up there with Halley on the mirror. He was everywhere across Stern. He was everywhere.

Now Edmund understood why the fire had been left to rage. Now he understood why the base was being allowed to fall apart. He realised it was all part of the plan. It had been part of the plan all along.

Click-click-click. Arachnoid arms were a hive of activity around the bed, rearranging wires, tucking in bedcovers, checking connections, while the hemisphere of a glass cylinder waited on standby above the full length of the body. Waiting to seal him in.

The auto-evacuation. Edmund drew in a sharp breath. He only had minutes. He tried raising his head—bracing a hand against the warm floor, slick with something he did not want to see—but vertigo sent it cracking back down. When he tried again, harder, this time his arm gave way with a jagged stab and a cry that tore his throat open. The room swayed, too much to be from his own dizziness. Behind him his legs were still malfunctioning, a puppet's, convulsing like plucked strings. When he forced his eyes back open it was to a world of formless colours, everything out of focus—flashes of motion, of light that blinded and dark that bloomed.

He scrabbled at the smooth floor with his fingernails, trying to gain some purchase. He had to get up. Orange was a wall to one side—a wall that came with heat, and with it the memory of more pain. In increments his focus returned, and with it,

365

recollection. He was in his father's hospital ward. The base was falling apart.

The wires snaked up behind the life support console. He could see them. He could . . . He dug his nails in harder . . . Gritted his teeth . . . Tried to drag himself . . .

He wasn't strong enough. He could run up the al-Idrises in two hours flat. He could calculate the precise sequence of genetic code to reprogramme a bacterium. He could build the machine to do it. But he couldn't raise his head from ground that burned.

Stern couldn't die like this. Its dream was already primed and incubated when Edmund first arrived, someone else's child, but that hadn't stopped it becoming his own. And even his father hadn't stopped it becoming something like home.

The spider-leg mechanisms retracted. The glass lid began lowering. Clavius Harbour was slipping away.

Edmund pushed back a leg, hoping to hit a wall, to propel himself forward—and met nothing.

Would Stern Base crumple inside the space it once occupied, as Edmund's chest was? Would Stern, too, feel its air pressed from it, feel its walls go cold, the lights behind the eyes of its windows go out?

He stretched out an arm—he could pull himself—he clenched his teeth together—stretched until his arm trembled like taut elastic—but the closest cable was out of reach.

Like the *Beacon* mission. Another memorial site. Edmund shoved the thoughts away, but they were vines snaking themselves tight. Another cautionary tale . . . One whose bones would lie beneath the wheeling stars of the aeons. The dream of calling Pluto home just that: just a dream. Mercury, Mars, Pluto. Another failed colony. Its survivors scattered and homeless, going their separate ways . . .

Nou. No home. No family. On her own. In a Solar System

where she had no one. She could never return home.

The surge of energy caught him too fast for conscious thought, and Edmund *lunged*. The cable was scarcely at arm's length but the distance was like leaping clear over a roaring river. Pulled rigid, it stretched straight to him from the back of his father's console—straight across the edge of the bed. The evacuation lid rose, sensing the obstruction, before trying again to close.

Edmund was on his feet. There was no vector from lying to standing; the world had been severed to discrete time intervals. His vision swung around him—the base swung around him—his legs were crumpling beneath him like paper—but again all superfluous action was cut from his consciousness. He was at his father's bedside, clutching the evacuation seal with both hands, and he was wrenching it back.

His father's breath was short, punctured. Muscles within his waxen cheeks were pulsing. His eyelids were flickering like boiling water. Even his fingers were twitching now, albino spiders' legs skittering on the sheets . . .

Edmund seized the wires behind the console and threw himself across the bed as his legs finally gave way. Red lights wheeled above him like crazed lighthouses. Beneath him, above him, on every side, Stern Base was screaming, screaming at him.

A rush between his ears like a rearing wave. Edmund tightened his grip and felt machinery as hot as blood between his hands.

He tensed his wrists and began to pull—then something grabbed him by the arm.

A hand had hold of him. A skeletal, paper-white hand. A shock of cold. The body lay limp, but the hand gripped him as tight as his own gripped the life support.

There was a monitor by the bed. The one Lucian had set up—the one that was supposed to display his father's words, and which never had. Except for now.

367

There was one word upon the screen. Lowercase. Sans serif. Three letters.

Son.

Edmund turned to the figure on the bed. Aged, shrunken, helpless Clavius Harbour. His last defence. He stared at the pulsing eyelids, and as he did he felt a quietness overcome him. His heartbeat slowed. He leant in, the better for the creature on the bed to hear.

'That was always your problem,' he breathed. 'You never understood that being a parent has nothing to do with genetics. It's something you earn.'

And he jerked back his hand and pulled every plug from the console.

Chapter 23

The crumpled metal shape was blanketed beneath snow. Nitrogen fell thick from clouds that froze as fast as they could form, each backlit by a blazing gold lining. Glassy plates crystallised, then disintegrated under the shifting shade, sealing then releasing the remains of the Sadge within the knee-deep nitrogen sea.

Lucian forced his lashes apart from something crusting them together, then squeezed them shut again as pain cleaved his vision in two. Every part of his body ached. His brain was spinning sickeningly inside his skull, and his legs felt worse even than the time he'd fallen asleep cross-legged after a mate's stag do. He tried to move them—and tore his throat open in a scream. Not quite cross-legged, then. A little—he pressed his lips together but couldn't keep from whimpering—a little more than that.

He was hanging upside down in his seatbelt, and from what he could tell, the hull was miraculously intact. He must have blacked out from the g-forces—it was coming back to him now—he'd been hit—his wing—the cliff—Nou . . .

'Gen,' he croaked in a voice like gravel. 'Gen, access the panic button.' He raised a wrist to unclasp his harnesses, but for some reason his fingers wouldn't move. He pawed helplessly at the clasps, then realised there was no response. 'Gen?'

Why wouldn't Gen respond? Gen was always there. Gen was everywhere.

'Gen, could you—?'

'Yes, Lucian?' That bland, efficient voice. 'My apologies—I was experiencing technical difficulties. All systems have been restored. How may I help you?'

Lucian got the clasps of his belt undone and howled as his whole body dropped free. Had it got darker somehow? He could barely see. He pushed himself upright on arms liquid with adrenaline, wincing to keep his weight off his gloved fingers. Whatever had happened to them he didn't want to think about; now that his leg was quieting down, the alarm bells from elsewhere were growing harder to ignore.

'Get Nou's location. Get me walking distance. Tell her I'm coming.'

At Gen's release the effect was instantaneous: water exploded from sprinklers and steam spurted with a deafening hiss to fill the room; the base stopped inching lower as some support mechanism hurtled into action; a powerful whirring started up—the air handling—a sound so ubiquitous and so routine as to be usually inaudible. The force trapping Edmund's electromechanical nerves released him; the stillness was like the flicking of a switch. Even inside him, inside the prosthetics his father had built, there had been control. Edmund hadn't realised his calves were quite literally on fire until they weren't. Perhaps anyone else would have already been dead.

And a glance beyond a window confirmed what he already knew: that eternal night had returned to Pluto. Whatever hold his father had had—however he had managed it—Plutoshine's mirror was now one more dead star in the sky.

On the sopping mattress, water running in rivulets over eyes that would never again open, over lips that would never again curl back to unleash pointed canines, the body of Clavius Harbour was still. And Edmund knew: the time for murder had now passed.

He allowed himself to think that again.

The time for murder had now passed.

Just for a moment, he let his eyes fall closed. They stung from the smoke, and they were wet from the rain, but neither meant anything.

He turned away and tumbled to his knees.

'Gen . . . !'

He made to shout over the hissing of rain and steam, but a fit of coughing took him by surprise. Once he started he could barely catch his breath to stop.

'Get . . . Lucian!'

There was a medevac Sagittarius primed to go up ahead; Edmund hauled himself to his feet and limped over, and without a backward glance pulled himself inside the back end made for the hospital bed. The whole base shook beneath him as the ship door slid shut, sealing out the storm of sirens and steam. But something else came in with him: filling up the quiet was raw heat in his legs, and the tightness of skin crisped and shrunken, and a fire still burning beneath it. Edmund risked a touch at the tender space where his flesh became mechanism and pulled away fast enough to stumble.

'Edmund?' came a hazy voice over the ship's comms. A voice that sounded how he felt. 'Edmund. You're'live . . .'

'*Lucian.*' Edmund spluttered again, doubling over with it. His words sounded fuzzy, somehow, as though they were physical things with edges blurred and bleeding. He pulled himself towards the cockpit, but it was at the other end of a lengthening tunnel. 'Do you have her? Are you safe?'

Crackling over the line. Static, or laboured breathing, or maybe it was all in Edmund's head. Then:

'Got hit. Ship's stuffed. Going now. 'S not far . . .'

Edmund made the mistake of blinking—and forgot how to open his eyes. He was suddenly tired to the marrow of his bones. If he could sleep . . . just for a little while.

'Send me your co-ordinates.' He tried raising a hand to hit the autopilot, but it wouldn't move. 'I'm coming to get you.'

All his energy fled with the words. A tiredness he had never known was turning his limbs to wood. This time, when his eyelids came down, he was powerless to stop them.

The snow was coming down fast. He hadn't crashed far from Nou. It was all dark, starless, dark as space itself. The mirror had gone out and Lucian couldn't care to wonder why. He clutched the splints of his leg together, grey with pain, and staggered around toppled cliff fragments to the site of her last connection. The ice gave beneath his feet and the slush below kept trying to refreeze to seal around his legs. He would drag himself the length of this broken Heart if he had to.

He was clawing his way now, scrambling over rubbly ice blocks, fingers numbed to non-existence even over the heat of his gloves, until the sight of a broad notch in the collapsed cliff face of Pandemonium Promontorium stopped him dead.

She was there between the arch. A small, still form in a child-sized orange spacesuit, the only spark of colour in his observable universe. She lay upon a crooked ledge of ice. No. Lucian's lips parted as his eyes registered the sight. She lay cradled in the bough of a Whistler.

It was the tallest one. The bright silver one. It was bent across itself like an old tree. It moved at the sight of him. *The Whistler moved.*

Lucian slid an arm beneath Nou's knees, around her chest, and lifted her into his arms. There was no face on the creature, nothing but gleaming smoothness, catching the light of stars that were not out to shine. He nodded silently to it: a nod in place of words that would not come, from a throat that would not open. And Lucian could have sworn the incline of its crown was a bow in return.

He turned the way he had come and encountered only grey on all sides. Snow fell in walls. It felt as though half the Heart was raining upon them.

One hand clamping his weightless charge to his chest, the other clamping his leg, Lucian stumbled forward. To the Sadge. To shelter.

Behind him, already haloes fading to phantasms, the lights of the Whistler said their farewell.

The autopilot plunged Edmund below the cloud line. Ice particles sublimated in flashes at the touch of his ship.

Visibility fell fast as he did. Lucian wasn't answering; he had given Edmund co-ordinates, but if he'd gone after Nou he would have been caught in this blizzard.

A blackened hull below, barely visible under a rising tide of white. Swooping lower still, weaving around the looming debris. The twin specks of two figures huddled together . . .

Focus surged into place at the sight. Edmund flicked to manual and swung the ship around. He dropped beside the shapes, raising the airlock door as he did. And there, almost buried in a snowdrift, were Lucian and Nou. She was unmoving in his arms, sheltered tight against him, but Lucian raised his face to the light. The disbelief there—the shining red eyes—the stupefied wonder—would remain seared in Edmund's memory long after others of that night faded.

Their eyes locked.

'Inside, now!' Edmund yelled.

Lucian dived through the snow and on to the ship with Nou clasped in his arms. With a roar of *g*-force, Edmund shot them into the sky.

A hiss of air and the universal *beep* of pressure stabilising. Edmund kept his hands tight on the controls as Lucian and the unstirring form in his arms burst inside.

'Get her helmet off . . . her gloves . . .' Edmund's voice convulsed like a plucked tightrope. He steadied his breathing. 'Is she alive, Lucian?'

Lucian, in the rear-view mirror, was grasping helplessly at the clasps of Nou's helmet.

'I can't . . .' His fingers wouldn't bend. 'I can't . . .'

The tightrope snapped. '*Is she alive?*'

'I don't *know.*' Lucian's composure broke as his whole face crumpled.

'Check her breathing.'

Edmund turned his gaze to the streaming snow and fixed it there, flying them up from the white-out.

Behind him, Lucian had managed to unclasp his own helmet with the edges of his palms. He cast it aside and fiercely scrubbed his eyes before working on Nou's, hands clumsily snapping the locks loose.

Her face, once revealed, was blue like sunlight through ice. Sticky blood shone where one temple met her balaclava. There was an expression frozen in the tightness of her brows that Edmund could not discern. Something he had never seen there before.

Lucian's voice hitched.

'Breath—she's breathing!'

Edmund stared firmly ahead, not trusting himself to blink or speak, and nodded curtly to the mirror.

Lucian didn't catch it. He had pulled Nou into his arms and he was hugging her tight to him.

'I got you, kid. You're gonna be fine. We'll get you somewhere safe . . .'

They soared higher now, no trace of ground or familiar landmarks to be seen: Pluto was a snow globe. Edmund recalled the dust storms of Mars, infinitesimally fine particles choking the planet for months on end, then settling like silt on an abyssal plain. Under Pluto's gravity, it could be years before the true damage was revealed.

'She's cold.' Lucian had a hand pressed to Nou's cheek. 'Hypothermic. Is there . . . ? Ah . . .'

There was a kind of table at the stern of the ship meant for the evacuation pod. Lucian grimaced his way to his feet and laid her upon it.

At once a glass hood sealed itself over the length of her. Arm after metallic arm appeared and began to disassemble their patient, unclipping spacesuit fragments, running clawed hands up and down each limb. A sensor marked the temperature inside as incrementally increasing.

Edmund looked away from the rear-view mirror as his throat closed shut.

'You know why she was out here, don't you?'

Lucian was watching him, propped up against the pod's side. Through reddened eyes his gaze was steady.

He said, 'She showed you the Whistlers.'

Edmund lowered his eyes, then showed Lucian the courtesy he deserved and returned them.

'Yes.'

'Then how can you possibly call them contamination? Why don't you believe her?'

Edmund swallowed hard and propelled out his words on an exhale.

'I do, Lucian. I always have.'

Lucian's lips parted, then clamped shut in a hard line.

'I knew it. I knew there was no way you . . .' His eyes caught fire. 'So you lied? You knew Pluto had life and you . . . you just chose not to tell the rest of humanity?'

'Let me explain—'

'*Yeah*, I'll let you explain,' Lucian spat, voice rising, hobbling over, 'to the Court of Planetary Protection! And worse,' he added, voice pure venom, 'she *trusted* you.'

Edmund forced himself to look: Nou, boneless, broken, probed by cold, sterile hands.

Something was wrong with Lucian's leg: he was gripping it with clenched teeth, his skin visibly greying. He sat down in defeat where he stood.

'If she showed you that place under the Heart, then she trusted you to do the right thing.'

Edmund did not flinch. He let himself be flayed raw.

'I know.'

'Then *why* . . .?' Voice cracking. '*Why* —?'

'Because it wasn't just me who saw the Whistlers.' He drew a deep breath, light-headed with sudden urgency, but Lucian spoke before he could continue.

'What do you mean?' he said quietly. Then, 'You mean your dad, right? She showed you both?'

Edmund knew the moment the words left his lips what their consequence would be. This was not a story he could only tell by half. Except now, after all those years accumulating secrets, he was ready. He realised this was what he wanted.

So he said, 'I found the person responsible. The saboteur. Moreno's employer.'

'What?' Lucian wasn't getting it. 'I don't care, Edmund. We're talking about Nou.'

'I am, Lucian,' Edmund told him. 'If you'll listen. Will you hear me out?' Then, closing his eyes as he swallowed his pride, 'Please?'

They were out of the danger zone now, along the deep blue line where sky became stars; the autopilot could take over from here. They probably didn't have much time alone: it wouldn't be long before the villagers would try to contact him, contact this ship, contact Lucian's ship. There was so much that needed to be said.

Edmund undid his harness and pulled himself to stand opposite Lucian, biting the insides of his cheeks as he forced the cracked burns on his legs to bend. The terraformer watched this—eyes flicking from limbs to face—and while there was no savage pleasure in his expression, concern was equally absent.

'My father made it no secret he was searching for life,' Edmund began. The words came from him fluently, as though prepared. 'He hired the Solar System's best xenobiologists under this pretence—that he wanted certainty the terraforming wouldn't harm any bio-heritage. What he did keep quiet was what he intended to do with life if he found it.'

Lucian ripped off his balaclava and scrubbed his shock of wiry hair in every direction, but only listened in silence.

'He was always very clear to me on his policy. We already had proof of extraterrestrial life with Europa and Enceladus. Adding Pluto to that list would tell us nothing new about our place in the universe, but Plutoshine would be indefinitely frozen.'

'The terraforming?'

Edmund nodded. He kept his words short, staccato, to the point.

'I had been raised to follow him. To obey. You don't understand the kind of man my father was. To the rest of the world he was an altruistic genius. To me, to *us* . . .' He sought words of description, but none came that were strong enough. He pressed

377

on. 'When life was discovered around the Gas Giant moons, all human activity ceased. All mining, all terraforming. Even scientific activities were limited. My father had given twenty years to Pluto's colonisation. He wouldn't allow that to happen to his world. So he planned to seek out life and exterminate it, then keep the xenobiologists on goose chases until Plutoshine was complete.' He looked down at his hands. 'There was just one flaw in his plan.'

Lucian shook his head. 'I don't . . . I can't believe what I'm hearing. Everyone loves Clavius Harbour.'

'I know, Lucian.'

'What was the flaw?'

Edmund felt his shoulders drop. 'There was one person searching for life harder than he was. Someone both of us underestimated every time.'

Between his words, like the air between the snow they ascended through, was pure silence.

'I don't know why my father never cared for Nou. I can't say for sure he has it in him to care for anyone. When her mother got out, I took it upon myself to be both her parents. Yes, we were once very close,' he said, at Lucian's transparent surprise, 'but she never stopped wanting her father's love. Even when he . . .'

Edmund stopped. This was something he had never shared with anyone. Lucian only watched.

Edmund considered his words carefully.

'He never *physically* hurt her. It would have been easier if he had. It would have been easier for others to see. But . . . it was always very apparent when he had got her alone. I don't know what he would say, or do. I only saw the smallest part of it. She would come to me afterwards and she would be unable to speak, sometimes for hours. But if it was anything like what he did to me when I was her age . . .'

It was a sort of magic trick of his. Clavius Harbour's. He would quirk his brows, fix his eyes on you, and watch you with rapt, warm attention. There was something inescapable about it, something in that expression that made you feel like the most important person in the universe. This most wonderful, most clever, most accomplished of men—and it was *you* he had made time for. It was *you* who maybe, just maybe, got to occupy the smallest corner of his fearless heart. Perhaps, safe and wanted in that corner, you might be worth something. Perhaps he thought you were worth something.

But the reverse was equally true. A man who could elevate you to something worthwhile, something meaningful, just by looking at you, could make you question all that through as little as a flick of his eyes. Make you value your worth, your meaning, your very existence, all in terms of how important you were to him.

Edmund knew all this at first hand.

'I thought long on the reasons for my father's behaviour. My only guess is that he saw her devotion to him. Whether he wanted to test it, or toy with it, I can't say. Or use it when she grew up, as he did with me. It's, ah.' A burning in his cheeks; Edmund almost raised his hand to them in surprise. It made sense that a conversation he never meant to have would raise emotions he never wished to feel. 'It's so much easier to rationalise maltreatment when it happens to you. I accepted my treatment as a child. I believed I deserved it. But when that same treatment fell on someone I loved . . . To watch him hurt her, as I had been hurt . . . It was unbearable. I would have done anything to make it stop.'

Still Lucian watched him with reddened eyes—staring at him now as though he was someone wholly new.

'All I knew was I had to get her away from him,' Edmund continued. 'The day she showed us the cavern, I came prepared. I had already sabotaged his suit, to make it seem an accident. I never wanted Nou involved, but with her as witness I would be free of suspicion, and the two of us could leave on the very ship you arrived on.'

'But it didn't work,' Lucian whispered.

He shook his head.

'Why not finish him off?'

Edmund looked up, startled at the sudden edge to the voice.

'You could have prevented all of this.' Waving a hand to the snow, to the pair of them, with open splits across cheeks and bruises bleeding under skin. 'You could have still got out. Why didn't you just unplug him, smother him, *inject* him? You're a *biochemist*.'

'Hydrofluoric acid,' Edmund said flatly. 'One drop to the scalp. Instant heart attack. No one will find the burn, no one will know the cause.'

Lucian's mouth slipped open.

'I've had a long time to plot murder, Lucian. And to think through its consequences. Cutting suit pipelines in a cavern hosting extraterrestrial life forms was scarcely the only chance I had. There were many. Every day. But let me ask you something.' He folded his hands together. How remarkable, how ridiculous: to discuss this in the same manner he would his latest review paper. 'Have you ever thought in utmost seriousness how it would feel to murder another human? Even knowing what you do now about my father. Could you make one moment in your life become the moment you ended another's?'

Lucian did not answer, and Edmund did not expect one: he had been asking himself that question for years, and hearing only silence in response.

'I have,' Edmund told him. 'More than the moment itself, it is the afterwards I think of. An empty space in a room because of my actions. Shaking hands with strangers, or smiling with friends—knowing I have it in me to do the same to them, if only I want it enough.

'I'm a coward, Lucian,' Edmund explained. He was so tired. There was a dull thudding in his head, growing worse with each word. 'I couldn't find a second attempt within me. Every day I saw him there, and every day I did nothing. I told myself it was safer to wait for the two-year anniversary, the deadline when all life support would be terminated. I calculated the risk and I took it. There was no evidence to suggest he would improve. Except, as that deadline approached, he did. And still . . .' Edmund stared ahead. 'Still I did nothing.'

'But why not just *leave*?' There was exhaustion in Lucian's voice now: as though he knew it could never be that simple, but desperately wished otherwise. 'Why not just . . . just go hide on Earth, go to your livestream . . . ?'

Few days passed when Edmund did not ask himself the same question, checking to see if his answer remained unchanged.

'Had I left with Nou and my father had awoken,' he said, 'he would have known what I had done. He would have known I had revealed Nou's secret, and he would have hunted us to the ends of the Solar System. And had I stayed and disobeyed his direct orders—had I revealed Pluto's life, to the cost of Pluto-shine—he would have punished me. Her, specifically. So I hid it. And . . . I silenced the only witness.'

Lucian closed his eyes. 'Nou.'

'She had to doubt herself. Enough to stay quiet. Just until . . .' Edmund pressed his lips together. 'Just until I could figure out what to do.'

His eyes slid to the small figure in the medical pod. Body covered over now, aluminium blanket snug, rising and falling with each breath. Hard white polyethylene for a pillow. The sight of her blue lips, the purple hollows under her eyes, drew a long line of pain somewhere inside him.

Lucian was shaking his head, but when he spoke the bitterness had bled from his voice.

'I suppose that's why you've been looking a little peaky of late.'

'Have I?'

'You look like when they defrosted the *Beacon* crew.'

'I hadn't . . . I suppose I haven't been feeling my best, Lucian, no. It's been a difficult few years.'

'She thinks you can't stand the sight of her, you know.'

Edmund stared firmly into the snow outside.

'That's what she had to believe. If I'd loved her, I would have listened to her. I would have believed her. Only, in my urgency to ensure her silence, I went too far . . .'

'Vasily will be here shortly,' he hears himself say, but there is no *him* in the voice. His throat is raw from shouting. 'Do as he says and be a good girl. You will not discuss this with anyone, do you understand me? You will never speak of this day.'

It is not the same Edmund of that morning who looks at the crumpled child on the floor. A kind of metamorphosis has entered his bloodstream. A chill. Pressing him on all sides into something new, something hard. Something necessary.

Nou does not respond, and that is when he catches the scarlet on the floor beneath her cheek.

He did that. He hurt her. And he will have to hurt her much more.

Edmund turns on his heel before he does something he will regret. In the airlock he calls Vasily—location, task, now. Outside on the Heart, he runs. He runs too fast for his thoughts to catch him, and he runs south-east, opposite to Stern, opposite to civilisation, towards the constellation shaped like a question mark. He runs towards emptiness and wilderness, oblivious to the burn of his thighs, oblivious to the warning lights, to his own sunsickness, the glow of the ice like fresh snow under a full moon, a full moon on Earth . . . On . . .

Home.

He has no recollection of the series of actions that brings him to his knees, and that breaks him. There he sobs, helmet in his hands, and raising his throbbing eyes he sees the stars are wheeling around him, the ice wheeling around him, and he knows then he should have left—why hadn't he left?—Why hadn't he taken Nou and run away with Maiv? Clavius would have chased her, would have chased them all, but they could have been free, and now . . .

Don't you ever! Edmund had screamed, and Nou had cowered before him. *Don't you* ever *defy me ever again!*

Nou, weeping before him; he had made her do that. He had become his father, and part of that was acting but part of that was the genuine cracking of a levee somewhere inside of him—the cracking of control. Now, and for evermore, he can no longer say where he ends and everything he loathes begins. Clavius's backup, installed in its new host.

Lungs gripped shut, no space left for air. He gave all his air to Nou. Flashing warnings wash over him. All he has to do is wait . . .

And if he does, he will never see Earth again. If he does, he leaves Nou alone against a father who could awaken at any moment. If he does, Clavius will win, after everything.

Starlight, shut out as he falls forward on his face. Edmund lets the emptiness fill him whole, and lets the metamorphosis complete.

It is only then that he returns to Stern, and when he does, Edmund Harbour is unrecognisable.

Back in the ship, Edmund closed his eyes.

'I never meant to hurt her so much.'

'But you stopped him, right?'

Edmund willed his lashes apart.

Lucian went on. 'You said you found the person responsible. And the mirror's gone out. So—you stopped him.'

383

Bluish hollows around eyes. The spiderlike network of lines across the backs of eyelids. Skin visibly whitening. Relief. All he had felt, looking at the body of his father. It was relief.

'Yes,' Edmund said simply. This was it. The moment he confessed to murder. 'Yes, Lucian. He is stopped now. And when the time comes I will take full responsibility for that.'

Exhaustion overcame him swift as depressurisation. The years had desensitised him to the weight of that truth. Now, high in space where weight was just a concept, it was more than just his body that floated free.

The snow was winking with light outside, tiny flashes like static, or the stars that spark behind drowsy eyelids. He needed sleep. How many hours had passed since the switch-on? When had he last . . . ?

He blinked sharply. The lights were not in his eyes. They were outside.

'Edmund.' Lucian, quietly.

All perspective of the world upended as the two men registered the sight beyond their window. Within the snow, steadfast as the stars, were the lights.

Edmund called them xenocryophiles, but that was only for something to call them: *xeno*, alien; *cryophile*, cold-loving. Really, he didn't know what the creatures he had found on his boots the day of the accident were. In the laboratory he had witnessed their tendency to flocculate, long gossamer threads knitting together, stark scarlet against the white of his Petri dishes. Seeds? Each strand a pillar? Each pillar a tree? Each tree but a limb to one singular, interwoven organism? As a scientist he'd been driven mad with the temptation to return, the yearning to know.

The scarlet threads in the snowfall cleaved like cobwebs across the ship's bow. Even as Edmund and Lucian watched, the broken ends connected again to one another, or reached out, fumbling for others, lighting the dark across three dimensions. All glowing, glowing red.

It had been years, but his memories were etchings in clay: the more he had retraced those grooves the deeper they had become, until a landscape had emerged. Edmund saw the cavern as vividly as reality. Pillars in a cathedral, lit by candles of flowing scarlet underfoot, overhead. Something dynamic, alive.

Edmund tried to estimate the volume beyond his window in cubic metres, then cubic kilometres, and failed. Some part of his scientific mind rationalised that the creatures must have been uprooted with the ice chunks; must have been lofted high into the atmosphere, dandelion seeds carried on a wind; must be spread far beneath the Heart; must be far, far more numerous than the colony of Nou's cavern . . .

His heart seized then, in sudden, instinctive fear that relaxed as fast as reason could catch up. There was sound crackling over the radio, first a whisper, soon as clear as the day he first heard them:

One-two-three.
One-two-three.
One-two-three-four.

Like a bird call, or an SOS. Like a hello.

'I don't think anyone can doubt it now, Edmund,' Lucian murmured.

They watched together in silence as the scene stretched on, as the ship climbed higher, as the snow lessened, as the threads thinned, as—maybe over minutes or maybe hours—the lights graded into those of the star-speckled sky. Would they rain back as snow? Would they lightly dust the planet's surface in a pulsing lattice of colour, before seeping down like rainwater through soil? From space the snow globe of Pluto must appear a

385

white haze, crackling with filigree lightning in the most delicate of traceries. Pluto would shine, perhaps even to the telescopes of Earth itself, and it would shine through light of its very own.

Quite suddenly, violently enough to startle, Lucian began to weep.

Edmund jumped in alarm, then again at the resulting stab of pain behind his eyes.

'What is it? Lucian, what's wrong?'

'I knew I was forgetting something!' Lucian cried, head in his hands.

Edmund let out his breath. 'Lucian, the mirror wasn't your fault. Nobody was to know.'

'It's not that.' Lucian looked utterly wretched. 'I left Captain Whiskers in the base.'

'Who in Earth's name is Captain Whiskers?' Edmund demanded.

'My *cat*! I just *left* him there, how could I do that? He must be so scared!' He might even . . . He could be . . .

Edmund bit the inside of his cheek. Comfort was not his speciality—or at least it had not been for some time.

'It's, ah. It's been a long day, Lucian. We're both overwhelmed.'

'And I still don't get the *why* behind all this.'

Edmund felt his eyebrows lower. '"Why"?'

'The motive.' Lucian rubbed his hands across his face. 'Sabotaging your own master plan. Plutoshine was Clavius Harbour's baby. Why would he want to—?'

A burst of static on the radio. Then:

'*crrrrk* . . . read me? This is Grace Halley, do you read me?'

'Halley!' Lucian cried.

'Lucian Merriweather, by all the stars in the sky, that had better be you!'

Edmund launched himself in free-float to the radio.

'Grace Halley, I read you, this is Edmund Harbour. Thank Earth you're alive.'

'*Harbour*.' It was impossible to say if the voice was exasperated or slackened in relief. 'It's about time you called in.'

'I have two passengers, Nou Harbour and Lucian Merriweather, aboard and alive. Do you copy?'

'Halley, I don't believe it, you're OK.' Lucian's eyes were redder than ever, and there were little globes of liquid catching on his eyelashes. 'I don't know what I'd've done if you weren't.'

'Copy that, Harbour, and copy that, too, Lucian.' The smile in Halley's voice was palpable. 'You all in one piece, lad?'

'I don't know about that.' Lucian's breath hitched in what was debatably a laugh. 'I think some of my fingers have snapped in half, but that's pretty standard for the coldest surface in the Solar System, right?'

'Rite of passage. And Nou, how are you doing?'

'We'll need a medical team upon our arrival to Charon,' Edmund interjected levelly. 'She's unconscious and severely hypothermic, but appears stable.'

'They'll be ready.'

'Halley, how are you alive?' Lucian had pulled himself over and slumped into the co-pilot's seat beside Edmund. He smelled like cool water—a scent Edmund had never thought to connect with Pluto, with the ices of the Heart. He himself stank of smoke. 'The Sun, the mirror, what happened? It all went dark.'

Halley harrumphed—or maybe it was just the signal crackling.

'The mirror may have been overridden by whatever broke our defences, but not its escape pod. That counted as a separate entity. The eject function was part of the main hab, so that was locked off—but the thrusters worked just fine. I set it on a burn that pushed the mirror into the atmosphere. Not sure what happened to it, actually, I rather lost track of it all . . .'

'But how did you *survive*?' Lucian stressed. 'You were heading for the atmosphere, there'd have been *g*-forces, you'd have been burning up . . .'

At once Edmund saw it all as though in the seat beside her: flames engulfing the hab; clamouring into the little pod as they rushed at her heels. Testing the eject function, knowing it was futile. Vibration sweeping up her limbs as the thrusters engaged; craning her neck, swivelling from window to window, every move a sharp jerk, watching stars wheel. The lights dimming; the mirror darkening. Euphoria for the success; despair, crushing despair, beyond the word's meaning, for what remained of the future.

'As for how I survived,' Halley continued blithely, and Edmund blinked the nightmare back, 'I was hoping you could tell me. Depending on the partial pressure of the additional gaseous volume sustained by the night's events, I was looking at either burn-up or cryo-braking, as you once so succinctly phrased it, Lucian.'

Pluto filling her vision. The pod jerking and jostling. Moving to wipe her eyes; hitting helmet glass . . .

'I was waiting to pass out, in fact. A death like falling asleep. Many dream of it.'

Hand coming off the thruster. Pressure forcing her back in her seat. A glow beyond the window, the glow of ionising atmosphere, of scorching metal . . . Closing her eyes . . .

'Next thing I know, Gen's back online saying *access authorised* and I'm being blasted loose while he tells me I've got seventy-three missed calls. Do either of you have any clue what in the worlds happened this fine evening?'

Lucian was watching him. Now was the moment, Edmund knew. The moment it came out. He straightened his posture.

Raised his chin. Kept his hands loose, neutral, in his lap. He opened his mouth . . .

'Well, I suppose there will be a full inquiry,' said Lucian slowly.

He kept his eyes levelly on Edmund—and Edmund, searching within them for contempt, for cold satisfaction, found only something he could not place. Something out of place.

'Until then . . .' Lucian shrugged, and Edmund realised what the look was. He realised it was something mild. Something warm. The terraformer looked him right in the eye as he said, 'Until then, I suppose we'd better get used to speculating.'

His eyes were blue. Vivid blue, almost shocking, as unblemished as a high noon sky above a snow-swept Earth. It seemed so absurdly improbable that Edmund had never noticed them before.

Lucian nodded to him, just the once.

And Edmund, all but frozen, inclined his head in turn.

'Unfortunately, you may be right,' Halley said unconcernedly. 'Anyway, now we all appear to be alive, I've got a bit of news for you.'

'I think we've got some of our own, but you go first,' Lucian said with a wry smile.

'I'll wager mine's worth your while. By any chance, did you know there's extraterrestrial life on Pluto?'

The words drew a surging jolt through Edmund's body, a physical shock that raised the hairs on his head and convulsed the tips of his fingers. For a moment it seemed more plausible he was dreaming.

He heard a hiccuping laugh, jarring him to the moment, then Lucian's giddy voice.

'Did you hear that, kid? You hear that, Nou?' Laughing, laughing, throwing back his head with it. 'All the worlds know it now!'

All the worlds. Earth, Europa, Enceladus. Pluto. Almost three E-years, quarantining a secret until it could be contained no longer. And now it was raining from the sky.

Despite those years, despite Plutoshine, and despite himself, Edmund felt his lips twitch.

Phase 5

Chapter 24

The people of Stern stood upon the shoreline where the ice of Sputnik Planitia met the mountains of their home. All eyes were across the ice and all ears were tuned to one of many communal channels of conversation.

'So what do you think, Harbour?' called Halley across one. 'A total of four operational hours—shortest terraforming mission in history?'

'The most successful failure?' Lucian tuned in.

'The most circuitously successful mission in history.' Edmund smiled. 'Even if it was at the expense of the mission itself.'

'T-minus forty minutes.' Parkin, in the makeshift command module, broadcasting on every frequency.

Before them on the ice was a modest little ship, only a class or two above the Sadge. Most of Lucian's team were already assembled at its foot for boarding, anonymous in their suits at this distance. The small craft was a tender for the real interplanetary spaceship, safely in orbit beyond Acheron, with its twin tori to prepare passengers for tougher gravities.

Lucian didn't envy them that.

'Any last-minute pangs to join us?'

The voice came across their personal line; Lucian turned

until he found Halley, looking up at him with eyebrows raised and arms folded.

In earlier years he might have faltered. But in answer, his cheeks curled in a smile.

'I'm petrified of getting reverse-sunsick. Dark-sick. Or maybe of our newly minted Doctor Stan stealing my job. Rightfully stealing, I might add.'

Halley nodded sagely. 'It's only a matter of time, that is true.'

'Either way, Pluto needs at least one terraformer to help clean up after the party.'

This was certainly true. While the Heart and its surrounding plains looked to have stabilised for now, they would need extensive seismic surveying for years to check for longer-lived effects. The melted crescent scar right through Stern's longitude would have to be fully examined, and the wreckage of the mirror recovered from wherever it had cryo-braked. And Stern itself would have to be rebuilt from the ground up.

It was a right mess. It was the morning after a house fire. But Lucian did love a new project.

'You're really serious, then?'

Halley watched him with her mouth pulled in something like disappointment, and for some inexplicable reason it only struck Lucian now just how very *short* she was. He was thinking, as he nodded back at her, that if he tried to hug her she would be angry.

'And you're heading back to Earth, right? You've got family there?'

'One or two.' Halley nodded. She smiled. 'I've been promising to head back for . . . oh, a good few years now . . .'

'That sounds good!' Lucian enthused, pleased. 'Bit of time out, bit of nature. You can read Hartdegen's other series—'

'. . . and there's an old colleague not far down the coast, he's been trialling micrometeorite disintegration over West

Antarctica. Seems to make a nice solar shield if you can get the clouds thick enough, and apparently they're one terraformer short.'

'Terraforming Earth? Making Earth more Earth-like?' Lucian blinked at her. 'You know, if anyone's earned a bit of retirement, Halley, it's you.'

'Don't insult me, lad.' She waved her hands dismissively. 'Terraformers never retire, you know that. We die in the saddle.'

'And there was me worrying what on Earth we were going to do with our lives after a project like Plutoshine.' Then, more soberly, 'You know, you spend a decade working on a thing, and wanting the thing so badly, that you don't even stop and think what'll happen when it ends.' He blew out a breath on his shrug. 'Whatever we do, it'll be a tough act to follow.'

'It might be a once-in-a-career thing,' Halley agreed, 'or it might not.' She leant forward, the better to look him in the eyes. 'So keep up the good ideas. Earth only knows we need more of them.'

'I'll see what I can do,' Lucian promised her. Then, eyes drifting ahead, 'I reckon I've got at least one or two for now.'

Following his gaze led to two figures atop the rise of a methane dune. Nou Harbour stood in silence, staring into the stars. She was searching with cross-eyed concentration for one in particular.

Her brother watched her from one side before taking her hand and shifting it slightly left. Nou smiled up at him, then away as quick—still shy, still uncertain, but she was trying. She was twelve Earth-years old—soon she would be 0.05 by Pluto's calendar, that special age for their people that marked the end of childhood. Edmund smiled back at her—then away as quick. He, too, was trying.

'That one?' Nou asked, and there was no trace of a quaver in her voice. It had been a month since she had last stumbled for words, even for him.

Edmund bent down to her height, sighting along her arm.

'Yes,' he said, voice intimate in her ear across the helmet intercom. 'Don't lose it.'

'T-minus thirty minutes.'

Edmund straightened up as Lucian appeared before them. With an excusing smile to Nou, he turned, and the two men fell in step together. Stan bounded over as they did and began signing something to her—redundant now but a sort of secret code between friends, too fast for Edmund to catch; despite months of quietly teaching himself, languages never were his strength.

He would keep trying.

'How is the Captain?' he asked. 'It seems my father's sealed resting-pods have already saved lives—though I doubt he imagined all those would be a cat's.'

'The bubble-pods?' Lucian shook his head. 'Old Whiskers was safer than anyone in there. I might have to patent that anti-depressurisation cat flap. I honestly think he slept through the whole thing.'

They lapsed into companionable silence. In unspoken agreement they walked away from the crowd, from the Bow—the nickname for Pluto's temporary housing structure while Stern was rebuilt.

'You'll have heard by now that Yolanda Moreno had a lot to add to my father's case,' Edmund said conversationally once they crossed some intangible threshold. 'We have her on record swearing Clavius Harbour paid her to sabotage Plutoshine, and furthermore threatened to halt funds to her radicals if word ever got out. I believe there were also threats to colonise Enceladus. In his words from her words . . . ah . . . "*and you can damn well bet no one will stop me.*"'

'Damn.' Lucian sucked air between his teeth.

'Mallory Madoc was also eager to share information, once we requested a check of her finances, too,' Edmund went on with a wry smile. 'So she'll testify, my father rather handsomely funded her research elsewhere in exchange for the pretence of a xenobiology survey. From corroborating her story with Moreno's, it sounds as though both were also—and unknown to the other, I might add—required to thwart their counterpart's search attempts.'

Lucian whistled. 'The two greatest xenobiologists in your pocket, pitted against each other. Your man sure knew how to get stuff done.'

'Indeed. However, after his . . . incapacitation . . . it seems Mallory saw a business opportunity.'

'Have her cake and eat it, too? Take his money *and* the glory of finding life?'

Edmund nodded. 'Right, exactly. It appears that's why she latched on to you and Nou, as leads.'

'Man.' Edmund understood the look on Lucian's face. 'She was up to the exact thing you accused me of.'

'Yes,' Edmund winced, 'and I have apologised for that.'

'You're welcome to do it again.'

'I'll certainly think about it.'

For a moment there was only the young ice crunching beneath their feet, the still hazy stars above through a choked atmosphere. It took tens of thousands of years for the Heart to convect; the scars would remain intact for their lifetimes and many more.

'Mallory must have been as worried as you, then,' Lucian pointed out, 'when it looked like he was recovering.'

'Hm.' Edmund nodded in thought. 'I always assumed it was you who suggested plugging my father into the gauntlets.'

'Oh, *that's* why she asked . . .'

'To monitor him, I would imagine. And get out if he looked close to waking and realising he'd been double-crossed.'

'Rather her than me.'

They had been climbing uphill and now reached the crest of a little rise, looking on to the excitement below. Every human on Pluto was on the ice for today—all except one. The body of Clavius Harbour was inside the ship and destined for Earth, where anyone who cared to could bury it at whatever ceremony they saw fit. There would be an inquest, of course. And there was the very real possibility Edmund would be trialled by Planetary Protection as an accomplice.

But Edmund had only to recall Nou's face the day she awoke on Charon to know he would take their verdict without regret. Her face not just when she saw the slender, shining bodies of her Whistlers waving from every crevice across the Heart, across every glasspad, across every world, but when she had seen his own. His hair in tufts, light stubble on his cheeks as he awoke from the chair beside her.

'There's just one thing I can't shake.'

Edmund raised his eyebrows. 'What's that?'

'Why'd he do it?'

There was no need to ask who.

'Why sabotage your own master plan?' Lucian turned to his companion in earnest. 'Any polymath worth their salt knows terraforming's a marathon over millennia. Sure, you speed things up a little. Bit more light from the mirror—bit more thermal energy from an asteroid impact or two. Bit more terra-forming a bit sooner. Except you run the risk of getting the whole thing cancelled—which has now happened.'

Edmund was silent as Lucian went on.

'All I keep thinking is, if he was trying to turn a whole population against terraforming and remind the Solar System *again* why it's a risky business, then he did a bloody good job

398

of it. A very expensive job, too. Never mind getting Plutoshine cancelled—Stern will vote down *any* plan now. I don't think it's from fear, you know,' he added. 'I'm not even sure if it's because of the Whistlers. Or *Whistler*, singular. Still haven't figured that one out. It's more like'—he twisted his hands, grasping for the word—'*pride*. Like . . . Like Pluto's worth protecting, just the way it is.'

Edmund perused him beneath eyebrows heavy with thought.

'The plan was straightforward,' he said eventually, 'and you're absolutely right. That was the goal. To malign the very act of terraforming. To ensure a world where its people were content with the darkness.'

Edmund had thought it through. This was not a story to be told incomplete. And, that night with Lucian in the snow, he had left out the last ten per cent.

'Doesn't it strike you as odd?' He kept his voice wholly neutral. 'Terraforming the coldest, darkest, most uselessly distant place in the Solar System? Of course my father told me,' he said simply. 'Not everything—but enough. That way I, too, was incriminated. I couldn't ever betray him without handing myself over, too. Yes.' He drew in a sharp breath through his nose. 'I knew of the plan from the start. I was no bystander.'

Lucian had gone very still.

'The sabotage?'

'My understanding was for it to never to cause harm,' Edmund explained. 'Styx, the gards, the final switch-on . . . they were all of them to be near misses. The intention was never to harm—only to exemplify the proximity of harm. That deviation, at least, was something he withheld.'

'You knew about Moreno? The whole time?'

'No.' Edmund shook his head firmly. He couldn't have told himself why, but it felt of the utmost importance that Lucian understood. 'I only knew there would be *someone*. For some time I was actually convinced it was you. With regards to Mallory Madoc, for that I was entirely in the dark. I was only trusted with what was necessary.'

Lucian looked . . . aghast. There was no other word for the look on his face. Edmund had braced himself for more anger, like on the ship, but this quietness—this disappointment—was worse.

Lucian stared at him for a long moment.

'Did you . . . ? Did you plan for Halley to die?'

'No.' Edmund shook his head again. 'No, Lucian, I did not, and that was why I sought Moreno out that night. I was convinced there had to be a second operator. Even then it did not occur to me it was my father himself.'

'But *why*? I still don't get it . . .'

Edmund looked at him for a moment.

'Why stay here?' he asked in response. 'Why build suns and create skies, when we could be out exploring new ones?'

Lucian blinked at him. 'What? What do you . . . ? You mean, like, interstellar travel, or something?'

'Did you know my father had a sister company that designed ships for exactly that?'

'I . . . Yeah. Yeah, I did, actually.' Lucian looked as though he'd just been hit in the face from twenty years ago. 'I had the playing cards.'

'They were his dream,' Edmund said. 'He worked on those the way other men work on model railways. But they were never built. Once terraforming caught on there was no demand. No interest.'

Lucian pressed his palms over his helmet bubble.

'Most people would've just bought the damn train set.'

'Clavius Harbour was not "most people".' *Was.* Past tense. Finally. 'Everything he did was carefully planned, often over decades. And he was a man used to getting what he wanted.'

'Do you think they'll buy it?' Looking below them, at the people jumping, the people running, the people chatting. 'You really reckon these guys, right here, will be the ones to get the interest going again?'

Edmund bowed his head. 'You were the one who said it. About pride. I am ashamed to have been part of my father's plan, and please, Lucian, believe me when I say I wanted no part in it. But . . .'

He looked up. Stars, innumerable. Blurred and hazy, as though from the bottom of a pool of water. Places within places. Planets, worlds, homes. Anything, anyone, could be looking back.

Edmund said to them, 'Now, more than ever after Nou's discovery, do we have cause to wonder what else is out there.'

There was silence. At their feet, spread out across the snow-white of the Heart, all of Stern had come out for goodbye.

'Bit of a dick move,' Lucian said idly. 'Killing off a fourth emergence of life just on the off chance you'll further a personal goal.'

'Fifth, including Mars. And yes,' Edmund agreed. 'I thought the plan would end right there the day Nou showed us the cavern. It was one of my many mistakes.'

'Edmund, why are you telling me this?'

Lucian was facing him straight on. The expression on his face was . . . strange. Edmund thought back to his first confession, the other ninety per cent; the look on Lucian's face was unchanged. Where was the anger?

He took a breath.

'You have covered for me thus far, Lucian, and I am . . . I am very grateful, even without understanding why you do it. But when the depth of my involvement becomes known, and I am removed, I want you to look after Nou.'

'What do you mean, "becomes known"?'

'What?' That was not the answer Edmund was expecting.

Lucian cocked his head slightly.

'How would they find out? Your dad's dead, and Gen's records traced the hack straight to the hospital. As far as the court'll care, they got their guy.'

'Yes.' Edmund was nodding even as his brows furrowed. 'But—'

'You think *I'll* tell?'

'No, but . . . Well, you . . . You would be within your right—'

'Edmund.' Lucian brought his hands up in two parallel lines, as though to take hold of him but thinking better of it. 'That kid doesn't need anyone else for a dad. She's got you. OK? No one's taking that away.'

The two men held each other's gaze. Slowly, Edmund nodded.

'T-minus twenty minutes.'

'We'd better . . .' Lucian indicated the crowd. 'Got a lot of goodbyes.'

'Yes.' Edmund took a breath. 'Lucian . . .'

He extended his gloved hand.

'Thank you. For—'

Lucian's hand was already around his own.

'You too, mate,' he said as they held on, 'now I'm all caught up. Oh, and, Edmund?'

Edmund raised his brows.

Lucian shrugged.

'You know, I thought you played some pretty mean piano when I overheard you one time. If you ever fancied starting a band, I'm planning on having quite a bit of free time.'

They found the rest of their friends beside the ship, and now the goodbyes began in earnest. People bounded from one to another, shaking hands, touching helmets, holding close, too fast to switch between personal lines, and the air was abuzz with snippets of laughter and promises and fond farewells.

Lucian was swamped in a bear hug by Kip, then clapped on the back and pulled in by Joules, too. Stan he just held wordlessly to him. The act made little sense within suits that transmitted only the ghost of such contact, and within helmets that hindered entirely the closeness of a chin upon shoulder, or the scratch of hair against cheeks, but that didn't matter. He caught a glimpse of Mallory hovering on the periphery, somehow both haughty and hesitating as their eyes met for just a moment, before she turned and floated without another glance aboard the ship.

Halley folded her arms firmly across her chest as he approached, and Lucian hastily rerouted his outstretched arms into a ruffle of helmet in place of hair.

'I'll look out for Stan,' she told him with a curt nod. Then, pointing a finger at him, 'Keep in touch. Don't get sunsick. And *please* try not to get yourself almost killed again.'

'Love you, too, Halley,' he mumbled.

'What was that?'

'I said I'll leave you to it, then, and I'll come visit some time.'

'You'd better.'

Now the crowds were pulling back, and the last interplanetary traveller had disappeared aboard, and the doors of the little spaceship were sealing them inside. Now *T-minus ten minutes* was sounding, but as it did another voice reached Nou's ears:

'Has anyone seen a scrawny little girl, about yea high? She's the tiniest thing, so she's a bit hard to spot—oh my Earth! Is that her?'

Nou tried to swipe a hand over her smile and met only glass.

'But this can't be Nou Harbour!' Lucian cried, and there he was as she turned. 'She's much too big, she looks far too big even to . . . !'

And with mock-grunts of effort he swept her up and spun her around and around to the sky, and Nou Harbour shrieked with happiness as her world fell away, and the scarred young ice blurred into creams, and the veiled stars opened their arms to her.

Lucian kept both hands on her shoulders as—like jumping from a merry-go-round—they came to a dizzying stop.

'How's the Whistler-whispering going?' he asked excitedly, and Nou loved him in that moment for the secretive hush in his voice, the way his eyes locked on hers in artless fascination.

She nodded and nodded up at him.

'He's got a lot to say,' she told him, a little breathlessly; just remembering their conversations tended to do that to her. 'And he's started doing this new thing.'

'Oh yeah?'

Nou blinked and was right back there: out on the shoreline that morning, out among the graveyard of collapsed cliffs. Rising between them, like shoots between paving flags, was her Whistler. Pillar after pillar, strung along the horizon, each somehow *taller* outside of the cavern, their greens greener, their blues bluer. There were hundreds upon hundreds of them, and though the atmosphere was not yet clear enough for satellites to confirm, Nou knew they had surfaced across the entirety of Pluto.

She blinked the vision away. Her friend—just the one, she was sure, one mega-organism—had been revealed as stranger and more magnificent than she could ever have conceived.

'I didn't even know he could—he's never done anything like it before—but it's not just meanings I get now. I get . . .'

She hesitated, reddening again. But if there was anyone who would believe her, anyone who would be as awed as she, it was Lucian.

'I see things,' she told him, her voice hushed and fervent.

'You know when you see a memory, and it's like you're seeing two things on top of each other—one thing in front of you and one thing in your head?'

Lucian only nodded, willing her on.

'It's like that. I get to *see* what he's thinking now, too.'

She fell silent and watched, anxious for his reaction. It didn't come immediately.

'I'm trying to think what to say without swearing,' Lucian finally said. He was staring away behind her, and had to shake himself back into focus. 'That's . . . What do you see? What do they show you?'

Now it was Nou's turn to think what to say.

'I'm not really supposed to tell,' she admitted, the toe of one boot drawing a figure of eight in the snow. 'He wants to show you.'

'Show me?' Lucian stared at her. 'Like, show *us*?'

He gestured about—at the people laughing, chatting, bobbing around; at humanity.

Nou nodded.

'He wants to show all of us. He wants us all to understand.'

'T-minus seven minutes.'

Nou glanced up at Lucian; all of a sudden she was ten years old again, shy before this big man who built suns.

'You're really staying? You really mean it?'

In answer, he placed his hands on his knees and bent to her height. The distance had shrunk in the past two years; she was growing like a sapling in the Sun. Their helmets made contact.

''Course I'm staying, Spark,' he said, words that Nou felt as much as heard, passed not just through comms but through the atoms of glass. 'You'll be needing an apprentice, right?'

'An apprentice?'

His eyes flicked up, just beyond her shoulder, then back. His smile was confiding.

'You really think I'd take off now, just when we're getting to the good bits?'

Hands on her shoulders; Nou looked up, and there was Edmund. It was time.

She pointed one finger to herself. Covered both hands across her heart. Then extended her finger across to Lucian.

And Lucian, straightening up, signed it right back as snow began to fall as fine as flour.

The minutes passed like seconds until, across every channel, the people of Pluto were counting down as one. Then, with a rumble beneath their feet and enough power to ruffle the air, air far thicker than when they had arrived, the Sunbringers returned to the sky.

Nou hesitated, gathering all her heart's conviction, then reached out and took her brother's hand within her own. Beneath their feet shone the lights, their familiar hues of red coiling and swirling within the ice. To the north at the Heart's shoreline, every last branch of the being called the Whistler swayed at the spectacle as though caught in a light breeze.

Edmund kept his hand tight around hers.

Acknowledgements

To all those who made the *New Horizons* mission possible–to all who brought Pluto down to Earth for the rest of us–and in particular to Alan Stern. To St Edmund Hall and the memory of Bill Miller of the William R. Miller Scholarship, for granting me the most beautiful home in all Oxford in which to quietly work; to Alex Grant and Belinda Huse especially, for going out of their way. To Linda Davies, the Hall's then-Writer in Residence, for being the first person to read this who didn't have to be nice, but who was anyway, and for continuing to be a mentor.

To Julie Crisp, my agent, for loving and believing in Nou. To Marcus Gipps, my editor, for reading on when he really didn't have to. To all the team at Gollancz, as credited, for style and professionalism. To Natasha Carthew and Andrew Cartmel, for encouragement and advice. For technical accuracy: to Tashi Chadwick, for sign language insights; to Dan Spencer, for back-of-the-envelope fluid dynamics; and to Tim Gregory, for mathematical, astronomical, and cosmochemical checks–and the rest. To BehindTheName.com, for being the onomatologist's best friend. To the European, Austrian, and UK Space Agencies, for funding my time in Alpbach and teaching me how to design space missions–though I doubt this was an intended output from such training.

To Andrew Lockington, Steven Price, Mark Mancina, Jasha Klebe, and Jacob Shea, whose music knew what I had to say, and said it better. To the memory of James Horner, whose music taught (and still teaches) me how to write.

To my sisters and first editors, Katie and Hannah, and to Mum and Dad, for putting up with unsociable teenaged years tucked away and tapping away.

To the gardeners of the Oxford University Parks—to the sequoia grove.

Credits

Lucy Kissick and Gollancz would like to thank everyone at Orion who worked on the publication of *Plutoshine* in the UK.

Editorial
Marcus Gipps
Áine Feeney
Brendan Durkin

Copy editor
Steve O'Gorman

Proof reader
Jane Howard

Audio
Paul Stark
Jake Alderson

Contracts
Anne Goddard
Tamara Morriss

Marketing
Folayemi Adebayo

Production
Paul Hussey

Editorial Management
Charlie Panayiotou
Jane Hughes

Finance
Nick Davis
Jasdip Nandra
Afeera Ahmed
Elizabeth Beaumont
Sue Baker

Sales
Jen Wilson
Esther Waters
Victoria Laws
Rachael Hum
Anna Egelstaff
Frances Doyle
Georgina Cutler

Operations
Jo Jacobs
Sharon Willis

Publicity
Will O'Mullane

Design
Nick Shah
Joanna Ridley
Nick May